D0859697

HOUSE
of
MARIONNE

ALSO BY J. ELLE

Wings of Ebony

Ashes of Gold

Against the Tide

A Taste of Magic

HOUSE

of

MARIONNE

J. ELLE

RAZORBILL

RAZORBILL

An imprint of Penguin Random House LLC, New York

First published in the United States of America by Razorbill,
an imprint of Penguin Random House LLC, 2023

Copyright © 2023 by J. Elle
Map copyright © 2023 by Virginia Allyn
Art on pages 405–413 adapted from Adobe Stock

Razorbill & colophon are registered trademarks of Penguin Random House LLC.
The Penguin colophon is a registered trademark of Penguin Books Limited.

Visit us online at PenguinRandomHouse.com.

Library of Congress Cataloging-in-Publication Data is available.

ISBN 9780593527702 (hardcover)

ISBN 9780593698129 (international edition)

1st Printing

Printed in the United States of America

LSCH

Design by Alex Campbell
Text set in Adobe Garamond Pro

For the first of their name heiresses of nothing,
the different, and the wandering.

A Note from the Author

The fictional settings and events in *House of Marionne* are inspired by various parts of the world. None is intended as a faithful representation of any one event, culture, or people at any point in history.

HOUSE OF MARIONNE
SPECIALTIES OFFERED

ANATOMER

Transfigurer of anatomy

AUDIOR

Transfigurer of sound

SHIFTER

Transfigurer of matter

RETENTOR

Remover of magic

CULTIVATOR

Transferer of knowledge

DRAGUN

By invitation only

Sanguis electorum dives est.

The surest measure of our stewardship
will be in our elasticity as one body,
for the weight of responsibility magic requires
would fracture divided shoulders.
Thus, I sign this Sphere Commissioning Pact,
on this 14th day of June in the great year of 1781,
and gird the yoke of burden in the maintenance of unity
and faithful duty to each other.
This endeavor shall either be
the greatest achievement of the living world
or the perpetual ruin of us all.

Westin Alkomae,
Upper, Seven of Twelve, First of Blood,
The Prestigious Order of Highest Mysteries
1740–1781

Château

Secret Wood

Belles Wing

Guard Shack

Entrance Gate

THE DRAGUN

Yagrin ran a finger along the blade and sucked in a deep breath. He hated this part. The scent of dumpster trash wafted under his nose, and he pulled his coat tighter around himself. He stuck his head out between the bauble shop and pastry bar where he was lurking.

"*Memento sumptus*," he chanted to himself as if that would slay what felt like eels wriggling in his stomach. His gaze sifted between the traffic.

And there she was.

A pink striped beanie sat tucked tight on her head, curly locks blowing beneath. She wore slender jeans and a bright green sweater with kimono sleeves. His nerves lodged in his throat. His foot wouldn't stop tapping.

But his fingers tightened on the dagger in his pocket.

It was a nimble weapon, its opulent metalwork sculpted to fit the curve of his palm. His fingertip moistened. He rubbed the blood on the lining of his pants, waiting for Pink Beanie to pass so he could blur into the crowd behind her. He would be patient. Careful. That's why he'd put off doing the job for weeks. *To be stealthy.* The House name, after all. He had to keep up the House name.

First he'd have to get her alone. Isolated.

You're not a killer, Yagrin, the voice inside his head argued, but he tamed it with recitations written on his heart. *Secretum.* Pink Beanie was a direct threat to their way of life, whether she knew it or not. And for it, she must die.

She strode by. He tidied himself in the window across the way before hopping out of the shadowed alley of the bustling retail district to stay on her tail. Her hat bobbed through the crowd; her face pressed to a phone. He couldn't quite make out her expression, but she strode slow and easy, greeting each person she passed who made eye contact.

His fingers twitched as he replayed his plan over in his head. The magicked dagger would be cleaner. Quieter. He pulled out a round coin, flipping it in the air. *Tails. Give me tails, dammit.* He shouldn't be superstitious; superstition was pretend magic, and he didn't need to pretend. He had the real thing. The coin glimmered in the sunlight and landed on heads in his palm.

"Rats," he muttered. Whatever his endeavors were for the day would be favorable.

If it weren't him, it'd be one of his Dragun brothers, he told himself. His insides sloshed. He clenched the coin in his hand. Sweat beaded on his forehead, and he stepped aside at an intersection to let a dog walker with a collection of tangled leashes swish by. Pink Beanie stopped for a coffee, and he let her, careful to stay out of sight.

While she folded over a chair, sipping a cappuccino, he tapped his phone, standing a little taller as if this moment of mercy somehow made it better. Made him better. Redeemable for this life that had chosen him. She liked it with cinnamon and extra whipped cream. She loved it cooled all the way down, too.

His finger hovered over "Mother" in his phone, not the one who bore him, the one he was sworn to. He gulped, tapping, and it rang. He tapped again, hanging up, knowing what she would say. *Duty is the honor of the willing.*

He scanned the area for witnesses, gazing over the crowds in and out of shops. A pair of lovers sat with arms pretzeled around one another sharing a muffin. A curly-haired girl with freckles on her face sat at a bus stop, tugging at a key chain.

He felt a chill sweep through him. Today did not feel like a day for killing.

A little girl waddling by faced off against a triple scoop of ice cream about as tall as she. It toppled in her fingers, and he reached to steady her hand. She smiled at him in thanks, and his lips split in a smile. But he wiped it from his face. He didn't deserve the joy it brought him.

He gulped, clenching his fist. *The more he did it, the easier it would get.* But he'd never found any of it easy. Not when he accepted the task. Not when he was inducted into the Order. It was pretending that got him through it then. He'd done the motions, worn the silk-lined tux, donned the mask, held the dagger, pressed it into his heart. Bold he might not be. But clever. Always clever.

The cracking of dagger against bone had been something he'd perfected. Tricking the ears, transfiguring the form and notes as sound moved in the air came easily to him. Making Mother and the rest of them think he'd stabbed himself was simple. If it made the sound and looked as it should, it would appear he'd completed Third Rite. No one needed to know he was truly a coward.

But pretending wouldn't work today. He had to kill the girl.

And then another, and another. It was beyond time he got used to the gig. He searched for the pink beanie, but found her table empty, except for her mug. His heart leapt in his chest as his eyes skimmed the crowd, brimming with conversations. Briefcases swished between legs.

"She was just here," he said to himself.

Loitering near a rim of hedges on the café's patio, he smelled her before he saw her. Vanilla and cinnamon, a garden of jasmine. A tiny hill of whipped cream on her lip.

"Sorry, I was just . . ." She switched up her feet, trying to get by. Her eyes were deep ebony and yet somehow as bright as the sun.

"No, excuse me, sorry."

"Have we——?" She smiled, tucking a hair behind her ear. "You look familiar," she said, finally working her way past him.

He walked in stride with her, hand tucked in his pocket, firmly gripping the metal.

"Oh?" He smiled. "I mean . . . I'd like to believe we've met . . . or that we were supposed to."

She blushed and it tugged at him in ways it shouldn't. But this was a job, so he stuck to the plan: *Earn her trust.* They walked, and he hung on her words, dotting in responses with smiles and head nods. She talked a million miles a minute, warming up quickly. He dropped details he knew she liked . . . like teacup puppies, cable-knit sweaters, anything apple flavored. Each deepened the creases around her eyes.

"It's like kismet," she said.

"Must be." He felt sick. "If you have a moment?"

"For?"

He shoved down his quivering gut and let the monster he was bred to become take over. "There's this really quaint café off the beaten trail, that way, with the best beignets you've ever had." He pointed toward an alleyway nearby, past the crowds, past the noise. "Should we maybe grab a bite?"

She hesitated, checking her phone. *Put her at ease, Yagrin.* He forced his lips into a kind smile, making sure he showed his teeth, pushing his cheeks up so creases hugged his eyes.

"They're really delicious."

Her lips pursed in consideration. The twinkle in her eye shifted from curiosity to anxious excitement. "Okay, for a moment. Sure."

He led her away from the bustling crowds of lunch patrons and down an alleyway, laser focused. "It's just down here."

She nodded. The deeper they walked, the more the shade shifted into shadows.

"Is it much farther?" she asked, hugging herself.

He could hear her heart pumping faster. "Just a little farther. Down this way."

She craned to see. Yagrin felt the familiar grainy heat blustering through him: his magic, warming up. He'd grown to hate the feeling. But now it burned him with the courage he lacked, reminding him of who he was. Twelfth of his blood, magic was strong in him like his father and grandfather before him. Twelve generations of his family, all Draguns. He took a breath and let muscle memory take over, like he'd learned in training. Then he opened his hand, drawing on an icy chill in the air. He held still, the cold clawing its way into his palm, up through his arms. He tingled all over with magic, turned into himself, and disappeared into a cloud of black.

She gasped.

He saw his House sigil on the back of his eyelids and gulped down the dregs of his regret. He pressed into her. She screamed. He tightened from his center, grabbing hold of the Sun Dust coursing through his veins, and plucked invisible threads from the air. Her shrieks of terror turned to laughter, his warm magic bewitching the sounds, note by note. It seemed somehow sweeter that way. He closed his eyes, imagining her smile, the way she smelled.

"I'm sorry," he muttered to her, limp in his arms. And he was.

But duty was the death of freedom.

PART ONE

ONE

I used to believe that magic was glittering, fanciful pretend.
Then I realized magic *is* real.
But it is dark and poisonous.
And the only way to hide from it
Is to not exist at all.

"Quell, are you listening?" Mom squeezes my hand as our car jerks to a stop outside the French Market on North Peters.

"Yes, get my pay for the week, in and out."

"That's my girl. Hurry now. I'll circle." She brushes my loose curls from my cheek with a cautious smile before I slip out of our '99 Civic, a junkyard find, its blue paint dry and peeling. Before this car, it was an old yellow truck. And before that truck, it was the bus, everywhere. But Mom didn't like not having a way to get up and go—*run*—at a moment's notice. So she made sure to get really good at fixing up old finds.

Really good at hiding me.

Fourteen schools. Twelve years. Nine cities.

Every place is the same: a backdrop I blend into. Anytime Mom gets suspicious someone might know about the poison running through my veins, she stuffs our entire life into a tiny yellow, hard-shell suitcase. It's perplexing that my entire existence can be tucked into something so small and shoved into the trunk of a car. At first, I'd stuff everything I could into my bag. Now, I just grab my tennis shoes, a phone charger, and my lucky key chain. The countless places we've moved and the blur of faces I'll say goodbye to are the white space between memories, ellipses strung between unfinished sentences. I stopped asking where we're going a long time ago.

Because running's been a destination all on its own.

Humid air, thanks to the roaring Mississippi nearby, assaults me, sticking to my clammy skin. The back end of our rusted hatchback blares red before disappearing around a corner. With only two weeks of high school left, I'm trying to work as much as I can to save up enough for the big plans Mom and I have.

To finally move somewhere and *stay*.

If a caged bird sings of freedom, and a song can be a wordless utterance, a wish, a burning desire, then I sing of salty air and sand between my toes. Of a home that's not a moving target. After graduation, our plan is to find some small beach town—a real beach, not like the muddy water we've been around these last six months in New Orleans—and blend in with the sand.

Only a couple more weeks.

I graft myself into the afternoon commotion of the congested Market, and it's like slipping into a worn pair of shoes. I disappear into the throng of shoppers in the outdoor pavilion with my chin to my chest, hands tucked in my pockets.

Be forgettable.

Mrs. Broussard should have my money for my shifts last week. She is a local confectioner whose family has been in the business of pralines since there was such a thing. The Market buzzes with an energy that slows my steps. Too many people. The usual spot where Mrs. Broussard sets up her table of goods is taken up by a person peddling various levels of heat—hot sauces. My pulse ticks faster at the hiccup.

I weave in and out of the crowd, avoiding curious eyes and looking for a bandana covering a head of pinned gray hair. My fingers prickle with a cold ache, a familiar sign that this curse in my veins—my toushana—is stirring. I swallow, urging it back down, pleading with it to calm. It's safer to be invisible; it's safer to be no one.

"Quell?"

I flinch at the sound of my name.

"That you, girl?" Mrs. Broussard waves me toward her, and the line snaked at her table parts. My skin burns, feeling her customers' stares. *No eye contact.*

"Tonta'lise got here before me, yeah. Had to set up my whole show ova here. She know damn well I use dat spot eva day. But here she come, tryin' to get my customers." Her hand rests on her hip. "You come for ya money?"

I nod and Mrs. Broussard pulls an envelope out of her apron. This is the first job Mom ever let me have, because we need the money and Mrs. Broussard doesn't ask a lot of questions. She pays me in cash and has only ever asked my name once.

"You gone do extra hours for me next week?"

"Not until school's out."

"Very good. Don't linger 'round these parts, che. Gone get outta here before it get dark, ya hear?"

The thick envelope in my hand soothes my nerves. I count it. Twice. My lips curl as I thank Mrs. Broussard and turn to go. The crowd has thickened like a nice roux. *Be unpredictable.* A cluster of tourists lodge in the entryway and I scan for another exit. Away from the vendors, near an abandoned pop-up tent full of fleur-de-lis candleholders, is a sign for the bathrooms. A red exit sign blares next to it and I head that way. Mom will worry if I take too long.

The winding hallway toward the bathrooms twists and the light bulbs overhead flicker. Small exit arrows glow red, urging me farther down the hall. I expect to spot the bathrooms but don't see them yet. The Market pavilion is open to the outdoors, so there should be sunlight up ahead. The fluorescents flicker again and I walk slower. This doesn't feel right. Worry bites at me and I turn to go back the way I came.

But there's a wall there.

A shape of something, like a shadow or trick of light, forms a fleur-like shape on its stuccoed surface. I blink and it's gone. My heart stumbles; my toushana unfurls in my bones, dancing with my panic, threatening as it does in warning that it might rise up in me soon.

I turn, but in every direction the walls have shifted or closed in. There are no bathroom signs, no blaring red light pointing toward an exit anymore.

"*Memento sumptus*," someone says. The voice is coming from a narrow door that blends seamlessly with the wall. Caution tugs at me like a tether. Pressed carefully to the door, I listen, hands hooked behind myself just in case. Strained voices tangle around each other in a whispered argument. There are a pair of men, it sounds like. I listen again and hear several more. I teeter forward on my toes ever so slightly, pressing my weight against the door to ease it open a sliver.

Inside, dark-robed men encircle another bound to a chair. Around them are rows of stacked barrels marked with a thorny branch coiled around a black sun and words in a language I don't understand.

"Go on, Sand," one says after refilling a barrel with a pale liquid. "We'll clean up."

A blond fellow lassos his arm in the air and the dozen barrels tremor. A haze fills the air, rippling like rain on a window. It clears and he does it again, and this time the barrels disappear. I squint, my heart lodged in my throat.

I glare at my hands in confusion, and I can still picture the wisps of darkness that bleed through my fingertips when my toushana shows itself, destroying anything I touch. When I was little, I'd called it "the black." Then as I grew to know its nasty nature, "the curse." Mom finally corrected me a few years back after someone overheard me complaining about it. Toushana is its name. Some genetic malfunction, Mom had said. She's lying. But Mom does that. I've heard her mutter to herself about this poison I have.

She called it magic.

But whatever these men are doing appears quite different. My nails dig into the door's frame as I peer harder into the dimly lit room. I've never seen magic that isn't my own.

"What was the order, Charlie?" asks Sand. The others in the room watch from the shadows.

"No prisoners. Not today." Charlie plants his hands on his knees and glares at their captive, now at eye level. "May Sola Sfenti judge you fairly."

"Screw you and your Sun God," the bound man spits as Charlie pulls deep from a fat cigar. He blows smoke into the captive's face. Then he does something with his fingers, too fast and too far away for me to make out. The bound man throws his head back, choking and contorting in pain, his wrists and ankles rubbed red from their hold on him. The smoke from Charlie's lips hovers like a cloud around his face, consuming and suffocating. The man gasps for breath and in moments, his writhing stops. His head lolls and I stumble backward, lacing my fingers, trying to slow my hammering pulse. *He's . . . dead. That man, they . . .*

"Fratis fortuna." The voice comes from behind me. I turn and there is a man in a dark suit, same as the ones the men I just saw were wearing. But unlike the others, a gleaming dark mask slopes across this man's brows, over his nose, its ornate carvings tapering off into his high cheekbones. His expression hardens at my silence.

I step backward, my back hard against the wall. There's nowhere for me to hide. His brows knit with intrigue and my heart patters faster. My toushana's ache deepens, my hands growing colder. I have minutes, maybe, until it will rip through my fingertips angrily like a spewing burst pipe. Pressure swells in my chest. *Run.* I step aside. His hand latches onto my wrist, but I feel it around my throat.

"What are you doing back here?"

My envelope from my job slips from my fingers, and I try to dash for it as it tumbles to the pavement.

"Ah, ah. Hold still." His long coat is tightly buttoned all the way up to his neck, and a round piece of silver gleams at me from his throat.

An image is engraved on it, a Roman-style column, with a jagged crack running across its front as if it's been broken in half. I squint, trying to remember if I've ever seen that symbol before. Thick brows shade his narrowed expression. "Answer the question."

"I got lost trying to find the exit. I thought it was near the bathrooms." I tug against his grip, but he doesn't let go. He glances just past me at what was a door, but is solid stone wall now. My heart hiccups. "I—I didn't go in there, if that's what you're thinking."

"In . . . *where?*"

"There was a door, but I could tell it wasn't the bathroom, so I turned around to leave. I *swear!*" A lie is too risky. People believe half-truths much more easily.

"What's your name?"

"I—"

The answer sticks in my throat, magic fluttering around in me like a moth searching for a place to land. Mom changes my name each time we move, cycling through the same three or four. Quell *Jewel.* Not Quell *Marionne.* Who lives at 711 Liberty Street. Born in a small town outside the city. New to the area. Whose dad's job requires him to travel a lot. Two parents means fewer questions. My script, the drill Mom has run through my head year after year, hangs on my lips. All lies seasoned with enough truth, the proper inflection, the warmth of a genuine smile, to make them feel true. To make the veneer of a life we've lived, I've lived, for as long as I can remember, real.

"I'm Quell."

His mouth bows in suspicion.

My fingers hurt as my toushana yawns like a cat stretching itself awake from a nap. Its claws run underneath my skin, sharp tendrils of ice scratching my bones. My breaths quicken. The mask on his face fades into his skin, seeping into his pores like dry soil soaking up rain. I blink and stuff down a gasp. But he doesn't even flinch.

"Your heart is racing. Your pupils are dilated. And if you move, that bile in your stomach might come tumbling up your throat. Something wrong?" He peers harder at me as if sussing out a question, but after a moment the crater between his brows disappears.

"No, nothing's wrong. May I go?"

He releases me.

"Better get a Retentor out here to take a look," he mutters to himself before smiling at me. "My apologies. I thought I knew you from somewhere. The exit is there, behind you."

I turn, and sure enough, behind me where there was a stone wall is now an arched exit that opens up to the avenue. That was *not* there a moment ago.

"Right. Thanks."

He smiles, turns, and I book it onto the street, grateful to put more distance between me and whatever that was. But my breath hitches.

My envelope.

I turn back, but stone has reformed where the archway just was. Some mangled mix of irritation and sorrow burns through me. That money was supposed to feed us for a week!

"Hey, let me back in, please?" I beat on the wall, and the icy chill of my toushana, already on edge from this whole tirade, seeps into my bones in a fury, rushing into my fist before I can pull it away. I groan at the burn of what feels like daggers tearing through my skin. The stone blackens under my touch, its facade crumbling with rot, brick by brick, inch by inch, until I'm standing before a decayed expanse of building that looks singed. *What have I done? What have I done!*

Muscle memory urges me into motion. I run. Back up Ursulines, right on North Peters. *Blue, Honda.* A horn blares and Mom is waving behind the steering wheel. Seeing her is a balm to my toushana. The chill in my bones retreats as I dart between traffic, yank the passenger door open, and duck inside.

"Go!"

"Did you get the money?"

"Go, Mom, just drive, go!"

Mom slams the gas, and the French Market grows smaller behind us.

I'M STILL GRASPING for my next breath when Mom tosses me one of those cheap disposable hand warmers and my rice pack. We keep one in the car and two at the motel. My toushana has worn off, but the throbbing ache that comes before and after lingers. *Those people. They used magic. They killed a man!*

"What happened?" She eyes her duffel bag on the back seat and white knuckles the steering wheel. Creases hug her eyes. Her pulled-back hair has grayed in spots, like threads of silver in a bushel of black wheat. Memories are buried in the folds of her skin, mysteries I'd give anything to understand. Like why I have magic and she doesn't. Who are we running from? But the curve of her lips as she merges into the thoroughfare tells me precisely what she's worrying about—whether it's time to leave again.

I bite down and find something outside the car window to look at so Mom cannot see the frustration on my face. I'm so close to graduating, which means some semblance of freedom. No more truancy checks. No more teachers breathing down my neck. Mom and I will just be able to *be*, hide in plain sight, much more easily in two short weeks.

"Well?"

"It was nothing." Those men at the Market didn't see me watching. And the one who caught me let me go. He didn't actually see my toushana destroy that wall. I'm not adding fuel to her fire.

"Do not lie to me." Her stare burns.

A shiver skitters up my arms. I'm just *so* tired of running. Mom exhales and snatches up a box of cigarettes from her purse and lights one as a string of museums I've only seen from the outside rush past us in a blur.

"You know that everything I do is to protect you?" Her expression softens. "We may not have much, but we have each other."

I look away. A house swallowed in flames flickers in my memory. I can still taste the smoke. We left our last place after this guy's house was burned down because he and I'd hung out after school. Even then, Mom offered no explanation. I know she loves me. But that's not the same as understanding. I could have been killed back there. If I knew more, I could be smarter. If I knew more, we could be safer. Maybe she thinks I'm too young to get it. She reaches to rub my shoulder, and I want to pull away. But I don't. I sit there and smile, so Mom feels like her best is good enough.

We continue the rest of the drive in silence, and I try to lose myself in one of the library books in my bag. But the car jerks to a stop in the parking lot of the motel, the latest spot Mom was able to secure for us, and I hurry out of the car.

Once inside our room, I can't hold it in anymore.

"Mom, I want to understand my magic. To understand why we're doing this."

She takes off her shoes, after setting her duffel bag right beside her, and for a moment I wonder if she heard me. "Quell." She takes a deep breath and the weariness carving her expression deepens. "I'm not even sure where to start, how to—"

"Just tell me the truth. I can handle it."

"You assume."

"I *can*. I'm seventeen, not a child anymore." My tone grates with irritation. "Please," I say, softer. She stills and sighs again. A long moment of quiet passes between us. And I sit in it because this time there's more than silence in response to my questions.

"Your grandmother is a very powerful and influential woman, Quell, in an entirely different world than we live in now."

My chest tightens with anticipation, hearing Mom mention Grandmom. I haven't thought about her—seen her—since I was little. Hope bubbles up inside me at finally getting some answers. "Does she have magic, like I do?" Mine must have come from somewhere. Maybe it skips generations.

"Growing up, our house was a training ground for a magical secret society." Mom wraps and rewraps herself in a blanket. "The Order." A smile wafts between us. "And life there at Chateau Soleil even in the off-season was . . ."

"Chateau Soleil?"

"Grandmom's estate."

"*Estate*? How big does a house have to be to have its own name?" We lived at my grandmother's until I was five. I can't remember it, really, or picture it. I have one cobwebbed memory. I was little. She pulled me up onto her lap. She smelled like birch and juniper. Sunlight poured into the room and everything seemed to glitter. She handed me some toy to play with. I felt safe. But Mom came thundering into the room, snatched it out of my hand and me out of her lap. The rest is a haze.

"Their magic is different from yours, Quell. They move in the world in a way that you never will because of your toushana."

My shoulders sink.

"All that glitters, darling—"

"Isn't gold. I know." Another question pokes my thoughts. "Does Grandmom know about my toushana?"

"No."

"Then why—"

Thunder claps quietly in the distance and the lights flicker. The suddenness silences both of us. Mom's brow pinches as if she's focusing hard on something. I know that look in her eye. That spark that won't die.

"Pack your things."

"Mom?"

"I need you to tell me everything that happened at the Market, Quell, right now. *Please*."

She grabs her duffel and something inside me fractures.

I tell Mom everything, about how I got lost leaving and saw them kill that man, that I ran into a guy with a mask that bled into his skin. How I dropped the envelope, and how my toushana rotted a hole in the stone trying to get it back. The longer I talk, the more her grip on her duffel tightens.

The far-off sound of thunder rolls again and her expression darkens. Mom stuffs the few clothes she has into her bag and my resolve falters.

"Mom, please." Hot tears sting my eyes.

I can't. Not again. We're so close. Two weeks.

She hands me the blue savings jar we made six years ago when we settled on our beach plan. I can practically see the house I built for us in my dreams. Two stories, a plain square shape, cozy with shutters. Salted air blowing through an open window.

"One more time, I'm sorry." She tugs on her coat.

It's always one more time. "I don't believe you!" I hate this. I hate it so much. How do I convince her I was careful at the Market? *I got away!* We'll be fine, like we always have been, for a few more weeks. I lock my knees and try to find a big voice.

"No."

"What did you say to me?" Her tone is sharp, but the grip on the bed rail says it's fear that strains her words, not anger.

"I said *no*, Mom." My tone is stronger this time, my song rising up in me. Magic prickles my fingertips, and I tuck them away to warm them, unsure of what it could do. I've never had it flare up when I'm this upset. The anger in her flickers, then morphs into something else, her eyes red with tears. She puts out her cigarette, then leans in so close I can taste it on her breath.

"You want the truth? That isn't thunder. It's magic."

My heart stumbles. "I don't understand."

A tear steals its way down her cheek. She wipes it away so fast I almost miss it.

"Those Draguns you saw . . ."

"Draguns?"

"Assassins for the Order. They're in charge of executing anyone with toushana." Her nails dig into my arm. "If anyone finds out your secret, they will *kill* you, Quell!"

Her words knock the wind out of me. I try to steady myself on a wall as the world sways.

Someone would *kill* me for a magic I don't even want or use.

"What if someone saw you at that Market?" She shakes her head. "We can't take that chance. One more time, Quell, *please?*" She curls her hand in mine as if holding on to it keeps her world in orbit. I know what I have to do, but that doesn't make it easy. If she's right, if this is the one time this so-called Order actually has found us, I have no choice. I empty the beach fund jar onto the bed and whatever pieces of me are left crumble.

"Okay," I breathe, taking on the yoke of her sorrow and blinking away my own. One more time. "I'll go to the convenience store and grab the necessities. Give me five minutes."

"That's my girl. And—" She lifts her skirt. Strapped to her thigh is a gold-handled dagger, covered in scrollwork and flecked with gems. She shoves it in my hand. "Just in case."

I blink in disbelief. The metal of the blade is twice the length of the handle, but somehow as light as air in my hand. Its ornate handle gleams gold and sparkles with jewels. I had no idea Mom even carried a weapon, let alone something so . . . exquisite.

"If I'm right and one Dragun has found us, there could be more."

I glare at the weapon in my hand. It's cold, like her words. Easily the most beautiful and dangerous thing I've ever seen. I meet Mom's eyes and finally, to some degree, understand the weight that hangs there.

"Five minutes," she says again. "No more."

I tuck the dagger away and hurry out the door.

TWO

————✳————

Outside the sky is dim but clear. Thunder or something made to sound like thunder rolls in the distance, and I hug myself tighter as I hurry next door to Stop 'N' Save.

"You're okay," I mutter. My fingers feel for the dagger tucked in my waistband. Just in case. I skirt bikes laid out in front of the store on my way in. Inside, the shop owner is behind a newspaper. He looks up and disappears back behind it.

There's no way to know how long it'll take Mom to find a new place. I grab the entire row of tuna cans, a loaf of bread, two tubs of peanut butter, canned beans, a bag of Skittles, and six bags of sour cream and onion chips, which Mom would tell me is a waste.

"Doesn't stick to you," she'd say.

But greasy chips make me happy. And with everything going on, I deserve some happy.

The bell attached to the door dings as more people enter, and I check my watch. I loop a roll of duct tape on my wrist and grab a tiny bottle of rubbing alcohol and one of vinegar. A line has formed at the register. The clock on the wall ticks and I feel it in my chest. I need to get out of here. *Fast.* I spot a familiar head of moussed blond hair, summer-tanned skin, and bright eyes in line behind me. A kid from the school where I've spent the second half of senior year. He catches me staring and waves. I groan.

"Hey, Quell, isn't it? It's me, Nigel, Nigel Hammond, from English Lit class." The Nigel who tries to bum all my answers because he's never done any of the reading. He's so close I can smell his brand-name cologne. "You need a hand?"

"I'm fine."

"You sure?" He grabs the bread, which I'm balancing perfectly fine on top of the stacks of canned fish.

"Really." I step away from him, and the line moves forward, thank goodness.

"Suit yourself." He hops into the back of the line even though his hands are empty. Maybe he wants something from behind the counter. I move forward a few spots before glancing in the mirror irked by the distinct feeling that someone's staring. But when I look up, Nigel is flipping a coin and cursing under his breath.

The line moves forward and finally I'm at the register. My foot taps. It's been seven minutes. This is taking too long. The cashier swipes everything and piles it into bags.

"Thank you." I reach for my money and my elbow bumps Nigel's chest.

"Really, let me help." He grabs one of my bags.

I pull it back. "No, really."

"I insist."

Dread finger-walks down my spine. I've watched Nigel at school. He surrounds himself with admirers. Once, a freshman dropped her books in front of him and he just rolled his eyes and kicked them out of his way. This is . . . odd. I pay the cashier and grab my bags.

"Thank you." I hurry to the door. But I can feel Nigel following me. He holds the door. I walk more quickly.

"I just want to talk to you." His footsteps echo mine, and I pick up to a run. I glance back to see if he's still there, and in the tinted floodlights of the parking lot, Nigel's face shifts. His slick blond hair morphs into a short dark cut, his face twisting from the comely countenance of Nigel Hammond to someone else I've never seen before.

He grows a few inches, soft craters dent his sunken cheeks, and long hair shields the glossed mask on his face. Something broken burns in his dark eyes and it unsteadies my steps. He approaches, fists clenched, his clothes shifting, too, their illusion wearing off. He flips his coin once more, and it snaps to the cinch of his collar like a magnet. On it is a familiar image. A column cracked in half. My heart squeezes. The man who I had a run-in with at the Market wore the same symbol.

Fear pins me in place. *Magic.* I reach for my weapon.

"Quell, is it? I've had orders to find you for *months*. You're quite hard to find, you know that?" He smirks and my insides quiver. His lips smile though his eyes do not. "That's your name, isn't it?"

I brandish Mom's dagger at him.

"Easy."

My foot nudges a pile of bikes belonging to those still inside the store.

"I'm not going to hurt you. I just want to talk."

I drop the groceries, snatch up a bike, and take off. I risk a glance backward. He is blowing air between his fingers, and more thunder rolls overhead. I swerve across the intersection where traffic has doubled at the promise of rain. My calves burn, pushing the pedals faster as I dash between rows of cars packed like sardines at a stoplight. Once I reach the motel parking lot, I dash up the stairs.

"Mom!" My fist connects with the door.

"Quell?"

It opens and I hurry inside, shove it closed, and lock it.

"Someone was at the store. And his *face*! Not the same guy from the Market. But another one. Another what did you call them?" I can't breathe. "Dragun."

"Slow down. Start over." Mom peeps out the curtains.

"At the store, there was someone I thought I knew. But then his face *changed*." I look for shock on Mom's face, but there is none. "He had a coin at his throat," I manage. "Like the guy from the Market."

"What was on the coin?"

I close my eyes, and his face shifting slithers through my memory. Outside, thunder booms, rattling the windows of our tiny room. The

Dragun is here. He has to be. I shudder, trying to focus on Mom's question. "A column. A cracked column was on it."

"Not a talon?"

"No."

"Beaulah."

She shakes her head, tsking.

"Mom—"

"Quiet! Let me think." She peeps out the window again. "That traffic outside came out of nowhere. It's stop and go, backed up all the way down the street. We couldn't even get out of the parking lot if we wanted to." She paces, the lines in her face deepening.

Knock. Knock.

"We have to get out of here." I tug at her.

"No, *you* do." She unshoulders her bag. "You go on. I'll get them off your tail."

"Mom, no! It's both of us, always." The rest of my words die on my tongue. She's right . . . Usually she flits, I follow, that's how it goes. But she has no reason to run.

She doesn't have poison coursing through her veins.

I'm the reason we've had to do any of this.

"Guard these things as if it's your life," she says, opening her duffel. She pulls out a journal and tears out the last page, where there is an address hastily written. "Go here. Hopefully, the safe houses are still intact." She digs out what I'd thought was a makeup compact and a tiny vial of glowing powder. She spreads it into a smooth shallow circle in the silver dish of the compact, tipping the vial all the way upside down until it's empty. "Should be enough." She hands it to me. "Whisper the place you want to go, then blow. It'll take you there."

"What about you? I can't—"

"Do you have your key chain?"

I pull it from my pocket.

She pulls out one just like it and squeezes. Mine glows. "Let me know you're okay by squeezing it. I'll do the same. It'll send me your location. So I can find you wherever you are."

I squeeze mine, and sure enough, Mom's lights up.

The compact is chilly to my achy fingers, my toushana stirring with something that feels like recognition. *Come with me,* I want to say, but the words won't form.

"I'll sort this out here, get rid of the Dragun, and come for you tonight." She zips my bag and nudges me to go.

"But—?" Tears swallow my cheeks. Running without Mom doesn't feel right.

"*Quell.*" She shakes me. "Get ahold of yourself!"

Knock. Knock.

"Open up, ma'am." It's the hotel manager. "I have someone here with me to see you. Says it's urgent."

"Just a minute!" Mom says in her plastic cheerful voice. To me, she whispers, "Buckle down. You know how to stick to the shadows."

I nod, saltiness on my lips as she presses her own to my forehead.

"Mommy, *please.* I'm scared!"

"You're a *Marionne,*" she says, her chin rising ever so slightly. "You can do this." She gives my hand a squeeze. The door handle jiggles, the lock clicking.

"Now, Quell!"

My heart hammers. Fear kneads my insides. I glance at the safe house address again. "Twelve Aston Lane," I whisper into the powder, and blow. The world tips sideways. A rush of pressure latches onto me and I feel it like a weight on my chest. Breath sticks in my lungs, and I lurch forward as if I've been punched, a thread of cold winding me tighter in its clutches. I blink, but the world fades into nothingness.

⚜

GRASS MUSHES UNDER my feet. The air is thick with the scent of woodsy pine and wet moss. Trees surround me like a thousand sentries. Between the rustle of foliage meddled by the wind is deafening silence. I move through the forest toward a break in the canopy up ahead. Though, there is no semblance of a roof or porch.

My foot catches on something, and clanging rings through the trees. I swallow a dry breath, holding still to see if anyone heard. Nothing moves but the broken lantern cracked under my shoe. *I'm close.* I hustle to a clearing up ahead where I find a house.

What's left of it.

My hopes for safety shatter like the wreckage I see: crumbled foundation, furniture in pieces, collapsed walls, and broken windows. Mom's given her whole life to keep me safe. This time, it's on me. I have to figure this out. For both of us.

"Watch it; that's my foot, you klutz," a whisper breaks through the forest. I wedge myself in the thicket between the trees.

"If your feet weren't so big, they'd be easier not to step on," someone else says. "Honestly, how do you even find shoes for those things?"

Two girls in long black cloaks lined with thick red fur pass, hoods slung over their heads.

"Dancing with you is probably like trying to woo a bear."

"Brooke, shut up!" She shoves the other girl playfully. "Keep talking, I'll turn your bones to metal. See how you like that."

Brooke laughs. "You think you're something special all of a sudden with more than one trick up your sleeve?"

"Mother says I could be."

"Ha, you wish."

"Enough, all right? Come on. Mother said make sure." She gestures at the rubble. "So get in there, make sure there're no traces we've been here. Draguns will be all over this place inspecting by morning." The girl's hand hovers above a small pile of rubble. Air ripples beneath her fingers and the pile shifts, stretching, twisting until it's turned into a heap of forest brush. I blink as she moves on to the next.

Amidst the wreckage, a cloud of black fog appears like a summoned ghost. The Dragun who is after me emerges from it. I gasp. *How did he track me here? Mom . . . Is she okay?* The pair of girls raise their arms as if they intend to defend themselves.

"Identify yourself," he commands.

"You first." Brooke flashes the Dragun something shiny. His fist hits his chest.

"Memento sumptus."

The girls lower their hands. *"Non reddere bis."*

"I'm looking for someone," he says. "A girl. I'm on orders from Mother herself. I had a lead that she might be traveling with someone older. But that ended up being a monumental waste of time."

I bite into my fist. *Mom got away.*

"Have you seen anyone come this way?" he asks, and the one with big feet inhales deeply.

"The levels of Dust in the air *do* suggest someone other than us recently traveled here," she says, rubbing her thumb and forefinger together.

I swallow, pressing deeper into shadow. I need somewhere I feel safe. *But there's nowhere I can . . .*

Chateau Soleil . . .

Grandmom.

I turn the compact in my hands, which thankfully have warmed.

"Shh." The Dragun raises a hand, and all three heads rotate in my direction.

She's my grandmother. Family. A kind woman from what I remember. And Mom said she doesn't know about my toushana.

"She's here." The Dragun rushes in my direction.

I flip open the compact. *Mom will come for me soon. Tonight, she said. I can hide my toushana for a few hours.* "Chateau Soleil," I whisper, and I blow, the last of the glowing powder dissolving into the night.

Hands reach for me as I disappear.

THREE

The powder transports me to the middle of a patch of dead trees. I latch my hands together to stop them from shaking. A gust of cool wind grazes my skin, and the earthy scent couldn't be more unfamiliar. There's no sight of the city in the distance. No neighborhood of houses. Only dense thick woods and musty blackened trees.

The buzz of barely getting away unsteadies my steps as I wander through the grove for some sight of Grandmom's house. The glow of evening has deepened by the time I spot a road that halts at a pair of iron gates. Attached to it is a stone guardhouse, where a line of cars waits to enter. The barrier towers there like hands raised in worship to the dusky sky, the words CHATEAU SOLEIL on its front. I swallow. Gates like that exist to keep people like me out.

I force my fidgeting fingers still and tap my dying phone to call a ride. It's linked to an account that probably has a few bucks in it. The wait drums my pulse faster. Will this actually work?

The driver rolls up after not too long and considers me with smooshed brows.

"You want me to give you a ride *through* the gate?" He twists his lips.

"I can pay extra." I flash him the money I have left from the store.

"Get in."

I slide into the back seat. The car juts into motion as the guard gestures for us to pull forward. I have nowhere else to go. I need to get through this gate. My grip on my bag tightens and I give my key chain a squeeze.

A second later, it glows in response. *Hurry, Mom, please.* Guilt hooks in my stomach.

We slowly roll forward to the guard, whose appearance is as approachable as his body language. His lips tilt down in a scowl as if they're just permanently that way. The high collar of his shirt is bound by a circular metal emblazoned with a single hooked claw much like a dragon talon. He plucks it from his neck, turning it in his hands like a coin. *A coin.*

"Is he a Dragun, too?" I mutter too loudly. I study the image on the coin again. Not a cracked column . . .

The driver's brow bows in confusion in the rearview as he eases to a stop. My window comes down, and I press back into my seat. I feel the gate guard's stare like a knife between my ribs. But it doesn't flicker with recognition. *The talon.* He isn't affiliated with the Dragun after me. He doesn't know my secret.

"Your name?" The Dragun's lips purse with irritation.

"Quell."

"One moment." His words slither from his lips. Beyond the gates, sweeping willow trees arc over the street, cloaking the already graying evening into deeper shades of gloom. I squint for a glimpse of a rooftop or building. But the road twists out of sight.

"I'm not seeing a Quell," the guard says. "Who are you visiting, exactly?"

"I'm here to visit Mrs. . . . Mrs. Marionne."

"*Mrs.* Marionne?" His eyes narrow, and I swear it's squeezing my throat.

"Y-Yes, sir."

"Another moment, please."

I try to sit up taller. I don't know Grandmom's first name. She's always been Grandmom Marionne. The guard returns and gestures to the gate. I exhale as it folds in on itself.

"Do you happen to have the house number?" I ask. "Like, which house is it?"

"It's the only house."

"Right, thanks." The car lurches into motion. The road winds through a tunnel of trees. I tighten my grip on the handle of the dagger Mom gave me, firmly, desperate for some sense of assurance. Some sense of control.

"Where do you want me to let you out?" the driver asks.

There's still no sign of a rooftop or anything besides brooding foliage and foreboding sky. "Just beyond these trees?"

Hair rises on my neck. I shouldn't be here. Memories play in my head on repeat, from times Mom and I have been in even more dire straits. My toushana is quiet at the moment, and I try to settle better in my seat. *We may not have much, but we have each other*, Mom says all the time. And it's always true. Until now. I peer out the window at the trees rustling, waving.

Are they saying welcome?

Or run?

As we exit the tree tunnel, the darkness lifts like someone pulled back a curtain. The ashen clouds have rolled on, and the evening's sky is a regal shade of pink. I press the button on the door, and wind whips inside the car. I inhale deeper and the knot in my chest eases.

The road curves around a sweeping cobblestone courtyard dotted with sculpted shrubs and statues like the garden of a fancy castle. Wispy grass sprouts between wide pavers and a stone fountain, which gushes water a whole story in the air, its droplets glinting in the evening sun. I stare, taking in the majesty of it all, and my grip slacks on the dagger's hilt. A steeply pitched roof is a speck in the distance buried in lush green and tall woods.

"It must be that way," I say, craning for a better view. The street snakes to a cul-de-sac, and that's when I see it: another iron gate with an *M* on its front. "There." I point. It's all so grand, like something I'd see on a postcard, a picture in my history books. Not a real place I could set foot into. Something twinges in my chest. Something warm, intoxicating, a little foreign. Something that feels like hope.

The car pulls up to the gate, and for several moments nothing happens. There's no guard tower or speaker box. The dark gable roof beyond it is no more than a break in the trees.

"Lady, I have to get going. I'm not getting paid enough to sit here all day."

This is it. It has to be. "Okay, thanks." I tip him and he peels off.

The gates loom over me like an altar waiting for an offering. Wind howls, turning my arms to gooseflesh. Cold seeps into my fingers, then creeps up into my hands. I clench my fists, then reach for my rice pack. My fingers snag on the zipper, seizing up. The ache morphs into a frigid chill, my toushana stirring. I wish I knew what provoked it. What wakes it up some moments and keeps it lying silent others.

"Hello?" I set my bag on the ground. They must have cameras. "Anyone here?"

Nothing.

Something swoops overhead, and the world darkens. But above, I only glimpse shadow, like clouds that have moved on but left their shade behind. I blink. It's gone. The dimness of the evening thickens. Wind grazes my skin, rustling the trees, and the slants of shade draw nearer, stretching across the pavement, reaching for me.

"Who's there?" I force down the lump in my throat and feel for the flap of my bag, eyeing Mom's dagger hilt with images of the Dragun after me still on the back of my eyelids.

Suddenly, darkness from above nose-dives toward me, and panic flares in my chest. My fingers graze the hilt of my dagger just before a force pummels into my back, knocking me forward, ripping away my breath. My knees slam the ground, prickling with pain. I reach again for my bag. The zipper sticks, but I jiggle it open, and a thick fog as black as night surrounds me. I steady myself for the blow, trying to see which direction it's coming from, but there is nothing, no one, only shadows.

The fog lifts, and my side throbs with the sting of a fresh wound. I hold the spot where it aches as the world tips sideways. The trees sway, watching in judgment, like the iron gates that wouldn't let me in. I scan for some indication of where the shadow went, where it will come from next, but only see tricks of light. Splotches of black on the ground that blur and shift.

"Please, stop!" My ribs quake with pain, as if they're being snapped out of place. I peer harder, grow colder, pins pushing behind my eyes trying to translate the darkness.

I blink, and the world glitches white. That's when I see him.

An outline of his feet, shaped by only air. He lunges toward me, but I'm ready. I grab his ankle, hold as tight as I can, and tug. He trips, but somehow catches himself before falling. The shadow he was blows away like sand.

What's left behind is a guy about my age dressed much like the gate guard with a glare that is a dagger of its own.

I gulp. *Another one.* A gleaming mask covers the top half of this Dragun's face as well. But it's much more ornate than the others I've seen, intricately carved along its edges where it fades into his skin. His dark coat and loose-fitted top are lined with red embroidery, much finer than any of the other Draguns wore. But the cinch at his neck where I expect to see a silver coin is only fabric.

"The gate guard already cleared—" But before I can finish, he's on his feet, nostrils flaring, before disappearing into a cloud of black.

"I—" I start, but I'm engulfed in a dark fog as cold as death. A fog of . . . *him.* Sharp pain pricks me all over like slashes with a fine blade. I blink, but everything is black. And red. I wail in pain. My toushana roars in me, a blanket of ice wrapping around my bones so insistent it burns. I bite down, trying to focus, and force my eyes open, looking for an outline. Some sign of where the Dragun's striking from. The fog shifts, rippling around his shape. I swing out my arm, as cold as a frozen log, slamming it into the back of his knees. He stumbles but recovers swiftly as the shadows lift, and he reappears.

His green eyes narrow.

I pull myself up and snatch the dagger, thrusting its tip straight at his face, Mom's warnings about Grandmom and this world haunting me.

"Touch me again and I'll slice you in half." The world frays at the edges, red rivers running between my fingers, down my arms.

My threat doesn't garner a response, but his gaze fixates on the blade. Warmth soaks my side and whatever he did to me makes it feel like something is ripping apart my insides. But I hold my dagger arm higher, firm. He won't touch me again. Tiny cuts stripe my arms, hands. Blood, there's so much blood. The mask on his face vanishes.

"Where'd you steal that?"

"It's *mine*."

He shakes his head with disbelief. "*Who* are you?"

I blow out a shaky breath. Words I've been forbidden to say my entire life rise like bile in my throat. "Marionne. Quell Janae Marionne."

FOUR

————*————

He holds out his hand and I consider my blade but tuck it away. My legs, scratched and worn out from the scuffle, feel like lugging lead. I stagger and he steadies me with a rough shake before wrapping his arm tightly around my back, pulling me to him. I stiffen against his hard chest as he leads me through the gate, wincing as his closeness presses against my wounds. A sprawling house not unlike a castle gazes down at us, lit up like a star in the distance, a blanket of rolling green between us and it. Like a manor in a world all its own.

"Hold on to me," he says, pulling me along faster. But the pain radiating all over my body sharpens and I can hardly keep up. He latches my hand on his arm and my heart thuds in my ears. His grip on me is somehow both gentle and tight. Closer to him the fabric at his throat is easier to see. What I thought was bare fabric is a stitched image of a hooked claw, a replica of the one the gate guard had on the coin at his neck. However, his is sewn in black thread. *A talon . . . Not a cracked column.* I try to exhale but can't because nothing about his hold on me says I'm safe.

"I've done nothing wrong. *Where* exactly are you taking me?!"

His grip on me tightens, his jaw working. "Do not let go of me." It isn't a request.

The world spins around us, and in moments, we're at the foot of the estate where pointed arch columns line the front. Along its stone triangular pediment, the name MARIONNE is etched. My insides slosh. *My* name. Beneath it is some sort of symbol, a fleur-de-lis and talon wrapped in words in a language I can't read. I catch a glimpse of myself in the window, and despite my bloodied clothes, I tie up my hair and dust off my freckled cheeks, but my hands sting, chafed from the pavement.

He pushes open the doors, tugging me along inside. The ceiling towers above, a masterpiece of gold leafed rosettes and crown molding like in the fancy castles I've read about in history books. Arches appear to be ripped right into it, reminiscent of an old, haunted church. He leads me through the entryway, past a maze of portrait-lined paneled walls, to a grand foyer where a giant sphere hovers midair like a black moon. Tiny speckles shine like constellations inscribed all over its glassy surface. Beneath them, darkness swirls violently.

"What is tha—" I reach to graze my fingers along its low-lying belly as we pass, but my hand goes right through it as if it's no more than an illusion. I rub my eyes, warming all over with awe.

He pulls me along, and I fidget in his grasp. "I can walk just fine on my own."

He holds me tighter. Music croons between a pair of towering carved doors as we pass. I crane for a glimpse inside. Bright lights illuminate an audience arced around a stage, some wearing masks, others with gold or silver tiaras on their heads. On the stage, a girl dressed quite fancily raises a dagger high above herself. I gasp.

"Eyes ahead!" My captor snatches me along before I can see more.

We go up one grand staircase, then another. Next, a long hall. Sweeping windows gaze out to a speckled sky hung over a sea of grass and sculpted plants. My wet shoes squeak, skidding on the polished floor. He urges us along faster, my mouth gaping, head swiveling at it all. How could a place so dangerous be so beautiful?

"Wait here," he says as we approach a pair of guarded double doors. He speaks briefly to a guard who also wears a talon-marked coin at his throat. The guard eyes my injuries with disinterest before letting us inside.

On the other side of the doors is a sitting room where fire crackles in a fireplace next to more tall windows swathed in fine fabric. I ball my hands into fists and exhale, grateful my fingers are warm, my toushana quiet.

A chandelier hangs from ornamental molding, giving everything a warm glow. The ceiling is so high, I have to tilt my head all the way back to see it. My mother grew up here. The wedge of guilt that's burrowed a hole in my heart widens. I took her from all this.

"Headmistress Marionne will be out in a minute," the Dragun guarding her door says. I squeeze my key chain, noting the tick of a pendulum clock on the wall. My captor puts the entire room between us without a word to me, irritation set in his jaw as his mask retreats back into his skin. Indoors, with better lighting, I can make him out fully. He perches in a corner of the sitting room like a Roman statue, broad-shouldered, looming like a god, perfect and poised. Pretty, even. Sculpted cheekbones and long lashes set off his deep green eyes. His nose curves ever so slightly upward above a pair of full lips that appear permanently puckered. He'd look as if he was pouting if it weren't for his cutting, broody glare. It's sickening how gorgeous he is. I smooth my threadbare shirt and finger the holes in my jeans that aren't supposed to be there, which only makes them worse.

He catches me staring and his edges sharpen. Something's under his skin. And that something, I suspect, is me. A knock at the door makes my back straighten. A girl with a petite frame and face enters, carrying a tin case. Dark hair curtains her warm expression. She wears a simple dress in a breathy fabric, and on top of her head is a thin silver tiara: coils of metal and stringy bits of silver stacked on top of a headband. It shines radiantly as her head moves, the silver bits catching the sconced candlelight. It's dainty and elegant, much like her.

She gestures at my arm, slick with red. "May I?"

I nod and set down my bag. For several moments, she works sharply focused over my wounds, smoothing her fingers over the cuts along my arm until they are new again. I glare at my hands. I really am broken.

My side cramps in pain as she finishes up with my arm. I wince, leaning on my other elbow, which is dug into a chair cushion that looks fancier than anything I've ever seen, let alone owned. The girl pulls her hair back into a bun. When she leans over my wound fully, I can see that her tiara is not sitting on her head—it's coming *out* of her head. I swallow my shock.

"Does it hurt?" I ask.

"Me?" Her brows touch.

"Yes, I mean the—" I gesture at her tiara.

Her cheeks dent with tiny craters. "Oh, you're serious? No, of course not." She works her magic around my wound as if she were pulling apart delicately small invisible threads until the skin on my arm is all healed. "This must all be so new to you. You can only see diadems"—she indicates the thing I called a tiara—"and masks if you have magic in your blood." She smiles. "Still, I can hide it at will, if I choose." Her diadem disappears.

"Whoa."

"It takes a little bit of control to learn how to do that."

I gaze up again at the show of magic arced above her head. "Wow!"

She blushes. "Was there anywhere else you were hurt?"

I lift the edge of my shirt.

"Okay, this one might sting a little." She cuts a glance at my captor, the Dragun, who picks dirt from his nails, his expression still rigid with annoyance. He could be a piece of furniture in this ostentatious sitting room with its silk lined walls and paneled wood. His mask, the one he shed outside, sits on his nose again, glistening in the sconce light.

My skin tugs and I brace for the pain.

"Hey," the girl says, pressing my shoulder down. "Try to relax. Here." She sticks out a hand. "I'm Abby, Primus, second of my blood, Shifter candidate, healer type." She dips her chin.

"Quell, uh . . ."

"You're a Marionne, yes?" she asks, tossing a glance at the guarded double doors. "I heard."

I nod stiffly.

My captor purses his mouth in disbelief.

"There have been five Headmistresses since this House's inception,"

she says, not seeming to notice. "Which means magic can be traced back
that long in your bloodline. So you'd say *sixth* of your blood."

"Right."

She grins and for some reason, I do, too.

"Nice to meet you. I should have you all fixed up in a few." My shirt
has worked its way back down, and she moves it out of the way. "Try to
breathe normally, okay? The magic works better when you're relaxed."

"Thanks." I force an exhale and set my eyes on anything across the
room other than my skin being put back together. Books line the far wall
secured in glass cabinets, affixed with a fleur-shaped padlock. I search for
meaning along their spines. But other than a talon or fleur here or there,
none of the terms or symbols are familiar.

"Almost," Abby says, and I glance back at her work.

The slice of red flesh zips closed, and I inhale through my nose, swallowing the nausea back down.

Creases hug her eyes as she cleans up the blood staining my clothes and
limbs. "There. Good as new. Could you put in a good word for me with
Headmistress Marionne about how I've done?"

"Sure."

She thanks me three times, before gathering her things and disappearing behind the double doors we came through. Just myself and my captor now. Feeling stronger, I rotate to face him. He stares into the roaring
fireplace. I slip my hand into my bag and feel for my dagger, keeping my
eyes on him and the door.

"How'd you do it?" He stuffs a hand in his pocket, his back still to me.

"Excuse me?" I tighten the grip on my dagger.

"Seeing me as I was cloaked. How?" He twists in my direction. His jaw
clenches like the words are rot on his tongue. I scowl at the man who attacked me, then dragged me in here like a criminal. He shifts his posture
and the light from the window cuts across his face. He isn't affiliated with
the Dragun after me and yet he dragged me in here as if . . .

"You thought I was *trespassing*?"

He tilts his head in agreement. Flecks of blue glint in his green eyes, and they remind me of a lake lapping a grassy shore. Heat rises on my neck.

"Well, I'm not."

"That remains to be seen." He turns his back to me dismissively. "The estate doesn't receive unsolicited visitors when Season is in, as a security measure." He is silent a moment. "And you didn't answer my question."

I rotate away in my chair, and to my great relief, the door to the Headmistress's suite clicks open. A woman whose skin suggests she's no older than twenty-five glides in.

"Grandmom?" I stand.

Her hair shines like polished silver, swooped backward and pinned in an updo, held together by a pearl comb. The diadem on her head is much taller than Abby's, not unlike a crown. It's encrusted with pearls and pink gems in a variety of sizes, all blindingly glitzy. Chunky stones are pressed to her ears, and matching ones hug her knuckles. The corset to her gown is shiny like silk, woven with a fleur-de-lis pattern. She is majestic.

"Quell." Her voice is soft and warm. A smile is pressed into her velvety skin.

I stand, hands clasped, not quite sure what's appropriate to do.

"Close your mouth, dear. You look like a trout."

I snap it closed. She moves toward me, and I'd swear she's gliding on air.

"Jordan," she says, addressing my captor. "This isn't how we welcome guests here."

"It's my understanding she wasn't invited."

Grandmother's nostrils flare, but her tone comes out measured. "Yes, but this is my *granddaughter*." She faces him fully, and his mouth parts in disbelief before he snaps it closed and it hardens.

"And," Grandmom goes on, "I would have liked her greeted properly. You might have debuted from your House, but you are *still* a Ward of mine until the end of summer."

His glare hits the ground.

I pull at my shirt. A Ward as in this isn't his House. As in he *could* know Draguns outside of the ones here. The Dragun after me . . .

" . . . you will abide by our way of doing things or find your duties overseeing security on these grounds revoked."

His cavalier posture stiffens, arrogance rising off him like steam. "You would do that? You would—"

"Do I strike you as a liar, Mister Wexton?"

"I . . . No, Headmistress."

"You might not be under my direct authority, but this is *my* House." Her stern demeanor melts back into a smile when she turns to me. "After all, we wouldn't want to give her a bad first impression, would we?"

"Thank you, Grandmom. He was—"

"You haven't been addressed to speak, dear."

My insides twist. This is not how I pictured this going. I'm making a fool of myself. She doesn't seem to like Jordan very much, but I'm not sure she likes me any more.

"Thanks to Abby, you look well."

I start to speak but nod and smile instead.

"You may go," she says to Jordan, and sits, somehow without bending her back at all.

Jordan starts to speak but moves to the door instead. He passes so close I expect us to touch. My breath hitches. But he grazes past me with room to spare and opens the door before turning back. He stares, piercing and sharp, his eyes gilded daggers that could cut right through me. My toushana flutters. *Does he know?* I shift in my seat and try to avert my gaze. But can't.

"My apologies to you, madam," he says. "Welcome to House of Marionne." He folds at the waist, his suspicion still fixed on me, before slipping out the door.

"Now." Grandmom pats a cushion beside her and I sit. "Let me get a good look at you."

Her stare bathes me in curiosity. She pulls at my clothes, grazes my hair. Every spot she touches tingles. She glances at my hands, and I flinch. They ache. In seconds, they could turn to ice, burn through all her nice things. Out my secret. I stuff them in my pockets and try to settle. After a moment, she sits back in her chair.

"What brings you here?" she asks. "I never thought I'd see the day."

In a rush, I tell her almost everything. How we've moved around often because Mom's work is always changing, *not* because we've been living on the run. I skip the stuff that happened in the forest and the Dragun on my tail. And explain that my mom told me she had some things to take care of days ago, left me at our apartment, and hadn't returned. The lie stings. I punctuate my explanation with smiles, the right inflection, enough truth, like I've always done. But her face is as stoic as stone as she listens. I smooth my clammy palms on my pants to warm them. I only need her to buy it for a few hours.

"And where is Rhea . . . your mother?"

My chest tightens. "I don't know."

"She has a way of making herself seen when she wants to be. Well . . ." She slaps her legs, before standing. "Season has already started," she says more to herself than me. "But you're my granddaughter, you can slip in and play catch-up. We have *lots* of work to do."

"Huh?"

"You don't think you're going to be on my estate idle, do you? You will enter induction for the Order." Her eyebrows kiss as if to ask how I could have expected anything different.

"I didn't need—"

"Did you not come here because you've nowhere else to go?"

"I did, but—"

"And I am saying, dear, you are welcome. But you will prove you're Marionne in more than just name and earn your place, like everyone else."

"No, no. I wasn't—" I blow out a breath. "I'm sorry. This is very generous. I wasn't sure where to go, so I came here."

She lifts a teacup from a silver-plated tray to her lips, sipping slowly, and I realize I have a fistful of chair cushion. She stands and walks to the window, her cup clinking against its saucer.

"What do you think your mother's last words to me were, Quell?"

I shift in my seat, reminded of the fine linen beneath me. The obstinate wealth, an entirely different life Mom would have had at her fingertips.

If it weren't for me.

"I don't know."

"Take a guess."

"'I love you, but I have to go?'" That seems sort of nice, maybe.

"She said nothing," she says, flinching a smile. "Left like a thief in the night. I tucked you in that evening. You liked me to read this story about a bear who lived in secret in the basement of an old house." She chortles. "So I read it twice. You insisted."

I have literally *no* memory of this. My throat thickens. A picture of little me on her lap pries its way into my memory. I replace it with one of dead magic bleeding from my hands.

"Afterward, your mother and I had a nightcap as usual. And then the next morning, she was gone." She pauses and the silence hovers like a guillotine. "She pretended."

I gulp.

"She lied."

I flinch.

"Despite all I'd given her, shown her." Her lips purse. "Would have given her. She took *everything* from me."

I look around at the scroll-armed furniture, the blanket of green outside. How is she the one with the short end of the stick? Grandmom must read my mind because her smile deepens.

"Don't be fooled by things, Quell. She took from me what no one could buy. My legacy. A daughter to love. A granddaughter."

A chill sweeps over me. "Family."

"Exactly." Grandmom's lip trembles for a split second, her composure cracking.

I hadn't thought about it like that, what it must have been like for Grandmom. I can't imagine just not seeing Mom again. Without a good-bye. Mom lost all this because of me. My grip slacks on the metal key chain hooked on my fingers.

Grandmom sits back down beside me, closing her hands around mine. I hesitate at her touch.

"You coming back here is a dream." She pats my arm. "And I intend to make you as welcome as she was. I do not coddle. I am firm. But there is always love behind my words."

She plucks a book so thick it requires two hands from one of her shelves. Its gold-lettered spine glistens: *Book of Names.* She opens it and turns past countless blank pages to one with a handful of names on it.

"It's our second chance." She smiles, and this time it reaches her eyes. "Sign here." She hands me a pen and indicates the next open space beside four other names, beneath the title: INDUCTEE ROSTER.

"I . . ."

"House of Marionne was the second-ever-created House in the Prestigious Order of Highest Mysteries to oversee magical instruction of prospects in the southern quadrant." She pauses, taking my silence, I gather, for my needing convincing. "There are four territories and thus three other Houses with their own Headmistresses who rule by Council." She steeples her hands. I'm not sure her nose could rise any higher. "Houses are run like a magical boarding school, if you will. There are no school year semesters here. We have one Season from May to August where débutants are able to officially join our societies. Since its inception, House of Marionne has held its own study and exhibition of magic as a cut above the rest." She rolls her wrist, unfolding her palm up. *"Supra alios."* Then she snaps it beside her, before unrolling her fingers to lie flat, and I realize it's some sort of official gesture. "Don't worry, you'll learn." She smiles and it tugs at something giddy in me.

I slide to the edge of my seat, eager to hear more.

"Since Sola Sfenti unearthed the Sun Stones in the ancient days, the Order has done what it must to protect and preserve its magic. For centuries, there was nowhere safe to grow or study it. Hiding magic was the only option. *Until* . . ." Her lips curl in a clever smirk. "The world shifted, capitalism boomed, and Britain began to tout itself as a world power. Within those *lavish* shows of disgustingly acquired wealth, the débutante was born."

"So the Order . . . magic has been around since forever?"

"If you don't know *true* history, dear, you *will* learn it here."

"History is actually the one class I never skipped." The honesty spills out before I can tug it back, my skin tingling with excitement. I bite my lip.

"We attend *all* our studies here, the intriguing and the mundane." She raises a brow, and I slink back in my seat. When she returns to my side, kindness has softened her expression, and I sit up a little straighter.

"We adopted the débutante concept, and of course put our own spin on it. But, Quell, those were the years everything changed for us." She cups her hand over mine. "We'd *finally* found a veneer to exist in the world, one to cloak our wealth, excuse our exclusivity, one to allow us to safely, *privately*, study and grow our gifts." She exhales. "That is . . . for those of us fortunate enough to be invited . . ." She pushes the Book of Names toward me.

Exclusive. Magic. Wealth.

I swallow. "I . . . I can't sign that."

Mom didn't tell Grandmom about my toushana. Instead, she fled, choosing a life on the run. There has to be a reason for that. I scoot away from her on the couch. "I'm sorry it's just . . . a lot, so fast."

Insistence burns in her eyes, and I pull my bag strap closer to me.

"You understand there is magic inside you, dear?"

"Yes, ma'am."

"And it *cannot* grow without the careful guidance of a Cultivator. That doesn't entice you?"

"I think I'm just tired."

Her stare deadens, and my throat goes dry.

"Of course. Forgive me." She slaps the book closed, her lips thinned. "You're probably exhausted."

"Yes."

"Very well, get some rest." She holds out her hand. "But I will require your phone. They're not allowed on the premises. This is a place of the utmost privacy and discretion."

"I—"

"Your phone, or I am afraid you will not be permitted to stay, dear." She straightens and I dig my phone out of my bag, thankful I at least have my key chain. I hand it over, and my heart skips a beat. It's like breaking off a piece of myself and giving it away.

"I'll have refreshment and fresh clothes sent to a room for you. We'll take up this conversation tomorrow, how does that sound?"

My fingers graze the spots on my arm Abby's magic healed, and a tightness unfurls in my chest at what *real* magic can do. I shove off the futile thoughts and meet Grandmom's eyes.

"That sounds good. Thank you."

By morning, I'll be gone.

FIVE

Outside Grandmom's door, I squeeze my key chain. It glows in response. I exhale and unfold the map Grandmom gave me. Room twelve of the Belles Wing, on the second floor, has a circle around it.

I hurry down the grand stairs and into a sconce-lit hall lined with glass display cabinets. In the first, a gold diadem speckled with radiant gems much more regal than Abby's or Grandmom's shines beneath spotlights. HEADMISTRESS CLAUDETTE MARIONNE, INAUGURAL HEADMISTRESS, HOUSE OF MARIONNE, 1874, the plaque reads. Beside it, in another display case, is a satin sash with frayed edges coiled like a snake, embroidered with the same fleur and talon symbol I saw on the front of this building. Its plaque boasts of someone else with my name that I don't recognize. Next to the sash is another. And another. The long hall is full of a dozen or more silver or gold diadems, some with tall spires, others with different shapes entirely, all encrusted with brilliant stones. Each as uniquely extraordinary as the one beside it.

I shove a fingernail between my teeth and wander deeper down the hallway, salivating at a world, a life, a history I should have known. The next case stills my steps. Unlike the other diadems in golds and silver, this one is blackened. I ball my hands into fists, reminded of the destructive secret coursing through my veins. Where the others are polished, their regality on display, the metal on this one is bent in several places and scuffed. The glass is cold against my skin as I squint at its plaque, where a sun is etched. The center of the sun is colored in.

THIS RELIC, VALIANTLY RETRIEVED BY
LEGENDARY SUNBRINGER ELOPHEUS THE DAWN,
WAS WON AT THE LAST KNOWN CONQUEST
AGAINST DARKBEARERS DURING THE SECOND AGE OF VULTURES.
CIRCA 1287 CE

"Won?"

"Yes," a low voice says, so close that I startle.

"Jordan." My heart hiccups, and the scent of him wraps around me as I turn to face him.

He's changed clothes. The top two buttons of his tuxedo shirt are undone, and a bow tie hangs around his neck, dangling on his chest. He stuffs something small and colorful in his tux pocket.

"That diadem was torn from the skull of a Darkbearer. They say the ghosts of Elopheus's victims still haunt the territories he razed."

"Darkbearer?"

"Night Bleeders, Death Walkers, Sons of Darkness, Dysiians. The names have changed throughout history. But they're all just another name for toushana-users who would pillage villages, torturing Unmarked. Elopheus once slew an entire hideout of Darkbearers in a single night. *By himself.*" He breathes a laugh. "Can you imagine?"

"No, I . . . I can't imagine."

"This was centuries ago." His expression sparkles with awe. "They're all gone, of course."

"And the Sunbringers? The ones who . . . hunted these . . . toushana-users?" My nails dig into my palm.

"Dragun was a nickname at first. The burning. The stories say the stench of Sunbringers disposing of Darkbearers, to make sure the toushana in them was dead, could be smelled as far as the next village over. The name just caught on after a while. But no . . ." He fingers the talon symbol at his throat. "We're still very much around." His eyes narrow. "You're nervous."

"I'm . . ." I glance both ways. Then back at the map. "Um, a bit lost, is all."

"Belles Wing is that way." He points.

"Did you follow me here?"

"I might have." Hard lines frame his inquisitiveness. "Is that a problem?"

"Hiding in shadows and attacking people are your specialties, I'm gathering?" The sass slips out as I put more distance between us.

"I was making sure you knew where to find your room."

No, you were spying on me because you don't trust me. The flickering hall light catches the specks in his eyes, making them shimmer. I start in the direction of the Belles Wing.

"You're being inducted, aren't you?" Jordan asks to my back.

"I don't mean to be rude, but that's none of your business." I walk faster.

"Everything here is my business."

I stop, his words slithering over me. "You're a *Ward*. A visitor."

"I am Jordan Wexton, Secundus, thirteenth of my blood, Dragun candidate, House of Perl."

I scrub my expression of whatever it might show and turn to face him. His mask seeps into his skin and his tousled hair is a sharp contrast to his tidy tuxedo.

"I don't need help to my room or your history lessons—"

"Don't you though?" He steps closer, but nothing reminiscent of genuine concern glints in his stare. Only suspicion.

"Get back to your party or whatever you're dressed for." I walk away from him, but he reappears in a cloud of dark fog in front of me, arm to the wall, a barrier in my path. His chiseled body hovers over me. I inhale, but there is no woodsy scent of paneled walls, oiled mahogany. Only him. Vetiver and olive trees. Vanilla and sandalwood. My heart patters. *Just get rid of him.*

"What do you want from me?"

He steps closer, his posture unyielding like that of someone who isn't often told no. I hold rigidly still. *He can't see me panic.*

"A truthful answer to my question. How did you see through my cloak?"

Words stick in my throat.

"Perhaps some sleep will loosen your tongue." He gestures toward the adjacent corridor. "Room twelve is that way. Rest well, Quell Janae Marionne."

I hurry down the hall to a gold-plated number twelve plastered to a door, grateful for more distance between myself and Jordan. I twist the knob open, and Abby stares back at me with one eye open and pinned hot rollers in her hair.

She pulls the door open wider. "Headmistress let me know you'd be rooming with me." She dangles an envelope with *Abilene Grace Feldsher* scrawled across it and a fleur seal at its back.

"Wow, she's fast."

"Order mail. Dropped in an outbox with a full name and proper seal, and it will travel right to the recipient, wherever they are, instantly. Tracer magic at its finest."

Inside, the room is oblong with two twin beds on opposing walls. Next to each bed is a door, one leading to a private bathroom and the other to a walk-in closet.

"That one's for you." She points at a tidy bed with a fluffed pillow, so nice it looks like it belongs in a magazine. Not something you actually sleep on.

"My roommate debuted tonight." Abby plops onto her bed. "So she's out of here."

I raise a brow.

"She finished the three Rites," she says. "Cotillion? Being presented to the Order as a member?" She spins in a circle, pretending to dance. I shake my head, full of questions.

"You'll learn." She smiles with a twinge of surprise.

Beneath a window on the far end of the room are two desks with an iron stand protruding from their center. A black-handled dagger lies on the stand on what must be Abby's desk. My hand instinctively moves to the shape of my protruding dagger handle in my bag. She catches me gawking.

"Honing."

"Huh?"

"Emerging. Honing. Binding. The three Rites." She tosses her dagger, catching it with her opposite hand. "To be inducted into the Order you have to complete them all. But Second Rite is honing your dagger, and it's a pain! Been stuck on it for two Seasons."

Mom gave me her dagger. I swallow, unsure what all this means.

"Good luck."

Her brow furrows. I set my bag on the bed, where I notice a stack of clothes with a note and a thin wooden tiara. I pick it up. Abby takes it from my fingers.

"First Rite is the easiest. Especially for you." She nudges me with her shoulders, grinning. "Your magic is probably so much more refined than anyone else's here. Being a Marionne and all."

I go cold all over, not my toushana, just bone-chilling angst.

"Once you start, you'll emerge in no time. But for now." She sets the wooden tiara on my head, and I pull it off, dread slinking through me. I told my grandmother I *wasn't* signing that roster.

I pick up the note on the stack of clothes.

Quell,

Forgive me for my haste tonight. To be quite transparent, Prospects are breaking their necks to be admitted here. I haven't found myself courting someone's interest in, well, ever. I strongly encourage you to explore the grounds, pop into classes, or sessions, as we call them here, if you like. Allow me to show you who you are, what you're capable of. Much of the world's mysteries are at your fingertips. Have a good sleep.

Warmly,

Headmistress

Tears well in my eyes. Underneath her title is a hand drawn fleur. She's wrong about me. Whatever potential she thinks I have like Abby, and the others here, that's not me. A part of me throbs with longing at the glimpse of a life, a secret magical life, I could have if I were like everyone else here.

"I am broken," I mutter, words thick in my throat.

Abby keeps talking, but I'm distracted by a small booklet that was underneath the note from Grandmom. I unfold it and remove a Post-it on it that reads, *Just in case. Inductees Rules and Responsibilities.*

"What'd the note say?"

"Nothing." I toss it and the rule booklet in a trash bin.

"Okay, well." She slides off my bed and back into her own, turned off, I guess, by my lack of enthusiasm and small talk. I feel bad. She's trying to make conversation. I blink and see a house swallowed up in flames. Why couldn't I have been in my own room, alone? Alone, I know. Alone, I can do.

"Breakfast opens at six, sessions start at eight," she says, painfully nice, despite my inability to reciprocate. "It's still pretty early summer, so sometimes sessions are outside. The last month of season, it's too sweltering for that. If we leave early, I can give you a tour. What time is your first session?"

I shift uncomfortably. The truth, that I'm sneaking out of here the minute Mom shows up, hangs on my lips. "I don't have my schedule yet," I lie. "But maybe I'll check out some sessions in the morning."

Abby wraps herself in blankets, turning her back to me. "Sleep well, roomie." She turns off her lamp, and I climb into bed in my clothes. Fortunately, she is already snoring and doesn't ask any questions. I bury myself in the blankets. My bag with the few things I brought is at the foot of my bed, and my key chain is beside me so I won't miss its glow. My fingers are warm and the cinch between my shoulders eases some. My toushana is settled, thankfully.

I shuffle under the blankets, restless before deciding to pull out the page Mom gave me with the address. I realize a postcard of a beach is clipped to its back. The water on the picture is so blue it can't be real. I settle down in the covers but avoid lying too flat. I don't want to doze off. Mom's going to be here soon. Guilt worms itself through me for the hard time I've given her over all of this. My toushana has ruined not only my life but hers, too.

Somehow, someway, wherever we go next, I have to make sure Mom is not in harm's way.

SIX

——✳——

A man reaches into my chest.
And pulls out my heart.
I fall to my knees, cold all over.
Clutched tightly in his hand, he tips the glass, pouring.
Blood spills onto the floor, dripping from the rim.
I shiver, pleading.
He licks his lips in a vile smirk, a coin glinting at his throat.
The glass, now upright, refills with a black substance.
With it filled to the brim, he squeezes and squeezes until the glass shatters.

I sit up, gasping. Cold sweat sticks to me. Abby's bed is empty and sun winks at me from the window. *Mom.* I feel through my covers for my key chain. It's over the edge of the bed on the floor. I snatch it up and squeeze. *Squeeze back, Mom. Let me know you're okay. That you're still coming.* I blow out a breath, hands shaking, cold, from my dream, I'm pretty sure.

Outside is green as far as I can see, the estate rimmed in morning fog. Right below Abby's window is a garden wrapped in shrubbery. Several pupils wearing diadems or masks in varying sizes and shapes gossip and gab over breakfast. It reminds me of a high school cafeteria where everyone's plugged into the drama for the day. Except here, no one's sitting alone.

Think.

Sharp aches bluster to and fro through my bones in warning, like winds before a winter storm, my toushana threatening to rise up. Mom hasn't come yet. I can't stay here. I slip on the plain scoop neck dress that Grandmom gave me so I at least blend in. It's a simple straight cut, embroidered with fleurs on its capped sleeves. My body tingles all over as the dress seems to tighten itself in places. The prickle of cold stabbing me sharpens. I can feel my toushana more clearly or something. When I grab my bag and dash past the mirror, I catch a glimpse of myself and still. The soft, fine linen is dusty pink, the color of the sky before nightfall. It fits as if it was made especially for me. I peel myself away from the mirror, ease the door open, and book it down the hall.

Down the stairs, I halt at a rush of people with no exits in sight. My toushana's ache deepens, pressing into me like a scrape of a knife on the underside of my skin. I knead my hands to try to warm them before it's too late. The hall is a cloud of conversations, and for a moment the world stops spinning. I'm surrounded by gleaming masks and radiant diadems, mindless titters and chatter behind gloved hands. Heads swim around me, and I'm pinned in the center of it all like a thorn in a bunch of hand-picked roses. My feet won't move. My heart won't slow.

"Excuse me," says a girl with a sharp chin and coiled hair down her back. The diadem on her head is angular and rimmed with small purple stones.

"Sorry." I step aside, out of her way, gaping at the showing of magic growing out of her head.

She and a friend hurry past, both in beautiful gowns much more or-nate than the simple one I and mostly everyone wear. I crane for a view of where they might be going dressed so fancily.

"Is that her?" someone behind me whispers, and I realize my staring has garnered attention.

"Headmistress's granddaughter returned from the dead," another snickers. My heart stumbles and I scan desperately for an exit.

"I heard she was back because Headmistress is sick and she wants all her money." I resist the urge to plug my ears, and I take off in the direction that looks most familiar. It was so dark when I arrived, everything looks so different now. Grandmom's a fixture in the busy corridor, ushering people to their sessions. She's the last person I want to see. I hurry, trying to blend into the blur of the rush to morning sessions as I look for the foyer we came through last night, the hovering sphere, *something* to orient me in this maze of a place.

The crowd moves down an expansive corridor of what appear to be classrooms: tall carved doors beneath arched thresholds with engraved inscriptions in a language that's unfamiliar to me.

Chill settles on my bones like a layer of morning frost, my toushana fully awake.

"Quell?" a familiar voice calls. *Jordan.*

Oh god, not now.

"Don't make this hard," he says, following me.

I pick up the pace to a light run, my heart racing my feet, knowing what the Order does to people like me. He can't see me, not like this . . . not while my toushana's this inflamed. I round another corner, and it's a dead end where an intricately sculpted sheet of stone eclipses most of the wall. It looks like a scene plucked out of a history book. The sound of panting is on my heels, but I don't see Jordan. Yet.

I wedge myself into the small space between the statue and the wall. The time between his footsteps lengthens as he rounds the corner. I rest on my heels, waiting, hoping he doesn't realize I'm hiding here. The wall is firm against my back.

Then it's not.

I fall backward, rolling right through the paneled wall, and hit my head on the hard ground. "Ow!" Darkness surrounds me. The only ray of light shines from a peephole in the wall. My hands rove the hard floor as I gape at the sturdy wall in front of me. The wall? I just went *through* a wall? Using the peephole, I spot Jordan, staring at the stone display with hardened frustration. But after a moment he turns to go back the way he came.

I dust myself off and look for some indication of where the corridor goes. Judging by the well-scuffed floor, it's a commonly used one. After several minutes, my pulse slows, my toushana retreats, and the rubbing of my hands finally warms them. I push against the wall that I fell through with my elbow to avoid using my fingers, just in case, and it gives like a trapdoor. I could go back that way. But if there's a way out of here that doesn't involve potentially running into people, Grandmom, for example, I prefer that.

Clack.

"Hello?" I tighten my grip on my bag, running my hands along the wall, feeling for some sort of alternative exit. I ease out my next breath to calm the anxiety pulling at me. The walls are all smooth. No archways, handles, or doors. I follow it until the peephole is so far behind me, my hand is invisible in front of my face.

Laughter flits through the air, dotted by footsteps. Several footsteps.

I follow the sounds, my feet much braver than my conscience, when a faint melody plays. High, strained notes. The music cries higher, and I press my ear to the part of the wall where I hear it loudest. There's no proper door, but there's something behind here. My fingers trace every divot on the wall, pushing, leaning into it. It shifts, and a door appears. I gasp.

Light splits the darkness and the music swells. I peek inside. The light flickers and the laughter is louder. Inside, a long table wreathed in chairs fills most of the room. Stacks of old leather books are piled in the corner. I look for a record player or some source of the music, but there's nothing like that. And no one's here. The hair on my neck stands. I heard people; I know I did.

I back away, and my foot nudges something piled on the floor. It spills, clattering. The thin long rods at my feet are slender with knobby ends like very large bones. The music stops. I gaze around, but only shadows shift in the corners. Goose bumps race up my skin. I turn to go back the way I came.

"You're early." The voice comes from the entryway, or trick door, rather, just as a busty woman with an earthy complexion and slick, dark hair appears. Black tulle gathers at her neck and wrists, cinched with a glittery fleur brooch. Her diadem is low to her head, covered in a cluster of blue stones.

"Cultivator Dexler." She sticks out her hand, and I take it, despite my confusion. "Your grandmother told the staff you might pop into some sessions today. I'm honored you chose to sit in on mine. No trouble finding the room, then?"

"I was—"

"Yes?"

"No, no trouble finding my way down here."

"Good." She claps me on my back. More file into the room, several with daggers in hand, and Dexler indicates a chair around the table for me to sit. I play the part, pretending. But when she dismisses us, I'll follow the corridor and see if it leads to the outside. From there, I'll try Mom again. I glance at my key chain, but it still isn't glowing. I chew my lip.

Next to me, someone wearing a bemused expression flicks her blue eyes in my direction, smacking on bubble gum. She pulls at her earring, eyes me up and down, and offers me a plastic smile before turning her attention back to a small black book. But I'm too distracted by the gold diadem, tall and ornate, stacked with gems arced over her cropped blond hair.

Dexler claps. "Now, where were we?" The word *Transfiguration* is on the wall behind her. "We'll start with recitations. Electus?"

"Ma'am?" a small group asks in unison, while the rest stay quiet.

"What is your charge?"

"Emerging one's magic," they chant. "Rich is the blood of the chosen."

"Very good," she goes on. "Primus, what is your charge?"

"Honing one's dagger." A different group speaks this time. "Arduous is the work of the laborer."

"And Secundus, what is your charge?"

Only a handful speak this time, including the blue-eyed girl next to me. "Binding fully with one's magic. Entrusted are many, proven are few. Duty is the honor of the willing."

"Excellent, and two more. Transfiguration?"

"To transfigure is to change," the group says in unison. "The core of magic is change. Transfiguring one thing to something else with regard to the Rules of Natural Law."

She snaps, keeping tempo with the cadence of the class's recitations. "And what is the First Rule of Natural Law?"

The session answers, their voices a blur of words and meaning.

"Superb." Dexler's gaze falls on me. I shift in my seat. *Please don't call on me. I know* nothing.

"Before we get started, hand up your independent study work on augratics." She moves around the room, collecting papers. I sit up.

"Today I'll be reviewing necrantics, a type of Shifting that deals with the transfiguration of dead anatomy, for those who need the refresher." Whispers swarm. "Remember, these reviews in sessions are only a fraction of your training. Magic is a kinetically acquired skill. Staring at me talking isn't going to grow your magical ability." She pulls her glasses off her face, eyeing each of us in the room. "You should be spending *hours* every day on actual independent practice and study. You Secundus, especially. Free time isn't for socializing."

Dexler shushes everyone and picks up a bone from one of the piles on the floor. It's longer than my whole arm. I hang on her every sentence, awestruck.

"Today's lesson is a bit more hands-on. First, you'll need your kor. Your energy source. Eventually you'll be able to summon your own energy, but for now, most often fire will do."

Fire. I swallow.

She secures a ring with a chunky purple stone on her knuckle before pulling a bunch of uncut taper candles from a box and separating one, slicing the wick close to the wax. Once she fits it into a candleholder, she rubs her hand over it, the purple stone glows, and the candle ignites.

I flinch, pressing back in my seat for a moment before leaning forward, gaping in awe. I realize I'm gripping the table so tightly, people are watching.

Dexler smirks at me. "First, I shifted the composition of the air to make it more flammable." She holds her palm face out and it's dull gray. "Shifted my skin to give it a layer of something complementary to the kor. For fire I chose magnesium."

Pencils scratch paper, but I can't tear my eyes away.

"Now, for the bone." She holds the bone, turning it in the flame, working her fingers up and down it, the stone of her ring still glowing. After several spins, she wraps the bone in a rip of fabric. Again, she turns it over the flame. I sniff for some sign of burning, but there is none. The fabric bubbles against the bone as Cultivator Dexler works her fingers, smoothing the bubbles out when the purple gleam of her ring stutters.

The flame swells larger.

"Ah," she shouts as the fire goes out, and she tugs the ring off her finger, wincing. "Well, it's a start. Magic is prickly." She returns the ring to its locked box, then sets the bone in the middle of the table, and everyone leans over it. The fabric wrapped around the bone has changed to cylindrical fibers, like muscle. "That's the leg of an ancient creature. And with enough time and focus and skill, we could recreate the entire carcass. That's the skill of a Shifter, a master at transfiguring one material to another. Common Shifters manipulate solids. The rarer complex Shifter can manipulate liquids and gases. They can change the air you're breathing into toxic gas with the right manipulation of their magic."

All around the room, mouths gape at her.

"So don't turn up your noses at the most prevalent specialization. Most of you will be Shifters, and they're quite impressive." She picks up the dead leg. "Now, if this creature were alive, to transfigure it, a Shifter wouldn't suffice. We'd need an Anatomer."

I stare in utter disbelief. She recreated the leg of a dead animal.

"Shifter magic is used to heal wounds. And to some degree, transfigure the body. So you Healer hopefuls, pay close attention. Your turn to try." She claps and the session jumps into motion, not the slightest bit confused. I, on the other hand, am stuck in my chair. *Can I do that?* I glance at the door, then my bag, but curiosity pins me to my seat.

Dexler works at a small table in the back, passing out materials, and I hop in line to try. She gives everyone a kor already lit, fabric, and a bone. Once I have mine, I settle in a corner of the room to work alone. I do my best to gulp down my annoying fear of fire and rotate the bone over the flame, like she did, slow and careful, then wrap the fabric around it. Suddenly everything in me goes cold. The white edge of the bone blackens, turning to rot. I drop it, my pulse thundering through me, glancing around to make sure no one sees. I could never do this. Toushana is the only sort of magic I can seem to reach. And all it does is make a mess of things. I'd probably kill someone trying to heal them.

"You need some help?" Dexler approaches.

I stumble up. "No, I'm good."

"Let me see what you've done."

"No, really, it's okay."

But she picks up the bone, turning it. I'm rigid with fear.

"Well, that's odd. I thought I gave you a fresh one. This one looks like it's rotted."

My heart thuds in my ears, too stressed to actually be relieved by her confusion.

"Here's a fresh one," she says, setting a new bone in front of me. My toushana rolls through me in a wave of chill.

"Now, again. Ready?"

Away, I tell my toushana, *please*, rubbing my hands together. As they warm, I replay the steps in my head. My fingers heat a moment, but chilliness chases the feeling away.

"The first time you use your magic, it burns a little," she says, her expression eager. "But if you push through it, the magic will listen."

Burns? My only experience with magic is bone-chilling cold.

"Thanks," I say, giving my fingers another moment to fend off the cold before grabbing the bone. *Warmth. Lean into warmth.* I close my eyes and picture my toushana, buried deep down. But an iciness wiggles its way into my hands and out toward my fingers. I hold my breath and the air tight in my chest swells against my ribs as if I might explode.

"Ready when you are, dear." Dexler hovers behind me, whispering, and I feel a hot rush of something seep into me, grainy and earthy.

It blooms, then crescendoes into a searing heat that thrashes around inside me like a pile of violently blown leaves. My toushana shifts against the inferno building in my chest. I focus hard, tightening my every muscle, imagining the feeling growing, *winning*. The wintry magic lurking in my veins retreats as my hands begin to warm.

Harder.

I clench my fist. My insides are fire. Again, I hold the bone over the flame, seizing the moment, rotating it steadily. The fabric ripples. *It's working!* I rotate the bone more vigorously.

"Yes, yes, that's it." Dexler grips my shoulders, tight.

My fingers get too close to the flame, and I hardly feel the fire licking my skin.

"That'a girl," Dexler says. "Steady now, just like that."

The place where Dexler is touching me sears. The fabric wrapped around the bone bubbles, shifting. "Oh my god!" The threads elongate and become rubbery and fibrous.

"*Yes,*" Dexler shouts. "The transfiguration is setting in nicely." She lets go of my shoulder and I rear back in my seat. "You did it."

"You . . . helped?"

"No more than I do with anyone. Cultivators can share a little of other magic"—she indicates the ring—"but I can only bolster what's already there. *You* did it. Quite easily, I might add."

I blink and blink again.

Oh my god.

I did real magic!

SEVEN

·· ——✳—— ··

My mouth is still wide open. Dexler squeezes my shoulders. "Don't be so surprised. You're a Marionne. Magic is strong in you."

I can access real magic.

I can access real magic!

It blew around in me like a vicious dust storm and fought off my toushana, I felt it. Excitement wells in my eyes. Maybe I'm not entirely broken.

"Very good." Dexler folds her arms. "Dare I say Headmistress will be ecstatic to hear it."

It's then I notice no one else in the session has managed to transfigure their fabric and bone to muscle yet. Cultivator Dexler's lips are pursed with the tiniest curl at the end. She's impressed. A weird feeling rolls through me. A smile tugs at my lips.

"All right, time." She passes out textbooks, pulling the class's attention back to the front. But I'm still reeling from what all this means.

"Who recalls the Second Rule of Natural Law?" Session moves on, hands shooting in the air.

"Magic strengthens with use," the girl with the blue eyes says, her book parted in front of her.

My ears perk up.

"Precisely, Miss Duncan," Cultivator Dexler says.

I sit up in my seat, flipping to the page they're on.

Dexler goes on as I find the text on the page.

2ND RULE OF NATURAL LAW

Magic strengthens with use.

When you bind to one sort of magic, it dulls your ability to reach other sorts of magic.

Wait. I raise my hand.

"Yes, Miss Marionne?"

I check the page again. "Does this mean that as I use one type of magic, it becomes easier to reach?"

"Precisely. When—"

I raise my hand again, and the session appears relieved to get back to their side conversations.

"Yes, Miss Marionne, another question?"

"Let's say I have an affinity for . . ." I check my book. "Necrantics. If I hone that magic, then try to transfigure sound one day, I won't be able to?"

"After you've bound, likely not. Once you bind with a certain type of magic, the others become extremely difficult to reach. They become atrophied, so to speak. Think of your magic like a piece of clay you mold," she goes on. "Once it takes shape and hardens, it cannot be remolded. So practicing your magic molds your clay. Binding hardens it."

"Binding?" I ask. "Third Rite, you mean?"

"Yes, Third Rite is Binding, when you are presented at Cotillion in your gown to the Order, officially welcomed into membership." She smiles at that part. "Your signature then transfers from the Book of Names to the Sphere's glass where it stays for the rest of your life."

I chew my nail completely off, my mind spiraling down a well of what-ifs. So if I keep practicing this warm, proper sort of magic, like I did here today, strengthening my ability to reach it, I can bind with it and bury my toushana forever? *No . . . no way . . . I must be misunderstanding.*

She returns her attention to the rest of the group. "Secundus, choose your magic specialty thoughtfully. You'll be stuck with it forever."

Heads nod, but I stare, blinking, stuck on her last words.

"Turn to page twenty-nine," she goes on. A collective groan rolls through the room and she raises her volume. "And copy down *all* twelve uses of acacia leaves. Secundus, you will also do a one-page analysis of the two magic specialties that you are most interested in."

Books slap open. I don't move, white knuckling my seat, as if I could hold her very words in my grip. The weight of them sits on me like a brick on my chest. I can lean into the sort of magic I did here and bind with it, getting rid of this poison in my veins completely! I steady myself on the table, reminding myself to breathe.

Did Mom know about this? *She couldn't have.* I glimpse the bone, still wrapped in shreds of muscle. I felt that other magic *so* strongly. It was different from the icy urge that haunts me. Everyone scribbles in their journals. Hope wells up inside me. The running, the hiding, the shadows. My chin hits my chest. We didn't have to live like that. We *don't* have to. We *won't.* Not anymore.

SESSION FINISHES AND I'm outside Grandmom's private quarters in minutes thanks to the map I grabbed from my room. Her maid lets me in. Grandmom is stirring a cup of tea, under a blanket by the fire.

"Good to see you, dear."

My insides are tight. I must do it now, before I second-guess myself. *Yes,* if the Order finds out about my toushana they'll kill me. But they won't. Hiding my truth is something I've done my entire life. I can do it here for as long as it takes to complete the Rites. This is the only way to put this cursed existence behind me. And it keeps Mom out of danger— *away* from me—until I'm no longer a risk to her. Wouldn't anything else be like treading quicksand?

Grandmom gestures to the chair beside her. "What brings you—"

"I'd like to enter induction, complete the three Rites, and become a member of the Order. If you'll still have me."

She sets down her cup. "You've come around?"

I nod and her cheeks swell.

"You're my granddaughter. Aristocracy is in your blood. Of course I'll have you." She flips through the Book of Names and pulls a pen from a wooden box and puts it in my hand. I hold it firmly, my heart ramming in my chest.

"Right there, beneath the others."

I sign and the ink thickens on the page.

"Once you complete the Rites, the Book will absorb your name and inscribe it on the Sphere, alongside the thousands of others, cementing your membership."

I struggle to move, equally certain and terrified of what I just decided to do.

"Aren't you thrilled, dear?"

My heart is in my throat. "Very much so."

She grabs me by the wrist uncomfortably tight and pulls me to her writing desk. "One more small matter." She takes my hand, and before I can snatch it back, she pinches the tip of my finger. She rubs her thumb and forefinger together and pulls backward, as if tugging an invisible string, and out of my skin comes a drop of blood.

"Ow!"

She blows on it, watching with wide eyes. After a moment, she exhales and drops it in a vial. "*Now*, there we are." She writes someone's full name on an envelope and drops the blood sample inside it before slipping it into an outbox on her desk. It disappears. "Mrs. Cuthers will get that all filed away. Welcome home, dear."

"Thank—" My pocket glows. I pull out my key chain.

Grandmom takes it from me. "I haven't seen this thing in years."

"It's Mom; I think she's trying to get me."

"Yes, I know how it works, dear. I procured it from a reputable Trader myself."

She did? There's so much Mom never told me. So much I still don't know. Grandmom sets the key chain on her desk. "I may be able to reverse trace the key chain's magic to locate your mother, if you don't mind leaving it with me for a bit." She gazes out the window, her back to me. "Would you like that?"

"You would do that?"

"Of course. After all, we have much to update her on, wouldn't you say?"

"I guess so." Guilt tugs at me, and I can almost see Mom's worn expression. She's sacrificed so much for me. An ugly, undeniable truth that I've shoved back down time and time again rises like bile in my throat.

The safest place for Mom is out there *away* from me.

I glare at my hands. I *have* to get rid of this poison. She would say my plan is too dangerous. But I know in my gut, I can do this. I was *so* good in Dexler's. I can't put her in danger anymore, not when this option is right in front of me. I blow out a big breath. *Away from me, she is safe.* When we're back together, she, too, will have a life. I didn't have a choice when we fled before, but I do now.

I have to do this.

To free both of us.

EIGHT

―――✳―――

YAGRIN

Yagrin appeared on the rain-soaked cobbled road that ran through Emancipation Park. It gave the area an Old World aesthetic. But it was more than mere architectural design. The quaint park near the west bank of the Mississippi was access for those who knew where to look. The freckle-faced girl had evaded him. But there couldn't be many places someone with her affliction could go. And he knew just the place to find out where someone like her might hide, a spot ripe with Order gossip—the Tavern.

Yagrin wanted an honest life. But the thought was laughable. Fear was the lifeblood of the Order, the shackle of duty. In the end, it was all about fear or being feared, his father'd taught him. And while he wasn't sure he bought it, here he was chasing another assigned target. Being the monstrosity expected of him. He kicked his boot on the rocky surface, shuffling through the muddy puddle, hoping it was just mud.

He pursed his lips, ruminating on Freckle Face, the odd way Mother spoke about this new target. The way she hesitated to give him her full name: Quell Jewel. His heel found the familiar spot, a loose rock in the path. He looked around. Lovebirds tangled around one another were on a park bench completely uninterested in him. Emancipation was still. The stone walls that wreathed its memorial courtyard and interior gardens stood like a sentry in the night's glow. He kicked the shifty pebble and sucked in a breath, letting his magic work its way into his fingers, up his arms. Heat swirled in him, and he tightened his stomach, holding in a breath, to shove it up to his head.

He directed his magic at the stone, and the ground opened like a dead man's throat, stairs descending into darkness. He took them one at a time, the Tavern's revelry swelling louder the deeper he went. It was *the* hangout for Order members in the southern quadrant. Usually teeming with eager students who hadn't yet debuted, prattling with gossip like baby birds anxious to leave the nest. Several recent debs, that is débutantes and débutants, hung there, too. And even a few dregs of older members popped in from time to time, but the desperate ones, never the classy ones. His parents wouldn't be caught dead in the Tavern. It was "beneath them." The thought put a pep in his step as he slipped inside.

Noise swelled like a balloon, and Yagrin skimmed the place for another of his kind, from his House. But he only spotted one Dragun from another House whom he didn't know well. Karaoke blared from a side room adjacent to a long run of gambling tables. A few loitered over drinks. He searched for a place to land out of the way of people, where he could size up anyone coming through the door. He felt like a maggot coming in here, stinking like death wherever he went. He scowled, but his heart thrummed as he fell into a chair at the bar with a sigh.

He undid the tie of his trench coat and scanned the crowd for someone worthy of interrogation. It was thinner tonight than usual, considering the Tavern was a notorious meetup for slimy Traders and their seedy customers. More magical goods were exchanged by covert handshakes, over card tables, and during drinks than money flowing in and out of a bank.

Yagrin's Dragun coin might still feel foreign at his throat, but he'd grown up in a powerful Order family, and his father had primed him, instructing him on how things were done. How to get what you wanted from people, until Yagrin came of age and was handed over to his Headmistress, who made sure the lessons stuck. Tonight he would let muscle memory take over. He intended to obtain highly proprietary information: where someone with toushana these days would look for safety.

Posted against the wall in a shadowed corner was a gangly bearded fellow with his fingertips tucked in his vest pockets. Yagrin smiled at the ripe opportunity. He knew if he snatched the stranger's hands out of those petite pockets, they'd be stained deep blue, nails bloody, some missing. A Trader.

The fellow's dusty brown eyes matched the bang swooping across his face. Yagrin stared and it unsettled the fellow's cavalier posture. Yagrin grinned. He'd found a guitar worth plucking. He approached, but the fellow moved, likely uninterested in a conversation with a Dragun. Yagrin needed to disarm his suspicion. Draguns were the enforcers of decorum in the Order, but he wasn't here to hem him up about the exploitive business he dabbled in.

"Feel like a game of cards?" Yagrin gestured to a nearby table where a dealer was two short. The Trader's eyes flickered with ambition, and after a moment he inclined his head. Challenge accepted. Trust was a fickle thing, and you could tell a lot about someone over a game of cards, his father had taught him. Their measure of judgment, how easy they were to read, and especially what winning meant to them.

Spades was Yagrin's favorite. Red had taught him how to play. His lips curled. He needed to make time to see her again. "It's all about hedging bets and winning tricks," she'd explained one night they spent camping, her body curled around his under the stars. She was more right than she knew. The truth was always in the eyes. That's what he loved about Red. She wasn't in the Order, knew nothing of magic, a daughter of a farmer who lived in the middle of nowhere. Her entire life plan was to figure out how exactly aquaponics worked and to ride a horse bareback without falling off. She was *sharp* but turned off by complexity. Detached is how she lived. Because she wanted to.

He pulled up a chair at the card table, and the Trader sat across from him.

"Wager?" the dealer asked.

"A favor," Yagrin told him.

The dealer smirked. Not every day a Dragun offered his services as a wager.

"And you?" the dealer asked the Trader. He was stoic. But Yagrin could sense his elevated heartbeat pumping with anticipation. Traders, by nature of their dealings peddling stolen goods, had many enemies. A favor from a Dragun wasn't an offer most would refuse.

"Source Enhancer. Ancestral quality, from the caves of Aronya." He held up a red stone. "Retrieved it myself."

That part was a lie. Traders stole anything of value they managed to get their hands on. But it was authentic; its hue and shine were unmistakable. There were many who'd pay generously for such a prize. When it was folded into a deb's dagger, its possessor could sense the presence of any magic, once bound. Broken down to liquid form by a complex Shifter, it was a powerful ingredient that could manipulate any elixir. Even an Anatomer could use it to cover their tracks.

Yagrin sat back in his chair, impressed. It was a perceptive offer. But tonight Yagrin was after the intangible: secrets. Ambition creased around the Trader's pursed lips. He *wanted* to barter.

"No deal," Yagrin said, pushing his luck. He waved his hand dismissively, and the fellow's confidence fractured.

"*This is—*"

"Not what I want."

He sneered, aghast.

"Match me favor for favor. That's it. Or no game."

The Trader's foot tapped, and an order of drinks made their way around the table. Yagrin cemented his expression, unreadable, like Mother—his Headmistress—had him practice time and time again in the forest, under the moon. He would be imperceptible. The Trader would look for a glimpse of Yagrin's eagerness but find none. Which would only further unveil his own desperation.

The Trader took a sip. "Fine. Favor for favor."

The dealer spewed cards from his hands, and Yagrin tightened his lips to keep from smiling. He had him. All he had to do was ensure he won the game. Yagrin's hand wasn't great, but nothing he couldn't fix. He pulled at the warmth simmering beneath his skin and called it to his fingertips. He eased his magic across his cards sneakily, and the diamonds in his hands shifted into spades.

"I have seven," the Trader said.

"I have nine."

The Trader unbuttoned his sleeves, tugged at his collar. If the dealer was on to Yagrin's tricks, he didn't make it known. He wouldn't want to be in a Dragun's ill graces either. Power wasn't Yagrin's preferred flavor of poison, but he couldn't deny it had its benefits. The cards were laid on the table in order. His turn, then the Trader's. And Yagrin slid more and more winning sets his way, until he reached twelve to the Trader's mere three.

"I win."

The Trader slammed his cards on the table. Victory bubbled up in Yagrin, but he hid delight from his expression. The Trader followed him to a shadowed corner of the bar just as a familiar face swept into the room. Felix, a buddy Yagrin had debuted with last Season. Felix landed at the bar and raised a glass at him. Yagrin's confidence shook. He hadn't counted on being seen with the scum.

He pulled the Trader by his collar deeper into the hallway, out of sight, fighting back the urge to apologize for roughing him up. He would project strength. He must, to get what he wanted. "I'll keep it brief and assume this conversation is confidential?"

"I owe you a debt. I can't exactly refuse, can I?" The Trader's hands shook though he kept his jaw mean.

Yagrin let go of him. "I just need some info. Relax." *I don't want to hurt you*, he thought, but he kept that to himself. "I'm Yagrin."

"Des." He stood up a little taller. "So let's get it over with. What do you want to know?"

"Someone on the run with toushana. These days, where could they go that's safe?"

After finishing Third Rite, target assignments came from Headquarters, from the Dragunhead himself, Yagrin's actual boss. But Mother kept her graduates close and didn't hesitate to call in favors. This was the second target this month she'd had him look for. Pink Beanie had been the first. Mother didn't elaborate beyond Quell's name. But she didn't have to. Nor did he care to know more about the girl he must find. The more he knew, the more doing the job would knot his insides.

"Safe houses," the Trader said.

A lie. Yagrin had just come from a safe house, and it had been destroyed. "If we're going to do this, you have to be honest. I'm on mission, but my friend . . ." He pointed at Felix, who was at the bar, leaned over a drink. "Isn't. He'd happily latch you up and take you in to answer for the treasonous dealings you dabble in." Yagrin grimaced; the taste of the threat was bitter. But somehow he had to maintain the upper hand.

Des swallowed. "Fine. The safe houses are being demolished."

"And?"

"And . . . so there isn't any real place to hide anymore. Unless this person knows someone who would keep their secret."

"Who would do that?"

The Trader's expression shifted, but Yagrin missed what it meant. "I don't know much, honestly. Look, things are in flux right now. My usual trading spots have been exploited. I'm having to reroute all my goods. And no one's talking anymore either. My usual whisperers have all gone silent."

Another lie. Yagrin scoffed, pushing Des into the wall. "Lie to me again and I'll debone you limb by limb, before I bury your body." *Fear or be feared.* It was as easy as breathing. He hadn't chosen this life, he'd been bred for it.

"I'm telling you the truth! Nothing's like it was. Even my customers are nervous. If I wasn't in dire straits I wouldn't have even joined you at that table," he spit, gazing far off. "Whispers of the Sphere changing have everyone nervous."

Yagrin stilled and eased off him a bit. "Changing how?"

"I heard it's all blackened now, like it's decomposing from the inside out or something."

Yagrin narrowed his eyes. "Have you seen it yourself?"

"I don't know if it's true, but if enough people believe it, does it being true even matter?"

Yagrin's brow deepened. That almost made him want to hightail it to his House to see the Sphere's state. An illusion of it hung in each House's foyer as a reminder of the Commissioning Pact that had forged it centuries ago. Its *actual* location was a mystery.

It had all been so wondrous when he saw the Sphere the first time on a visit to his House with his father well before he was old enough to even think about inducting. It was so vivid, its insides sparkling with glowing granules of Sun Dust, swirling back and forth like a snow globe. His skin tingled then and again now. Pride in knowing he was a part of something grand and special—the Prestigious Order of Highest Mysteries. *Magic.* Something his bloodline had a firm hand in shaping.

That was before it all soured. Before he struggled to show any magic at all until two years after everyone else his age. After he saw how furious that made his father. After he'd been deemed an embarrassment.

"Consider your debt paid."

"*What . . . I—*"

"I'm feeling generous tonight." Yagrin squeezed his shoulder before walking away. He could sense the blood rushing through Des begin to slow. Yagrin hadn't gotten the info he needed. But Des didn't have it. In his gut, Yagrin was sure of it.

But this news of the Sphere kneaded his nerves. He let his mind wrap around Des's words as the Trader blended into the crowd before dashing out the door. The Sphere was rotting from the inside. *If the Sphere's insides ever bled out . . .* He steadied himself against the lip of the bar, his heart thumping . . . *that would be the end of all magic.* In their lifetime at least. It would vanish from every person who used to wield it.

Yagrin fell onto a stool at the bar. How did something like this happen? Was something responsible, or some*one*? Only someone powerful could do something like that. *He* could do something like that. But there weren't many like him, with his bloodline's prowess for magic. He looked for Felix, but he'd already gone. He reared back in his seat and thought of Pink Beanie and the toushana that used to course through her veins. The acrid way it smelled, burning. The mission of the Dragun brotherhood was to preserve and protect magic, whatever the cost. But his missions didn't come with explanations. They were only orders. He sat up taller. Maybe it was better that way. His Headmistress would say his job wasn't about his enjoyment, only his obedience. For the sake of everyone and everything. The mere suggestion should sink his shoulders, soothe his guilt.

But it didn't.

Whatever was going on with the Sphere, whether it had to do with Pink Beanie or not, he didn't feel good about any of it.

He waved for a drink, stewing on his predicament, trying to appease Mother to keep her in the dark about his treachery, avoiding the Dragunhead altogether. And now this. He shouldn't even care. The bartender didn't glance his way. He had no regrets about cheating out on Third Rite. That wasn't the same as not caring if he got caught. But he'd made his choice when he met Red. He wouldn't induct all the way. He'd seen what it did to his family. He would do enough to get by, fly under the radar. He flagged the bartender again.

"Kiziloxer?" the bartender asked, smoothing his hands on a towel that hung from his waist.

"Water, actually."

"Got it. Sorry, I saw you earlier. Small crowd, but thirsty."

"No problem."

"I'm Rikken, by the way," the bartender said. He was a barrel-chested fellow with a thick short beard and reddish-brown hair. "Slated class of '15. House of Ambrose."

He didn't finish.

"Yagrin. Fresh out."

Rikken wound one hand around another and pulled at the glass. It stretched, growing taller in size. He gathered his fingers, rubbing them together, pulling at the humidity in the air, and water filled the glass, straight from his fingertips.

"How'd a complex Shifter end up working a bar?" Yagrin asked, taking the glass. Shifter magic, even its basic form, had always evaded Yagrin. Anatomer and Audior magic took him a long time to master, but they were much more his speed.

"My great-great-grandfather started up a pub to help out the Order and they let him in on things. But his magic never took good enough to be usable. So he stuck to business, expanded into a string of pubs. Once he died, the family got tired of the upkeep. Most of 'em closed. 'Cept this one. I had nothing else going on, so I told them I'd take it."

"Ah, I see." He pointed to the water filling his glass. "I'd like to see you do that on a dry night," Yagrin teased.

Rikken laughed and pointed to a very normal water dispenser behind him. "Backup."

It was so much easier talking to people he didn't have to threaten. "These whispers of the Sphere? You buy it?"

"Who's asking?" he asked.

"I'm asking."

"You or your Headmistress?"

"So you *do* know something."

Rikken wiped the counter and poured another drink for a crowd rushing the bar. Inductees by the look of it. Bright eyed and eager, diadems and masks shining like they polished them each night. Yagrin sifted through the crowd, his collar up, careful to keep his face difficult to see. Slim chance the girl could enroll anywhere with the poison in her veins. Still, he scanned for freckles and soft brown eyes just in case.

The students tossed back their fizzed drinks, and he watched, sunken in the shadows on the farthest end of the bar. But he didn't spot the girl. He checked his watch and tapped his foot. Mother would be hounding him for an update soon.

"Look, I'm just the no-name son of an Order dropout," Rikken said, returning with a handful of drinks. "I don't need any trouble. I try to stay out of it. I'm not one of you fancy folks anyway."

"But you've heard—"

"I heard a while back, before you had hair on your chest, that one of the 'Mistresses had a hefty wager on finding that Sphere's location. Now it's all blackened. You tell me what that means."

Yagrin sank into his seat, the insinuation tugging him down like an anchor. Rikken thought a Headmistress was behind the Sphere rotting? That made no sense. Their lives were tethered to the Sphere. How did the old saying go? If the Sphere broke, the Headmistresses croaked.

Yagrin finished the water, thanked Rikken, and backed away from the bar. He wasn't interested in tinfoil hat theories. He wanted something he could sink his teeth into. His insides sloshed, sickened, like he imagined the Sphere, swirling with blackened bile.

Again he glanced at his watch, resituating his trench coat around himself. If he didn't find the freckle-face girl or some whispers of her soon, he'd have to face his Headmistress empty-handed. He gulped. He couldn't let her figure out that he was effectively a pretender. He imagined his father's face twisting with contempt, learning Yagrin's traitorous secret. Would he defend him or cast him off as a traitor, too? Yagrin tossed back the dregs in his glass, revelry bustling around him. It wasn't a question. He knew the answer.

PART TWO

NINE

····──✳──····

I plant my knees on the velvet bench, careful to keep my head bowed and Grandmom in my sights from the corner of my eye. I am entering induction, officially. *Please don't let this have been a mistake.*

The auditorium is full to the brim of my soon-to-be peers, but not a breath can be heard over the hammering in my chest as Headmistress Marionne cloaks my shoulders in the ornate gold cloth of the House. Abby waves at me from the front row of the worship rotunda. The small prayer room on the east side of the estate is made of stone with wood accents. Sun-inspired detailing covers its walls, and above the altar, early morning light winks at us from colorful windows with images that seem to tell a story.

"Sit on your heels." Grandmom presses my back. "The robe should cover all but your head." Her lips thin in frustration. She sighs, and Jordan leaps from his seat and joins her side.

"May I assist, Headmistress?"

"No, I—"

"Oh goodness, yes, please." Grandmom smooths the edges of her hair, warily eyeing the audience. Jordan joins my side and my breath hitches. Grandmom steps away, addressing the growing crowd.

"Put your hands in the pockets of the robe," he says.

"I don't need help, really." I glare up at him, desperate to put as much space between me and him as possible before my toushana confirms his suspicions and his deadly magic is wrapped around my throat. "I mean it, I'm fine."

"There's no room for your pride in here. Humble yourself before Sola Sfenti's altar and take your anointing with some dignity."

"*Pride?!* You think—"

"Please, if you will quiet your voices," Grandmom says into a microphone. "The ceremony is about to begin." A bell chimes three times and low music croons from the distance.

"Pockets, *now*," he says in a barked whisper, and I bite down, stuffing my hands into the velvety pockets of the House robe.

"On the twelfth chime," he whispers so closely I feel it on my skin, "slip your hands out of your pockets, palms and eyes up in a show of submission to the Sun God." He demonstrates. "When Headmistress signals, stand." He moves backward to give me some space.

On the twelfth ting of the triangle I do as he says. Light throbs through the domed glass ceiling's faceted angles, speckling on the marble altar beneath me. Grandmom approaches with a wood-handled brush.

"Now you must choose, mask or diadem," Jordan whispers.

"Where will you take your anointing?" Grandmom asks.

"Um, uh, diadem, please."

Jordan's eyes widen and he mouths, *ma'am.*

"Ma'am."

She dips the brush in a gold-rimmed bowl, gently back and forth. The subtle disturbance unlooses a cloud of glowing dust, and a hushed gasp sweeps through the room. Grandmom's hand stills until the dust has settled.

"Sun Dust is ground from the sun stones Sola Sfenti discovered in the ancient days, the source of all magic," Jordan says. "Its slightest touch is sacred, its every grain powerful. It will sharpen, focus, and awaken your ability to reach magic."

I suck in a breath as the brush touches my hair.

"The words," Grandmom says, her blush robe shifting at her feet as she moves around us. "Are you ready?"

I nod.

"May I prove worthy," Jordan prompts me to parrot him. "May I prove to be a proper steward."

"May I prove worthy. May I prove to be a proper steward," I say as the soft fibers glide across the dome of my head.

"Again, keep saying the prayer, over and over until you feel something."

I mutter again and again as Grandmom continues dusting, eyeing me with brimming anticipation. My skin tingles everywhere, subtle at first, then all over, so prickly it hurts.

"I feel it."

Grandmom's tentative smile brightens as she returns the brush to the bowl. "Rise and face Sola Sfenti, daughter of Sun. Your time is now."

I stand bearing the weight of the cloak, the House jewels slung across my chest, and face the sun. The audience claps. Grandmom embraces me, kissing each of my cheeks.

"You'll emerge in no time." She squeezes my shoulder, and sickness sloshes inside me. I've done it. I've stepped into this world we've spent our entire lives running from.

There's no turning back now.

Shortly after the induction ceremony Grandmom handed me a schedule, plus several more dresses like the one she sent to my room last night, and urged me to get to my first session without delay.

"Magic circulates in the blood better wearing these," she said. "This is your uniform, here on out." The fine fabric still feels foreign on my skin. Since the ceremony, my dress has felt as if it's a part of me, amplifying the warm hum of magic beneath my skin. I turn in the mirror above the dresser but there's no sign of Dust residue in my hair.

"Emerging . . ." I mutter, grazing my scalp with tentative fingers, and cringe at what it must feel like to have a diadem poke through. I set the wooden circlet on my head before departing for session. People stare as I move through the halls. Several with shiny masks on their faces or studded metal arced above their hair. Grafting myself into the shadows at a new school is nothing new. But this . . . here . . . with my name invisibly plastered on my forehead makes my head swim. I decide to try smiling; sometimes that's more disarming. To my relief, those watching me smile in return. *I will blend in.*

The hall opens up to the grand entryway, sunrays throbbing through endless windows. It takes every bit of my focus to not gape at the rotating sphere hung in the grand foyer like a blackened sun, matter undulating beneath its glass angrily, choppy waves on a stormy sea. The dots on its surface sparkle like a starlit night. I reach for one of the specks and my fingers pass through the illusion. Then it shifts, expanding into a web of what must be hundreds of names written in such small letters I can hardly make one out. I marvel at the numerous members' names etched on the Sphere, before returning my attention to my map.

The map shows a way to Dexler's session that doesn't involve going through a hidden corridor. Dexler, as my assigned Cultivator, will be like a homeroom teacher or adviser, Grandmom had explained. Everyone gets two Seasons to work at their own pace, under the guidance of a Cultivator, and can apply for Third Rite when the time comes. For some it takes months, for others, like Abby, years. Many don't make it at all.

Dexler's room is past the foyer, down Sunrise Corridor deep in the North Wing. At least there'll be one person in this room I sort of know.

The doors open, and a powdery residue on them sticks to my hand. I step through.

And somehow I'm outside.

The fresh air sings notes of gardenia, whipping by, the breeze soothing to my nerves. The estate hovers behind me like a watchful mother, and fog rests on the blanket of green in the distance. Landscape crews tend the gardens in the midday sun, trim the grass, shape the hedges with nothing more than the glide of their hands. I hurry toward the makeshift classroom in the middle of what appears to be a small garden closed off by walls of greenery, with stone pillars for desks, fallen trees for seats. Dexler weaves her magic around a bit of bark, and it shrinks smaller and smaller while everyone watches with wide eyes.

"Oh, good," she says, waving me along faster. "I was worried the gateway would throw you. Come on, have a seat. We just got started."

I slide into the seat next to the blonde with the pixie cut and exhale. The session is a mix of inductees in robes like mine and others in pants with loose tops. A quick inventory eases the tension between my shoulders. There are three others without diadems and at least one without a mask. Who knows how long they've been here, but at least I'm not the only one who needs to emerge.

"Where were we? Oh, yes." Dexler cradles the bit of bark with both hands. It's so small now, I have to squint to see it. She clasps her hands around it and lifts them toward the sun. Her ring, a deep blue-stoned one today, glitters in the sun. "From one living thing to another." She opens her hands, and a baby bird takes off from her fingers.

The class gasps.

"Today's refresher is about Natural Path of Change, a branch of Anatomer magic. And a reminder that all magic has a cost." The hatchling flaps its wings in the air, and their span widens as it matures, aging from a baby bird to a full grown one right before my eyes.

"Part of your job is to weigh that cost."

The bird's wing tips gray first. Then its feathers fray as if withered with age. He starts his descent, struggling to keep himself up on the wind until he's flying, falling more like, straight for the ground.

"He's going to—" My teeth dig into my knuckle.

He pummels the lawn. Someone yelps. Dexler gathers us around his feeble frame. She rolls the dead bird on its side, horror etched on my peers' faces. "Know the cost of the mysteries you wield, or you too might pay a price you hadn't bargained for."

A shiver runs down my spine as we return to our seats.

"To begin, Electus, what is your charge?"

That's me. "Emerging one's magic," I say, ready this time, in unison

with the others who haven't emerged. "Rich is the blood of the chosen."
The words send a wintry echo through me. My toushana flutters. *Quiet,*
I urge it. *Please.*

Primus and Secundus complete their recitations and I glance at the
others who haven't emerged, trying to glean what they're doing. One
spots me watching, and I force myself to meet her eyes. She looks me
up and down as Dexler drones on about what we'll be doing today. Her
shoulders hang. Her chin rises. I know that look. She wants nothing to
do with me.

I fight the urge to shrink in my seat, and focus on Dexler.

"We'll be working with a different kor today." She points at the sun
overhead. "Hence the change of venue. Anatomer magic requires understanding how organisms function, how they grow and change naturally.
Similar organisms will have similar anatomical structures, making them
easier to transform. Changing from person to person is vastly easier. But
we are a cut above the rest, we don't settle for easy, do we?"

"Here." The blonde next to me tosses me a spare notebook and a pencil.

"Thanks."

"Shelby . . . Duncan." She offers me a handshake, but a question glints
in her cerulean eyes.

"Hi."

We shake. "Secundus, fifth of my blood, Anatomer candidate."

Nigel Hammond morphing into the Dragun who is after me unfurls
in my memory.

"You can shift your face."

"If I was basic, sure. With enough practice and a bit of their blood, I
can mimic voice and personality, too. I can become anyone. I've almost
mastered one person so far. But I still don't have this animal bit down yet."

"You're a Secundus, so you must know Abby, my roommate."

"Yeah, we were both here last Season. We're on track to finish together."
She pops her gum. "If she can get it together that is."

"I'm Quell Ma—"

"Marionne, I know. Everyone knows."

My cheeks warm at her response, the exact sentiment unfamiliar. Being talked about isn't new. But the curl of her lips, the way she doesn't smile at me so plastically this time makes it hard to look her in the eyes. A robust diadem studded with pale blue stones rises out of her head, setting off her eyes. Abby's was much smaller than Shelby's. But something tells me everything about Shelby is grand.

Say something else. Don't be awkward. "Nice to meet you."

She blows another bubble until it pops. "You, too."

"Do you mind telling me." I point at my head. "How the emerging thing works?"

She rolls her shoulders back haughtily, as if it wasn't already painfully obvious I'm the new girl. Marionne only in name, Grandmom pegged me right. But I will show her.

"I just haven't caught up yet," I say, trying to make my words come out more certain than they feel. "My mom didn't do any of this, so it's a bit new."

"Sure thing." She leans in for a whisper as Dexler wanders between the aisles going on about something I am almost sure I should be listening to. But I can't help but hang on Shelby's words.

"So emerging is the easiest Rite if magic is strong in your bloodline, which, I mean, for you it is, *duh*."

I can't help but smile. It's tempting to think I could be a member of this Order, a wielder of what Grandmom called the greatest mysteries of this world.

"Go on."

"Emerging happens by using a lot of magic in a short period of time. Because magic—"

"Strengthens with use," I recall.

"Yep, and you'll be using it all day for the next several days. Completing First Rite proves that your magic is strong enough to be useful to the Order. Don't sweat it. At most it'll take a few days."

"I see, okay, thanks." If using magic is what gets me to emerge, then using magic is what I need to do.

"Ready?" Dexler chimes, something green blooming in her hand. She passes out bunches of grass and jars of dirt. "Transfigure these items into a fresh Nerium oleander bloom. On my desk by the end of class."

Everyone around me seems to know what's happening, including Shelby, so I follow her lead. I pour the dirt on my stone and arrange the grass around it.

"I missed what she said. I have to grow an oleander flower?"

"Watch." Shelby shows me a seed. "Seed to flower is a natural path of change. But magic is wielding the *unnatural.*" She turns back to her two ingredients. How is this going to bloom into a flower? I watch, intent to not miss anything. Shelby traces circles in the grass, her expression suddenly very focused. The air around her fingers ripples and the grass dissolves into the dirt. Then she tugs at her pile of earth, pulling up. Out of it blooms a white flower.

"Wow. So you made the grass behave like a seed?"

"Exactly. Give yourself a break. It takes a little time to catch on." Smile lines hug her eyes, and I settle in my seat a bit more comfortably. I thank her and leave her to her own work before smoothing out my dirt again.

My fingers creep with a sudden chill, and I shake it off, shoving my toushana down. *Warmth.* I reach for anything inside me that feels hot. A tightness in my stomach ignites like a flame, and I imagine it growing. Heat streams up my body in a sudden puff of air, and it feels like tingly granules fluttering all through me. I set my mind on changing the grass to behave like a seed, its dewy surface cold to my fingertips. The air around my hand ripples and the tiny blade of green dissolves.

My heart thuds in excitement. I pinch a bit of dirt, and the bud of a stem grazes my fingers. I pull on it, and suddenly everything in me goes cold, chasing away the magic roaring in me properly. I shove my hands between my thighs. On my desk is a puny excuse for a flower. I breathe, in through my nose, out through my mouth, until the chill in my fingers ceases.

"Not bad, Miss Marionne." Dexler wanders over.

"Thanks, Shelby helped."

"Now, with me, again." Dexler cups her hand on my shoulder, and we repeat the lesson a few times with her magic bolstering my own until the flower that I pull from the dirt is much longer.

When she breaks our touch, she staggers.

"Cultivator Dexler, are you all right?" I steady her as she sways.

"I'm fine, don't worry. All magic has a cost. The one Cultivators pay is quite high." She snatches a clear-stoned ring from a box and slides it onto her finger, blowing out a breath. "Now, you, madam, must keep up that good work. You'll emerge in no time," she says before turning to Shelby to survey her work. "Flawless, Miss Duncan, as usual. Such a keen sense of touch and solid oration." She turns the ring on her knuckle. "That and your knack for teaching. I wonder, have you ever given any thought to cultivating?"

"Actually, Headmistress and I—" Shelby blushes, and their words drone on into the distance as I keep practicing. By the time session wraps, I have managed to pull three flowers out of my dirt, but none with full leaf and stem.

"Not bad for your official first day," Shelby says, tossing her things into her bag.

"Thanks." I tuck a strand of hair behind my ear, finding it a bit easier to look my peers in the eye.

Maybe I can do this.

TEN

—————✳—————

After a quick lunch, which I eat by myself back in my room, and a short study period, I hustle to my next session. As I enter Etiquette in the Grand Ballroom, I stuff my hands in my pockets. There are fewer students than the last class, and it doesn't appear that we'll be using much magic here. The rotunda towers with a domed ceiling. Slender windows draped with sweeping fabrics flutter at the glossed floors. Long tables decked in floor-length tablecloths run along the center of the room with tall-back chairs on either side. I set a foot forward, determined to do as well as I did in Dexler's. I should be able to manage eating "properly" even if it does involve way too many spoons.

Heads turn my way, but I keep mine down and find my name on a tiny card atop a gold-rimmed stack of plates. No one else is in a seat, so I blend into the small crowd.

There isn't a single familiar face among the dozen or so others. No Shelby, no Abby.

"Oh, excuse me," someone says, trying to squeeze into a back spot against the wall, away from the buzzing clusters of cliques. It's one of the girls from Dexler's who also hasn't emerged.

"You're the Marionne, right?"

The Marionne.

My toushana flutters through me, nudging my insecurity. As if even it knows the very idea of me here, in this world, is preposterous. More heads turn our way at the mention of my surname, and I fight the urge to look at my shoes, to shrink away. I force my head up. *You're not invisible anymore.*

"Yes, that's me." The words are foreign in my mouth, but I chew them up and force them down. I am a Marionne. Grandmom and I share blood. I clasp my fingers behind me, hoping my mannerism reads normal and not suspicious.

"I'm Rose," she says, something shading her expression. "This is a lot, isn't it?"

"Yeah. How long have you been here?"

"Since the very end of last Season but it was too late then to really do anything."

Something about what Shelby and Abby said made it sound like it happened quickly for everyone. She must read my mind because irritation sets her jaw.

"How'd you do with the oleander?" I ask, trying to change the subject. She looked a lot more confident in Dexler's than I felt.

"I managed to pull a leaf out of my dirt. No flower, though."

"I've heard it takes practice."

"Hoping so." She smiles before letting out a long breath.

"Have you—"

"Did you hear"—her interruption startles me—"how nice the Moonlight Mixer was?" She pulls at the threads of her embroidery. "It was at the Wexton Regency. In New York, you know?"

"I, uh . . . .no."

"The Season's opening ball is always unforgettable, but I heard this year's was especially decadent. Everyone who joined the Order last Season got an invite to kick off things this year, rub elbows with society's elite." She smiles but it tremors, then fades. "My parents made an appearance. My sister. But I of course couldn't go, not yet. They're always harping on me about finding a respectable man in the Order. Magic should marry magic, you know?" She scoffs.

"Oh?" A better response escapes me.

"But how exactly am I supposed to do that if I can't get this thing to grow out of my head!" Her cheeks ripen with frustration.

"I'm sure you'll emerge and get invited to one soon." I offer the best smile I can muster at the awkwardness.

She exhales a disgruntled sigh. "Well, it was nice to meet you." She moves away and I exhale. When the doors to the ballroom open, a gentleman in a dapper suit with a short coat and longer panels in the back enters. A sturdy black tie sits at his neck.

"Cultivator Plume," the crowd says, bowing and curtsying. I copy and move through to the front to hear better.

"Good afternoon." Plume gestures widely before folding his lean gangly frame at the waist. He moves like air, gliding closer to us, each step perfectly poised. The twist in his hips would put Mom's strut to shame. He is the epitome of elegance. "Well, we're missing a few, aren't we." He surveys the group, hands on his hips, then glances at his watch just as the doors behind him open again. "Ah, there we are. Please, find your name, take your seat."

I rush to the seat labeled "Marionne." But when a face dents my peripheral, I still, registering Jordan as one of the latecomers Plume was referring to. I press back into my chair. *Why is he here?* He's not in the slacks and top like the others. Instead he's in a tuxedo like Plume. One of the perks of being a graduate, I guess.

He crosses the room along with two others, both with statuesque diadems. His shoulders are squared, stomach in, and the table flits with whispers and fawning smiles. Whether or not he notices, I can't tell. His eyes find me as if he can hear my thoughts, feel my panic from yards away. I try to scrub the shock from my face and fix my glance on the plate in front of me, counting the ridiculous number of utensils and glasses. There are so many plates!

"Good afternoon, Miss Marionne." The chair beside me slides back and I feel Jordan's presence. I make the mistake of looking at him. His chiseled jaw hardens, etching the sculpted hills beneath his eyes. Craters in his cheeks soften his brooding expression. He is beautiful, criminally so.

"Do you have an answer for me yet? This morning didn't seem like the proper time to ask."

"And now is? I'm trying to focus. But I can't with your—"

"My . . ." His brow rises, and the insistence in his gaze pulls my chin over my shoulder to look squarely at him.

"Your *questions*." I still have no explanation for why I could see through his cloaking. My toushana flutters in warning the longer he stares. I warm my hands between my thighs, garnering a few quizzical glances.

"It's cold." I look ridiculous, especially in here. Like coarse wool next to fine silk. Jordan's expression narrows in thought at me, and I grip the sides of my chair.

Plume claps along the others who are too slow to get into their seats. Then he raises his glass toward the room, and it quiets. "I do not allow swine at my table unless it's on a plate."

My hold on the chair slacks at session starting, thankful to look anywhere else but at Jordan.

"We have a few Electus with us today, I see. So I'll do a quick refresher. You'll need to work hard to keep up." He eyes me and Rose, who's across the table. Her brows jump at Plume addressing us directly. She's a ball of nerves, too, and even though it's for a different reason entirely, it's comforting to know I'm not the only nervous wreck here.

"Look at the person to your right," Plume orders us newbies. Rose stares at someone who came in with Jordan. "If you have questions," he goes on, "they will help you keep up."

Seeing Jordan for the second time, I allow myself to really look. His eyes are darker today than usual, more blue than green. It's what I imagine gazing out at the sea would be like on an overcast day. He watches me as I watch him, lowering his gaze at first, then raising it above my head where I was anointed. He meets my eyes. The urge to look away bites at me, but I hold my head still as Cultivator Plume's instructed. I can't afford to mess anything up.

Jordan looks at me as if he could look through me, our gazes dance around each other, and my insides do weird things. *Please let this be almost over.* But Plume goes on about how surviving debut is not an individual activity. How we will need help and must ask.

"Your nose does this thing when you get flustered," Jordan says, enjoying the apparent discomfort staring at him brings me. "It crinkles."

Plume weaves through the room, stopping from time to time to adjust a fork or slightly shift a plate.

"You're making fun of me."

"I'm . . . observant."

"My discomfort intrigues you." I scowl.

"Your dishonesty, more so." He rears back in his seat knowingly, and bile bubbles up my throat. I put as much space between us as I can.

Plume pauses beside us. "Your place at my table," he says to the session, "like your position in this House, is *earned.*" Plume circles the table and grips the back of Rose's chair, and her eyes about pop out of her head. I would try to mouth some consolation, but I'm dealing with my own crisis over here.

"As my mother used to say," Plume goes on, "if you can't stand the heat, get out of my kitchen. The standards do not lower, you meet them or you leave. Some of you will dismiss etiquette as if magic is the only thing that requires practice. And you will be sent home. Those who recite place settings and meal courses until they haunt you in your sleep, who use correct posture so consistently that lying down at night makes your back ache, who dance until their feet are full of sores . . . will have the privilege of staying." He cocks his head, chin tilted up. "It's not my job to keep you here."

The room explodes in conversation, and chairs scrape the floor, pulling to the table as Plume's reminder sinks in.

"He's weeding people out," I mutter, hugging around myself as best I can in these stilted chairs. Jordan is quiet for once.

"Headmistress entrusts me to prepare you to be fit to dine with *kings.* To move like royalty. You will not embarrass this House. And you will not embarrass *me!*" Plume glances at me, then at Rose. The table is a tapestry of expressions, from humdrum to terrified. "With that, let's get today underway." Plume claps. "Servers. Knives."

We have at least two per person on the table already. And another tiny one too dull to really slice anything. We need more?

Butler doors sweep open on the far side of the room, and an army of serving staff marches toward us. Most balance hors d'oeuvre trays on their hands, but a few hold a bouquet of thin, short scalpel-like blades. I glance at Jordan, my helper for the day, and open my mouth to speak. But think better of it.

"You have a question." He shifts, careful to keep his posture erect.

"Nothing, I mean, no."

After Plume grabs his napkin, Jordan moves his own to his lap in one smooth motion, a swan on ice, controlled and elegant. He raises his brow in challenge.

"You think I'm not up to it." I bite my tongue too late. The last thing I need is more heat from him. *Head down. Mouth closed. That was the plan.*

He leans across the space between us. "If you're here for the reason you say you are," he says low enough so only I can hear, "then what I think doesn't matter." His words hang in the air over me like a guillotine. I close my eyes to soothe my angst. But all I can picture is his pointed stare. The way he tries to see through me.

"Others use powdery concoctions, but cloaking is imperceptible. Do you have an explanation for how you saw through my cloak?" he asks, breaking the silence as he pricks his toasted hors d'oeuvre with his fork.

I can't ignore him outright and make him *more* suspicious.

"No, I don't."

His jaw clenches. But before he can open his mouth, a server with a knife nudges me to lean forward.

"What are you—" I watch in utter shock as he affixes a blade to my chair, pointed at my back. Jordan watches, pensive.

"There we are, Miss." The server moves on to the next chair, skipping over Jordan.

I sit back a bit too much, and a sharp point digs into my spine. I huff in frustration, my chest rising and falling, telling a secret I'd like to keep private: I'm terrified of doing this wrong. And Jordan knows it.

I straighten and ease forward in my chair. The blade is there, but just barely, and as long as I don't slouch, it won't nick me. Which I realize is the point. I set my focus straight ahead, ignoring Jordan's brooding. I think of Mom, delayed for some reason in meeting me here. When Grandmom reaches her, I will have good news to share about my performance here. I *will not* fail. Too much is on the line.

The rest of class is six more courses with instructions on everything from how to bring food to my mouth, to how to fold salad *around* a fork, sip soup from the side of the spoon, and even how long to chew. Jordan, whose every movement is graceful and perfect, keeps an eye on me off and on without a word. My hands are achy, but not yet cold. At least my toushana is behaving.

Finally, a server takes dessert away, and my lower back throbs, but I hold myself still.

"And poached pears in a red wine reduction for our last." Plume motions for the waitstaff to return.

A plate is set in front of me, but I can't imagine eating another bite. Not because I'm full, because my gut is swimming with anxiety with Jordan looking at me every time I look up. No one else commands his attention as I do.

I detach my hand clamped tight on my chair and reach for the fruit, but a sharp twinge of chill stabs inside my fingers. I snatch them back. *Please! Not here.* By some gift of the universe, the cold actually flees.

Rose's wrinkled stare unsettles me. I offer her a smile, and she seems to buy it. I'm almost tempted to slouch in relief. Almost.

"You're not going to eat that with your *fingers*, are you?" Jordan asks.

"Of course not." *Um, yes . . . yes I was.* With the chill gone I slide my fork down the side of my plate and find my audience is still eyeballing me. *He won't be sitting next to you forever. Just eat the damn pear and get out of here.*

"Small slices, as you go." Plume moves through the room, adjusting wrists, bolstering others' ability to remain rigidly poised with his magic.

I grab my knife.

"Your wrist should hardly bend and be held gently, with your index along the top of the handle."

I hover my wrist above my plate, bending it back and forth until it's just so.

"Secundus, you should be helping your peers *without* them asking," he says to one of the girls who came in late with Jordan. She's in a conversation with another while Rose is holding her knife with both hands like a sword over her plate. I tighten my posture and glance at the door, then the clock, sweat slick on my neck as the ache returns, creeping from my arms into my hands.

I grab the knife with iron-willed determination, but my bones pinch with a stronger ache. I toss it back down. *Clang.* Heads turn my way. I smile timidly, and they return to their conversations. *I'm making a fool of myself.* I rub my hands vigorously to create some friction, some warmth, and the ache flees.

Again. I pick up the knife and Jordan watches intently. His knife is poised daintily in his grip, a finger resting on its spine as if it was a bird perched on his fingertip.

"Lower," he says, indicating the angle of my knife. Though whether he wants to help or is just doing it because Plume suggested, I can't tell. "Your wrist is bent too much."

I relax my arm and press the tip of my knife to the pear and slice it in half when my fingers are suddenly languid and loose.

My toushana tricked me; it's right there, a sudden, painful throb in my hands. I drop the knife before it has a chance to react with the metal. It hits the plate, and I swear it rings louder than someone slamming cymbals.

The room goes silent. My heart thuds, blood pooling in my ears.

My toushana burns colder.

I clench my hands.

Even the windows seem to glare in judgment. Plume clutches his chest, horrified.

"Miss Marionne," he barks. "Absolutely *not*."

Somewhere, someone snickers.

"I—I'm sorry, if you'll excuse me." I push back from the table and try to stand, but the tablecloth catches and the whole thing tugs. "Oh my god." Glasses fall over, and the table swims in ice water and sweetened tea.

My glass rolls toward the edge of the table. I reach for it but quickly realize I can't touch it or anything, not while my blood is running cold. I yank my fingers back, and it dives off the table edge, shattering on the floor. Jordan pops up from his seat but isn't able to get out of the way in time. His lap is soaked and everyone, including Rose, gapes at me.

"My *god*," Jordan huffs in exasperation, pulling out a sopping envelope from his pocket. He shakes it out, but judging by his smeared name on the front, it's too late for that. "Could you be any more of a disaster? And to think . . ." He shakes his head, his expression still scrunched in horror.

The room spins in motion, everyone standing and inspecting their clothes. A few glares fly my way, but I couldn't possibly feel any smaller. Voices and footsteps ricochet off the walls as people move around the wreckage. I back away, itching for some shadow to slink into. Some place to not be seen. How will I ever do this with this poison inside me? And Jordan breathing down my neck? This is impossible. I glare at my icy hands. I have to get a handle on this. *Think.* This isn't exactly the first impossible thing I've dealt with.

Jordan scowls, water dripping from him all over before he storms off.

"Are you all right?" Cultivator Plume stands over me now, the tone of his frustration softened. "Your teeth are chattering."

"I'm fine." I hold my cold hands tighter to myself.

"All right, well, go on and get out of here," Plume says. "Clean yourself up. You can reach out to your mentor about anything else you would've missed. He's done this all before."

"My mentor?" I freeze.

"Yes, your pairing wasn't just for today. Jordan will be your guide for the duration of your time here to ensure you debut. You're expected to work closely with him to—"

"I have to go." I rush out the door, and I could swear the walls are closing in. Working with Jordan will only ensure one thing—I end up dead.

ELEVEN

··——✴——··

Cultivator Plume's words linger as I dash up the grand stair to the third floor toward Grandmom's. She has to make Plume reassign me to a different mentor. She and I agreed to have dinner together each evening this first week while things are so new. I banked on having better news to share of how my first day went. And I'm early. Like, really early.

My hurried footsteps are the only sound on the top floor of the estate. The upper floor makes the lower ones look like servant quarters. The doors up here are much more ornate, with intricate woodwork and brass handles. I rushed up here before, but now in the bright daylight, I can't help but take it all in. Crystal chandeliers dangle overhead from the mural painted on the ceiling. Colorful, precise strokes depict an elderly man and his apprentice wandering through a golden field of glowing wheat. Familiarity nudges me. I've stared up at this ceiling before.

I blink, and I'm a small child again, my fingers wandering the carved molding along the walls. This is the private family floor. This is where I lived until I was five. This was home. I squeeze my eyes shut, trying to pull more from the cobwebs in my memory. But the only image I can conjure is one of tiny feet running across a sun-streaked floor to loud giggles. Then it morphs to fire. Suffocating, engulfing, searing flames, surrounding little me curled up on a ragged bed, hugging my knees in a strange, dark place nothing like this here.

I shove down the unfamiliar memory and urge myself faster down the long corridor. Its windows offer a picturesque view of the grounds' rolling acreage golden in the sun's glow. I pass another few doors, but don't recognize any one specifically that used to be mine. The hall halts at Grandmom's unguarded door. A stubborn hint of cold lurks underneath my skin as I knock. I tighten my fisted hands and move them behind my back just in case.

Her maid ushers me in. Grandmom's fireplace roars and I rush over to it to warm my hands, hoping I don't appear too eager.

"If you'll take a seat," says a woman with a thin gold diadem in a maid's uniform. "I'll get Headmistress for you."

I get as close as I can to the fire as I wait, straining to keep my back straight, remembering Plume's warning about making the cut. Heat wafts against me, lulling my angst, and then Grandmom's bedroom door opens.

"Well, you're quite early," she says as I stand to greet her. She pauses, eyeing my clothes. "Is everything all right?"

"Yeah. Just clumsy." I shift casually. "Spilled a cup."

She gestures for her maid. "Pull the drapes open wider, would you? And lighten them up a bit. I'm sick of the dusty old plum."

Her maid curtsies and hurries off, working her magic, shifting the curtains from deep purples to soft blues. Grandmom hesitates another moment before squeezing my hands, now piping hot, in greeting.

"I just finished etiquette."

The creases around her eyes uncinch the tangle twisting my insides. She's pleased. It's a small victory but I savor it. "Plume is the absolute best. Nabbed him from Isla, that ole hag didn't appreciate him."

"Isla?"

We move to a sitting area adjacent to a gallery of framed maps, and I notice my key chain on her coffee table.

"Isla Ambrose? Three leaves that intertwine?"

I shake my head, wholly fixated on the key chain. Mom.

"Oh, you *do* have so much to learn. Isla is Headmistress of House Ambrose. And well, Plume was miserable over there. I'll just leave it at that." She rings a bell and her maid returns. "Margot, would you please have them serve dinner in half an hour?"

"Yes, ma'am." She curtsies, then leaves.

"I'm sorry. I didn't mean to cause things to rush."

"It's no trouble, I—"

"Were you able to get in touch with my mom?" The desperation spills out.

Her gaze falls to the key chain, and I scoot to the edge of my seat.

"No luck." She sips her tea. "Now, tell me about sessions."

"Was there more . . . about my mom? She is okay, right? She should have met me here by now. But she was delayed for some reason."

She pets my hands. "No news as of yet. But I will tell you if I hear anything. Rhea is an expert at not being found when she doesn't want to be, you know that."

She's right. My chin hits my chest. "I just wish I could see her and explain myself."

"Soon, I'm sure." She tugs my head back up. "Today isn't a day for frowning, dear granddaughter. Any itching?"

"No."

"By tomorrow, I'd bet. Have you thought about if you'll emerge silver or gold? There's copper and rose gold that we see from time to time, but those are exceptionally rare these days."

"I'll just be happy to emerge at all." Perhaps that was too honest.

"Do not fret, everyone comes to love their showing," she says. "*The magic* chooses, that's the beauty of emerging. Each diadem is unique to its wearer." She strokes her own, its pearls glinting in the light. She lifts a teapot from a tray on the table and fills two cups and adds a splash of milk before handing me one.

"Quell?"

"Ma'am."

"You say 'thank you,' dear, when someone hands you a cup."

"Sorry, thank you." I've never had tea before and certainly not in this fancy of a cup. And I am thankful. The warmth of the cup is a welcome salve; I can't even sense my toushana anymore. I cup it with my hands like a bowl, and Grandmom grimaces. I rework my grip on the porcelain, tea sloshing over the sides. She takes an exasperated breath, fingering the hair at her hairline, as if watching my poor attempt is downright painful.

"Here." She wraps her arms around me and separates my fingers, looping two through the hole of the cup handle. Warmth, not the magical kind but another, wraps around me. "Your thumb. Use it to balance."

I try and the cup falters, but I tighten my grip and hold it still.

She curls my other fingers under the handle. "Very good." She hands me a teaspoon and takes her seat. I wish Mom was here, the three of us, a family.

I note how Grandmom stirs her tea back and forth, not in circles, and I copy. My spoon tings the side of the cup and I cringe at my mistake. I try again, and the smile lines around her lips say she's pleased.

Something shifts in me. It's an odd feeling. A tightness that releases. My lips crack an unrestrained smile. Heat flushes my cheeks. Something as small and so simple as tea in my grandmother's sitting room. Her showing me how to properly drink it. It's so insignificant, and yet I feel like a mountain's been moved. I have longed for this, in the most desperate way.

Mom should be here, too. And she isn't. Because of my toushana.

"Now, before you go slurping it like a cow, remember to sip." Grandmom demonstrates, slicing through my brooding. I lift straight up and take a sip, eager to do something right. She nods in approval. "But that's not why you came early, is it? To drink tea and talk about etiquette. You have questions in your eyes, child, speak. If you're going to draw attention to yourself, do so for good reason. Otherwise, mind your tongue."

"I'd like to have a different mentor."

"Ah, so Plume gave you your pair-up today?"

"He did, yeah."

"Yes. It has an s. And you're not pleased? Others work with Secundus. But Jordan has debuted. He's trained under my direct guidance as a Ward of this House for the last three years, on *and* off Season. He knows his stuff."

"He attacked me when we first met."

"As he would anyone presumed to be trespassing. I do hope he's apologized for that misunderstanding?"

"He has."

She reclines.

"In class, Shelby was really helpful."

"Shelby Duncan?" She sets her tea down on the tray and considers. Her gaze moves to the window and there's much written in the lines that form on her face. "No, I don't think that's going to be possible. I want you to be happy here. But I can't change your mentor."

The more she says, the more I feel like invisible hands are wrapping around my throat.

"Mister Wexton requested you, and I'm not in a position to refuse the request."

"I don't understand. You—"

"Relax, dear." She sets a hand on my shoulder, but it doesn't comfort. "I am so glad you told me. And if it were anything else, I might be able to. But this, we need to just leave. The relationship between the Houses is prickly at best. And hosting Wards is an effort to ease those tensions. A measure of accountability, so to speak, so each House has eyes in another House."

"But—"

She holds up a hand. "Mister Wexton gave good reason for his request, and I know the boy well." She crosses her legs, settling deeper into her seat. "Mentorship is no light matter. After you emerge, he must sign off on your readiness for Second and Third Rites before you can participate in them. And he holds himself to the *highest* standards. Someone like that is hard to please, but good to learn from." She moves on as if the matter is settled. "He will be in etiquette with you through Cotillion, as your partner, but if you want him to pop into Dexler's or any other sessions, be sure to ask."

"Can't you just say you changed your mind?"

Her posture stiffens, and the gentleness that smoothed her expression dissolves. "Taking it back could give the impression there are trust issues.

And his aunt, Headmistress Perl, is the last person who needs any indication I do not trust her."

I gape. "His *aunt* is a Headmistress?"

"You've much to learn, dear, about the inner machinations of an organization like ours." Grandmom stands and puts distance between us, her body language somehow more rigid than usual. I stand, too, because it feels like I'm supposed to.

"This discussion has ended," she says. "You will let this go." She gestures for her maid. "Is Mrs. Cuthers still here?"

"Yes, ma'am." Her maid returns with a woman with silver hair swept back and pinned beneath a silver diadem with small white stones. She carries a stack of envelopes.

"Yes, Darragh?"

"Mrs. Cuthers, please, see to my granddaughter." She turns to me. "She is my right-hand lady in this House. If there's anything you need and I'm unavailable, she'll see to it."

"Miss Marionne," Mrs. Cuthers says to me. "I can show you through to the dining room. I was headed that way."

It's not a question. I'm being asked to leave. I stand, swaying on my feet, unsure what to do with my hands. Something has shifted, again. The mountain or the whole earth I stand on. Grandmom turns without a goodbye embrace or anything, moving toward her bedroom door.

"And Quell, if you need to arrive early again, do send a note first. You're a Marionne and really must begin behaving like it." Her warmth is gone, as elusive as it came.

"Will I see you at dinner?" I say, my insecurity breaking through.

"Of course." Grandmom's lips flinch a smile before disappearing behind her door.

"Are you all right, Miss Marionne?" Mrs. Cuthers asks.

"I'm fine. Could I just have a minute, please? I'm sure I can get to dinner myself."

"The dining room is the second door on your left off the main hall."

I make my way out, trying to numb myself to the sting of Grandmom's words, but halfway down her private corridor, my steps grow heavy. Too heavy to bear. I let the wall hold me up and hug my knees, smoothing the tears streaming down my face. *It shouldn't even matter.*

"That's not why I'm here," I mutter, but the lump in my throat won't go down. It takes a short while, but once my eyes dry, I gather myself and make my way to the dining room. I need to be focused on getting a handle on my toushana until I can be rid of it completely. Nothing else.

I bury the hurt of Grandmom's rejection.

Deep down.

Somewhere dark.

AFTER A PAINFULLY silent four-course dinner with Grandmom, I hurry to my room to avoid seeing anyone else. I step inside and immediately pinch my nose. Something reeks, sweaty and pungent.

"Oh my gosh, hey! How'd it go?" Abby beams from her bed, folded over a slice of pizza speckled with something I don't recognize.

"Miserable," I say a bit too honestly. I freeze, worried I've gone too far. Shown too much of myself. But Abby's dark eyes are bright and wide, her expression entirely disarming. I sit on the edge of her bed. "I just hoped emerging would be easier." Opening up feels like a jackhammer dancing inside. "And I made a fool of myself in etiquette. I'm not sure I can do this." Abby's expression softens in concern. Saying it aloud is freeing. Having someone care to listen, even more so. "Then I found out my mentor is Jordan."

"Oh my goodness, stop!" She sets her plate aside, and I realize that horrid smell is coming from her food.

"*What* are you eating?"

"Pizza . . . with sardines. But it's good with tuna, too. Never touched a pepperoni in my life and I don't intend to."

I dry gag. "On pizza?"

"Hey, you want my help?" she teases. "No making fun of my food choices."

"Okay, deal." I rotate a bit more comfortably on her bed. Her grin is infectious, and she holds up three fingers.

"Okay, three things! One, you can't self-reject. Say it with me."

I roll my eyes. "We don't self-reject," we babble in semi-unison.

"Okay, and two, it takes performing a type of magic at least thirteen times before it even responds consistently. Sometimes it just doesn't work. You're being way too hard on yourself. Practicing is what ultimately helps you get it down. Repetition is key. Say it."

"You're unbearable."

"I'm waiting." She holds her plate nearer to me, threatening to make me smell her fishy pizza again.

"Fine, fine! Get that away from me." I laugh. "Repetition is key."

"Good."

"Seriously, dude, try pepperoni. It's so much better."

"Mmmmm." She takes a rebellious bite, dramatically savoring the taste.

"Okay, so don't self-reject, practice a lot. What's the third thing?" All this seems like a no-brainer, but hearing it from someone else is somehow affirming. Maybe it's not just me being a colossal screwup.

"Oh, three is omg, *Jordan*! He is *so* hot." She squeals and shoves me playfully.

"You're delirious."

"He's so . . ."

"Nope." I hop off her bed and dig out the notebook Shelby gave me. "Between your pizza choices and obsession with Jordan I'm officially nauseated. I'm going to start studying and get some practice in."

"You can't deny he's hot."

"He's . . . *dangerous.*"

"That's what I said." She snorts and tosses a pillow at my head. "I don't know a person in this place who won't be jealous when they hear *the* Jordan Wexton is your mentor."

Heat rushes to my cheeks, and the foreign feeling unsteadies me. I toss the pillow back, and I stick out my hand for a shake. "Hi, I'm Quell, have we met?"

She chuckles, and a laugh bubbles up my throat.

"He is good-looking, I will admit." I struggle to meet Abby's eyes.

"*And?*"

"And yet . . . terrifying."

She folds her arms. "I don't see the issue."

I roll my eyes. "If you have any notes on Natural Path of Change, I'd love to see them."

She snatches up her bag. "You're going to stress yourself out of emerging. There's a reason Secundus and Primus are *still* practicing that with you in class. It takes time. Magic can be stubborn."

"Tell me about it."

She hands over her notes.

Abby's kindness tugs at me. The disaster with Grandmom tiptoes through my memory. I feel like an outsider everywhere but in this room, it seems. "Are you going to hang out here awhile? I need to study, maybe we can study together or something."

"For sure. Hey, are you all right?"

"Sorry, was that weird?"

"No. You just . . . For a moment you seemed sad or something."

"I'm fine, really." I turn my back to her and skim the first page and immediately spot a problem with how I've been doing things. It suggests when I feel the heat of the Dust stirring in me, instead of trying to amplify it right away, I should latch on to it and just hold it there. Let it rev up like an engine to make it even stronger. I sit on my bed, pondering. I've definitely been latching on to the warmth and trying to spread it right away. So that it chases away my toushana. Maybe this can help.

"How long did it take you to emerge?"

"Sixty-three hours."

A little over two days. "Hmm."

"Oh my goodness, girl."

"What?"

Abby tosses her plate aside and primps in the mirror. "Come out with me?"

"Out. No, I don't—"

"You're way too uptight. You won't emerge if you're wound up like this. You need to relax." She squeals. "And I know the perfect place."

Going out is not my scene. I'm already in a fishbowl here. "No, really. I need to study."

"Oh, come on. There's hotties there," she says as if that's a dangling carrot that has any appeal at all to me. A strangled laugh escapes my throat at the ridiculousness.

"And gossip." She swipes my schedule from my desk.

Right, which is why I shouldn't be there. I laugh again, but she mistakes it for my being excited and throws an arm around my shoulder.

"*Please.*" She holds my schedule up. "You don't even have morning sessions tomorrow, so you can sleep in."

"I'd planned to use that time to practice and get to the library." I also need to get a better handle on my toushana. Its random thrashing inside me is going to get me killed.

"I'll take you to the library myself at eight. I swear!" She crosses her heart with her half-eaten slice and holds it up in salute. "You won't regret it, I promise. Literally everyone who's anyone will be there. It's better than the end-of-Season balls, and those are usually so wild they make *Debs Daily.*"

"Fine," I relent. "If relaxing will help, I'll go. But only for a couple of hours. I need to make some real progress."

"You'll probably emerge by the time you wake up tomorrow, *Marionne.*"

I sift through the closet of clothes Grandmom gave me for something that looks casual and not super noticeable. Maybe black. Or gray. Abby refreshes her makeup and slips into a dress that accentuates her diadem. Grandmom didn't give me any T-shirts or comfy pants. I settle on an olive top that ties at the waist and my same pair of dingy jeans.

"What's this place we're going called?" I ask, grabbing my bag.

"The Tavern, why?"

"I was going to leave Grandmom a note."

"Don't be dense." She takes the pen out of my hand. "The Tavern is obviously prohibited, which is precisely why we're going."

I groan. "This better be worth it, or I'm leaving," I say, following Abby out the door.

TWELVE

———✳———

The grand foyer broom closet has a trick back wall. Abby pushes it in several places while I swat at a mop that keeps falling over, slapping the floor and scaring me half to death. She finds the spot quickly enough before we go through.

"Are you sure this is the right way?"

"No, I'm leading you to your doom. Of course this is the right way."

"Couldn't both those things be true?"

She laughs. The dimness lifts the deeper we go. A bitter tang hangs in the hazy air lit by the glow of lamplight. Much like the corridor that took me to Dexler's the first time, the passageway is dark and long, and if it weren't for Abby reaching back, I wouldn't know where to put my next step.

"A little farther."

"Where are we?"

"There are only so many places we can really hang. Lucky for us one of them is not too far from the Chateau."

"We're leaving the estate?" The thought of being away, on the outside again, sends a prickle up my arms. With every step I doubt more and more that sneaking out to some prohibited place, likely prohibited for good reason, is a good idea for anyone. But especially for me. The Dragun hunting me is still out there. I can still vividly picture the cracked Roman-style column minted on the coin at his throat. I should go back, but if she's right and I'm stressing myself out of emerging, I have to at least try to unwind.

She cracks a latched door open slowly, pressing her ear to it. Then she pushes the door open wider and night sky fractures the darkness, crisp outside air sweeping into the corridor. I step through, my feet seeking purchase on the supple ground. Rogue branches strewn across the doorway tangle in my arms and tear at my skin. I manage to free myself from them with only a few scratches. A forest?

The cool, early summer night air reeks of wood and smoke. I peer around, expecting to see burning or some source of the scent. But the forest is no more than clusters of twisted trees scattered like broken limbs. *How far did we walk?* I turn. Between the nest of trees, far in the distance, sits Chateau Soleil, a sentry in the darkness.

"Where are we exactly?"

"Just off Headmistress's territory." Abby points toward lights and stone pillars in the distance. "It's a bit of a walk, just past the forest's edge on the other side of those memorials." She starts in that direction, but my feet stick in place.

"We'll leave as soon as I'm ready, promise me," I say.

"Promise."

The cobblestone path circles an old war memorial, then halts at a stretch of perfectly manicured grass. Abby eyes the path, where the stones grow smaller before fading into lawn, as if she's looking for something.

"Right about . . ." She moves her heel across the uneven ground until she finds what she's looking for. "Here." She glances around before hammering the rock with the heel of her shoe. The ground opens wide, stairs cutting into the rocks.

We descend the narrow stair, easing past several people coming up, leaving. One with a long coat has a staring problem. The nosy onlooker pauses a beat too long, and a chill sweeps through me. I swallow, and he doesn't move, his stare flickering with something I can't place. My heart stutters as I glimpse for his face, fearing the worst, but the collar of his trench coat and the shadowed stair makes him too hard to make out. I pull at Abby.

"Ow!" She rubs her fingers across the half-moons I've accidentally dug into her arm.

"I'm sorry, I just—" I glance back at him, but the man ties his trench coat and disappears on the spot. "Never mind. I thought I saw something."

"Remember, *relax*."

I nod. Inside, the Tavern is packed, alive with people hanging over tables, cash crushed in their fists. Some are more subtle with their dealings, briefcases parked next to their card tables, shades covering their eyes. But things, money, stuff is definitely changing hands. Diadems and masks sway through the hazy air. Most are dressed in plain clothes, but there are a few who look like they are here skipping out on some formal dance. The bar is sectioned off into rooms, one for lounging, another for gambling, and one in the back where a girl's squawking onstage into a microphone. A waitress passes through the crowd with purple rolled leaves on silver trays.

"Peckle?" she asks.

"No." I move along faster. Stares burn my skin, from every direction. My stomach flips and it has nothing to do with my toushana. This is so not my scene. If I could shrink smaller, I would.

Abby waves at someone as we push through the throng of people. A few smile, others stare. But I set my focus on the back of Abby's head like it's a target and let the rest move past in a blur. *I hate this.* I swallow my nerves and force myself to find a few friendly expressions in the crowd.

"So everyone here's an Order member?" I ask, making a conscious note to unclench my hands.

"Yep, our own little Misa."

My brows cinch. But before Abby can say more, she throws her arms *and* lips around someone. Holey jeans and a baggy shirt hang off his slender frame. He wears his hair long and it looks like he's in need of a shave, but I think that's on purpose. Beneath dark bangs a plain mask of sleek gray seeps into his skin as he kisses her back. Now I understand why she was itching to get here.

"Oh, sorry, this is—" Abby starts.

But he sticks out his hand before she can finish, and I can't help but gape at a set of tally marks tattooed on his skin.

"It's a 'Roser thing," he says, noting my staring. "Shows how many masteries we've discovered." He turns his wrists up. Two suns are tattooed on his veiny pale flesh. "Got these just for fun last week."

"Ah, I see."

"Mynick Luc Jarryn, Primus, Retentor candidate, House of Ambrose."

I rub my hands on my pants to be extra sure they're not chilly and shake his hand. "Quell."

"Sixth of his blood," Abby says to me. "And she's a Marionne," she says to him as if that fills in necessary blanks on the rest of our introductions.

His brows jump.

"Don't be too impressed. I'm new to all this. I haven't even emerged." I gesture at the wooden circlet on my head and realize my tone was a bit more desperate than I like.

"Still. Honored to meet you, Quell. Headmistress will be eager to hear."

"Isla?" I survey my surroundings but don't note any strange movements or people watching me. When I meet Mynick's eyes again, they've grown wide at the shock of my calling his Headmistress by her first name.

"Sorry, I mean Headmistress Ambrose. Yeah, yes." I stumble over my words, suddenly aware of what he sees in me: our House—Grandmom. "I've heard great things about your House."

Abby glances between us.

"Oh?"

Abby rubs my wrist on the sly.

"Sorry," I sigh. "Social anxiety is a real thing. Cultivator Plume finished at your House, right?"

"Class of '84. Repeated Primus phase twice by choice to finish with perfect marks. Great teacher. Cool to meet you, though. I can't imagine Nore, our Headmistress's heir, caught dead in a place like this." He rambles on about House of Ambrose and Abby hangs on his every word, her lips doing this pucker thing like she's so sweet on him she might burst, and I really can't take it.

The bass shifts and stringy guitar notes prick the air.

"Our song!" Mynick pulls Abby toward the partitioned room with the stage.

She gestures for me to follow. "You and me next?" She twists her lips in a pout.

"Have fun." I wave her away. She and Mynick push through the crowd, and in a small way, the bump of the music and hum of casual chatter corkscrews my envy. Here I am, a Marionne by blood, and yet a broken sconce on Grandmom's paneled walls. A shadow even here.

I look for a spot to land, and a mass exodus from the bar catches my eye.

Music blares as I sift through the crowd, looking for anyone or anything suspicious. Some reason to tuck tail and run out of here. But the glittering diadems, and masks for those who are showing them, steal my entire attention. They're all so different. Green gems set in silver arced over a braid of brown hair. Another girl's is gold, peppered with iridescent stones, each shift in its hue setting off a different fleck of color in her gray eyes. And the masks, some are rimmed in tiny stones, others are carved with detailing. I even saw one deb with a mask of gold. I plop onto a barstool because it's the only spot open that doesn't require sitting next to anyone. I wonder what my diadem will look like. How big it will be. Will it sparkle with gems or be metal, like Abby's?

The bartender glances at my circlet. "Ah, fresh meat. What can I get you—juice, soda, kizi?"

"I'm fine." I can't really spare the little money I have left for something so frivolous, even if it does sound delicious.

"It's on the house for Electus. You sure?"

"Um, okay. Soda?"

He shuffles off and then a man climbs onto the stool beside me, brandishing his tattered coat. Muddy bits fling off it and land smack on the bar.

"Oh, sorry about that," he says flatly. His dark hair hangs long and straight behind him. "It's nasty out there."

I get up, not in a mood for chatter.

"You want to emerge?" he mutters, not quite looking my way.

"Excuse me?"

"Sit." He touches my chair with blackened-bluish fingertips but retracts them quickly when he notices me staring.

"I'm fine, thanks."

"I have something," he says, gazing over his shoulder, "that could help." He doesn't wear a mask, and he definitely doesn't look like a Cultivator. His coat sleeves are rolled to hide its improper fit. Tally marks, like Mynick's, cover his arms and disappear up his sleeves. I meet his watery eyes. They are an ocean of drowned secrets. But desperation or something equally potent tethers me to my seat.

"You drink this." He slips a vial of a thick translucent substance from his pocket. "And you'll emerge in *hours*." His rotten fingernails wrap around the bottle, and every rational thought in my head screams, *Get up and run.*

"Who are you?"

"*Who* isn't really your concern, is it? Why, perhaps. But not who."

"Fine. Why are you offering me this? And don't say money. There are people here who practically smell like money. And yet you're talking to me."

His mouth twitches a smile. "You sure you're a Marionne? Not Ambrose, eh?" He rotates in his seat to face me fully. "I didn't mean to alarm you. I overheard you and your friends."

"Eavesdropping isn't helping your case that you're just trying to help me."

He pulls the hair back from his face, revealing his thirsty skin. "The name's Octos. Trader. My ancestors ran Misa's shipping yard." He widens his posture, and I realize I'm supposed to be impressed. "Through the war," he clarifies, reading my expression.

I have no idea what he's talking about. But I keep my mouth shut because I don't want to come across as a clueless idiot. Had enough of that today.

He chuckles at my apparent confusion. "Misa was our region. A place where magic was in the open, before the Houses," he continues, sensing my intrigue. "But the Order was worried that because the world was obsessed with expansion, our little private piece of the globe would be discovered. It was safer to learn to blend in. Well, not everyone liked that idea, and a big war broke out. In a week's time, Misa was gone." He snaps. "Erased, just like that. My family's business sank with it."

I try to picture an entire city like Chateau Soleil, with magic everywhere, out in the open, but the pieces don't come together. "So what did your family do since the family business wasn't an option?"

"Well, the Houses were the *new* way." He rambles on in that way people do when they like to talk because they don't often get the opportunity to. "Before, my great-grandfather took a test and boom." He slaps the bar and I jump. "You're official: complex Shifter, Cultivator, Retentor, whatever, as long as you pass. But the war changed all that. So when it was my time, I enrolled in a House." He toys with a napkin, trickling a tendril of magic on its edges.

"Ambrose, I gather." I eye his decorated arms.

He twists his magic, and the napkin shifts into a white rose. "Aye. But they didn't appreciate my skills, I don't think. Wasn't pious enough. Or maybe I picked the wrong House." He broods, tugging at his worn coat. "They kicked me out of there as Primus. Couldn't quite hack the dagger honing. Tricky little devil." His fingers trace the slopes of his face. "I finished First Rite, so I didn't lose all my Dust. Though I lost my ability to summon my mask years ago." A flicker of something burns through his stare. I recognize the sentiment; I know it well. I lived it my entire life. Longing bleeding into desperation. I gaze around. Maybe I'm still living it. It's written in the lines of his face. The way he boasts of who his family was, trying to impress me. He pretends he's okay with being the outcast. But he's not.

This isn't about money. Whatever he wants from me has to do with my last name.

"But the drink works. I got it from an old 'Roser buddy myself."

"And you would just give it to me? For nothing?" I narrow my eyes.

"In return, all I ask is that you spare a little change to get me a drink. Rikken's tired of my freeloading." The hunger in his posture, the way his nails are dug into the lip of the bar says he's holding back.

"And?" I press.

"And . . . one day, if it ever comes down to it, you remember my name—Octos. That I did you a favor when you needed it."

Because I'm a Marionne. He reads me like I read him. I'm not sure I like that. He holds the vial out to me when the bartender slides a soda my way.

"Octos, schmoozing the fresh meat already, are you?"

"Just making her acquaintance. Letting the nice lady know if she ever needs a favor, I'm her guy."

"Give him a soda, too, please." I pay Rikken, and a moment later he slides Octos a drink, with much hanging on his lips that he doesn't say. Octos gulps it down and sympathy nudges me. I'm not sure many here would even give him the time of day. I sip my soda, eyeing the vial.

"So we have a deal?" He pushes it toward me, mistaking my silence for agreement.

I spot Abby across the room. Her and Mynick's duet has ended, and she's in his lap gabbing with a bunch of other Secundus. She catches me looking and waves.

"Give it a smell, see." He unstoppers the glass, wafting it under my nose.

If I take it and it works, I'd pass First Rite. But that's cheating. My fingers twitch. But I ball them into a fist. His offer is tempting. But I can't. It's not right. I belong here, and emerging the right way proves it. I won't be any stronger or have any more control over my magic if I cheat on this first one. I reach for the vial to stopper it back up and refuse him, and then several things happen at once.

An explosion of black fog blinds me.

The vial is snatched from my grip.

Someone grunts.

I stumble off the stool, startled, blinking through the clearing haze. Jordan towers over Octos. The roistering in the Tavern stills, everyone watching.

"Jordan? What are you—"

He stalks to a nearby potted plant and cuts me a sharp glance before tipping the clotty liquid into the soil. Its droplets burn through the plant's leaves like acid, then through the pot. I try to swallow, to move, to say something, but only a sputter comes out. Jordan meets my eyes, his jaw hardens.

"That could have . . ." *Hurt me.* I step forward, reaching for the plant in disbelief. But Jordan's arm stops me, stiff against my torso.

"The off-gassing can even be toxic." His words are rigid like the lines dug into his face. But his arm across me suggests maybe he's more than just steel on the outside.

I glare at Octos, who's gaping at the plant, shaking his head in disbelief, pale as if he's seen a ghost.

"Rikken, some help with this mess." Jordan's mask hardens on his face as he rotates his wrist, calling on his magic. He grazes the stem of the plant with his fingertips delicately. Though his arms tremble as if fighting off some invisible force. He bites down, straining, and thrusts once more. Darkness unfurls from his hands, and the clay pot shudders, then collapses into a pile of charred dust. He exhales, breathless.

I stumble backward, gaping at the mess on the floor, then at my own hands and back at the pile that's reminiscent of my own dark secret. The bartender shoulders through the crowd with a broom and mop to sweep up the decayed mess. Jordan lifts Octos by the collar, and the room parts to let them through. The doors creak open, and I lose sight of them.

"You all right?" It's Abby.

Blood pools behind my ears as I stare, unmoving.

"Quell?"

Abby says something else, but I'm halfway out the door on Jordan's heels.

THIRTEEN

Outside, the night has cooled and the scent of the rain lingers in the air. Octos is nowhere in sight, and Jordan's stomping off through the park back toward the estate. The forest looms ahead and I follow.

"How did you do that?" I demand, still shaking from what I witnessed.

"What do you mean how?"

Careful, Quell. "I mean, how . . . did you know that guy was trying to harm me?"

He ignores my request, and I have to practically run to keep up with him. My shoes stick to the mud, and cold rain trickles on my skin.

"Answer me!"

He doesn't give any indication he's in pain. Or deathly cold.

"You shouldn't be here."

"You're still a Ward, so should you?"

"Trust me, I don't come this way unless I absolutely have to."

I follow at a stomping pace, urged by my need to know what I just saw. What it meant. What it could mean for me. He destroyed that pot, like my toushana could have done. And no one scorned him for it. He didn't shiver or look like he was going to pass out. He wielded whatever it was—as dark as it was—with *control*. A control I lack. I rush ahead of him, blocking his path.

"I asked you a question!"

He considers me a moment, his jaw ticks. "Do you have any idea how many would kill to be in your shoes? To be in mine?"

"What?" I step back in confusion, the word *kill* sticking like a lump in my throat.

"For every member the Order debuts we turn away a thousand who aren't good enough. They don't even get to set foot on the property. Let alone grow the magic. Have you even considered what that's like for them? What it *does* to them?"

I think of Rose, the girl in etiquette who still hasn't emerged. "I hadn't considered that, no."

"You think it's all fine silks and glittering balls? There're droves of families out there excluded from this life. Who don't exactly approve of the way we do things." He steps so close to me, there is no air. I breathe and it's only him. "You think they all just swallow their frustrations and grumble about it over dinner? If you do, you're naive."

"Octos. You're talking about Octos."

"Of course I am. He *knew* hurting you would hurt the Order. He wanted revenge." He spits the words, and I'm taken aback by the ferocity.

A thirst for revenge? I'd read it as something else entirely, that Octos and I share something in common. But the destroyed plant suggests maybe I was wrong. I've been grafted into this world. My gaze falls, painfully aware that I should be one of the rejected thousand, not the accepted few.

"I hadn't thought—"

"I can see that. You haven't thought about a whole lot. What do you think would happen if a Headmistress's own flesh and blood was killed or even severely hurt? You have any idea?" He sighs, exasperated, and walks off. It makes sense that my last name would put a target on my back. Such irony, considering the drastic shift my life took just days ago.

"I'm sorry. I was just trying to—"

"Cheat." His words are sandpaper.

"No." I block his path again, making him look at me. "I'm not, I wasn't going to—"

"Well, to me it looked like—"

"Well, if you *listened* half as much as you *assumed*, you would know!" I snap, and my tone silences him. "I considered it for maybe a second. But no . . . that's not who I am."

He studies me a moment, then gazes off into the distance, hands stuffed in his pockets.

I can't tell if he believes me. But the knot of dread that usually cinches me in his presence loosens some. Duty fuels him, clearly.

"You're innately so powerful, and yet have *no idea* what you're loyal to." A strangled laugh escapes him. "To think I was concerned you might have been a calculated threat." He moves hair off my shoulder, and the suddenness of his feather-soft touch brushing my skin sends a shiver up my arms. "A missile strike and a deadly hurricane couldn't be more different. Or more dangerous."

"Jordan—"

"I'm saying I've misjudged you, Miss Marionne."

A response escapes me, but the drum in my chest slows. Wind gusts between us, and the heat of the moment blows away with it. We stand there for several beats under the moonlight, silent. The park rings with a string of nuzzled laughter. Somewhere puddles splash. He sighs and it sinks his posture. His mask dissolves into his skin, and I can almost feel the weight of his worn expression. He is a storm brewing that I don't quite understand. But like the night that surrounds us, even when I peer hard, I can't make out his shadowed parts.

"All I'm trying to get you to understand is that *you* are the House. I am Perl. You, Marionne. You are what you represent. An ideal. A standard. Above reproach. You should be best in all your sessions."

I swallow, pressure cracking the pieces of myself I'm barely holding together. As if every part of me wasn't already full to the brim, ready to burst. It's too much, and it's me who walks away now, pacing.

"You should be untouchable, Quell." He follows, his tone gentler.

Like him. The way his energy commands any room he's in. The way people step out of his way without him asking. The way everything about him is calculated with precision, perfect. He moves with dominance, a confidence that's entirely foreign. Always in control. I glare at my hands, fury rising up in me. *That's not me.* But I can't say that . . . I can't let him see just how much these shoes I'm squeezing into don't fit.

"If *you're* reachable, then *the Order* is reachable."

So that's what it's about then. Frustration swells in me. All this pressure, carrying the Marionne name out in the open. I turn, and he's there right in front of me, not hovering in his usual ornery way. And for the second time tonight, I stare into eyes that are as heavy as a summer rain.

"Because I'm your mentor, your performance is a reflection of me. Our success is tied."

"I am trying. I swear."

"Try *harder*. Be smarter."

I suddenly realize how close he is, and heat flushes through me. I step back.

"Do you know Octos?" I ask to fill the silence. "Those marks on his arm . . ."

He opens his mouth, and I expect some of the good intentions to bleed through, soften his sharp edges. But his words come out as cold as before. "Not particularly, no."

"Then how'd you know what he was trying to sell me was bad?"

"He's a Trader, they're all the same." He glances at my furrowed brow and his jaw tightens with impatience. "There are twenty-three known elixirs: ones that can sedate you, stop your heart, echo your thoughts so others can hear them, and a whole host of other illicit things. But Ambrosers claim they've discovered more." He sneers. "They tout those marks on their arms like trophies."

Abby's beau Mynick had a dozen or so tallies tattooed on his arm. But something about the way Octos had pulled at both his sleeves in my presence suggested he must have many more. "Why do you say it like that?"

"House of Ambrose is always trying to push the limits, exploit magic to give more credence to the notion that they're superior to the rest of us. They don't understand the concept of duty. *We* serve *magic*, it does not serve us. You can't trust people like that."

"How do you know all this?"

He meets my eyes and my heart squeezes. "Why is *that* your concern?" He radiates with annoyance.

"Well, you stepped in back there and—"

"I shouldn't have to step in in the first place. Using magic like that off the grounds isn't ideal."

My patience breaks. "Then why did you!"

"Get back to the estate before you wander into more trouble. *Good night.*" He storms off.

Ugh! If he thinks I'm such a screwup, so bad at all this . . . "Why did you request to mentor me!"

He's far enough that I yell, and my voice echoes off the stone memorials in the park. He doesn't even look back. Irritation burns through me as he disappears into the forest in a cloud of black.

I stomp the entire way back to the Tavern to grab Abby and go home, fuming less and less with each step. Because for as crappy as this night was, there's one silver lining, one that could help me get a hold on my unruly toushana. I can't shake the image of Jordan's magic turning that plant to ash.

I will find out how he did that.

FOURTEEN

———✳———

Abby's a great friend, the best roommate, super smart, but *not* at all a morning person. She didn't wake up at eight to take me to the library and was still in bed snoring when I slipped out of our room at eight thirty. Fortunately breakfast was grab-and-go ready, and despite some possible indigestion later from eating so quickly, I'm at the library's entrance by nine.

It's on the second floor between the dining hall and yoga studio. Its carved doors with half-sun handles tell a story. Inside, shelves are stacked floors high with clusters of study tables peppered among them. Walking inside feels like slipping on my favorite cozy socks. The first place Mom and I visited after each move was the local library. I skim an electronic catalog hungry to figure out what exactly Jordan did to that plant in the Tavern, and *how*. Any books on Dragun lore should be shelved in the Secundus section. Signs lead me to a small room with its own set of glass doors where a woman with mousy brown hair is repairing the spines of worn books with the shift of her hands.

"Excuse me," she chirps, removing her cat-eye glasses. "I need to see a permission slip to check out books in here."

"I don't have one."

"It's fine, Mrs. Loudle, she's with me."

I turn and the precise person I didn't want to see, all six foot something of him, is right behind me. My grip tightens on my bag strap as he walks past. His skin brushes mine. I jerk aside to get out of his way a bit harder than I mean to and knock over a stack of Mrs. Loudle's books. I pick them up hastily.

"Quell." He dips his chin in greeting.

The way he stormed off last night makes me prefer rolling my eyes, but I think better of it and dip my chin back. "Jordan."

"Mister Wexton," the librarian, Mrs. Loudle, says. "My bright and early bookworm, find anything good today?" She turns to me. "This boy reads more than anyone I've seen in my thirty years here."

He likes books?

"I did find a few this time actually," he says, showing his stack to Mrs. Loudle, and I peek for a glimpse of their spines. He catches me watching, and I promptly look away.

Mrs. Loudle smooths a thumb across a badge, and my name appears in bold black ink. "Here you are." She hands it to Jordan.

I reach for it, but my fingers crash into his. He takes my hand and gently unfolds my palm and sets the badge inside it.

I clear my throat. "Thank you."

"Are you surprised I like to read?" he asks.

I snatch my hand away and loop the lanyard around my neck.

"You wear everything you're thinking on your face, Quell."

"Not everything." I grind my teeth. "Thank you, Mrs. Loudle. I shouldn't be too long. Session is starting soon." I hurry off, hoping to avoid any questions from Jordan about why I'd want to peruse the Secundus section.

"So have you been busy with . . . you know?" Loudle asks. "Nasty whispers about the Sphere, I'm hearing. Do you know if toushana has something to do with it? Darkbearer days are gone, they say. But 'they say' a lot of things."

I slip past them inside. Hopefully she'll keep him wrapped in conversation for a few beats longer so I can peruse without a stalker on my heels.

The Secundus section is much quainter, with lounge chairs for reading. It's completely empty, which is a small relief. Shelves cover every inch of wall space. There's even a decorative ladder of blankets in a corner. I pick a section and scour the book spines, periodically checking to be sure Jordan's still tied up in conversation outside. Nothing on Draguns.

I graze another row for anything even close to toushana, Dragun lore, or Order history. A set of cracked leather spines embossed with gold lettering catches my eye on a low shelf. *The Rare Breed.* I have to get down all the way on my knees to pull them out. They are unyielding when I tug, like they haven't been touched in forever. I pull harder, and one gives.

The rest of the letters on the spine have worn off, but inside, the title page is intact. *Draguns: The Rare Breed*, vol. 1 of 3. I grab it and the two others, creating a small stack in my arms. I glance back again, and Jordan's pulling away from Mrs. Loudle. My heart thrums faster as I move to the checkout table. I slip the books under the scanner and shove them in my bag, and then a low voice spins me around.

"So you like to read, too, I gather? Only bookish people are impressed by that."

"Who says I'm impressed?"

"Your surprise—"

"I'm *surprised* you do anything for fun."

For a moment, he says nothing, his mouth parted. "It's good to see you up and at it early," he says.

By all indications, nothing about him seeing me pleases him, other than his persistent ability to get in my way.

"I have to get going," he says.

"Oh, I'm so disappointed." I could kick myself for letting his annoyance bait me.

He taps the lanyard on my chest, ignoring my snide remark. "You're welcome."

I offer nothing more than a tight smile.

"Remember, your *best* today, protégé." He turns on his heel and leaves, and I stay and read as long as I can.

When I get to a section on "Dragun Legacy," I skip over a few parts about "Early Wars" but stop at "Draguns: Multifaceted and Lethal." I pull the book closer, my eyes flying across the words as my brain tries to sift them into meaning. *Draguns are a brotherhood that spans Houses and supersedes House loyalties. Their universal sigil is a single, hooked dragon talon. Draguns have the unique ability to master multiple areas of magic.* I twist my shirt hem between my fingers, remembering the cracked column at the throat of the Dragun after me. Who was he if not with the brotherhood? I bite my lip and try to remember what Dexler said on my first day. Binding with one form of magic usually dulls the other forms. *Draguns are the exception.*

I sit up and flip the page, looking for examples. Some comprehensive list of the types of magic Draguns wield. The dark kind, especially. But I find nothing but a pressed mosquito, guts smashed on the page. I slap the tome closed, and I realize the time. I toss my books into my bag and hurry to session.

I arrive to Dexler's room and crash into my seat. Despite being a few minutes late, things haven't started. Today's my second shot at proving I can do this. I can't afford any screwups.

"Easy there, tiger. We don't do track tryouts here." Shelby tosses me a bubble gum.

"Funny." I tuck it away. "I didn't see you at the Tavern the other night."

"Oh, yeah, this guy and I were out doing stuff."

Rose flings herself into the other chair beside me, apologizing for her tardiness—still no diadem on her head.

"I was actually going to ask you about emerging," I say to Shelby.

"Nothing yet, huh?" She glances at my head.

Rose flinches, eyeing our conversation, and guilt hooks in my stomach.

"Never mind," I say. "I'll ask you later."

Shelby gives me a you're-too-nice look.

"You didn't miss anything," I tell Rose, trying to change the subject when I notice puffiness under her eyes. "Are you all right?"

She doesn't say a word, and that says everything. I glance at her disheveled hair and the rest of her. Wrinkled clothes, the same she wore yesterday, are stained with makeup on the sleeves.

"Rose, I'm sorry. Any itching?"

She shakes her head, her eyes watering.

"How long do you have?" I whisper when Dexler calls everyone's attention to the front.

She points to her desk.

"*Today?!*"

Shelby nudges me with her elbow to keep it down as Dexler glances our way. But it's too late.

"Miss Marionne, what did I just explain?"

There's no way out of this one. "I wasn't listening, I apologize."

"Is that because you don't think what I have to say is important or…?"

Cold flickers through me. "No, it absolutely is. I—"

"Then I expect you to act like it."

The tongue-lashing leaves me hunched over my paper of notes, fixated on every next syllable out of Dexler's mouth. Rose is stiff next to me and silent. I think of Octos, hoping it doesn't come to the worst for her.

The way things unfolded with Octos still doesn't sit right with me. Something about him was so genuine, so honest. The way his shoulders shrugged with pride when he spoke of his family. The surprise on his face when he saw what the elixir did. I'm pretty good at reading people, and I'm not sure Jordan's pegged him entirely right.

When our materials are passed out, we're arranged into groups. Shelby, Rose, and I link up and scoot our chairs to an island of our own in the corner of the room.

"Decomposing," I say, spacing out our materials. Two different types of bones and a beetle. "We have to fossilize these ingredients and collect their ash in a jar."

Rose broods, her hands shoved in her lap.

"You want to ready the kor?" I ask her. "It's fire again today."

"What's the point? Nothing's helping. I've tried everything."

Shelby glances between us, sighing before grabbing the kor. I don't miss her slight eye roll. She works her fingers over the wick to ignite the kor. I grab the bone, rolling it in my hands. It's light and fragile. A little bendy. I shiver at the thought of where it could have come from.

"The closest natural path, remember," Shelby says.

My toushana could turn this to dust in one point three seconds, but that's not going to fly. I search for a glimmer of warmth, turning the bone over the fire. I picture it decomposing under soil, the sped-up process of time. The warmth in my fingers hums louder as I tug at it.

It crumples at its edges, pieces falling away. I tighten my grip, determined to hold on to my proper magic. But something causes it to stutter and the heat dissolves. *"No!"* But the flicker of progress is lost and the bone is an unchanged log in my hands.

"What's wrong?" Shelby asks.

I shove back from the table in frustration.

"Here, let me." Shelby works her magic over the bone, turning it in the flicker of the kor as she focuses intensely on the ingredients. Its edges crumble a second before the whole thing collapses into dust. "See?" She eases it off the table into a funnel attached to a jar.

"You make it look so—"

"Agnes," Grandmom says from the doorway, and I smooth the edges of my hair.

"Headmistress," Dexler says with an inflection that suggests she's just as surprised to see her as the rest of us. "Ladies and gentlemen, we have a visitor."

Chairs scrape the floor as we all stand. "Good afternoon, Headmistress Marionne."

Hearing my name in a chorus pokes me with an unfamiliar sensation. They're not talking to me. But still, it's weird.

"To what do I owe this treat?"

Grandmom enters, and there isn't a single eye in the room that would dare look away. Awe swivels every neck, flattens every back against its chair. Grandmom's gaze finds mine, then quickly shifts to Rose. She whispers something to Dexler, who glances at Rose as well. Her posture sinks with disappointment.

"Ro—" I start, but she shoulders her bag.

"Good luck to you, Quell, I mean, not that you need it."

Grandmom guides her through the door with a dainty hand cupped on her shoulder. As it swings closed, Rose glances back at me, her face pinched with sorrow, reminiscent of a lonely Trader in a bar. I look away, but her despair lingers like a bad perfume. I turn back to my materials, but time and motion seem out of balance. Rose's exit replays in my mind over and over except it's my head on her body.

"Well." Dexler's voice snatches me from my spiraling gloom. "Staring isn't going to get those ingredients decomposed." She claps. "Back to it! Once you turn it in, you're dismissed. Remember, practice independently, seek out your mentors. You have much to master."

Session buzzes with whispers about Rose being kicked out.

"What'll happen to her?" I whisper to Shelby.

"She couldn't cut it in the House she's zoned to, so unless her family relocates to a different territory, she's done," Shelby says with equal measure of disinterest and surprise. "Shunned, barred from growing her magic."

"What'll happen to it?"

"It'll become stunted and eventually unreachable."

My chest aches for her.

"You want to try the beetle? It should be a little easier since it's still alive. I can do the others."

"Sure." I don't mean it to come out so dreary, but it does.

"Hey," Shelby says, sensing my sullen shift. "It happens. It gets easier."

I don't know if that's true. But I need to focus on this lesson, do it well.

"I'm serious. I'm a *Duncan*, Quell. No one in my family's been inducted for decades. But I wanted to, and Headmistress knew my grandmother personally. So she gave me a shot. Four other girls started the week I did. We got close, fast, made a pact to stick together, determined to survive. My Cotillion is in just over a month. I'm almost out of here, and guess what . . ." She picks up her ingredients. "I'm the only one of my friends left."

"That must have sucked."

"Sort of. You begin to understand, you're different. And you can either own that and step into it or be tortured by everyone else's failure for the rest of your life. Rose is gone because she didn't deserve to be here. *You* do." She walks away and my resolve fractures.

But I don't.

Head down, I carve out a work space for myself away from Shelby and everyone. My hands shake as Rose's departing stare and Shelby's words tangle together into a nightmare.

Focus.

Rose was here one day and gone the next.

I blow out a breath and bite down with new determination. A texture of warmth hums to life beneath my skin. I clench my every muscle, holding it there tight like I read in Abby's notes. The beetle writhes on his back, moving slower. I grow hotter, my proper magic revving up as what feels like bits of sand spread from my head to my toes. Each place they settle tingles with heat. A quiver of cold tugs at me, but the magic burning through me sends it back to the pitless depths from which it came. I hold on to the feeling, and magic sears through me like a furnace, raging and in control, hotter than I've ever felt it.

The beetle snaps flat. *It's working!*

I tighten, pulling harder at the sensation of my magic all over me. *Now, decompose.*

But the heat shifts like a cool gust on a summer day. My insides quaking with fire, then shuddering cold. Back and forth, the oscillating temperature of my magic threatens to unsteady me. I strain, urging my toushana deep down. But it fights me back with a frigidness like I've never felt before. The world blinks white, and for a moment a cold like death seizes tightly in my chest. I think of Mom and her strong hugs when she would whisper in my ear: *There's good in you, Quell.*

Something shifts, and I latch on to it.

I warm a little.

There is good in you, Quell.

Now hot.

So close.

Harder, I urge, pulling from my core, imagining those Dust granules piling one on top of another until I'm warmed to the brim. When suddenly everything bleeds cold.

The beetle erodes into a tiny hill of ash, my toushana decomposing its little body at warp speed. Then, it retreats as quickly as it appeared. I shove out of my seat, blinking in disbelief. I gaze around, but the cyclone of panic only swirls around me.

I couldn't fight it off. I tried and it fought back. My throat is a desert and swallowing doesn't help. My freak-out garners pinched glances and I tug at the ends of my hair to keep from clawing my skin. *Remember where you are.* I clear my throat and try to slow my breaths.

The mess on the table looks . . . correct.

Decomposed dust from a beetle.

I did that with my toushana.

"Quell." Shelby grabs me by the arm. "Are you okay? You're as pale as a ghost."

I snatch my arm away. "I'm— Yes. I'm okay."

She coaxes the dust into a jar. "This looks great. You sure you're all right?"

I clear my throat, still chilled all over. "Yes, I'm good."

"Okay, I'll turn it in."

"Thanks."

"Catch you later in the dining hall if you're around?"

"Sure thing."

Shelby gathers our supplies and takes them to Dexler. She beams, inspecting it, but it doesn't ease the nausea welling in my gut. I couldn't stop my toushana. No matter what I tried.

I shoulder my bag and head out the door. I distance myself from the crowds lingering in the hall, and when I round on the Belles Wing where my room is, the coast is clear. I pull the book out of my bag that I borrowed from the library, thumbing through it for any mention of toushana. It's a long shot, but I'm desperate.

"Oh, hey, there you are." It's Abby.

I slip the book away.

"Want to grab a bite? Sorry about this morning. I was wiped. I want to hear more about what happened the other night. You didn't say much on the way home. I saw you follow Jordan out of the Tavern and—" She reaches to brush up against me playfully, but I move away. "Why are you being weird?"

"Sorry. I have a headache. I'm going to go back to the room to lie down. Can I have some alone time?"

"Sure. Jordan was looking for you though."

"If you see him, can you make an excuse for me? He's just really intense about this mentor stuff."

"Ugh, not mine. I rarely hear from her." She folds her arms. "Fine, but I need the entire rundown on what's going on with you later."

By then I should be able to make up something believable. "Deal."

"Feel better." She turns. "And drink water!"

I hurry to our room and shut myself inside.

I move to my bed, tucking myself under my covers, and bury my head in another book, trying to find something I can use. Something about toushana, something about controlling dark magic, or even emerging. But I turn and turn and turn, and it's just more about how Draguns were created and why.

To kill people with toushana in order to "protect the integrity of magic."

I drift off to sleep to the image of being ejected from session with a dagger at my throat.

Down the corridor,
Through the dark halls, something chases me.

Up the stairs to the balcony's ledge,
Air whips beneath me.
I stare at the ground so far below, breathless.
My foot slips on the edge,
but I catch myself, nails digging into the unforgiving stone.

I gasp for breath, my ceiling solidifying in focus. Abby's faint snores ease me into the present. *A dream. It was just a dream.* I try to sit up, but my head throbs. I reach for my temples, rubbing circles into my scalp.

My fingers touch something cold and hard.

I throw off the covers and dash to the mirror above my dresser. I flip on a lamp and see coils of metal snaking up from my scalp, tall and robust. My diadem sparkles, speckled with gems. But it's not gold, or silver, rose gold, or even copper like other diadems.

It's black like death.

Black like rot.

Black because of my toushana.

"Oh my god." *I'm strengthening the wrong magic.*

FIFTEEN

I snatch the lamp's cord. My heart pounds, and it's all I hear in the darkness. The glass display cases of diadems in the hall. The black one was ripped from someone who'd had toushana. Abby twists in her covers, and for a second I don't breathe. Her snores return and I snap to my senses, grabbing my shoes. No one can see me like this. A bright number two blares at me from the wall clock as I try to formulate some sort of plan. *Think.* Jordan crosses my mind. *Think of something else.*

The walls close in, and I rip through the moonlit room as quietly as I can to find something to cover my head. I pass my mirror and stop. Despite the dimness, my diadem glitters like a thousand stars. It's as big as Shelby's. Bigger maybe. The coils of black metal twist around one another like a nest of curls. Short narrow points rise around them like spires, and the whole thing gleams with dark pink gems. But, because of the black, the stones almost appear red.

I've emerged. I steady a hand on the dresser, gaping in the mirror.

My curiosity tries to morph into admiration, but I look away. I give the metal coming out of my scalp a gentle tug. My brain pulses with pain as if it's being pulled apart at opposite ends, and I bite my cheek to stifle a scream.

Abby rolls in her covers, and an idea nudges me. I could try trusting her. But I don't know how deep friendship loyalty goes. Shelby? No way. I hug around myself as Octos's worn expression slinks through my memory. I shift on my feet, warring between impossible options. The gravity of what I'm actually considering tugs me down, and I sit on my bed. He said if I ever needed a favor . . .

I bite into my knuckle and glance again at Abby. I don't believe Octos tried to kill me. I know the stench of desperation, and he reeked of it. I snatch up my jacket, Mom's dagger, and a scarf of Abby's before I talk myself out of what I know I have to do.

The halls of Chateau Soleil are so silent I fear the broom closet door's creaks will awaken all three floors. The trick wall responds to my pushing easily enough, and I squeeze through and sprint down the corridor, holding my scarf in place. The door to the forest is latched shut, and I work my warm magic around it, just the way I saw Abby do. I shove down all the reasons this could go horribly wrong and step through. I'm out of options.

I don't have the privilege of reason.

Outside, I manage to slip through the tangled branches concealing the door with only a few scrapes, and once I set foot on the ground and glance back at the estate, my pulse ticks a little slower. The cobblestone path that runs through the forest is swept with leaves, and I follow them all the way into the park. The stone memorials signal me where to stop. *How did she do it?* I kick my boot on the rock. Nothing happens. I try again, peering harder at the stones for some indication of which rock is the trick one. I run my fingers across them until they ache with a chill, and then I graze a raised one.

"Is this it?" The cold in my bones rears up, and I can feel my toushana nestled inside me like an ache I can't shake, a cramp in my side. I rub the rock again, and my destructive magic flutters. The urge to wriggle at the sudden feeling of my magic heavy and present in my body, like a lead ball stuck to my insides, bites at me. But instead, I give the rock a kick, angle my magic toward it, and the ground opens. *It actually worked.* I start my descent, Mom's dagger clutched tight in my fist.

The Tavern is a dead zone with only dregs of a crowd shuffling to low music on the dance floor. The game tables are empty and the lights are dimmed.

"Last call was ten minutes ago," the bartender says, without looking up. Octos isn't anywhere in sight.

"Excuse me?"

"I said, last—" He looks up. "Fresh meat, you're out mighty late."

I tighten my grip on my scarf under my chin. He slides a wet rag across the bar as his barback starts busing tables.

"I'm looking for the guy I was talking to the other night. Worn coat, long hair, in need of a shave."

"You come in here this time of night looking for Octos?" He folds his arms across his barrel chest. "What kind of trouble are you trying to get into, girl?" He glances at the door.

"Is he here?"

"He's slept on that couch there for the last few nights. But I haven't seen him tonight yet." He tosses a towel over his shoulder. "I have to close up. You should get home. Being out here alone like this isn't smart." He turns and disappointment sinks in my stomach like a stone in a river.

By the time I exit the Tavern, the dance floor has cleared. The bartender flips the lights, and when I climb the stairs, I hear the lock click behind me. The ground closes up with a slight rumble. Night buzzes with the crackling vibrato of bugs, and I gaze in every direction, hugging my arms around myself. Maybe this wasn't my brightest idea. The distinct feeling that someone or something is watching me urges my feet faster.

"You looking for me?" a voice says when I make it back beneath the forest canopy.

Octos's face is shadowed between branches. He steps out and I grab Mom's dagger. He backs away. "If you've come here for revenge, I swear I didn't know."

I stand a little taller, careful to keep the weapon between us. "I came with a request."

He moves into a patch of moonlight and I can fully see him. He's as haggard as before. The worn lines that trace his face are deeper tonight, with dark pockets under his eyes and a sullen droop in his shoulders.

I lower the dagger. "I have an offer."

"I don't understand."

"I have a hunch you know things. Things . . . you probably shouldn't."

He stuffs his hands in his pockets. "And?"

"And I need to know if there's any sort of magic to transfigure a diadem."

"I'm not getting anywhere near you and emerging." He throws up his hands in surrender. "I tried selling you that elixir, and that went to shit. I still owe a debt to the merchant trash who traded me that rotten vial," he spits.

I knew it.

"You said if I ever needed a favor to find you."

He tilts his head. "Go on."

I step closer, out of the shadows, willing him to listen. "I've emerged."

He gazes up at the scarf wrapped around my head very obviously hiding something. "What exactly do you need? And what are you offering?"

There's the Octos I hoped to find. I lay my mother's dagger across my hands, making sure its jewels catch the moonlight. "This belongs to the Marionne family and would probably make you rich beyond your wildest dreams."

He reaches for it but pulls his hand back. "Why would you offer something so valuable?"

"For someone who deals in illicit affairs, you sure have a lot of questions."

"I make it my business to know the kinds of people I get into deals with. Especially lately."

"I'm the granddaughter of Darragh *Marionne*." The strength of my words flattens my posture. "A cornerstone of the Order, a purveyor of influence." I circle him, mimicking Grandmom's air, squaring my shoulders, holding up my chin. My body rebels at the discomfort. But I hold myself there, my best impression of who I am to him, hoping he buys it. "I'm a powerful ally."

He eyes the dagger, pursing his lips.

"So we have a deal?"

"I don't even know what the task is yet."

"Do you need to?" I pull back his sleeve. His arm is a colorful collage of a tri-tipped sun and tally marks, way more than I'd even imagined. "Don't these represent the twisted things you're capable of, your discoveries while in House Ambrose?"

He snatches his arm back. His lips tighten. "I can do whatever you need," he says, pride loosening his tongue. "But my price is the dagger plus something else."

"Name it."

"I want a Location Enhancer. It's a pale blue stone. The Cultivator supply room should have some on hand."

Stealing one seems a small price to pay for my life. If it's a common enough stone to be kept on hand in a supply room, it can't be terribly hazardous.

"Deal."

"Well . . ." He gestures at my scarf. "Show me how bad it is."

I begin to untie my scarf but hesitate. *I hope this isn't a mistake.* I remove the covering, and he sucks in a breath.

"You can change it to some other metal, can't you?"

"Curses," he says under his breath. "Sola Sfenti has not looked upon you with favor, has he? He would punish us both. Bring me the stone before sunrise. I'll need to use the moon's kor."

I'm BACK ON the grounds in no time, slipping down the stairs to the lowest floor, underground. Dexler had mentioned lugging supplies up from the storage room in the basement of the estate. The stairs creak no matter how gently I ease down them. *I can't believe I'm stealing.* But the trepidation kneading my nerves doesn't stop my descent. It's steal once or be killed.

The stairs deposit me in a spiral hallway of doors. The supply room should be at the center of the spiral. But the end of the maze is a dead end. This hall is half as long as it should be. I push the wall, letting warmth curl in my fingers in case there's some trick to getting through. But the stone doesn't budge.

I count the doors again, then push the same spot on the wall harder this time, and the stone shifts a little. Warmth blusters around in me, a dust storm settling, feisty and hungry. Then it shifts—the warmth of my magic washed away by an ice storm. I clench my fists.

"That's where it should be." A voice ripples down the hallway, and my heart hiccups. I'm trapped with nowhere to go but *toward* whoever is down here or *through* this stone wall.

"Where it should be and where it is could be two completely different things," Jordan says, puncturing my resolve, his steps growing louder. I can't breathe. I can't think. My toushana could get me through the wall. But it would make a colossal mess. And I'm already strengthening the wrong—

It will work, my magic whispers, and I hear it as gooseflesh spreading across my skin.

"What do you want from me?" the person with Jordan huffs, exasperated. "I've told you what I know."

Their voices are just around the corner. Hastily, I smooth my icy fingertips along the wall, praying my instincts are right and it won't make a crumpled mess right here on the floor. A heap of ash like my very own bloody fingerprint.

The stone shudders, then splits in half like a curtain. Beyond it is the rest of the corridor with the missing doors. I twist the handle of one labeled SUPPLY ROOM. Inside, crates of serveware and rows of hung linens are crowded into what smells like a laundry room. But there's no sign of a washer or dryer. A sea of tarps hang like sloping waves over furniture as far as I can see. I ease the door closed with the slightest click and listen.

"Just show me," Jordan says. The door handle twists, and I scramble for a place to hide.

"Get this over with," the other person says as the door opens. I wedge myself between two lumps of furniture beneath a tarp and clamp a hand over my mouth.

"If Headmistress catches me down here . . ."

"Hush," Jordan urges.

I don't breathe.

"Did you hear something?" he asks.

"No, did you?"

"No, but I sense—" Jordan's shoes click on the stone in my direction. He stops. "*Hmph.* I guess not. Go on, then. Show me where it is." Shoes shuffle. Fabric rips through the air like it's being unfurled.

"There's what you were looking for," the other says. "Over there. See. Safe and tucked away." Heavy wood groans as it's dragged across the floor. "Right where I said it was."

My pulse ticks faster.

"No word to anyone about this," Jordan orders.

"What's your aunt up to anyway?"

"That's Headmistress Perl. And none of your business."

"Right, my apologies."

Footsteps are faint until the door clicks shut. I pull the drape of fabric off me and fall into an old velvet chair, trying to calm my racing heart. The room's changed some, furniture uncovered, but there is no indication of what Jordan wanted to make sure was down here. His sneaking under Grandmom's nose for his Headmistress doesn't sit right with me, but I don't need another reason for him to be on my case.

The stone. Octos.

Dining tables, chaises, armchairs with broken legs and ripped seats surround me. I remove cover after cover but find nothing that could house stones. I sift aisles of bureaus and storage furniture, but each is empty. Until I spot a cabinet on curved legs with rows upon rows of tiny drawers inconspicuously hanging out in a corner on its own.

I tug one open, and polished stone shines back at me. LUMEN ENHANCER is inscribed on the inside of the drawer. I close it and pull out another. This one is greenish yellow. DECIBEL ENHANCER. I hastily open others, several at a time, peering for some glimpse of pale blue, and my thoughts drift to Jordan. I file away seeing him snooping for later use in case I need it and force myself to focus on the dilemma at hand—the blackened metal growing out of my head.

The enhancer chest's rows are endless, but by about the fiftieth drawer I open, I finally find a powder blue stone. LOCATION ENHANCER. I grab it and hurry out of the room.

I take the stairs two at a time, the stone clutched in my fist. I push the door open to the floor above, and the ground trembles. *What in the world*—I steady myself on the wall as a chandelier above rattles, its crystal baubles slipping off and shattering against the polished floor. The stone slips from my grasp, rolling away, and my heart skips a beat. I cling to the wall for footing to gird myself against the shaking ground.

Then I dash for the stone when the quaking stops. Commotion spills into the hall as bleary-eyed students pour out of their beds with questions. With it tight in my fist I cinch my scarf tight and rush to the grand foyer and through the broom closet, ignoring the earthquake. I have bigger problems.

Please let Octos be true to his word.

I push open the door and step into the thick forest air.

SIXTEEN

—— ✳ ——

"Octos?"

 I tighten my fist on the stolen bauble and skim every shadowed corner of the forest for some glimpse of him.

"Here." He comes out of the bramble.

"I have what you asked for. Now do what you promised." I smooth my clothes and press my shoulders back, then open my hand. He looks at the stone, stare alight with veneration. I close my fist.

"What does this mean to you?"

"Questions weren't a part of the bargain."

He's right. But his expression drips with yearning. It's a Location Enhancer; what is he trying to find?

"If you know anything about Location Enhancers, you know that it takes a dozen of them at least to do anything."

"I only have one."

"Which is all I asked for." He holds out his hand and I place the stone in his open palm. "We still have a deal or—"

"Yes, but let's be clear, whatever trouble you're trying to get into with this, leave me out of it."

He agrees. "If you'll remove your scarf, Miss."

I do. And it's only then I notice how much shorter than me he is. He tiptoes to get above my head to take a closer look at my diadem.

He hands me a thin flat branch. "Bite down on this and be still." He winds his hands in a smooth circular motion.

"What do—" My head throbs, and I shove the bark between my teeth a beat too late. "Ah!!!"

"Shh!"

I bite down, regretting not listening immediately. But the world blurs from the pain. I sway, stumbling sideways.

"Don't move!"

I hurt, all over. Bark is a wall at my back, holding me up, thankfully, as my senses weaken. I'm not in a forest. I'm not a person or body at all. I'm a head swimming in an inferno. I bite down harder, swallowing every utterance that grazes my lips.

"Almost," he says between his teeth.

I stagger as a surge of sharpness rips at the inside of my head like the world's worst migraine. My eyes feel like they're being sucked into my skull, and my brain is being squished. Then a rush of calm breaks over me. The feeling of the world being ripped apart comes to a halt.

"There." He stumbles back, panting for breath. Sweat beads on his face. He sits down on a stump and takes a long swig from the water at his waist.

I blink, confused by the absence of pain, and reach for my head, only to realize I should have brought a mirror.

"Here." He pulls himself up, despite his exhaustion, and digs out a shard of mirror from a bag hidden beside a tree. He holds it up. I gasp at coils of what was just black metal now shining in rose gold above my head, dotted with almond-shaped gems the color of happiness, pinkish crimson. It sparkles with every twist of my head, and it steals my next breath like an endless field of spring's first bloom. I try to speak, but my hand is cupped over my mouth.

"How long will this last?"

"As long as you keep that rotted magic you're carrying under control, forever."

Forever. "It's so . . . beautiful."

"Always was. It's just gold now."

"Thank you." I roll my neck, unwinding the frazzled mess that I am. "A-And I apologize if things were tense there for a moment. I just—"

"No explanation needed." He gulps down a deliberate breath, his chest still rising and falling loudly.

"Are you going to be okay?"

"I'll be fine." He gathers his coat and the dagger, which I realize, in the chaos of everything, I dropped.

"You're quite talented. It's a shame your House didn't let you finish."

His eyes meet mine.

Octos has saved my life. The words hang on my lips, but I hesitate to show my full hand. He rolls his jaw as if there's something he wants to say.

"Yes?"

"Most wouldn't give me the time of day." He turns the dagger in his hands.

"Before I came here, me either."

We shake. "Pleasure doing business with you."

I offer a tight smile and watch him go. When he reaches the edge of the forest, I go back inside and tuck the scarf away.

THE ESTATE HAS quieted as I sneak to my room, and my eyelids are heavy, demanding to be closed. My head swims with the chaos of the last couple of hours. But I urge my feet forward, the warm sheets of my bed calling to me. When I wake up, maybe this will all have been a bad dream. It's a lie, but without it I'm not sure I'd be able to put one foot in front of another at the moment.

I could have been *killed*.

I claw at my throat, willing it to unclench. My fingers reach for the metal on my head again, and I ease out a breath. It's rose *gold* not *black*. My secret is hidden.

Broken glass litters the halls, swept aside as if cleanup is in progress. Whispering somewhere freezes me on the spot, but it's too far and too faint to make out. I ease around the banister and up the grand stair to the Belles Wing, my head still pulsing with a minor throb. It's hardly noticeable compared with what it felt like ten short minutes ago.

When I enter our suite, Abby's wide awake, shifting the fabric on a long gown.

I stop, a ball of tightness and nerves.

She gasps at the showing arced above my head, and the dress in her hands falls to the floor. She rushes to greet me, shaking my shoulders.

I force them to sink and try to relax my arms as I close the door behind me. It takes every bit of focus not to look down at my shoes.

"*You!* It's so tall and . . ." She steps back with sweeping dramatics, brandishing her arms in every direction. "Magnificent, regal, resplendent, grand!" She swings me around and curtsies.

Shame burns in my chest. But I force myself to look at her and smile. To step into this world of make-believe where I am actually worthy of this fawning affection.

"Well go on, curtsy like a *proper lady*!" She scrunches up her nose and I laugh, a burst of joy rushing up against the dam of my indignity.

I copy to appease her, but my heart is not in it. My knees go all wobbly when I get too low. "That's harder than it looks."

"Plume will whip you into shape, don't worry. You'll be the talk of the entire Season!" She pulls me to the mirror, and I suck in a breath as I take myself in fully. Despite the events of the night, the stranger who stares back at me holds her shoulders squarely; her chin doesn't point to the floor as it usually does. I look away. *She's a liar. A cheater.* Disguised as someone deserving.

Abby rotates my head, making me stare into the mirror. "Ladies and gentlemen," she says, mimicking a stuffy announcer's voice. "I present Quell Janae Marionne, granddaughter of Darragh Marionne, Headmistress and Cultivator *extraordinaire*." She laughs, and the bubble in me somehow resurfaces, spilling out in bashful laughter.

"You're ridiculous."

"You just don't seem nearly excited enough. First Rite, down. Two to go!"

"I am, really." I shrug. "There's a long way to go to Cotillion, that's all."

She sits on her bed and pulls her dress across her onto her lap, her magic shifting the shiny purple fabric to a deep shade of green.

"That looks nice."

"Oh, thanks. The nice thing about being away from home is I don't have to listen to my parents nagging about how Vestisers are a frivolous waste of shifting ability." She rolls her eyes. "I like fashion. They act like that's a crime."

"Well, I'm glad here you get to be yourself."

She slips her dress onto a hanger before climbing into bed. "I have honing exam tomorrow. Finally. It's taken me forever to even qualify to sit the exam. Like two entire summers. Give me all the good juju to pass."

I wiggle my fingers in her direction. "Juju sent. You'll do great though. I'm sure of it."

She reaches for the lamp with a yawn as I climb into bed.

"Thanks, Abby. For sticking by me and being excited and stuff."

"You just wait. This entire House is going to bow at your skirt."

The light clicks, and my insides swirl with nerves. A different kind than I've felt before. Angst, yes, but rooted in something strangely unfamiliar. I hadn't thought about what people would say. My diadem is beautiful. More glorious than I could have even dreamt up. Even when blackened, it was stunning. Maybe even more so.

But the truth—that this isn't the real diadem—needles me.

You emerged, my conscience whispers. *That matters.*

I stew on the thought, and something uncinches in me.

"I belong here." I mutter the mantra to myself, but it sounds hollow. I squirm to get a bit more comfortable with this thing on my head. Careful to not shove it into the pillow too hard. I pull the covers tight to my chin, and my thoughts shift to Octos, the tally marks all over his arms. The rogue life he lives. But I have my own self-destruction to fight off. I hug my pillow and obey my heavy eyelids.

"I belong here," I say again, low enough so Abby can't hear. I have to say it until I believe it. I have to say it so I can face tomorrow.

PART THREE

SEVENTEEN

———✳———

Morning comes entirely too soon, but despite my heaviness from too little sleep I pop out of bed. Abby's already gone. After a bit of curtsy practice and table manners studying, I'm up and dressed and out the door for etiquette. But downstairs, the grand foyer is set like an auditorium with chairs arced around a podium.

"You're here." Abby hooks her arm into mine, guiding me to a seat.

"What is all this?"

"She called an assembly this morning because of last night."

"My diadem?"

She snorts and points to the Sphere, which hangs above the impending meeting, its blackened matter tossing to and fro treacherously. The tiniest crack lines its surface.

"Was that crack always there?"

She shakes her head. "Happened last night."

As we move to a pair of seats in the back, I quickly realize the foyer isn't swarming just with students, but with adults, too. *This is serious.* I clear my throat and press back into my seat. Fear wells up in me. My diadem emerged the same night the Sphere cracked. I hope that is a coincidence.

"It's a big deal, seems like?" I say to Abby.

She faces me, thunderstruck. "A *huge* deal. If the Sphere ever empties, magic is gone. For half a century at least."

I stiffen, her words ricocheting through me. "Gone?"

"Yep. Gone. No magic. Anywhere."

I'm sure it's hard for her to imagine a world without magic. But the thought doesn't sit with me the same. If there was no magic, I'd be free in a way.

"*And,* rumor has it, the Headmistresses of the Houses would pay the price." Her countenance pinches with the hint of something sinister. She slides a thumb under her throat. "I mean, it's only a rumor, but still."

I'd say execution seems a bit severe, but those who've earned their place, built their trades around magic, would be livid. They'd expect someone to pay for it.

"Is there a way to fix it or patch it or something?"

"No idea. No one even knows where the Sphere is. When it was made, it was hidden for the protection of all magic."

The crowd is a sea of golden and silver diadems, and the events of last night pick at me. The Sphere commands my attention. Its tiny specks— names—etched on its surface seem to gleam angrily. Blackened matter crashes against its glassy surface, ferocious and thrashing as if it intends to claw its way out. I bite down knowingly. That's how my toushana feels.

My hands twinge with a hint of chill as my worry unfurls. I rub them together, fixated on the Sphere hovering like a foreboding storm. I press my feet more firmly to the floor and urge away the cold seeking purchase in my bones.

"It's so angry," I say, before forcing myself to look away.

Abby cocks her head. "I hadn't thought of it that way. I guess it does sort of look mad. My father told me the stuff inside used to be clear with glowing granules of Dust."

"So the Sphere's been changing for a while?"

"Guess so, yeah."

Then it couldn't have anything to do with me.

"My parents are up in arms about something disturbing the balance."

Her words are lasso and hook around my throat. I raise an eyebrow, as if to ask for more information.

"The Sphere represents the balance of all magic being used, including the forbidden kind. So whatever happened last night somewhere in the world upset it."

My heart races as fear takes me tightly in its grip. I lean forward, gasping. "Quell? You okay?"

"I need air." I walk off, back toward the stairs, to quiet, a hallway without eyes and people. *Whatever happened last night disturbed the balance of magic.* I know what happened last night. I pace until the ice in my veins melts. I catch a glimpse of myself in the glass of a portrait on the wall. My diadem is still so radiant to behold. Like the moon on a clear night, I can't imagine staring at it will ever get old.

This can't have anything to do with me or my toushana or my diadem. It just can't. I'm *one* person. Abby said the Sphere encompasses all of magic, like, everywhere.

"There's no way," I whisper, peeking back around the corner at the crowd as Grandmom approaches the stage.

"Excuse me," someone says, rushing past me to find a seat.

I scoot out of the way. Then hastily set a foot in the same direction. *I belong here.*

I look for Abby in the spot we were just sitting but she's gone, and it's filled with someone else. I grab another open chair just as Grandmom takes the microphone.

"Ladies and gentlemen, if you'd take your seats," she says, and a barrage of people swarm into the seats. I cross my ankles and pull at a loose thread on my dress.

"Thank you for appearing on such short notice." She surveys the crowd. "I . . ." Her gaze lands on me and her lips purse in a restrained grin. She sees my diadem.

My lips curl in a smile.

"Sorry, where was I? I am happy to report, but for a few cherished heirloom chandeliers, no one was harmed in last night's incident."

Grandmom clasps her hands, and I recognize it as nerves. I sit up taller. Maybe the rumor Abby mentioned is true. What else could make Grandmom sweat?

"The Sphere, as you can see, has been cracked. But the Headmistresses and I are working around the clock to figure out how this has happened.

I assure you, everything is under control." She tugs at her blazer. "Your patience is greatly appreciated as we sort out answers. The *good* news is that we do have eyes on the problem."

A hand shoots up from the crowd.

"Yes, sir?"

"Does this mean the Sphere's location has been discovered?"

"Yes. But as we all know, it's designed to protect itself."

Chatter erupts.

"I don't like this," someone whispers next to me.

Grandmom huffs, flustered. I squirm in my seat, watching it unfold. Cultivators line the front row, each hanging on Grandmom's words in silence. Plume twists his bag strap around his finger, over and over. Winding and unwinding.

"So you're saying it has not relocated itself, or—" the parent presses.

"I'm saying." Grandmom's tone rises. She wants to be done with this public interrogation. "We have it under control. All signs indicate that it's an accident tied to some random natural disaster."

I sit back in my seat, and the air in my lungs expels. The relief chases away any remnant of chill.

"Each of us four Headmistresses takes this very seriously. The Sphere will not crack further. When we have more updates, we will share without hesitation." She tucks her clutch under her arm. "Now if you will, your children have a full day of practice and studies ahead. Please, let them get to it. I bid you all a good day." She exits the stage, ignoring the next questions thrown her way.

The meeting adjourns as quickly as it appeared, and Grandmom beckons for me to meet her beside the stage.

"You are *exquisite*." She air-kisses both my cheeks and turns me around, taking in the diadem on my head.

"I'm so glad you're pleased."

"I am more than pleased, dear. This showing will be in the Hall of Excellence one day, mark my word. It's . . ." She turns me again and whispers, "Astounding."

"Thank you. Any word on my mom?"

"Actually, yes." She digs out my key chain from her pocket.

My heart skips a beat.

"I tried the key chain a few times with no luck. So I sent a few letters but those garnered no response either." Her nostrils flare. "So I had the Dragunhead send a few of mine to look for her, discreetly, of course."

"And?"

"And she was spotted about forty miles from here. I insisted my people not get near her so as not to alarm her. She didn't appear to want to be bothered."

Mom is staying close by. I reach for my key chain. She hands it over. A part of me unwinds, then tangles up again. "Then why wouldn't she respond to your letters?"

Grandmom grimaces. "Who knows why Rhea does what she does? I just wanted you to know I took care of it, as promised." She eyes the key chain, but I stuff it in my pocket.

"What's my mother's middle name?"

Grandmom's lips thin. "I don't see how that's helpful."

"I would really like to know."

I pull harder at the thread of my dress until it comes out completely. I don't want to upset her, but Mom might not respond because the letters are coming from *her*.

"Marie," she says, begrudgingly. "If that's all. You should be getting along to sessions." She departs before I can respond, but I don't miss the disappointment in her tone.

Unsure what to do to smooth things over with Grandmom, I scribble a quick letter to Mom updating her on things, telling her my plan, that I've emerged, and drop it in Mrs. Cuthers's outbox before booking it to session.

CULTIVATOR PLUME IS already there by the time we file in. Whispers accompany me as I move across the ballroom toward the small crowd of waiting students. Eyes follow me, but not gaping at my face or my clothes, my ratty shoes, the stains on my zip-up. The things I know how to walk past and ignore. These stares gawk at my diadem. My lie. My foot hesitates at my next step, the urge to run whispering to me like an old trusted friend.

"Oh, the rose gold and her eyes," someone whispers, her tone sparkling with awe more than disdain. "Michelle, did you see?"

"What did you expect? She's a Marionne." Michelle, whoever that is, twists her mouth in contempt.

I watch my shoes the rest of the way across the glossed floors.

Until I spot Jordan.

He's unfurling a microphone cord next to a speaker. It hits the floor when I pass. Our eyes meet and he sits there crouched and frozen. The air in the room buzzes, and the floor beneath my feet must vanish because I feel as if I'm standing on air. His lips part and I still, his attention a tether, holding me in place.

"Quell," he says. The word falls from his lips as if unbidden. I search for something in his expression to ease my nerves and find none of the usual hard lines there. The curve of his lips tugs up, softening his jaw. His heavy brow, typically pinched and low, has widened, as if he's seeing something new for the first time. His chest rises a bit faster than normal, and for some reason it makes my breath patter faster too.

Is he going to say something?

But his eyes trace me like a drawing he's paying the utmost attention to, around every curve, careful at each dip so as not to make a mistake. So as not to taint the art. When he does finally meet my eyes again, the green in them has deepened. My breath catches. *Look away.* But my body doesn't listen, my gaze as transfixed as my feet at the way Jordan Wexton is staring at me.

Say something.

But courage escapes me, and the moment seems to render us both speechless.

"Jordan," I manage feebly, wondering if he can sense the weirdness in my tone. But his gaze doesn't falter. Those green eyes hold on to me tighter than a grip, warmer than a hug.

"Very nice, Miss Marionne," Plume says, inserting himself between us. He ogles at my diadem, then spins me around. "It's simply regal. Headmistress must be beside herself at such a strong showing! How are you feeling?"

"Good. Different. It's all so new." Warmth rushes into every part of me that's usually knotted with angst. "It just happened last night."

"Sounds like you had a better night than the rest of us."

The Sphere, he means.

"Yes." I pull harder at the hem of my sleeve. "I guess so."

"Well, go on, with the others."

I hurry to blend into the crowd, waiting for my insides to twist tighter. But I'm halfway across the Grand Ballroom floor and none of it comes. The urge to look down pulls at me, but Jordan's stare plays on repeat in my head. By some miracle, my chin holds parallel to the floor, and the others pointing at the gems on my diadem, commenting on their size and type, the rarity of the metal, are easier to ignore. I set my shoulders back and tuck my stomach in for proper posture. I move nearer to the front and ready myself for instructions. My days of blending in are over. I'm one foot into this world of magic, and there's no going back.

Jordan finishes his business with the speaker cord and joins the rest of us. I risk a look his way, for some foolish reason, and he's still staring. Maybe he'll back off some now.

"Posture is what we're working on today, and proper movement," Plume says, sashaying front and center. There's no table set up today, instead the floor is marked with taped lines. He points a toe and glides sideways. "You are an art form at your debut." He slides a foot back and bends at the knee. "Curtsy, keep your head up, *float* down." He holds the curtsy position. "Now bow your head, eyes to the ground." He lowers his chin. "Now come up, finish on the back foot." He moves in one even motion. "Slide, cross, slide, again."

Music hums from the speaker in a melody with an even cadence. He assigns each of us a line on the floor. Jordan is a fixture at my side, his energy entirely different than usual. He's quiet, for starters. The music drums on and I mimic Plume's moves. The knee bending and balance proves to be the trickiest part.

"Now slide, cross," Plume chimes from the front. My feet tangle, and I trip over them, stumbling into Jordan's arms. He catches me. A beat passes as we gaze at each other before I pull away from him.

"Sorry." He clears his throat and looks away.

"It's fine."

"Imagine an invisible string pulled up from your head," Jordan says. "The motion is silk. You slide . . ." He demonstrates, and he's shockingly graceful. "Like you're being pulled, not like you chose to."

I throw a foot out and try it. "Like this?" I hope my body is doing it, but I feel like an octopus trying to imitate a gazelle.

His lips tilt up ever so slightly.

"I'm trying, hard."

"Here, let me." He moves behind me, careful to keep distance between us. His scent wraps around me, notes of smoky vanilla and cedar tickling each one of my senses. He pinches his fingers above my head. "Now picture the string."

I bend into a curtsy, following his lead.

"Good, now bow your head, in one even motion. Don't stop, float on the movement."

I let his instructions seep in. He lowers the string, and I dip with it. Then up again, and he slides to my left. I follow, imagining I'm a feather on the wind, fettered to his will. He shifts and I move, the space between our bodies almost nonexistent.

"Now cross."

I slide my foot over, his hand stroking the air. I emulate the motion, imagining his hands in control of my body's every flinch.

"And one more slide."

I finish breathless. Pride tightens around his lips, and it does something to me, inside.

"You're a good teacher."

He folds at the waist. Plume claps us to attention.

"Jordan, if you could," he says. "Quell's doing nicely. Hallie is sick today, and poor Evelyn needs some help. Could you?"

He departs quickly, without a word of goodbye. The flutter of the moment burns me with shame at how foolish I'm being. I give Plume my undivided attention. For the remainder of the lesson, we curtsy and cross and slide until my thighs ache from holding the stances so long.

When it wraps, I'm actually sweaty. I look for Jordan but he's still helping someone else. I'm shouldering my bag when my name is called. As some of the class departs, a bunch head in my direction. People who haven't given me more than a side-eye are eyeing me up and down. Mostly up. At my diadem. *Breathe.*

"Congrats on First Rite," one says. Lavender stones set in silver metal arc above her head.

"Thanks, I—"

"That's a strong showing," someone else whom I've only seen in passing says, his bronze mask seeping into his midnight skin.

"Thanks." For once in my life, my cheeks burn hotter from excitement and not shame. I force myself to meet their stares. I'm cornered, but skimming their warm expressions keeps my panic at bay.

"The Tavern, tonight," another says. "Don't be late."

"What for?"

But the circle breaks and they're gone. I hurry to the dining hall, trying to hide the ridiculously huge smile plastered on my face.

EIGHTEEN

———✳———

I thumb through the closet of clothes from Grandmom, but everything is either too formal and stuffy or too clearly says, "I'm desperate for friends." I've settled on a dark plum dress when Abby bursts into the room in full song and dance. She twirls her dagger.

"You passed Second Rite!" I don't mean it to come out as a scream, but passing First Rite felt like fighting off a slow death, and I only worked on that for a week.

"The Latin portion almost kicked my butt, but *I. Did!*" She screams in delight, and for several moments, jumping up and down shouting seems to be the only thing I can do.

"I'm so excited for you! Third Rite is next. So, fancy dresses, a lot of food, and dancing? Is that really it?" There has to be a catch. Rites one and two are tough, so the third's got to be—

"And plunging this bad boy into my heart at Cotillion." She presses the dagger tip to her chest.

I guffaw. But her expression doesn't change. "You're serious." I take her blade, turning it in my hand, and I'm reminded of the glimpse of what must have been a Cotillion going on the night I arrived here.

"It's not like actually stabbing yourself. It's magic." She smooths her hand along the blade's surface and its metal ripples dark black and red. She presses it into her finger and the tip disappears. "When you press it into you, as long as your heart is *sure*, your blood binds with magic, sharpening your instincts, amplifying your abilities. It's sealing your magic to you, forever."

"And if your heart isn't sure?"

"The blade doesn't shift to air, it stays metal . . ."

I drop the blade.

My heart is sure. Binding with my magic is what I want.

"I've heard of people who were kicked out before Binding and missed Third Rite," Abby says, picking up her dagger. "For most of them magic just lies dormant and eventually becomes unreachable. But for others . . . it's *bad*. It can get unwieldy and torment them, sometimes to death."

I think of Rose, then Octos. That won't be me. I will complete all the Rites.

She eyes my dress and flashes me a wicked expression. "Scandalous."

"They invited me out." Admittedly it's shorter than I'd prefer to wear and the whole back is exposed. But it's the least frumpy thing I have.

"I'm coming with, give me fifteen." She yanks a black dress out of her closet and disappears into the bathroom. Her dagger is fitted in the holder above her desk, and the spot where Mom's used to be on my desk is empty. Guilt twists in me for getting rid of something so precious.

I glance, as I pass my mirror, at the stranger reflected there. Her head glitters with gems and golden metal. Her shoulders hang a bit differently than before. Her chin holds steady, instead of pointing toward the ground. I slip the dress on, wrapping the strange girl in even more foreign layers. The shiny material is soft on my skin. My fingers trace my collarbone, but my gaze is fixed on the girl in the mirror. I don't know her, but damn I'd like to.

THE TAVERN BUSTLES with energy. Abby immediately makes a beeline for the karaoke stage, and I, seeing the size of the crowd, how many heads turn my way, begin to regret my decision to come here. I find the bathrooms and splash water on my face. That girl in the mirror eyes me again, and I struggle to look away.

The lights flicker.

I reach for the door, but it doesn't budge.

Creak. The stall door behind me rocks back and forth.

"Hello?" My heart stutters.

The lights go out, and I blink, but I can't see in the darkness. A hook tugs in my stomach. Something moves nearby and the hair on my arms stands. A warm hand reaches from behind me and clamps my mouth shut. Arms lift me off my feet and drag me out the door.

NINETEEN

et me go, I try to yell, but the hand across my face muffles my screams. I claw, scratching at the arms wrapped around my limbs.

"Primus, relax." Their voice lilts with mischievousness, not malice, and the thump in my chest slows. I can hear the Tavern's revelry faintly in the distance. A door creaks, and I land on my feet. Something hits the back of my knees, and I fall into a chair. I blink, but the dimness is thicker than the velvet robes hanging on the bodies encircling me. A flame erupts near my shoe and my grip tightens on my chair. It flickers, dancing as if on the tip of a candle. A robed figure works his magic over the flame and it stretches into a thread of fire, tracing the edges of a sun carved into the floor around me. I draw my knees to my chest as the flames encircle me, my mind and heart racing, trying to make some sense of what is happening.

Heat wafts against my skin from the fiery barrier now between me and twelve faces glowing beneath their hoods in the flames. Daggers hang from their belts. Some wood-handled, others leather, or bone, and a few in shiny metals embedded with jewels. Firelight dances on their razor-sharp edges.

"What is this?" I ask.

"Primus, what is your charge?"

"Honing one's dagger. Arduous is the work of the laborer."

"Aye." A chorus of table-beating ruckus follows my answer but there are no tables in sight. One robed figure steps over the flame, and I blink in horror, waiting for his robe to catch fire, but it doesn't. He hands me a shard of metal and a block of wood.

"What someone is given, they may never again find," he says. "What they earn, they will have a lifetime. Areya Paru, Mother of Magic, *Journal of Inscriptions*, volume one."

If they intended to hurt me, they would have done that by now. I take the items tentatively.

"You must prove you can make the dagger you will hone for Second Rite." The hooded figure gestures at the table. *"Mereri."*

Wood for a handle, metal for the blade. I suddenly understand: I have to transfigure it into a dagger here in front of everyone. My throat closes at the thought of demonstrating my magic in front of someone. So many someones. I grab the wood and the flat piece of metal, turning them in my hands. The shifting I've tried so far has worked for the most part. *Please, magic, behave. Don't fail me now.*

I rotate the block of wood over the flames, imagining it changing. Heat swells in my gut as my proper magic answers with the fury of a sandstorm. I shift at its intensity, holding firmly in place, rotating the metal steadily over the kor. For several moments the only sound in the room is the thud of my heart knocking against my ribs. Suddenly the silver flat of metal shifts, elongating. It stretches, thinning. I slide closer to the flames, salivating with anticipation at my magic working swiftly and properly. The blade stretches to a point until it forms a sharp dagger tip.

The faces around me are still, stone expressions. Now, to attach its handle. I rotate the blade, careful to keep my fingers away from its sharp edge, and press it to the wood, letting the kor engulf it on every side. The flames lick my hands, and the dusty magic inside blows about violently. I hold it there.

"Come on."

My magic obeys and the wooden block shifts, molding to the curve of my palm, into the shape of a handle as it affixes itself to the blade. The wood softens against my skin, shifting to a different material. Leather, by the feel of it. I tighten it in my fist, overcome with a smile I can't push away.

I hold the dagger up for everyone to see. It's plain but correct, and

I'm jostled with rumbling applause. The lights lift and I can see, finally, everyone around me. They pull back their hoods and the kor flickering around the room disappears.

"Catch," a robed figure with long locs says. "Put it on."

A bundle flies toward me. "What is—" But it unfurls in my hands. It's a dusty pink cloak like the rest of them are wearing. I throw it over my head, and they surround me in ceremonial precision. Hands set on my shoulders, one after another, like a link of chains, pushing me down to my knees. I kneel and turn my palms up. I'm not sure how I know I should, I just do.

"May Sola Sfenti forever illuminate your path," the one with locs says before nudging me. "The prayer."

"May I prove to be a proper steward. May I prove worthy."

"Pray that twelve times, every night." He helps me up. "Welcome, you're nearly there. *Supra alios.*"

"*Supra alios,*" the room chants.

The crowd takes turns offering me handshakes.

"I missed your name," I say to the one with locs.

"Casey, seventh of my blood, Retentor candidate. I'm social chair this Season, responsible for transitioning all the noobs after First Rite." He hands me a short stack of books. *Latin Primer*; *Declensions for Beginners*; *Journal of Inscriptions*, vol. 1. "You'll need these to get you started. There'll be more later." He sets a small box with a ribbon on top. "And this is a little something from all of us."

Inside a speckled, milky stone glimmers.

"It's a Reactor Enhancer. Extremely rare."

"Wow, thanks," I say, realizing I'm still smiling embarrassingly large.

Casey takes my dagger, examining it. "You shifted it nicely, the handle's even changed materials. Not bad. You'll need to push your magic into it to pass Second Rite exam . . . among other things, but your mentor will guide you on all that." He glances at my diadem.

I fight the urge to flinch. I've earned this. I've forged my blade fair and square.

"You're off to an impressive start." Casey joins the others, and the crowd moves to the door. It opens to darkness, but when we step through, we're back in a long corridor at the Tavern.

I'm tugged along, jostled with revelry, arms slung over my shoulders, shaking hands, thanking each person kind enough to say anything to me at all. I make a point to look into the face of everyone who talks to me without looking away, stubbornly determined to soak up every dreg of this moment.

"Rikken, a round—kizi," I shout.

The crowd parts for us, and as they shed their robes and ease onto the dance floor, I do the same and grab a blue fizzy drink. Abby finds me in the crowd and raises a toast.

"To Quell! Miss Badass Extraordinaire!"

I let the senselessness take me and toss back the kiziloxer. It's bubbly going down like drinking soda too fast, and a ripple of calm breaks over me, my muscles going languid. Every inch of me soothes, like a knot coming undone, and I stare at the cup with pinched brows.

"Don't worry, it's magic, not liquor." Abby laughs. "Rikken is an entire rule follower. Ask me how I know."

I giggle. "I feel . . . so . . ."

"Relaaaxxeed?"

Laughter bubbles up my throat. We signal Rikken for another round, and I spot a brooding figure. Jordan's perched over a table alone in a dim corner. He raises a glass to me and I'm not sure if it's the kiziloxer or the way he looked at me in etiquette, but I don't sense even the slightest hint of indignation. He is legitimately proud of me. I raise my glass to him but turn my back so the huge, bashful smile on my lips remains a secret. What's come over me? I glare at the glass. It must be the blue drink.

Hours later I'm standing on top of a table, balancing on one leg with the entire Tavern crowd as an audience. A girl from House of Oralia with an eccentric diadem of silver and multicolored stones watches me, folding her arms. The world has been a bit fuzzy around the edges since about kiziloxer number . . . actually I've lost count. But I'm not sure I've ever felt more alive.

I finally make my way back to the bar, where a stern-faced Jordan is hovering. The top two buttons of his shirt are undone, and stress lines mar his perfect skin. He straightens at my approach and starts to speak, but instead his expression hardens.

"You're ruining my vibe." I wave for Rikken.

"Your *vibe*?" Jordan asks.

"Yes, my vibe. You're brooding."

"I'm not brooding, I'm just watching."

"Your watching *is* brooding."

Rikken slides a drink my way.

"I'm perfectly relaxed, thank you. This is my natural state."

"That's unfortunate," I say, reaching for the drink, which is intercepted by Jordan.

He pulls a large bill out of the pocket of his blazer, far too large for a single drink. "Thanks, Rikken, but she'll pass."

"Hey, I wanted tha—"

He steps closer and he's so tall I have to look up to really see him. "Walk with me." His voice is silk this time, and low, as if he's sharing some intimate secret he wouldn't want anyone else to hear.

"I—"

Hunger unfurls in his eyes. "Just outside." His words are a breath and yet hit me like gale force winds. I nod but stand frozen. Not from fear, from something else I can't quite put into words. "Please." There's a song between his words. He walks off leading the way and I follow, foolishly curious to dance to it.

Outside, the night is chilly, but I'm warm all over, either from the kiziloxer or just the thrill of emerging and earning my dagger still buzzing through me. We walk past the park, farther than I've ever wandered, until we reach a marble courtyard of towering pillars etched with names. Jordan stops at one, tracing some of the names with his fingertips.

"Unmarked assume this is another war memorial. But this one's ours." He presses his fists together gently to his chest.

I don't recognize any of the names. "These are people in the Order who've died?"

He inclines his head. "In service of protecting magic."

I don't know what to say, and after a moment we keep walking. Jordan glances at me.

"You should drink some water. It'll help."

"I feel amazing."

"Yes, but in the morning."

"You wanted to take me on a walk to tell me to drink water?" I fold my arms, the boldness coursing through me altogether foreign.

"I wanted to take you on a walk to—" He stops, and those hard lines meet the challenge in my expression.

"Yes?"

He glances at my diadem, then keeps walking. "You need to keep your wits about yourself. You're different." The lilt of disdain I usually find in his tone isn't there. He speaks with respect, admiration even.

Because I emerged.

"I thought you never come to the Tavern."

"I don't, only when I have business there." He rests on a railing wrapped around another memorial.

"You were alone at a table looking like you'd lost your best friend. What sort of business were you onto tonight?"

He looks at me but says nothing.

"*I'm* your business?"

We walk another beat in silence.

"You're not drinking."

"Does that surprise you?"

I sneer at the rhetorical comment. He points at his eyes, then mine. His tone shifts. "You need to be observant."

"I notice more than you think." *Because I've always had to.*

"Oh?" he asks with a challenge.

I clear my throat. "You were in the Tavern tonight because you wanted to be, not because you had to be. Though you have convinced yourself otherwise. You carry around some kind of candy in your pockets, which is just *weird*. You haven't had a haircut since I met you. *And* you haven't been able to meet my eyes without looking away since I've emerged." I gaze right at him.

He, predictably, looks away to keep from smiling.

"Impressive, though you're not as right as you think you are. Add humility to your goal sheet."

"That's comical coming from you."

He huffs and it's almost a laugh. "You have no . . . filter."

"Maybe you just have too much of one."

Suddenly, hushed voices slice the air in the distance. Jordan stops me with his arm. My body buzzes at his touch. I move back a bit, to put some distance between us. We spot a couple biking through the park, and his posture softens. Slightly. We keep walking.

"So tell me, what's it like being a Dragun?" I ask. Maybe now he'll tell me what I really want to know: Does he use toushana? "I read you must master three types of magic."

He doesn't respond.

"What are yours?"

He stops.

"If you can share."

His hand rises ever so carefully, halting just before touching my face. I take a deliberate breath because it seems I've forgotten how to.

"Close your eyes." The tips of his fingers brush my eyelids, and his touch is gentler than a breeze. "Now listen."

"I don't hear anything."

"Yes, you do." He's so close I can feel his breath on my skin. It's warm and inviting, and the urge to curl into him tugs at me. "Describe what you hear."

"Wind and rustling leaves."

The crinkle of leaves morphs into a flit of bird chirps. One at first, then more until the breeze whipping through the trees is soundless and I could swear I've been transported to an aviary. I open my eyes, looking for a bird, some source of the sound. But only find Jordan, blowing air between his fingers.

A dark memory stalks through my mind and I take a step back. The Dragun hunting me could manipulate sound, too. I dig a nail into my palm to stay in the present. "You can transfigure sound?"

The chirps fade, his magic wearing off.

"An Audior is the proper term."

"Was it hard to learn?"

"It's in my blood. Headmistress Perl is my aunt, so our magic is strong."

"And what about your other two strands?" *Why does one of them look like toushana?*

"May I touch your hand?"

The question catches me off guard. The gentleness of his tone, the lack of expectation. He's entirely confusing, and my insides swim with flutters. My hands are warm, the curse in my veins at bay. The idea of letting him touch my hand, on purpose, unsettles something deep inside me in thrilling way.

"Never mind," he says. "I didn't mean to make you nervous."

"I'm not nervous," I lie.

"Sure, Miss Marionne."

"Call me Quell."

"Quell." My name rolls off his tongue like suede, with an inflection, a smoothness I could listen to over and over again.

"Watch closely." He drags a thumb down the center of his face, and his skin morphs as if it's being unzipped to reveal someone else behind it. His green eyes bleed to brown, his features twisting until he's completely unrecognizable, several inches shorter, with a long beard and hooked nose. He holds the disguise a moment, straining. Then he releases and the disguise dissolves. He groans.

"Are you okay?"

"Feels like your head's being squished between metal plates." He pants. "The longer you hold it, the more it hurts. And the more disguises you master, the more taxing it is to use them. I've only taken two personas—face, body, voice, the whole bit, which required a long time of studying them, their mannerisms, their personalities, *and* a bit of their blood. But after I used the face I just showed you for the first time, I was in bed for a week." He shudders.

He's an Anatomer. "I didn't mean to make you—"

"I wanted to."

Something shifts between us.

"Well, it's very cool and a bit creepy."

That almost gets a laugh out of him.

"And the third magic?" Hope cinches in my chest, eager to hear what he might reveal.

"Tell me what you've done to prepare for honing."

I bite down, trying to hide my disappointment.

"Honing is difficult, Quell. I hope you're focused."

He's definitely evading telling me what I want to know. But he's opened up a bit.

"I bet I could be a Dragun." I scrunch my face in the meanest expression I can muster and push my lips out. "Watch me brood." I wrinkle my forehead and narrow my eyes before lunging a punch into his arm.

"That *actually* hurt."

"Told you."

"That's all you think we do is brood and fight?"

"That's all you show me."

He shifts on his feet. "So you think that's all that's there?"

"I don't know. But I've got those two parts of it down." I punch him again, and he reaches for my wrist to try to stop me. But I twist away. "Ooo and I'm faster, apparently!"

He reaches for me, but I dart out of his reach in the nick of time.

"Would you calm down already? You're going to draw attention." He plants his feet, determined not to run.

"Make me."

He snatches at the air for me again and misses. I run back toward the Tavern, gasping with laughter, and then a cloud of black swallows me. I chill down to my bones as Jordan reappears right in front of my face.

His hand wraps around my wrist. "I win."

My laughs settle into breathless panting as I realize how little space there is between us. He stares, and it's like standing too close to a flame.

"Still." I step back. "I had you for a minute."

Moonlight illuminates the rigid angles in his face. Each chiseled with absolute precision, rhythmically carved, a work of living art. Suddenly I notice the tiniest scar on his eyelid. And that his nose is ever so slightly crooked. A smile tugs at my lips.

"We should get you some water."

We walk back to the Tavern in comfortable silence, and I smile the whole way. His lips brush the back of my hand when he tells me good night, and I hold on to the feeling until I'm back in bed.

It feels a bit like playing with fire.

But, more than anything, it feels good.

TWENTY

—————✳—————

I wake and there is a gong inside my head. *Bang.* I steady myself against the dregs of kiziloxer before standing to shake off my deliriousness. *Bang.* Something flicks at my window. I hurry over, and there is Mom, two stories below in a dark coat, her hair pulled back.

"Mom!"

Abby stirs as I stumble into my shoes and out the door. How did she know where my—*the key chain.*

Downstairs, the night's air bites at my heels as I rush to the courtyard below my window. I weave around the maze of tables and chairs to the gate where Mom was just standing. But there is no one there. My heart ticks faster.

"Mom?" The night is silent. Empty. Tears burn my eyes. *"Mom!"* A dog howls somewhere far away, followed by a chorus of snarls and barking. In the distance I see her, and my heart leaps. She's a dot against the forest's edge, sprinting away.

"Mom, wait!" I say, dashing her way.

"*No, Quell,*" she shouts in a strained voice. She waves her arms, gesturing for me to turn around and not follow her. I don't understand. I shake my head, unlatching the iron gate to run after her, and a letter with my name tucked between its rods tumbles to the ground.

"Mom, please, come back!" But I can hardly see her anymore.

The air thickens with an eerie fog, the night darkening. Draguns. I slink back into the shadow of the Chateau and hurry back inside to avoid being caught outside after curfew. Once in my room, I rip open the letter to her familiar handwriting.

I'm so relieved to hear you're doing okay.
Darling, someone is onto you outside of these gates.
Stay at Chateau Soleil until it is safe.
Stay. Whatever it takes.
Remember, there is good in you, Quell. <3
—Love, Mom

I climb into bed but toss and turn, Mom's letter playing on repeat in my head. She didn't even mention my plan to get rid of my toushana. I stew over her words again and grab a paper.

I wish I could have talked to you! And okay.
Don't worry, Mom. After I complete Cotillion, it'll be safe.
Then we can go wherever we want.
—Quell

I write her full name on the envelope and read the words a few more times, then drop the letter into my bag to mail tomorrow.

SUNLIGHT PEERS THROUGH my window before my alarm goes off, and I hop out of bed with a renewed sense of determination. After an hour of posture and curtsy practice and reviewing the table manners Plume has gone over, I grab my dagger and slip out the door.

Second Rite starts today. It took Abby *two years* to pass this thing. As if mastering magic, and hiding my toushana, isn't hard enough, a Dead Languages session has been added to my schedule. Somehow I have to familiarize myself with basic Latin before finishing. The halls are a traffic jam as I sift through the breakfast line before rushing down Sunrise corridor to session.

Dexler's room is arranged differently today. Round tables are set around the room with a pile of colored stones in the centers. There are more seats than usual, but everyone present has a diadem or mask. I recognize a few from last night at the Tavern, but there are tables full of faces I've never seen. I spot a square of bubble gum on a table and I head in that direction looking for Shelby. Her bag is under the chair.

"Primus, what is your charge?" Dexler asks, surveying her box of rings before plucking a gray one.

"Honing one's dagger. Arduous is the work of the laborer."

Secundus performs their recitation, and then the door opens and Shelby rushes in.

"A bit late, aren't we, Miss Duncan?"

"Sorry, ma'am." Shelby slides into her seat, pale as a ghost.

Dexler rolls up her sleeves. "Daggers out."

I set mine in front of me. It's simple and plain compared to most of the others with fancy handles, some gilded, others with silver filigree, another sleek and nimble with a curved handle wrapped in leather. Each style seems to complement their diadem or mask. My insides shrivel. I hope I don't need Octos again.

"I have a special guest to help us understand honing," Dexler says.

The door opens again, and a handsome guy in a dark gray coat with piercing blue eyes and unkempt hair strides in, moving with a poise not unlike Jordan's. Something about him is familiar. Beside me Shelby turns rigid.

"You okay?" I ask, but she doesn't answer, her fist white-knuckled on her dagger.

A pair near the front giggle, eyeing our visitor, and I roll my eyes. He slips out of his jacket, and a silver coin marked with a cracked column shines at his throat. My nails dig into my desk at the familiar mark. My sleeping toushana tremors. But he looks past me without a flicker of recognition.

"Felix happened to be on the grounds today. Please introduce yourself."

"I'm Felix. Class of '23, Dragun, House of Perl." His mouth tugs sideways in a self-assured grin.

My grip on the desk tightens.

House of Perl.

That's Jordan's House! I guessed it was some rogue group after me, not a *leader* in the Order. Someone in a position like Grandmom. Last night unfurls in my memory, and the hairs on my neck rise as I replay every exchange Jordan and I have had since I arrived here.

"I'm a complex Shifter." Felix works his magic, pulls his hands apart wider until a woodsy pine scent fills the air. "I can sweeten the air you're breathing or shift it to a toxic gas if I want."

His mouth is moving as he roves around the room, but I'm too pre-occupied with thoughts of Jordan. Is that why he keeps a close eye on me? For his House Headmistress? But if Jordan knew I had toushana, I'd already be dead. That I'm sure of. So either he and the Dragun after me don't know each other, or he and his Headmistress aren't close. Or she only has the one Dragun on my tail.

"My magic is more developed and easier to reach because of the en-hancers I chose for honing. Whatever you fold *into* your blade affects your magic," Felix goes on, rounding on my table, and I realize I'm be-hind on taking notes. He grabs a purple stone from Shelby's and my pile.

"A Strength Enhancer is going to double the impact of your magic. I folded six of these into my dagger."

"Six! Heavens," Dexler says. "Headmistress Beaulah is quite militant, isn't she?" She pulls at her blouse.

Beaulah. I know that name . . . Mom mentioned it when we parted ways.

"*In manu exercitus tui merces legatorum.*" He knocks his fists together, one on top of the other, then pounds them to his chest. "At the hand of an army legacies are formed."

Dexler's brows slash.

Felix plucks a few more stones, detailing which and how many he used with a lilt of arrogance that's actually nauseating the more I listen. "A demonstration." His eyes find my diadem. His lips part as he marvels, taking all of me in.

"That's quite impressive," he says. "Might I see your dagger, Miss . . . ?"

Once more, I search his face for some seed of recognition. Some slight tell that he knows my secret, but nothing even close simmers beneath his expression. Headmistress Beaulah hasn't told him. He's here for some other reason. *Could she really only have the one Dragun after me?* No one else seems to recognize me as if I'm on some shared hit list. But if that's true, why would a headmistress keep that a secret? Why not run to the Dragunhead and turn my name in so everyone knows? The truth occurs to me so suddenly I have to steady myself on my chair. *Because she isn't absolutely sure I have toushana.* A wrong accusation of that magnitude would *not* go over well.

I hand Felix my dagger.

Shelby fidgets under the table.

"Shelby?"

But she ignores me, picking at a scab over and over.

"Today's your lucky day." He takes the purple stone and sets it on the flat of my blade and glides his hand over it in one smooth motion. The purple stone melts like butter into the metal. He hands it back to me. "The stones can be stubborn. Some are just harder to fold in. But that's the gist of it. Choose your enhancers carefully, a dagger can only hold so many."

"Ah, Mister Felix forgets that in our House, the enhancers you're given are a set list," Dexler says.

"Right, forgot." His eyebrows bounce. After a bit more fawning from Dexler, Felix takes a bow and winks at Shelby. "Maybe I'll see you tonight." He leaves, and Shelby exhales.

I almost ask her if she's okay, but it's obvious she isn't and she doesn't want to talk about it. Dexler parts a thick leather tome. "On page six hundred thirty-three is a list of what each enhancer does. You must memorize them all. And by tomorrow, the first three must be folded into your blade successfully. Understood?"

Heads nod.

"I laid out a few others for your *observation only*."

I take out the speckled enhancer from Casey at the Tavern, trying to remember what he said it did.

"Any more Strength Enhancers?" someone asks.

"I'd like to see a Lumen one, you have any of those?" another says.

I gather the three stones first on the list plus the one from Casey and set my dagger on its side.

"I'm out, okay? Good luck with honing." Shelby shoulders her bag before I can respond, and she's gone. *I should check on her later.*

Light catches on my dagger as I turn it in my hands, its steel rippling purple. I study the stones. One's a jagged red rock that gleams silver in its crevices. An Endurance Enhancer, which helps magic last longer, according to the book. Another is a deep blue like a glassy ocean. A Purifier Enhancer, which wards off magical impurity. And the third is spiky and green and apparently unique to House of Marionne, mined from the caves of Aronya in a precise location only our House knows.

"Binding Enhancer," I read, under my breath. "It aids in binding magic to the blood with far greater longevity and precision. What on earth does that mean?"

"It means Marionne puts out the best stock!" Dexler winks. "A cut above the rest."

"A cut above the rest," I repeat. The House motto. "Right," I say, still confused about what that has to do with this green stone. Dexler moves on and I pick up the enhancer unique to our House, turning it in my hands, picturing how to set it on my dagger. Then the red one. It's radiant and deep with various hues, depending on tricks of the light. I hold my dagger next to the green and the red one, trying to decide which to do first. But the blue stone, the Purifier, grabs my attention. It's by far the prettiest.

Felix made it look so simple. I set the others down and hold the blue in one palm and reach for my dagger.

My hand stiffens as my fingers graze its handle. My heart patters faster.

I try to stretch my fingers, to close them around the dagger, but they're rigid. Cold. The blue stone burns my hand and I drop it, pushing up from the table. The cold in my bones retreats.

"Miss Marionne?" It's Dexler, and at the sound of her voice every head in the place turns in my direction. "Everything all right?"

"I . . ." I flex my fingers, and to my surprise they move, as if nothing ever happened. I glare at the blue enhancer on the ground. Then my dagger. I grab it first, then bend down to pick up the stone, but my toushana shudders through me, threatening to rise up again. It won't let me touch them at the same time. I skim the page for a description of the blue stone again.

Wards off magical impurities.

"Miss Marionne!"

I realize that in my haste to get up I knocked my chair over.

"Yes. Sorry, I'm fine." I swallow. "Did you say we could work on this in lab?"

She nods, and I gather my things and toss them into my bag but wait until my magic has settled all the way down before grabbing the Purifier and hurrying out the door.

I dash down the hall toward my room and bump into a tall carved frame.

"Quell?" Jordan's gaze twists in surprise. "Session's out already?"

"No, it's not . . . I—I mean yes. Sorry, yes, session is out."

Jordan's brows cinch and I notice he's not alone. Felix is with him.

"You know this one?" Felix asks, and I swear I see Jordan's jaw clench. "She wouldn't tell me her name. Feisty." Jordan eyes Felix and something shifts between them.

"Anyway, I better be going," he says. "Good chat, Wexton. Next time answer the damn phone so I don't have to come all the way to this sweaty armpit. See you in the field in no time." They do some sort of handshake. "I'll tell Mother you said hello."

"Mother?" I ask as he walks off.

"Headmistress Perl, he means."

I put more distance between us. "Are you and she close?"

His eyes narrow. "Why?"

"As a Ward, I'm sure she likes a good check-in. Is that why Felix was here?"

"He was here . . . on Dragunhead business, if you must know."

I can't tell if he's lying or giving me half-truths. But if Beaulah is anything like my grandmother, she wouldn't just let her nephew *be here* without keeping tabs. His stare deepens, his head cocked, but he says nothing for several moments before checking his watch. "How is honing?"

"I was going to skip lunch and work on my dagger in lab . . ." On my own. When no one's around. I start in the opposite direction.

"I'll come with."

"*No!* Sorry, I have a handle on it so far." In a perfect world I'd be able to ask him for help. But he can't be near me with my toushana reacting to the enhancers. Also I'm not sure how much I can trust him.

He tidies his coat and shifts as if his ego is wounded. "The next offered honing exam is in five days. I've signed you up."

"Five? You've set me up to fail!"

"Hardly. I've set you up to shine."

None of my peers have to deal with this. "What do you get out of this?" It has to be more than a reputation as a good mentor.

"Who said I get anything out of it?"

"Something I've picked up on from being so *observant* is that you're very calculated. You requested me specifically, you shadow me almost everywhere I go, now you're pressuring me to finish well and fast. The only reason that makes sense is if my performance is somehow tied to your own."

His brow bows up in surprise, but his chin rises in its familiar arrogance. "It doesn't matter. You shouldn't need a reason to push to be exemplary. You should *want* to be. You're a Marionne, it's expected."

"I appreciate the help, but I've got this."

The severe angles of his face sharpen. He steps closer.

"If you take my insistence for altruistic encouragement, you gravely mistake me, Miss Marionne." His stare darkens. "There is *much* on the line here, for both of us."

I was right. He doesn't see me; he sees my performance. The idea of me. He pulls my chin up to his, and a stranger stares back at me. He is not just the boy who walked with me through the park. Cold and heartless, he can turn off his humanity like a light switch. *He is a trained killer.* Trained to hunt people like me.

"Five. Days."

I shove his hand away and storm off.

TWENTY-ONE

—✳—

"There you are!" Abby waves a paper in front of my face as I return to our room, before I lose the fight against bawling my eyes out. "What's wrong?"

"Nothing." I snatch the paper from her and gasp at its swirly letters announcing she's been cleared for Cotillion. A satin ribbon is cinched across its center, embellished with a jewel.

"Headmistress Darragh Marionne is commanded by the Council of Mothers of the Prestigious Order of Highest Mysteries to summon Abilene Grace Feldsher to an Afternoon Presentation Party at Chateau Soleil's Annual Magnolia Ball, on Saturday, the second week of June," I read. "Your invitation, already! Where's the rest of them? This is only one. I want to come!"

"It's only a sample. Duh. You have to prepare your own invites for your guests. But Headmistress formally sends one to each of us officially inviting us to be presented for membership."

"This is so exciting. Did you tell Mynick?"

She deflates. "Yes, but Headmistress would never let an outsider escort me." She perks up. "At least I'll get to go to his. His House doesn't have the same stuffy rules as Headmistress Marionne." Abby slaps a hand over her mouth. "No offense! Please don't tell her I said that."

"Oh, Abby, I'm so happy for you!"

"But that's not the best part!" She shakes me by the shoulders.

"No?"

"My name's been circulating society, *finally* now that my Cotillion date is set, and *look!*"

She shoves a stack of envelopes addressed to her in every color into my arms. "I've been invited to all of these!"

I scrunch my nose.

"Can you believe it?" She flips through the envelopes. "The Chadwell Ball, Senator Beaumont's Summer Soiree, the Rose Ball, and is there one for the Tidwell?" She flips faster, gets to the end, then frowns. "They have *real* swans there. It's usually at some swanky hotel in New York City or on old man Tidwell's wine country estate. *Swans*, Quell! And they let you drink *real* champagne. Nobody asks your age."

I've never seen Abby so excited about anything. She throws herself on the bed beside me. "Quell, there are 'the rich' and there are 'the *wealthy*.' The wealthy live in an entirely different world. A world that because of the Order"—she gestures at the opulence around us—"we fit in." She shimmies the envelopes at me.

I laugh at the ridiculousness. "You're serious?"

"The world is opening up to me. It's my time to experience all of it. What use is magic to me if it doesn't help me have the life I want?"

We serve magic, it does not serve us. Jordan's words trickle through my memory.

"Doesn't your family have, like, two homes? I would guess those stones in your ear are actual diamonds. What's so impressive about going to dances with stuffy people?" I try to stifle the laugh, but it slips out.

"Four homes."

"See!"

She rolls her eyes and loops her arm in mine. "My deda was brought here as a baby with nothing. He scraped together what he could and worked his way up to becoming a lawyer. He met my grandmother. She was a nurse at the time. Sometimes I lie and say she was a doctor, but don't tell anyone." She elbows me. "They did well. But then my dad got my mother pregnant before he finished high school. And around the same time, he showed signs of magic. Deda was ashamed of him. He and Grandmother took me and kicked him out. But then my father entered induction here, and *everything* changed. Quell, my father moved into this fancy gated neighborhood shortly after he debuted. I don't know how, he hadn't even gotten a job yet. He proposed to my mother with a *fat* rock literally the day after his Cotillion. Deda used to say my dad had gotten into drugs or was running with a bad crowd. He wouldn't let me go live with them until he realized that wasn't true."

"I thought your dad was a banker."

"Yes, *now*. Someone in the Order set him up with the position. But between you and me, he's home more than he's at his office." She whispers, "He has framed degrees on his wall from colleges he never even went to."

My eyes widen.

"The Order takes care of its own. It's like a golden key that unlocks access to . . . options. You're a Marionne, you must know what I mean."

My skin turns to gooseflesh. "It was a bit different for me since I didn't grow up here."

"That's what I'm saying. Because I grew up with Deda, I saw both sides of it. And I know which side I intend to land on."

"Your parents must have money set aside for you." Isn't that how rich families stay rich?

"It's not about the money, it's the experiences, the circles you run in, the way people look at you." She folds her legs under herself to face me more properly.

I shake my head, unsure what to say.

"I mean, what, do you suggest I *not* use the privilege my position affords me?" She folds her arms.

I can't picture a future as gilded as Abby imagines for myself, but she *is* my friend and I want her happy. "You deserve everything you can imagine. I'm happy for you, Abby, really."

"This one is tonight!" She shows me the invite before rushing to her closet. "I wish you could come with me."

My stomach sinks.

"But you haven't passed Second Rite, so you can't."

I exhale. *"Rats."*

"You're such a bad liar." She snorts. "But enough about me, how was honing today?" She works her magic over her dress, adding detail to the corset and fiddling with the hem before laying out a matching pair of shoes.

I bury myself in my pillows, groaning. For a second I'd almost forgotten my own nightmare. I unfurl myself from my covers. It isn't going to get any easier.

"There was this Dragun there from House Perl. He gave a demonstration." I shiver, loading up my bag with anything I might need. "He was a creep."

"Draguns are like swarming sharks. More of them around isn't a good sign." She fiddles with the dress, holding it up against herself in the mirror. "I wonder if it has to do with the Sphere. My parents *still* have their panties in a bunch about the Sphere cracking. Is this dress too much for tonight, you think? I don't want to overdo it."

"It's perfect. But don't add any more jewels. It's already a bit over the top sparkly." She holds her hands up and the magic buzzing around her fingertips dissolves. "Do you think it's true Draguns dabble in dark magic?"

"No one knows how they do what they do."

I nod my head and latch my bag closed. "I really should get to honing lab."

"Good luck getting a table at this hour."

"What time is it dead, usually?"

"Hard to say. The stoners like to wander in there at like two a.m." She laughs. "Maybe try during dinner while everyone's eating."

I put my bag back down. I can't exactly go to a crowded lab and get anything done.

"I'm not the best person to give honing tips because, alas, I wasn't great at it. But you can talk to me if it's stressing you out."

"No, I'm not spoiling this day for you. I want to hear about all the things and help you get ready for your very first society ball." I don't get the big deal, but my friend is excited, so I am thrilled for her. I notice a stack of oversized parcels in a corner half opened with fabric spilling out. "What is all that stuff?"

"Samples my parents sent. They're flying in a whole host of Vestisers from all over. I need to narrow this down from, like, two hundred samples to, like . . . thirty." She rolls her eyes. "My mom is a lot. She didn't debut, so this is big for her."

"Why not?"

"She could see diadems and stuff, but her family didn't know anyone in the Order until my dad finished, and by then it was too late." She shrugs. "So she and my dad were *all* over me when they realized I had a shot. Deda still refuses to come anywhere near this place."

Why? I wonder, but Abby keeps talking. The itch to get moving tugs at me.

"Are you listening?"

I nod.

"I was ready to quit a year ago, but she refused to let me. She said I'd be here every Season, May to August, as long as it took. I didn't burst her bubble and tell her you only get two. You know how hard it is to get a private prep school to let you out of school *months* early to 'study abroad'?"

"I went to public schools. I don't think they care very much."

"*Lucky.* Anyway, now I'm glad, of course."

She loops her arm in mine. "*So* you'll be by my side for all the Cotillion planning and everything, right? To help me fend off my mother at the very least. If I have the excuse of hanging out with the Headmistress's granddaughter, she'll back off, I'm sure."

I really should be spending every free second I have working on my dagger. And trying to get control of my toushana.

"Sure," I say, still not quite certain what exactly I'm signing up for. But it feels like the right thing to do. I check my watch before dumping her mountain of samples onto her bed. "I think we have some time to sort through these." I plop beside her on her bed. "But by dinner I *have to* get to lab. I have three enhancers to fold into my dagger by morning."

She squeezes me and I warm all over, not with magic, but something else just as foreign and special.

THE LAB ON the basement floor of the estate is as silent as the dead when I descend the steps. Inside are tables like the one in my room. I ease the door closed and lock it. For good measure, I drag one of the tables and barricade the door. I don't know how ugly trying to fold in this Purifier Enhancer is going to get, but I can't have any surprise visitors. I set my bag down and center my blade on the stand. The stones in the bottom of my bag glisten at me.

Here goes nothing.

I start with the red one, setting it on the blade, and slice my hand over it. Magic prickles in my palms, then gushes in a rush of granulated warmth like tiny particles crawling beneath my skin. The stone brightens, then bleeds into the metal. I exhale and repeat the process with the green one, which takes some repeated swiping motions to get to meld in completely. But it eventually goes.

I reach for the blue one, and I'm cold in an instant.

It doesn't want me to touch it.

My toushana rolls around inside, and I hold the spot where the chilliness throbs, imagining I can subdue it, hide it, shove it out of me. I pace, then try again, reaching deeper into the bag, my fingers grazing the glassy stone. Bitter cold magic crashes over me, and I stagger at the sheer force of it. Toushana expands in me, and I can feel it slinking through my body, dragging itself along with icicled claws, bone by bone, from my trunk, up to my chest, then through my arms. A spur of warmth flutters in me, and the cold strikes at it like a snake protecting its nest. The heat disappears.

I stuff down a scream, pushing past the pain, and close my hands around the blue stone. I blink and the world bleeds white, my insides so frostbitten they burn like fire. *Let it go,* my magic seems to whisper, my toushana edging me off a frozen cliff. But I tighten my fist. *I have to do this. For Mom. For me.*

I'm so *cold.*

A cold that sings like a lullaby from death's own lips.

A cloud forms at my next breath as I summon all my strength to drag myself to the table, hoping I can browbeat this poisonous magic into letting me set the Purifier Enhancer on the blade.

Toushana rears in me. A scream rips from my throat. My insides quiver, but I picture Mom the last time I saw her and drag one stiff foot in front of the other. I lug my dead weight to the table, my toushana fighting to turn me to ice limb by limb.

I hover the stone over the dagger, and a stabbing pain rips through my stomach. My knees slam the ground. Victory hangs like a dangled carrot just out of reach. *Up, I have to get up.*

I steady myself on shaky legs.

Despite my bones feeling like they're being pulled apart, I reach for the dagger, imagining it's the doorknob to a beach cottage, with the Purifier Enhancer clutched tightly in my hand. The world sways from the throbbing pain. My hand is a breath away from the dagger. I grab the table to anchor myself, but my grip on its edge falters.

The wood in my hand turns to dust and the rest of the table collapses in on itself, shattering my hope with it.

I stumble to the floor, knocking into a chair. It grazes my chilled hands and blackens with rot. My dagger skids across the room, my hold on things spiraling out of control. The world drains of color. Sickness swims in me. My brain throbs as if it's splitting in two. I tighten my grip on the stone and try to picture a weathered door with waves lapping outside its windows, but it's buried beneath blinding pain. *It hurts too much.*

I drop the stone.

And curl into a ball on the ground, hugging my knees. *Breathe.* I inhale deeply, and the air fills me up like tight arms wrapped around me, a pat on the head. A reward for folding to my dark magic's will.

I exhale and take another sharp breath in, my fingers warming. I flex them and rub my eyes as the world's haze clears. *I can't survive my toushana, let alone fight it off.* My stomach churns and a rush pushes up my throat. I'm on my knees, acid burning up and out of my mouth. I sob, a mix of tears and bile dripping from my lips. *I can't do this. I'm just not strong enough.*

The handle to the door jiggles. "Weird," says a muffled voice beyond it.

I try to pull myself up, but my arms are unsteady.

"Hello?" The handle jiggles again and I freeze. "Anyone in here?"

"Didn't you say it was open?"

"I guess it isn't. I don't know. Try later."

Their footsteps disappear and I fall to the floor, like a bird with clipped wings. Hot tears sting my face. Shadows taunt from the darkest crevices of my soul: *Why am I this way?*

"*Please,*" I mutter between tears. *Someone, please, anyone, help me. I'd give anything, anything to get this poison out of me.* I try to turn off my tears, but the more I push them down, the more they break free. I shake, sobbing until I have nothing left.

I don't know how much time passes. My eyes are dry and swollen when I pull myself up. I don't know what I'm going to do about honing, but I have to get out of here. Panic flits through me at the decaying wooden table I ripped into. I bite my lip, ruing the only thing that makes sense. As foolish as it feels, it's the only sure way to get rid of this mess.

I glance over my shoulder at the door, shove out a breath, and call on my toushana. The cold answers instinctively, yawning from its moment of rest. I hold my side and I feel it shift, stretching through me, rushing into my hands as I rub my poisonous magic all over the table until it's a pile of ash. My breath hums in me steady and even, a dirge of sorts. I've never been more focused, and yet I've never done anything so dangerous—using my toushana on purpose.

I take the chair in my hands and it collapses around me like a dropped bucket of sand. *That's about enough* . . . I pace a few moments until the chill in my fingers slinks off, my magic finally obeying me for once.

I grab a broom from a closet and sweep the entire mess until the room looks as it was. I remove the barricade from the door and resituate the tables so it's not obvious one of the tables is missing. *The bile* . . . I grab a towel from the lab sink, clean my face and hands, then scrub the floor. Back and forth, my knuckles white from the force, until the floor shines. I rinse everything and survey my work.

I was never here.

I exhale.

Cold prickles through me. It moves like a thread, coiling up my spine, my neck, and through my hair. Not consuming or grating, somehow gentle and inviting. My head feels dizzy for a second, and I dash for a mirror. My diadem twists, its rose gold coils lengthening, growing more robust and ornate. Gems bloom like budding roses against the metal on my head. I gape at my diadem, more statuesque than any I've ever seen, watching as my desperation fuels my doom.

Using my toushana did this.

It's growing stronger.

TWENTY-TWO

Shame burns my cheeks as I ascend the stairs; dinner with Grandmom starts in ten. She will expect an update, and I have nothing to give. I keep my head down as I hurry through the halls. A throng of Primus greet me as they pass, but I can't look at them. I've told myself I belong here, but maybe believing it isn't enough anymore.

I arrive to Grandmom's sitting room adjacent to the dining room. Her maid ushers me inside.

"She's in a meeting; she'll be out in a moment and you can go through."

"Thank you." Whatever I do, I can't let on that anything's awry. Get out of here quickly and get back to honing. That's the plan.

The room is as stilted as the rest of Grandmom's quarters with its high-back settees, crystal chandelier, and towering drapes. I warm myself by a fire, still haunted by the blue stone I tried but failed to fold into my blade. Everything just seems to get harder the closer I get to Cotillion. The truth weighs me down like an anchor, and I immediately regret admitting it to myself.

Servants dip their heads in and out a few times, offering me refreshment. But I'm not in the mood to drink, or even eat. I should have faked being sick and skipped dinner altogether. *There's no letting up. No mercy.* Just the weight of my toushana closing the walls in around me. Frustration knocks me between woe and fury like waves on a stormy sea. *I hate this. I hate all of it.* Jordan's face flickers through my mind. I try to blink away his brooding gaze, but it lingers like a stain.

"Quell?" Dexler exits a door on the far end of the room.

"Cultivator Dexler? What are you doing here?"

"Oh, nothing. Just a meeting." She averts her eyes and I'm immediately uneasy. "Honing going all right? On track to have everything worked into your blade by morning?"

"It's going fine."

"Very good, then. I'll see you." Dexler waves, then wrings her hands as she leaves. Was she here about . . . me? I jump to my feet and press myself to the door, listening.

"It's unnerving, but I'm not getting my drawers in my ass about it," someone with a fruity voice says.

"Are you some sort of mongrel or a lady? I honestly cannot tell," a husky voice chastises. "And as far as this issue goes, the situation is being handled; I've told you I'm looking into it."

I chew my lip.

"Forgive me, but I don't trust your House to handle this by yourself," a third person says.

"Then have your Draguns join in the search, Isla, if you must!"

I press closer, my ear flush against the wood.

"We should all put a few from our Houses forward. Put it to a final vote."

"I'm not sending my Draguns after some pipe dream for glory."

"This isn't about Houses, Litze," Grandmom says. "If that crack worsens, all our lives, all our magic, are on the line."

The Sphere. Of course. I sag against the door a bit too hard.

It creaks.

The voices hush as the door eases open.

My heart stumbles.

Footsteps patter toward me. "Oh, look at the time. Ladies, if you'll excuse me." The handle jiggles, and I turn to dash.

"Quell?"

Too late.

"Grandmom." My chin rises, parallel with the floor, channeling everything Plume has taught me. "I was looking out the window. The view from up here is breathtaking."

"You are simply *regal*, child." She turns me, admiring my diadem again, and I spin, a feast trapped in Grandmom's web. I try to calm my racing heart. Trying to forget I was sobbing on the floor no more than an hour ago. And put on my best everything-is-fine face.

"I'm just finishing a Council of Mothers meeting. But you *must* come inside and meet everyone! They're all dying to meet you after . . ." She smooths her blouse. "So many years."

Meet them . . .

The Headmistresses.

"All of them are in there?" I swallow.

Inside, fresh flowers tied with pretty ribbons fill vases around the room, and a tea cart full of artsy confections is parked beside three women who couldn't be more different. Each sits cross-legged around a table. The blond woman with a brightly colored diadem set in silver doesn't even look up when I enter, tapping on her phone. Her pantsuit is widened at the legs, and her blazer does the same, giving her petite frame an oddly modular appearance.

The gangly woman beside her, with a face and complexion that reminds me of carved bone, wears a scowl. Her brownish-red hair is pulled back in a tight ponytail and bangs shade her eyes, which match her drab gray dress uncannily. A sleek diadem hovers above her head, unadorned and minimalist without a single gem. We meet eyes and she folds her tattooed arms across her chest. *Isla Ambrose.*

"My, my, aren't you a sight," the woman with the husky voice says, standing. I don't have to guess which one of the Headmistresses is most intrigued by me. I face her as pleasantly as I can. A crown of silver hair coiled in a bun sits on top of her head and fur is wrapped around her shoulders. Her frame matches her voice. Her diadem is statuesque, a bronzy-gold color, adorned with deep honey-colored gems. She moves closer, and a brooch in the shape of a cracked column glistens from her scarf.

I take a tiny step closer to Grandmom, who hovers nearby like a queen watching her finest peacock spread its tail feathers.

The woman who sent her Dragun to kill me catches me staring and holds out her hand, knuckles swallowed in black and red gems. "Beaulah, Headmistress, House Perl."

My heart thuds in my throat as I kiss her hand, then slide a foot back, fold at the knee, and let my head dip like the falling crest of a wave at sea. *If I am perfect, what could she possibly suspect me of?* "Pleasure to make your acquaintance, Headmistress Perl, I am Quell Marionne."

I scrub my face of expression and catch sight of Grandmom, lips parted, watching my curtsy, which, I've practiced enough now to know, is absolute perfection.

"I must remember to give Plume my compliments when I see him," she says. "He's turning this granddaughter of mine into a work of art worthy of her name."

"Such poise," Beaulah says, her words curling with curiosity more than admiration. "You must be beside yourself, Darragh."

Grandmom's lips pucker, smugly, at the Council staring awestruck. *"Supra alios."* She winks and my cheeks warm; pride hangs in her posture kindling my own.

"So it's true." Headmistress Perl pulls her fur tighter over her shoulders, her tone sharp yet cautious. I've seen her type before. She plays coy as a cover. She doesn't like Grandmom, but she's hesitant to outright cross her. "An heir to this House has finally returned."

I search Grandmom's face for some flicker of truth at such a proposition, but she's as stoic as a statue. *Heir.*

The fruity-voiced Headmistress rises, her blond hair swishing, and extends her hand. "Litze Oralia."

I greet her, followed by Headmistress Ambrose, whose heavy brow sags with derision.

"We should adjourn," Grandmom says. "I'm late for dinner."

"Pleasure meeting you, Quell," Headmistress Oralia says. "Watch these old hags, they'll get you all flustered for no reason if you let them."

A chuckle stuffs its way up my throat, and despite my best effort to swallow it, it comes out as a smirk. She winks at me before exiting.

"May your intellect shine brighter than the rest of you, Miss Marionne." Headmistress Ambrose follows Litze out.

Beaulah takes me in once more, up and down, and Grandmom's lips twitch in delight. Jordan's Headmistress rounds me, and my pulse quickens.

An achy warning pricks my bones, but I keep my expression soft and unflinching.

"I look forward to your honing exam," Beaulah says. "I expect you will continue to impress."

I curtsy once more. "I certainly hope so, Headmistress." The door closes behind her, and I could collapse on the floor. I steady myself on an armchair instead. Grandmom circles me, beaming.

"You were *magnificent*." She pinches my cheek.

I can't do anything to ruin this portrait she's painted of me. This granddaughter she believes I can be. In Grandmom's shadow, I am safe. Here in her home, it seems Beaulah can't touch me. Or won't. Even if she does know my secret, once I've rid myself of this poison, once I am free, she won't have a credible thing to hold against me.

Now, if I could actually pass my honing exam, *that* would be great.

"You know, I think this calls for something." Grandmom pulls a velvet box off a high shelf and slides its top aside. Inside is a collection of stones in glittering hues. She selects a mint green one. "Longevity Enhancer."

The stone gleams in different colors, depending on how the light hits it. "It's beautiful."

"It's *as rare* as it is beautiful. A Marionne family heirloom, given to me by my own grandmother."

"You would give this to me?"

"Who else should have it but my granddaughter?"

She gestures toward the door and we make our way to the dining room, which is set with an elaborate table of gold-rimmed plates and fresh flowers. "I hear you're sitting the exam Friday?"

"I am, yes."

"Are you nervous?" She lowers herself into her seat, and I mimic her form, determined to keep whatever this is we have going and not ruin it this time.

"No," I lie.

"Very good. Confidence is a débutante's finest accessory." She rings a bell, and servers stream into the room, platters in their hands. And I spend the rest of our time together careful to chew with my mouth closed and cup my glass properly, nodding in the right places, smiling when prompted, keeping my posture stiff as Grandmom goes on and on about Cotillion and everything to come.

ONCE I'M OUT of Grandmom's presence I hurry to the Belles Wing. I halt when I spot the Sphere, its guts thrashing in the way my insides feel. Closer to its illusioned surface, the hairline crack is much larger than it appears from far away, the length of my arm, easily. I imagine my name soon to be chiseled on its slick surface, another sparkle among the thousands of others. My toushana tremors the longer I stare, and out of the corner of my eye I spot Jordan having a conversation with Headmistress Perl.

"Miss Marionne." She smiles tightly as I pass, faster. Jordan and I meet eyes. His are stone. Once I reach my door, I stuff myself in my room and sag against the door in relief.

I have to hone my dagger.

Whatever it takes.

I pull off my shoes, and my bag gawks at me in judgment. I dump my things on my bed and run my fingers across Mom's letter. The blue stone taunts me. I reach for it and my fingers flicker in warning. How am I going to do this?

Knock. Knock.

"Who's there?"

"It's me."

My heart stutters.

"What do you want?"

The door handle jiggles before black fog seeps between its seam, and Jordan forms before me, rigid with annoyance. "Here." He hands me a book. *Discite Latina.* I reach but pull my hand back. *I don't trust him.* "It helps make everything simpler to memorize."

I take the book and set it aside.

"Honing. How's it going?" He glances over my shoulder.

"It's harder than I thought it would be. I just need more time."

"Time you do not have." His insistence stokes me like kindling a fire.

"Breathing down my neck *doesn't* help." I ball my fists, as the culmination of the entire day boils over. Grandmom's expectations, my toushana destroying the table, Beaulah. *It's too much.*

He grabs my dagger from the bed, turning it in his hands. "Hold it up," he says, his tone gentler. I begrudgingly raise the dagger.

"Higher." He motions for me to raise my arm, but I let it fall when an idea lassos my heart into a tight squeeze.

I glance at the blue Purifier on my bed taunting me and gulp down a breath of foolish courage. "You think it's so easy, huh?" I turn my back to him and grit my teeth to reach for the blue stone. I will have *seconds* once I touch it before my toushana betrays me. But if I can bear its sear against my skin for a sliver of a moment, I just might be able to get him to do what *I* want for a change.

My fist closes around the stone and the hum of my toushana awakens in a fury, swelling in my every crevice, frost scratching against my bones. I bite down until I taste copper, and almost toss the stone and dagger at him.

"*You* do it."

I fold my arms, trying to resist the cold teasing its way through me.

"*Fine.* Watch closely this time." He holds the blue stone over the dagger and the world teeters on the edge of a cliff. *Please let this work.* "It's like a magnet, you have to set it on there just so or it'll repel." He moves the stone in a roundabout motion, pushing it lower, closer to the metal. "When it gets stubborn, hold firm. Let your magic know you're sure about what you want. It will give in. The more enhancers you've folded into the blade, the harder it is to fold in another. But these are only your first several, so it shouldn't be difficult for someone like you." He glances at my diadem.

I swallow a retort because he's doing exactly what I want him to. He eases the enhancer lower, and I realize I have a fist full of my skirt. The stone shimmers and finally snaps to the blade.

"Now you *ease* it in." His glides the flat of his palm across them, and pressure hooks in my chest. The blue stone bubbles, contorts, then flattens until it fully dissolves, disappearing into the metal. He hands my dagger back at me, its blade rippling blue, then purple.

"It worked." I clutch my chest.

"Of course it worked. One down, two to go."

"I've actually already done the other two, Mister Observant."

He suppresses a smile. "My apologies, then."

I purse my lips. "Thanks." I grab the last enhancer I have, the milky stone Casey gave me.

"Try it."

"Now?"

He gestures for me to get going.

I hold up my dagger and ease the white stone onto it. My stomach rolls with nerves.

"You're holding it wrong. Not so flat, angle the cutting edge of the dagger up, just a bit."

I tilt my wrist.

"That's too much." He's close, so close. Warmth slinks down my neck. His fingertips brush my skin. Then he curls them gently around my wrist. He bends it a fraction, his thumb caressing the back of my hand. "Like this." His voice is a gentle breeze, and it snatches my next breath.

I push away from him. "I have it from here. Really." He hesitates a moment but, to my relief, moves to the door.

"The next time I knock, answer." The door shuts behind him, and I collapse against the shut door with my blade, holding it at the angle Jordan told me, and the stone's milky surface darkens, stretching before disappearing into the dagger. I bite away the smile forming at my lips. I still have so much to cram in before I'm ready for my exam.

The door handle jiggles, and I snatch the door back open. "I *told* you—"

"Quell?" It's Abby, arms full of fabrics.

"Sorry, I thought you were Jordan."

"I saw him just leaving." She grins wickedly.

"Don't even. I can't stand him."

"It doesn't look that way." Her brows jump as she comes inside. "When you talk about him, that is."

"It's complicated."

"I'm listening."

"I don't know if I can trust him."

Her lips twists in confusion.

"Because . . ." *He hunts people like me.* "He's hard to read. I don't know what he's thinking. Not truly. Sometimes he seems to like being around me. Other times, I feel like a job to him. None of this makes sense." I scrub a palm down my face. "Ignore me." I laugh.

"Boys are not complicated. They're like puppies."

I snort. "With Jordan, it feels like he sees me in a way no one else does. But when I don't match this picture he has of me in his head, he's frustrated with me."

"Do you *want* to match the picture in his head?"

Part of me wants to believe this person he sees in me is actually there. I try to picture myself controlling magic the way he does, having a position in a great magical House, belonging somewhere. But the other part of me is terrified that my worst suspicions of him could be true. That he could be working with Beaulah. Or that his interest in seeing me debut well is a cover for something sinister.

"I don't know, Abby."

"Well, in my professional boy-expert opinion, he's into you. You just need to figure out if you care. Don't get too attached, but if you want to have fun, have fun." She nudges me with her elbow before dumping her load on the bed. "Word on the street is Draguns don't really get involved romantically with anyone anyway."

"Really?"

"The running joke is if the Order wanted them to have a partner, it would issue them one."

A feeling I can't quite put words to nudges me.

"Help me with these, would you?" she asks, finally unloading the bags draped over her arms. Shoes tumble out. I take out an armful of bedazzled shoes from her bag only to find she has three more full bags.

"*How* many of these things do you have?"

"A lot. A few of those samples Mom custom ordered. I have to narrow these down tonight."

"Geez!"

"I make a big deal, but it's sort of nice. She's usually drowning in work. Now I can't get her off the phone. Did honing go all right?"

"I think so. Jordan's making me take the exam Friday."

"As in the end of this week? Quell, are you going to be ready? You don't get a second chance, you know that?"

Wait, really? I join her on the bed.

"You can't fail, Quell."

Oh, I know.

"In fact." She takes her shoes out of my hands. "I can do this."

"No, I want to help. We're friends, right?"

"Yes, silly. Go study. I have fittings all day Thursday, you can help me with that."

I sigh. She's making sense even if I don't want to listen. "Only if you're sure."

"And try to talk to Jordan about sitting a different exam date."

Grandmom knows, and she's already told Council. There's no way that's changing. The expectation has been set . . . etched on my tombstone. "I'm not getting out of this exam this week, Abby."

"Then *be ready*."

TWENTY-THREE

———✳———

Despite fatigue, I was first in my seat in Dexler's in the morning. She fawned over my blade, praising me for how good it looked. Then dumped a bag of thirty-two more enhancers in my lap.

"These need to be done before your exam," she said, and I died a small death inside. Still, I somehow managed to fold in three during class, but Jordan wasn't kidding when he said each subsequent stone gets harder to fold in. Thankfully the Purifier he folded in doesn't seem to be giving me any trouble. However, I fought with a translucent gray one for an hour before my toushana flared up and rendered me useless for most of the day. Then I went back to the gray stone only to realize it required four specific enhancers to be folded in *first* before it could bind with the metal. *What a headache.* And it's already Tuesday. Three days left.

I grab my book as Dexler's class wraps, shoulder my bag of stones, and make my way to a full day of specialty classes that have cropped up on my schedule: Latin, Knowledge-Strand Location, Body Binding, Elixirs 101, and Magic Exhaustion and Rejuvenation. I was hoping to get into Advanced Paths of Change, but no luck.

My brain is mush by the time I stumble into etiquette. My toushana lurks beneath my skin, and I wrap myself tighter in my sweater. I glance at the pile of stones in the bottom of my bag. I'm so close.

"Quell." Casey and several others say hello, wrapping me in their small talk.

"How's it going?"

I update him on making headway toward the exam.

"Any tips you can give? Like, what's on the exam exactly?" I've been studying everything, all my notes.

"You'll figure it out. It's tradition." He winks. "Just remember, stay calm. That's key."

Has he met my mentor?!

Casey's Cotillion partner hooks her arms around his waist, and they take their places. "Good seeing you, Marionne."

I can't let Jordan frazzle me today.

I will be *perfect*. He'll have nothing to say!

I stand on my name, written on a small rip of tape on the floor, and wait for him. Head held straight up, I tuck my chin, making sure my ears are over my shoulders. I imagine my body is a statue, intricately carved. I hold air tight in my chest to keep my posture just so, and I feel a presence behind me.

Jordan steps into position, his warm body hard against my back.

"Afternoon," I say, creating some distance between us.

"This morning went well, I assume?" He eyes my posture. "With your new schedule?"

"It did." The shrill cry of a violin pierces the air before Jordan can interrogate me further.

"Places, everyone." Plume waltzes into the room, critiquing postures. "Today we'll be working on the basics of dance. It's all about finding synergy with your partner." He snaps and a few stragglers find their marks on the floor. I tighten my center. "Miss Marionne," he says, circling me. "Absolutely *flawless*."

My chin rises.

The knot at Jordan's throat bobs.

"The event involves three dances: First Dance; the Cotillion dance, which we do as a group; and a Sunset Waltz. But before any of you can even think about the proper form, you first have to understand the *language* of dance. It is *led* by one partner. The other *follows*. You can't have two people stumbling over each other who don't know their knee from their toe. To demonstrate." He beckons for Jordan, who joins him at the center of the ballroom. "And who would you like to have with you?" Plume asks him.

"Miss Marionne of course."

"But I don't know the steps—"

"That, my dear, is the point," Plume says. "Dance is all about moving with your partner *instinctually*. Part of the reason you're paired with a mentor who out-seasons you is to prepare you for dance."

But the plan was to be perfect . . .

"What are you doing?" I mutter to Jordan, joining him in the center of the room. "I'm going to royally embarrass you. *And* me." A mix of stares surround us, some ripe with curiosity, others with amusement, and a handful with jealousy.

"Not if you trust me." He tries to take my hand, but I snatch it away. He could literally not ask anything more impossible from me.

"Annnnd . . ." The music bursts into motion like a fireworks display, and my body refuses to move. "One, two, three, one, two, three, one—" Plume claps us along but I still can't move. Eyes in every corner of the room stare. "One, two, three, one, two, three, one—"

Jordan circles me, close, his breath brushing my ear. "Let yourself go."

I take his hand. The music croons and Jordan moves as if under the spell of its rhythm. I watch his feet, trying to predict his next move.

"No." He lifts my chin to look him in the eyes. "Be here. With me."

We ease into the dance, turning, twisting, mimicking the reverse of each other's steps, arms folded behind the other's back. I hold my form perfect, counting in my head, focused on keeping in line with him and the music. I set my focus on those viridescent moons beneath his lashes and imagine myself bathing in their moonlight, letting myself go wherever they take me.

"Two, three, four . . ." Plume chants, clapping with the tempo.

Jordan's hands curl around my waist, pulling me closer to him. I stutter for breath, frozen inside, as if a single exhale could shatter me. I warm all over, and it has nothing to do with magic. And everything to do with him and me. *Let go.* I exhale and melt into his grip, trying to find his rhythm.

He moves like silk, pushing my hips back, then forward, and I follow like a tousled breeze, moving with the slightest request of his hand. His lips curl in a full smile. The first I've ever seen.

My arms are slung over his hard shoulders as I move with him, a part of him. I see his intention in the direction of his hips, and my body moves in anticipation of it. He releases me and for a moment I quiver at the loss of his touch, but his fingers lace tightly to mine. The world spins as he turns me out. *Now back to me,* his body seems to say as he tugs on my hand, and I flee to him, spinning in his grasp, until I'm tight against his chest. It feels safe.

The music's pace picks up, and Jordan moves more quickly, asking more of my body, and I give in to his every request, twisting and turning, until Plume, the ballroom, and the world fade away. And all that's left is me, twirling across those rolling hills in his eyes, untethered. *Free.* The feeling fills me up in a way I've never felt, and my grip on his lapel tightens. I give in to the urge I felt last night and press our bodies closer. His arm curls around me tighter in response. He smiles again, so close his breath licks my skin. I feel it in my soul, a warmth, a wanting, a twinge below my navel. I take a deliberate, deep inhale. I will be alive in every beat of this moment.

"Now back," he utters. His fingers trace down my back, my spine curling at his touch. He dips me, his mouth brushing my exposed neck. He holds me there, tight in his grip. I'm not sure where he begins and I end.

"You're *magnificent*," he breathes.

I don't know what to say, and I realize the entire class is applauding.

He pulls me up, and I finish in a deep curtsy, him in a bow. Applause drowns out the sound of my thudding heart. He squeezes my hand. But I keep my head straight ahead, for fear of what my expression might show.

"I see you've found your match, Mister Wexton." Plume beams. "Take notes, ladies and gentlemen. That's how it's done. Now, places . . . again. I want to see Cotillion starting positions."

Jordan reaches for me, but I step back.

"I need a minute." I rush to my bag, pretending to look for something just to have a moment to catch my breath. *What's come over me?* I know the answer, but it's so ridiculous, so unwise, so *dangerous*, I don't believe myself. Once my breath eases, I return to the dance floor and fall in line with the group routine. This one doesn't require as much one-on-one, which helps my pulse simmer down. Jordan glances over at me every few minutes, but when I catch him looking, he promptly looks away.

We finish the session, and I can't bolt for my things fast enough.

"Quell?" Jordan follows.

No, every second I'm around him confuses. I walk faster.

"Quell, listen . . ."

"Look, I have a lot of enhancers to work on." I force myself to face him so he knows I mean every word. "I don't have time to talk, really."

His expression is a far cry from last night, and the shock of it snaps my lips shut. The frustration and contempt have melted away, and I'm reminded of the first time he looked at me this way. When he saw that I'd emerged.

"Have lunch with me."

"No."

"Quell, I think you're . . ." He tugs at his shirt. "What I'm trying to say is . . . I know I'm hard on you." He sighs.

I twist my bag strap into a knot.

"Can we start over, please? Lunch, we can eat wherever on the grounds you like."

"Me making a choice for us for once?" I shift on my feet, but the humor doesn't buffer as I hoped it would. I stare back at him, and my insides do weird things. He slips his hands in his pockets, waiting. My skin tingles remembering the way his arms felt, *he* felt, around me. How I could live in that feeling, die in it, and I'm not sure I'd have any regrets. I've never felt more alive. I gnaw at my lip, trying to chew off the foolishness on the tip of my tongue.

"Say yes, please."

It's just lunch. I nod, reshoulder my bag, and follow Jordan out the door.

TWENTY-FOUR

✳

The cafeteria is too crowded, so after we grab our food, I ask about checking out a glass building just past the gardens.

"The conservatory is off-limits, so we should have privacy."

"Then how can we get in?"

He dangles a ring of keys, and I remember he oversees security.

The conservatory is a tapestry of flowers and herbs. Delicate white flowers cover plots on the ground, and winding greens hug its windowed perimeter. Above, light pours through its glossed windows, the sun chasing away any lingering chill of morning. We stop near a pair of stone benches next to a fountain of a mother and two girls hugged against her legs.

I settle on the seat with him but not quite next to him. I need my head on straight if I'm going to get through this lunch without raising his suspicion. *Distance is good.* He pulls a bag of colorful candies from his pocket and pops a green one in his mouth.

"You're going to eat that before your actual food?"

He bites into his lunch. "There, happy?"

"I was just asking. It's weird, right? To go from sweet to savory like that? I don't know."

He gazes off in the distance somewhere. "We weren't allowed sugar growing up."

A laugh that's more shock than amusement spills out. "Wait, are you serious?"

He pulls another bag of candy out of his pocket and shows me two more in his leather satchel. He pours candies into his hands and I expect him to offer me some, but he doesn't.

"I'm not actually hungry yet either." I pull my dagger out of my bag and pile the twentysomething stones I have next to it. I don't have time to waste.

He glances up at my diadem. "You know, I'm not sure if I've said it, but you're very impressive, Quell. Your level of ability is quite rare. It's been incredible watching you come into your magic."

"You have a funny way of showing it." I pluck one of the smaller stones from the pile and ease it onto my dagger.

He looks off again, and it's like he's somewhere else entirely.

I slide my hand over my blade and summon warmth to my fingertips. The teal stone bubbles down into the dagger without too much trouble. I grab another. "How can you tell?" I ask, trying to bring him back from wherever he's run off to.

"I can sense it. Are you feeling more ready for the exam?"

"I'll be ready. I'd actually like to get out of here as fast as I can."

That swivels his head around, back to me.

"What?" I ask, pressing another stone to my dagger. This one melts in slower than the ones before it, but it still goes, the metal shimmering yellow once finished. I grab a couple more.

"I can't imagine itching to leave this place." He parts his lips but closes them again.

"And why is that?" I ask, unable to bury my curiosity.

He lets the silence swell before speaking. "I've been groomed to be a Dragun since I was very young." He faces me, and for a moment I consider scooting closer to him. "My House is run a bit different than things here. The training is more rigorous, for lack of a better word."

"Did you have to go there because your aunt is Headmistress?"

"Partly. But we also live within her territory. Sola Sfenti illuminated the magic in me for the first time when I was eight. And my father handed me over to Headmistress Perl right then," he says more to a flower nearby than me.

"As a *kid*?"

"In my House, that's how it's done. To honor the Mother of Magic and the children she lost we commit more time to mastery of magic, not just study. Much was sacrificed to shepherd magic through the centuries, and the Mother of Magic paid a lot of that cost. Her children and their children lived their lives on the run. Can you imagine?"

I look away. "That sounds awful."

"If you look at history, whispers of magic have incensed every ruler since the beginning of time. And for what? So that they could dabble in it, play with it like a toy to put on a shelf once they're bored of it? In my House we start priming prospects for magic *six* years before the rest of the Order does. One year in honor of each of the Mother of Magic's children. Headmistress Perl inspects children in our territory around age ten, and if they show the potential to access more than one strand of magic, she takes them in right away to help their chances of becoming a Dragun."

"Like you live with her? As an orphan?"

"Sure."

"You call her Headmistress, not Aunt." *Perhaps they're not close.*

"And you call your Headmistress by her title as well."

I don't know what to say to that.

"I've known what I would do for as long as I can remember. I can't imagine coming here as you have later in life. That doesn't sound ideal."

I stare at the Dragun, trying to see the boy behind him. There's a wariness that carves the angles of his face that I hadn't noticed before. A deep sag in the set of his shoulders. I hadn't really thought about how where he comes from likely hangs his posture and sures his steps, as so much of where I've come from has etched my path into stone. He slips another green candy into his mouth.

"I wish I had known about this place." The truth slips out, and it seizes my heart. His expression crinkles as if he's sifting through my words for treasure.

"So it's true, then? Your mother's departure from here was more than a sabbatical?"

I flinch. "Is that what people say?"

"I'm just trying to understand you, what your life was like."

He takes off his coat, offering it to me. I'm not cold, but for some reason I take it, considering the earnestness in his expression. There's only honesty there.

"Forget I asked. What are you thinking of specializing in? Cultivator like Headmistress?"

"I haven't thought past debut, to be honest."

"You're serious?"

My chest tightens, and I see the stern-faced Jordan who towered over me just yesterday. The Jordan whispering in the halls with Beaulah. *And yet.*

"I want to live on the beach one day, near the bluest ocean, in a modest house with small windows. Like really small and square with little planters outside of them. It probably sounds like a silly little detail I know, but . . ." *It's the one I've dreamt of since I was little.* "That's just how I picture it. My mom and I—" Nerves buzz through me, fluttering for a place to land. "That's where we said we'd move one day. It doesn't have to be anywhere fancy. It just—"

"Has to have the tiny square windows. I got it."

"You're patronizing me."

"I'm not, really." His lips crack a smile, the second one today, and I have to look away to not smile, too. "I think it's incredible that you're inspired by where you want to be. I've never really thought of things that way."

My turn. "And what about your magic? Maybe I should consider something like that."

He puts away his candy, his mouth arced in amusement.

"What? I'm serious. You said *be open.*"

"You don't choose this life, Quell. It chooses you."

Dead end. Yet again. "So you always knew you'd come here? To my Grandmom's House, as a ward?"

"Headmistress Perl dropped me off at the Chateau's gate with my things at fifteen."

"That sounds mean."

"I won't hear insults about my House," he says sharply, but something else glints in his eyes.

"I didn't mean . . . My apologies." I let the silence balloon.

"My parents pushed hard for me to get the position; Headmistress worked tirelessly to prepare me. I have no regrets. I was eager to do my part." He looks away. "Am eager to do my part."

"Is it hard being away from your home for so long?"

"Home is where you make it. There are many things I like about Soleil." His gaze finds mine and heat rushes up my neck.

I grab my dagger and start working again to do something with my hands. It might have started as a lunch, but neither of us are even eating, really, and I've told him more in the last several minutes than I've told anyone in my life. My hands work faster over the blade, grasping for something I actually can control, and I accidentally knock my bag off the bench. One of my library books from school spills out of my bag. Its tattered edges have been taped together. I grab it, and so does he.

"I love her," he says, noting the author.

"I didn't take you for someone into novels in verse," I say, letting him thumb through it. "You seem like a pure action and adventure kind of guy, no offense."

He hands it back before folding his arms behind his head, biting away what I think is a laugh. "I just love stories," he says, more amused than he's been the whole afternoon. "Historically inspired is my favorite."

"Because it's the best of both worlds," I say, working another stone in. "It's storytelling, but with bits of reality."

"Exactly. What else do you like to read?"

We talk about our favorite books until the sun has started its descent. I work through my stones at the same time as he offers advice. He even laughs a few more times. By evening, I'm somehow sitting closer to him on the bench, when my toushana flares in my chest. I stand. *This is foolish.*

"Was it something I said?"

"No." It's all of him. The way he looks at me. The way we move when we're together. The way he commands the darkness of his magic without it consuming him entirely. His control, his focus, the thundering storm that wages in his eyes. The way this conversation only makes me want to be here longer. Know him more. The boy who would kill me if he could really see me.

"Then please, sit back down." He asked me to trust him when we danced, but his stare asks even more of me now.

My fingers prick with an ache, my toushana reminding me it's awakening. I fidget over my dagger, and a ruby-colored enhancer on top of it slips off.

"I should probably go." I pick up the stone—as the pain in my bones grows, my time before a flare-up shortening—and set it back on top of the blade. This will have to be my last one for now. I work my magic and the stone bleeds into the metal, which gleams a moment.

Then the metal grows longer.

I gasp and drop it, and the sound of it thudding against the dirt stops my heart. I'm up on my feet, watching in horror as my dagger contorts its blade, curving it to a point like nothing I've ever seen. The memory of my diadem growing from my head as black as death squeezes my heart.

I glance at Jordan, his eyes narrowing with intrigue.

Pink gems bloom on its handle here and there, and I can't tear my eyes away. Something or someone says my name, but sounds blare in my ears as Jordan picks up the blade. *Run.* My toushana rears up in me unbridled with force, lassoing my feet to the ground. *I can't think. I can't move.*

Jordan holds the dagger out toward me, and I close my eyes, bracing for him to slice right through me. "Quell?"

I blink.

"*Quell?* Do you hear me?"

I blink again, and Jordan's holding my dagger by the blade, offering me its handle.

"This is what I meant. That Amplifier Enhancer you just used is a finicky one. Your magic has to be really strong to get enough out of it to shift the shape of your dagger."

I take it from him, turning it in my hands, staring at what I was sure was evidence of my brokenness. "I thought I'd ruined it and messed up my chances at honing altogether." That's as close to the truth as I can get with him.

"I haven't seen a dagger this impressive since my own." He marvels at the speckled beading up and down its grip. "It is stunning. *You* are stunning."

I reach for words, but I have none, so I grab my things to prepare to go.

"You were about to work yourself into a fit, it looked like. I'm glad I was here." He holds the door open to the conservatory for me to go through.

"I am, too." I bite my lip. Silence lingers between us. I don't know where to look or what to say. So I just walk away.

TWENTY-FIVE

———✳———

I sit, hovered over my dagger, tangled in my bedsheets, being judged by a half-eaten jumbo bag of chips and a bazillion chocolate candy wrappers. Honing exam is tomorrow, and I have hardly left this spot. Scrawly handwriting on a note catches my eye.

Are you ready?

I read Jordan's foreboding words once more for the millionth time before knocking it into the trash. The truth is I'm not sure if I am. My fingers ache from holding my blade just so for so many hours yesterday. I flex them before grabbing one of the two final enhancers I need to fold in. The metal blade hasn't contorted anymore either. The Amplifier Enhancer I used in the conservatory was apparently unique in its ability to change a dagger. But I've spent so much time folding in the enhancers that my note cards on what each actually does are collecting dust. The good news is I have my first and second declensions down backward and forward.

I eye the clock. Fifteen minutes until Abby's fitting. I have time to do these *last* two. I glance at my notes, easing the bronze stone down onto my blade, one inch from its narrowest point. I press, but it shifts sideways, missing the precise spot it needs to bind to the metal.

Again. I hover it over the blade once more, careful to angle it up, and finally the stone snaps to the blade properly before folding in.

After reviewing a few handwritten notes in the margin of my book, I grab my last enhancer. *Sealer Enhancer: helps homogenize the composition of the other enhancers in the metal. Do this one last.* I steady the black stone over my dagger and in moments it coats my blade like a glaze of melted snow. I turn it in my hands, watching the blade absorb the sealer until it shines bright again.

I retie my unruly curls and roll my shoulders, which have been knotted since I woke up, thanks to not enough sleep. Then I sit up and hold my dagger firmly by its handle, ready to finally try pushing magic into my blade. I'm not sure how it works exactly, but I conjure warmth, and a swarm of heat gathers deep in my belly, granule by granule, until a weight sits like heated lead against my ribs. I focus on the handle firmly in my grip. Magic moves through me like live wire, pulsing with urgency, up my torso, through my arms. I tighten my hold, and I feel energizing magic coursing through me toward the handle in my hands. *Now, into the blade.* Nothing happens. I catch a glimpse of the clock again. *Argh. I better go.*

Today's Abby's dress decision day, and I don't want to be late. I'm two steps down the stairs when I spot Jordan.

"Quell," he says, just as I turn to go in the other direction. It's been two days since our evening in the conservatory.

I stop and he catches up to me. "Jordan, I'm almost late for Abby's fitting." I fiddle with my bag to avoid looking at him.

"Did you finish?"

"The enhancers? Yes. I still need to practice pushing magic into my blade so when I take the exam, I can demonstrate without incident. And study for the written part." I hold up a brick of note cards.

"Pushing magic into the dagger is the easy part. You just—"

A clock chimes. "I really have to go."

"I'll find you later."

"Maybe, I don't know." I hurry off.

The room where Abby has me meet her is a quaint sitting room with a glorious view of the sweeping estate. Abby cradles a teacup, watching as trays of jewels are being set out in front of her.

"Quell, you made it!"

A Shifter curating a pot of tea with a pile of fresh herbs and rose petals offers me a cup, and I take one, looping my fingers into the handle the way Grandmom showed me.

"We're just getting started. Here, come sit by me."

The room is a traffic jam of racks lined with dresses in every color and fabric. Some glitter, others shine. Dazzling necklaces and dangly earrings are splayed across furniture.

"Is *this* the friend I've been hearing so much about?" A woman who could be Abby's twin, only slightly older, sets down a stack of dresses and extends a hand. "I'm Teresa, Abby's mother. You must be Quell."

"Pleased to meet you, Mrs. Feldsher." I curtsy.

"Oh, no, no. I should be curtsying to you," she jokes, glancing up at my diadem. "She's every bit as lovely as you said, Abs. Thanks for being here to support her. This has been a long time coming."

"Mom, really?" Abby shoos away a server offering her a tray of iced cookies. "See why I need you here?" she mutters.

"Which one is your favorite?" I whisper.

"These are my two picks from the swatch samples." Abby's mom dangles a gold sequined gown and a shiny red one with embroidered fleurs on it. "And they have reinforced lining along the torso for stronger magic retention. What do you think?"

"Mom, I don't like those." She pulls me over to a rack of dresses in dark purples and blues that are simply stunning, and for a moment I imagine what it would be like to be in her shoes. An ache of sadness writhes in me, watching Abby and her mother fawn over the options.

"Quell?"

"Yes, sorry, did you say something?"

"I said I think these colors go better with my diadem." Abby indicates a purple sequined one.

"It's too humdrum and doesn't have all the fortifications these do." Her mother holds up her two favorites beside Abby's. "We need function *and* maximum sparkle."

"Mom, I don't care how it functions. I care how it *looks*."

"Let's put it to a vote. Quell?"

"Oh gosh . . . I sort of agree that the gold ones go better with Abby's diadem. But the purple and blues are gorgeous, too. But I think *that's* the one." I point to the purple one Abby's wiggling ever so slightly and she grins.

"I should have known I'd be defeated against you two." Her mother dotes on her with such sweetness that I have to look away. *I'll never have a moment quite like this.*

Mrs. Feldsher checks the label. "This one is Civaolin. Let me see if my people can get his people on the phone. We need this done quickly."

"Can't you just wear this one?" I smooth my hand on the silk gown, trying to blink away thoughts of Mom.

Her mother guffaws. "She's funny, too! I need a quiet room to make this call. Abs, can you work on accessories and such next?" she asks before leaving.

"Thanks for having my back." Abby loops her arm in mine as we survey a collection of statement necklaces with fleur-de-lis shaped jewels dangling from them.

"Your mom is really nice."

"She's a lot."

I reach for my key chain, which isn't there. It's in a drawer by my bed, in my room. *Mom, I miss you.* "It's just really cool that you get to do this together."

Abby goes on and on about all the preparations they've been making, and I muster as much enthusiasm as I can. But eventually, longing stretches the spaces between my words until I'm all out of them. She shows me more fine things than I've ever seen, but it becomes a blur, morphing into one big heavy feeling.

"You're quiet."

"Sorry." My bag weighs a ton and I eye the note cards. "I actually should go, if that's okay." The words feel like sandpaper on my tongue. She isn't even halfway done picking out her things. Abby deserves better.

"All right, I guess," she says, her jaw working.

"Please tell your mother it was nice meeting her."

Abby nods, her shoulders slumped in disappointment. I apologize again and hurry out the door.

TWENTY-SIX

I rush through the halls, ignoring every look and word tossed my way, trying to forget—for at least a moment—the way it felt being in there. And the way Abby looked at me as I left. The feeling trails me like a ghost, pushing one hurried step in front of the other, past the corridor that leads to my room, past the library and yoga studio.

Through the dining hall and into the courtyard. *So many people. So many eyes.* I keep going, farther, until the estate is small behind me. Until I can finally breathe. I traipse toward the gardens, where I spot the towering glass walls of the conservatory. I tug on the handle. *Closed. I knew it would be.* I peer through the windows for some glimpse of a familiar Dragun with keys.

No luck. I opt for the rose garden beside it instead. I settle on a bench inside and let the cool morning air soothe my nerves. I imagine myself blowing as it does, directed by its own wiles, free. And the tangle in my chest unwinds. I'm doing this for her. For both of us. But I can't pretend it wouldn't be nice to fit into this place and have her by my side. Abby's slumped shoulders tug at me, but I uncoil the guilt from around my throat. If she knew Mom's and my story, if she knew what I was fighting for, she'd want me to get out of there and practice, too. She's that kind of friend.

I pull my bag to my lap and slide out my dagger. Grandmom might see my passing Second Rite as a ticket to furthering her legacy. But it's my ticket to a life that's my own. Failing isn't an option.

"Now, we're going to try this again." My pulse ticks, even and calm, and my toushana is quiet. I clear my throat and dig for magic. A tendril of warmth coils in me, and I hold it there, letting it grow hotter. With a double fisted grip on on the dagger's handle I imagine the heat in my limbs siphoning into my hands. The curl of magic tightens like a cord pulled taut, and I am tingly all over. "Now, *into* the blade." I squeeze my hands. The demonstration is supposed to show that I can focus my magic enough to push it into something at will. But my magic quivers, its fire dimming. "No, no, come on." I resituate my grip. "*Into* the blade."

"That's not going to work," a voice says, sending my heart racing.

Jordan.

"I heard someone talking, so I came here to check it out. You're doing that wr—"

"*Wrong*, of course."

"Quell." My name from his lips pulls at me like a song, the other night playing on repeat. He sets a hand on the garden gate. Past the garden's shrubbery, through the glass walls, I can see the fountain we sat beside just days ago.

"I only want to help you," he says.

I'm not sure if it's the lilt of his tone, the kindness webbed around his eyes, or that I'm parched to believe someone, anyone, would be on my side in all this. But I actually believe him. "It's not that simple."

"It actually is."

I should say something, send him away, but deep down I'm not sure I want to. I'm still not certain how close he and Beaulah are. And with my toushana flaring at will, distance from Jordan is wise. But my feet betray me. Because somewhere deep down, I want him here. I lift the garden latch, and he steps inside, and my heart leaps in my chest.

He moves behind me, so close I can feel the thrum of his heart against my back. "Hold it here, even with your hips." He tucks my elbows tight to my side, drawing a line with his hand from my elbow down to my waist. "Angle it toward the nearest kor to help conduct your magic."

I raise the dagger's point toward the sun.

"Now, from your diaphragm." His fingers start at my waist and follow my ribs to where they meet, just below my breasts. He presses there, but I feel his touch all over my skin. "Now call to your magic, and when you feel it, direct it using *all* the muscles in your body to tell it where to go."

I do and lean into the rush of heat that answers. It swarms inside me violently, and I let it whip around freely, exploring every part of me. *Into my blade.* Magic thickens, growing heavier, moving slower, trudging through me as if each grain of the Sun Dust has magnified in size and weight. I cinch my ribs with my elbows and my magic tugs sharply into my arms in one smooth motion. I stagger and Jordan holds me closer.

He moves my hair to one shoulder and whispers, "*Focus.*"

My breath hitches, and I tighten every muscle in my arm. Magic tugs harder, as if pulled by a hook, through my wrists. I tighten my grip until it burns, magic streaming into my hands. The blade throbs with light.

"*I did it.*"

"Look at that," he says, still holding on to me when my fingers suddenly prickle, like cold droplets of rain on a raging fire.

I shove myself away from him, my toushana unfurling, and search his eyes for knowing.

"What's wrong?" He reaches for me.

"*Don't!*" I say. "Don't touch me." I grab my dagger from the ground and back away. He may be helpful, and perhaps trustworthy, but I must do this on my own. I have no choice. What I might feel doesn't matter.

His mouth parts.

"You asked if you could assist. And my answer's no, Jordan. Just . . . *please*, if you want me to succeed, the most helpful thing you can do is just . . . leave me alone. You said we've started over, so *those* are my terms."

"As you wish." His words are as steel as his revised composure. But in his eyes I see the boy who sat with me on the bench just a few days ago. I have wounded him.

"Thank you." I take off before the thunderclouds in his eyes deliver on their promise of rain.

⚜

I COULDN'T EAT dinner because of nerves over my exam. I couldn't sleep for the same reason. And I wasn't ready to see Abby. So I stayed in the library going over my enhancer note cards until they kicked me out at two a.m. Then I found a settee in the hall not too far from the exam room, and that is where I wake.

I pull at a thread in the cornflower-blue cushion before fully realizing what I'm doing. I try to smooth it back down, but it doesn't go, so I yank the rogue thread out, which only rips the fabric more. I put my bag over it and try to forget about it. I have bigger issues, such as how I'm going to keep my toushana calm as I push proper magic into my blade. There are seven others waiting to take the exam. Their daggers, all a bit different, rest on their laps.

"Good luck," I say, when I make eye contact with one of them. They smile nervously and return the encouragement when our names are called.

"Could I see your daggers?" Dexler greets us with a bright smile, collecting our blades. "We inspect them first just to be sure there's no funny business."

I look over it once more before handing it to her. Then I force myself to think of positive things. The minutes tick like days and finally the doors open again, and we follow her inside. The exam room is a sparse classroom with a raised platform and podium. In the back, all of the Headmistresses sit at a long table. None of them smile in greeting this time.

"Where emerging shows one's propensity for strengthening magic, honing demonstrates your measure of control." Grandmom paces the length of the room and no one next to me moves. "Having access to magic is dangerous if you are not able to command it. The exam is one hundred twenty questions; you must finish them all. You will have one hour."

I try a smile at Grandmom, but she only points at one of seven desks in the room. I slip into the chair and feel the Headmistresses' stares fixed on me like sweat all over my skin. The hour winds by, and I answer each question with more certainty than the one before it. The Latin portion is much easier than I anticipated, but I still am careful to take my time, finishing last, and checking it over thrice before handing it to Grandmom.

She gazes over it. "Very good. The oral portion consists of four random questions, one from each of us. We'll start with Quell." She addresses the others, "Please take a seat back in the hall and await your name being called." The door clicks following their patter of timid footsteps. "Do you need a moment?" Grandmom asks me. "Shall we proceed?"

"I'm ready." Her brow rises. And I nod, assuring her that I am.

As ready as I'll ever be.

"Take the podium just over there. We'll go around the room, starting with House Oralia, then Ambrose, then Perl, finishing with myself. You have three minutes to respond to each question."

"Good to see you again, Quell." Headmistress Oralia throws her blond hair back over her shoulders. "My question is *which* enhancer is steeped in argala tea as a part of its mining process and why?"

I know this one. "Brazen Enhancers are mined from a volcano in a toxic region of the Kenetan Rainforest. It's steeped in argala tea because the anthraquinones in argala have a neutralizing effect on any toxins that may have been absorbed by the stone during the mining process."

Headmistress Oralia smiles, sitting back in her chair.

"Miss Marionne." Headmistress Ambrose fixes her mouth in a clever smirk. "What are the limitations of known elixirs?"

Elixirs. The marks all the way up Octos's arms turn on like a bulb in my memory. *This is a trick question.* There is a "known" limit for the rest of us, but not for House Ambrose because they aspire to surpass the bounds of the *known*. I can't answer her in a way that makes me seem naive. I also can't answer it in a way that suggests I know more than I should about the intricacies of her House. I clear my throat.

"The only limit is ours. There are twenty-three *known* elixirs. But with commitment to astute study, the possibility of discovering more is undeniable."

"Mmm. Yes. I suppose that is correct," she says, crossing her legs. Grandmom winks at me and my insides flitter.

"Quell." Beaulah stands to administer her question and my heart knocks against my ribs. "What strands of magic are forbidden? And why?"

Grandmom's expression at Beaulah narrows.

"Could you repeat the question?" I dig a nail into my palm.

She restates the question.

Know too much, and she'll see right through you.

I twist the end of my dress. "I only know of one forbidden strand. Toushana." I can count on one hand how many times I've said that word aloud. I hold still, careful not to flinch. "And it's forbidden because . . ."

"Yes?" Beaulah rotates a ring on her knuckle, and I imagine her wringing her hands around my throat.

"You have one minute left to answer the question," Dexler announces.

"Because it is destructive in nature."

"Anything else to add?"

"No, I don't know much about it. Only what's been mentioned in session a few times."

Beaulah resituates her fur on her shoulders, fingering her jewelry, apparently done with her questioning.

"And Quell, *my* question is, what is our House motto?" Grandmom asks.

"A cut above the rest!"

"Brilliant." She winks. "It's only fair to get an easy one from your own House. You've done very well," she says. "Dexler has outdone herself preparing you."

"Your dagger was inspected and found without any abnormality," Dexler says. "You've honed it beautifully. Now, if you would, show us you know how to push your magic into it. If done correctly, the blade will glow to some varying level of brightness. And then I believe we're done here." She hands me my blade, and Grandmom's grip tightens on the arm of her chair. Beaulah leans forward.

Please cooperate.

"You have three minutes, starting *now.*"

I grip the dagger firmly in both hands, forcing myself to look anywhere but at Beaulah. I latch on to a flicker of warmth, incensing it with my focus. My toushana twinges. *There is good in you, Quell.* I dig again for the warmth that I've felt so many times before, urging for it to unleash. Proper magic that I know is there, but my bones answer with an ache.

"Two minutes," Dexler says, tapping her pen on a clipboard. Beaulah clears her throat.

"Come on," I mutter. Again. I call to my proper magic, tightening my midsection, holding on fiercely to it, imagining it combusting in a cloud of fire and smoke, burning everything in its path. A gust of hot swells in me, but my magic doesn't bluster around or grow heavy. Instead, a knot of cold unspools from my side, clawing its way through me. The world blurs.

"One minute."

Grandmom stands. Her glare and Beaulah's ghost of a smirk spurs my panic, and my slick hands slip on my dagger. The gnaw of cold in me grows to a tide, rising up, then falling back, but growing closer with each lapse. I shudder, unable to feel even a single granule of warmth. The rush of cold pools, swelling until I am ice, all over. *Heat, I need heat.* I call to it, copper spreading on my tongue as a sudden fever blooms in my belly like a rose in the middle of a winter storm. I pant in anticipation. The feeling stretches, and I tighten all over, every muscle within reach, trying to grab hold of it. My throbbing side softens, my toushana being tugged back into the crevice of death it emerged from. *It's working.* Hope beads on my forehead.

I groan. The world dents at its edges, color bleeding away as my toushana plays to win. But I'm so close. *"Please . . ."*

"Time," Dexler says.

"She's almost got it, *hush.*" Grandmom nips at her knuckle.

"The rules are the rules, time is time." Headmistress Ambrose's smirk has returned, reminding Grandmom she's not the helmsman here.

"It's obvious she can't do it," Beaulah says.

"No, wait," I plead. "Just a few more—"

"I'm sorry, dear." Dexler's hand cups my shoulder. "Passage of Second

Rite, denied. Discourse for expulsion will be scheduled per the Council's availability."

Something bangs as her words drown me in a tide of chaos, a rush of hollowness that unsteadies me on my feet. The Headmistresses are up from their seats arguing with Grandmom, but it blares in my ears. Everything came down to this moment.

And I failed.

TWENTY-SEVEN

—✳—

Time must still because I can't feel anything. No air swells in my lungs, no drum beats in my chest. All I hear are Dexler's words. *Expulsion.* The Headmistresses circle Grandmom, who talks with her hands, insistent and sharp. Chatter swarms around me, a tangle of hushed conversations, but I can't make sense of it, the last several moments replaying like a song I loathe stuck on repeat. *Breathe. Say something.*

I wait for tears, but they don't come. They're wound up, a knot in my chest so tight it'd probably take a lifetime to be undone. I pull myself up off the ground. My heart ticks, and I focus on its hum, grasping for ideas about how to fix this. The places we've lived roll like a reel in my head, and calm breaks over me, muscle memory taking over. First, Mom. I have to get to her.

A tight grip grabs me by the shoulder.

"In here, *now*." Grandmom squeezes, and I wince as she urges me into a neighboring room. Once the door is closed, she faces me, her nostrils flaring in and out with the sharpness of her breath.

"I don't know what you're playing at," she seethes. "But you've made a *fool* of this House!"

"Grandmom, I—"

"*Silence!* Understand me *well*, Quell. I've crossed a line I never thought I would have to in order to fix this for you." She spits the words, and I taste their poison. "The Council has agreed to give you *one more* chance to demonstrate pushing magic into your blade. *One.* Tomorrow, at eight a.m. Which is entirely against the rules, and *all* protocol . . . You will tell *no one* about this. I will speak to Jordan myself. He is due for an earful and more!" She takes in a long slow breath, and her nails dig into my arms.

"You're hurting me."

She tightens her grip.

"You will *pass* tomorrow, or I swear you'll regret the day you ever stepped through my doors." She releases me with a push, and I stumble back into the wall as the door slams shut. Tears uncinch from their hiding place, stealing their way down my cheek. I hold my arm to my chest, smoothing the half-moons dug into my skin, wishing I knew how to shift them away.

Head buried between my knees, I weep until my chest aches. *I can practice all night, but would it help? Will my toushana ever behave?* I tug at the roots of my hair just to feel the pain somewhere else. My fingers feel for the familiar lump of my key chain. But it's not there. I clean my face and hurry through the halls to my room. Inside I find a sullen Abby shifting the neckline of a gown. *Great.* I don't know what to say to her, and it doesn't even matter. When Mom responds, I will get going tonight and explain everything. How I'm not good enough and this wasn't a good plan in the first place. How it doesn't feel safe here, not anymore.

"Hi," she says, and it's ice.

I offer a smile instead of words for fear they might crack and say too much. My fingers hover over stationery to write to Mom. *Too slow.* I grab my key chain, stuff my book into my bag and the T-shirt I had on when I came, but shame stops me at the door handle.

"I'm sorry, Abby. I'm really sorry about how things went."

She looks at me but doesn't respond, so I leave without another word and set my sights on the uncertainty ahead. *Come on, Mom. Answer.* I squeeze my key chain and head down the halls. It's probably best to exit out of the back door rather than the front. Or maybe the forest?

I head toward the foyer, where the broom closet is, but my key chain still hasn't lit up. I'll tell her all about my magic, how it sometimes works and sometimes doesn't. I'll show her all we can do. And maybe we can use some of what I've learned here to hide us? I squeeze the key chain again. *Please, squeeze back.*

I close myself in the closet, waiting, staring at the ring on my key chain. If she doesn't respond, where am I even going? If she doesn't respond, how can I leave? Mom knows more about getting around out there, evading the Order. I glare at the metal key chain. *Glow, please!* The urge to cry again pulls at me. But I exhale away the tears, white knuckling my key chain. I squeeze again and again until my hands ache. Until I'm numb to the scratch of my nails in my fist. Until the truth slaps me so hard in the face the wall has to hold me up.

I can't run.

Those days are over. Running the way I used to is done. I don't know where Mom is. I want to believe she is okay, nearby and waiting for me to finish like we'd planned, but what actual proof do I have beyond Grandmom's word? *None.* The only thing I can count on is what I *do* know. Which is that Headmistress Perl knows exactly who I am, what I look like, even *where* I am. But here, under Grandmom's nose it seems she can't get me. Mom must know that because she wants me to stay here now, too. I have to be here. Or Beaulah has to at least think I am.

My safest option is to pass this exam.

Which at the moment is impossible.

I'm reminded of a certain someone as I finger the hem of my dress. His advice has been the only that's truly helped.

I just can't trust myself around him. Because I *like* him. I sag against the broom closet door. It feels good to admit it. *I like Jordan.* My stomach does something weird below my belly button as I stew over a million reasons going to Jordan for help is the worst idea. But I can't forget the way he showed me how to fold in those enhancers, made me realize my dagger transfiguring was a good thing. The way he taught me how to dance a dance I'd never done in my entire life because we are *good* together.

"Arrggh!" Frustration burns through me, colder than my magic, and I slam my fist to the floor. I'm *out* of options.

"I need him." I hug around myself. As swiftly as he'd end my life if he knew my secret, I need his help to survive. I know what I have to do.

I leave the closet and hurry out onto the grounds toward the guard shack at the gate down the hill, when a Dragun spills out of the shack. It takes me a second to realize I recognize him. Felix.

"What are you doing here?" I ask, before I think better of it.

Felix disappears. *I could ask you the same,* his voice seems to say in my head, but I blink and only see dark fog. My heart patters faster. "I'm here to see Jordan." The strength goes out of my legs as I grow cold all over. Not my toushana, but whatever this Felix guy is doing to me. "Please. Just tell him I'm—"

"Jordan's busy. Anything I can help you with?" Cold fingers trace down the side of my face. I blink and blink, but I still can't see.

"What's going on out here?" It's Jordan.

The world returns, Felix appears in front of me in his regular form.

"Quell? Are you all right?" He casts Felix a wary glance that hardens on impact.

"I'm fine. Just cold."

He shoves Felix's shoulders hard, but his friend laughs.

"You play too much," Jordan says to Felix. "You didn't have to scare her like that."

"I wasn't scared," I lie.

"Just having some fun with the little heiress," Felix says.

"Get back inside," Jordan barks.

Felix disappears inside the guard shack, and I swear I hear muffled groans. My brows dent.

"If it's a bad time—"

"It's a fine time. I'm just surprised to see you."

My gaze falls.

"I heard," he says.

I meet his eyes, thanking him for not forcing me to say it. I'm ashamed enough as it is. I *needed* to do a good job, but I *wanted* to do a good job, too. Would making my House proud of me be such a terrible thing? Is that selfish of me?

"Headmistress was able to get the Council to give me a second chance." His edges harden as he pulls me away from the guard shack.

"She said it wasn't customary."

"I want you here as much as she does, but—there are rules, Quell."

He wants me here. "I didn't ask for a second chance."

"But you would take it," Jordan says.

"She didn't give me a choice."

His jaw clenches.

"So I have to try again. And——" *Just spit it out.* "I need you—*your* help practicing how to push magic into my blade, until I've solidly got it down."

Jordan listens without a word until a commotion in the guard shack pierces the quiet that's settled between us. He sighs. "I have to go. But I'll do it. You're going to be ready for the exam. You have my word. Meet me in the conservatory at dusk."

I stare a moment longer at the disturbance coming from inside the guard shack but can't surmise a cohesive thought because I'm tunnel focused on my exam. Jordan leaves, and I try to sit in the comfort of the promise he just gave me. He strikes me as someone who doesn't make empty promises. I'm relieved he's willing to help after I've done my best to push him away.

But what will the danger of his company cost me?

NIGHT HAS FALLEN when I arrive to the conservatory. The gardens are empty, and the only sound that can be heard is the ring of crickets and the bluster of wind. Each step sinks my shoulders as I realize out here, I'm truly alone. Except for Jordan, of course. I spent the day practicing on my own, but I've been such a ball of worry, my toushana quickly grew agitated. After my fifth attempt, I decided to rest in my room during Abby's afternoon sessions to prepare myself for the long night ahead. I don't want Jordan to go easy on me. For once, the anticipation of him being hard on me quickens my steps. Whatever it takes. I have to pass.

Jordan is nowhere in sight when I reach the glass house. I peer for a look inside, but its windows are slick with fog thanks to the humidity. I twist the handle and step inside. Instead of brick paths trimmed in ivy, my shoes crunch on sand. I run my fingers through its coarse grains. The inside of the conservatory has been changed entirely. There are no plants at all. Instead everything is open air, sandy shore, and a moon grazing the water's edge. There's also a weathered facade of a white house with small shuttered windows sitting on the shore. I suck in a breath and ease an unbelieving step forward.

"What is all this?"

Jordan's hand grazes the back of his neck. "Just trying to help."

"I don't understand. I—" I can't be standing on a beach with salty wind blowing through my hair. "Where are we?"

"We're still here. On the grounds." He walks toward me, leaving a trail of sandy footprints, and I shake my head in disbelief. Jordan blows between his fingers, and the sounds of crashing waves and squawking seagulls titillate each and every one of my senses. A lump rises in my throat, and I'm overcome with the weight of an emotion I can't put into words.

"Magic." I'm breathless when he reaches for my hand. But I hesitate to take it. Instead, I walk to the small house, running my fingers along its coarse wood, and a splinter slips into my finger. I laugh.

"You did all this . . . for me?" I face him.

He dips his chin. I inhale a deep, long breath, taking in the world around me once more. My toushana doesn't flicker. My pulse slows. The soothing ocean rhythm gently lapping the sandy shore lulls me to a calm I've never felt. *This isn't real.* But I blink, and my eyes call me a liar.

"Why?" I breathe.

"Magic is unwieldy by nature. It thrives on indecision, panic. You need control, Quell. That's what it takes to push magic into your blade. I couldn't think of a better way to remind you of why you're doing all this."

"I don't know what to say."

He stares deep into me, the etched angles of his face washed in moonlit glow. The boy behind the mask stares back at me, and I search for something to say, but no words come. He did all this. For me.

"Thank you," I manage. "Those seem like too small of words to explain all that I feel." My gaze meets the sandy ground, cheeks burning at how honest I've been.

"We should practice," he says.

We move toward a flatter area, and it's too cumbersome to walk in sand with shoes on, so I go barefoot. He maintains some distance between us, which I appreciate. The last time we were alone together I was a ball of anxiety. But here, with him like this, I don't think I've ever felt calmer.

He tosses my dagger into the sand and steps closer to me, holding up both his hands, palms facing out. "I want to feel your magic course through you. Put your palms on mine."

I hesitate.

He's asking me to touch him on purpose. I raise my hands, halting before his, like a sullen glance in a mirror, worried what will happen when our skin kisses. If it'll unsettle the monster sleeping in my bones. Or worse, if nothing will happen and I thirst more for little touches like this.

This is foolish. I swallow, refusing to look away. *I can do this.* I can stand here and do this magic and shove off the rest of whatever I feel for him.

I press my fingertips to his, savoring the warmth of his skin. His touch is always softer than I remember.

"You're trembling."

I breathe a laugh, unsure of what to say.

"Are you afraid of me?"

"No." *I'm afraid of me.* His green eyes shine under the glimmery night sky like a boundless meadow washed in sunshine. A place with endless summer where it never rains. A place I would run to if I was brave. Or foolish. *I shouldn't. I won't.*

"Now, the magic," he says.

I search for my proper magic, a burning deep inside. My pulse ticks evenly, my toushana slumbering, completely undisturbed. I find the warmth of my magic, hot and throbbing, and tighten my core.

"That's it," Jordan whispers.

He shoves my dagger into my hands. "Now move it into the blade."

I urge the burning to rip through my hands. It shoots through me, and the flat on my dagger pulses with light. "I did it!"

Jordan smiles, and rays light up the darkest parts of my soul. I fight the urge to throw my arms around his neck and scream. I really did it. With control. My toushana didn't have anything to stoke because I was calm.

He settles on the sand beside me and nudges me with his shoulder. "Good job, protégé."

I nudge him back. "Why, thank you, mentor."

He reaches for his shoes, and I grab his wrist.

"Stay, please."

"Sounds like you want to amend our starting over terms again, then?" He plucks a bag of candies from his bag.

"Yes, I do."

He pops a green candy in his mouth.

I sit up taller. "The amended terms are *friends*." I offer him a hand. Instead of shaking my hand, he pours a few candies into it after removing all the green ones.

"Have you tried a purple Skittle? Much better."

"Sacrilege." He pulls at my fist of candy, and I tighten my grip on them. "Give me my candies back. You're not worthy."

I toss them down in one mouthful, laughing.

I pick up the dagger. "Let's do it again."

He nods, and I flex my fingers, letting my magic cool down before starting over. We go again and again until the night yawns and I ache all over, muscles tight. We rest, settling on the sand, the earth cold to my legs.

"You did well," he says.

"Thanks for not telling me to go take a hike."

"I wanted to help in a way that would actually reach you. We think so differently."

I dig my toes in the sand. "How long until the magic wears off?"

"Another few hours."

"Is it silly that I kind of want to stay here?"

"We can stay as long as you like. No one will disturb us."

"Will you be there tomorrow?"

"As long as my being there is a help to you."

"I mean, I wouldn't mind you there . . ." I look away to keep from smiling. "If you happen to be free."

He smiles without hiding it. "I think I can arrange to be free."

"Well, good. I have another amendment, actually."

"An amendment to the amendment?"

"Yes." I put on my serious face. He smiles tightly, undeniably that time, and I guffaw, which unspools something inside of me. I fold my legs under me. "*Really* good friends. Those are my terms, take it or leave it." I offer him a hand.

"You drive a hard bargain, Miss Marionne." He pops a green candy in his mouth. "But I suppose you have yourself a deal."

TWENTY-EIGHT

———✳———

The door to the Headmistresses' suite shuts, and the walls seem to close in around me. I gulp down the lump forming in my throat. Each Headmistress sits around Grandmom's fire, their eyes glued to my every step. Jordan escorts me, tugging me forward, but my feet stick to the ground.

"You've done this practically a thousand times, you have nothing to worry about," he says, but I hardly hear him.

"Over here, near the window, dear." Grandmom beckons for me.

"She attempts to cheat with kor," Beaulah retorts.

"As if we need to *cheat*," Grandmom spits.

"Isn't that what this is? Giving her more time than the others."

"I *told* you she was ill."

"So we make an exception?" Isla Ambrose says, countenance deadened with contempt.

"Isn't that what we do, when our own blood is on the line?" Grandmom's steel glare meets Isla's gaze, then Beaulah's. Headmistress Ambrose sits back in her chair.

"You're ready, I presume?" Grandmom approaches, her sequined dress dangling to the floor.

I nod, and she glances at Jordan, a statue on the wall.

"The Council doesn't look happy about this," I say.

"Never mind them. I've kept worse secrets of theirs." Her nose rises. "Let's knock their socks off, show them an heir worthy of the title has indeed returned."

Heir. There is that word again.

She pats my cheek before crossing the room to her judge's seat, and I picture last night, my pushing magic into my blade over and over again.

Beaulah rises. "I'll be proctoring today, just to be sure everything's in order."

"For inspection." Jordan hands Headmistress Perl my blade and for a moment I don't breathe. She twists it and makes it glow, then measures it at every angle. Headmistress Oralia crosses her legs and shields a yawn.

"No abnormalities found," Beaulah Perl says over her shoulder to Isla, who scribbles down a note in a record book. She hands me my dagger, handle first.

"Thank you," I say, but she doesn't let go. I tug harder but she holds the dagger so tight I expect to see blood. Her lip flinches and cold flutters through me. I swallow.

"If you'll let go, I'd be happy to demonstrate that I'm quite capable of pushing magic into my blade." My toushana quiets like a melted snow-flake. I almost regret my tone, its lilt of arrogance, until Beaulah's mouth twists at the challenge.

"Is that so?"

"Quite so." I curtsy to soften the sting.

"I guess we'll see then, won't we?" She shuffles her fur around her shoulders.

Jordan watches, his knuckles grating against his jawline.

"Whenever you're ready."

I can do this. I did the magic last night. He helped with posture and form. But *I* did it. *Me.*

My belly burns with warmth and I don't even have to call on my proper magic. It is there, ready and willing. I grip the blade tightly and order magic into my hands. Heat curls through me, stretching itself awake. I bite down, holding still, urging the temp to rev up more. Hotter until my skin feels like fire. Until I blink and expect to see flames. An inferno answers, coursing up through my core, shoving through my arms and into my hands.

"Now *into* the blade," I command, and I've never felt more sure of anything in my entire life. Searing magic pools in my fingertips like tiny needles pushing against my skin. Gentle at first, then more insistent until the sharp pricks break through.

The leather handle of the blade throbs bright and red. Magic churning through me tugs like a chain. There's no me or it anymore. I *am* the blade. Magic erupts from the dagger tip in an explosion of light. I jump at the suddenness, and blood spreads on my tongue. But it tastes like freedom. The room beams as if the sun itself is between my fingers.

A swarm of gasps and thundering applause surround me as I call my magic back into me and the brightness retreats, siphoning back into the blade. Grandmom gapes. Jordan and all the Headmistresses stand.

"Well?" Grandmom shakes off her shock and addresses the Council. Beaulah gestures in agreement.

"Passage of Second Rite, granted."

A sash is slung over my head, and creases hug Grandmom's eyes. "Get Popper from the library this minute." She rings for her maid, then rolls her wrist doing the House gesture, nudging me to do it with her. "Oh! And tell Mrs. Cuthers to let the servers know to move forward with the reception."

I did it? I really did it!

Second Rite down, one to go.

Tears sting my eyes, my pulse still racing, not in panic but in unbridled joy. In minutes refreshment is brought in on platters.

"I don't understand, I thought you didn't want anyone to know I got a redo," I say to Grandmom.

"You sorely underestimate my cunning, dear granddaughter. After the exam yesterday, everyone wanted to know how you'd done. Where you were. And I told them you did fine but needed to rest. The celebration would be tomorrow morning." She winks.

I shake my head. "But how did you know I'd pass?"

"Because getting kicked out of your new home, with all this at your fingertips, isn't something you were going to risk."

My mouth opens, then snaps closed.

"Now go on and grab some refreshment. Popper will be up in a minute."

I almost ask who that is, when I spot Jordan perched against the fireplace mantel, a pride tilting his lips that he couldn't wipe away if he tried. His eyes say more than his words ever have. I grin, rushing over to him, and his hands hook around my waist. He lifts me into a squeezing hug, and for a moment everyone and everything else disappears. Gold glints in his eyes and his mouth curves in delight.

He sets me down, clearing his throat. But the tingle of his touch still dances on my skin.

"Sorry," he says.

"Quell, he's actually here now." Grandmom pulls at my arm. "If you'll excuse me, Jordan, my granddaughter is needed for pictures."

"Of course," he says, but I don't look away from him until the curtain of a crowd closes between us.

Grandmom parades me in front of the room, her grip tight on my arm as more and more file in, asking me if I'm feeling better, offering their congratulations.

"Smile now." She points toward one camera, then another. "A little more teeth."

I do.

"Too much." Her hand presses my back. "And watch your posture."

"What's all this for?" I manage to ask after the millionth camera flash in my face.

"When an heir passes Second Rite, news goes out immediately."

"It'll be on Page Six along with our internal post, *Debs Daily*." Popper hands me a card. *Rudy Popper, Audior, Debs Daily.* "Don't hesitate to reach out."

"Thanks for rescheduling on such short notice, Popper."

"Happy to." He tugs at his royal blue bow tie. "The Order could use some good news with all the rumors about the Sphere going around." He flips open a notepad and holds his fingers in the air mid-snap. "And how do I spell Quell?"

"Q-U-E-L-L." His fingers are pressed tightly together, as his magic transfigures the sounds to written letters on his paper. "But it's short for Raquell. Use her full name. So, R-A—"

"My name's Quell. Not Raquell."

Popper opens his fingers, which stops the writing in his journal.

Grandmom pinches me. "It's as I've said. She was named after my mother, Raquell Janae."

I was?

"Got it." He flips his pad closed. "That name, young lady, will be at the top of every exclusive social event invite list before you can blink. You've made this House quite proud." He turns back to Grandmom. "And the dates are set for Cotillion, I saw. I'm showing about a month out."

She nods. I pinch myself on accident from the excitement.

"Can we get a quote for the piece?" Popper's notebook is back open as he stares expectantly.

Grandmom's eyes meet mine, and they are a sea of many things, desperation, fear, hope, and, somewhere underneath all of that, joy. This is a moment for which she's hungered for so long. Her enthusiasm digs deeper into my arm.

"Quell, I—" she starts.

"I got it." I set my hand on hers.

She nods, her teeth pulling at her lip with worry. As if everything she's worked for amounts to this moment.

"I'm overcome with so many feelings. If I had to sum them up, I'd say I'm eager to make this Season unforgettable for myself, my House, but especially for Headmistress, my dear grandmother, who has worked tirelessly to prepare me for this day."

Grandmom's lips part and she digs in her bag suddenly, flicking away something at her eye. If I've embarrassed this House before, I've certainly made up for it now. Popper's magic jots that down, and he wishes me luck before departing.

Shelby hovers in the doorway. She waves before tossing back a whole flute of champagne.

Grandmom clears her throat. "You have a whole host of people to talk to, but let's meet this afternoon. I have something for you."

"All right. I'll see you then."

Grandmom departs, bidding the other Council members who haven't left goodbye just as Dexler hugs me and hands me a wrapped box. *"Fratis fortunam."*

"A fortuna. Thank you, you shouldn't have."

"It's tradition. Open it whenever. No rush." Dexler departs, and I spot a familiar diadem atop long dark hair and a kind face.

"Abby—"

"Quell—"

We say at the same time.

"This is for you, congratulations." She hands me a small box similar to Dexler's.

"Thanks, Abby. And I'm sorry." The apology expels like a much-needed release. "I should have stayed. A friend would have stayed."

"When you left, it honestly felt like you didn't care that it was a moment about *me*. But when I thought about what it must have been like for you . . ." She sighs and I grab her hand. "What I'm trying to say is, I noticed you don't ever talk about your mom or your life before here. But I can tell you miss her. Thinking back on it that day, it was written all over your face how uncomfortable you were. I feel bad that I didn't think of that. I'm sorry."

"I've never done this before, so I'm sorry, too. If I was insensitive or selfish. I felt bad leaving, really. It just was a lot at once."

She squeezes my hand back. "Fortunately, perfection isn't on the list of requirements for being my friend."

I snort. "Friends?"

"Friends." She slings an arm around my shoulder.

A FIRE BURNS in Grandmom's sitting room, and evening glows outside the windows as a gentleman with sooty fingers hoists a large frame onto her wall. I've settled in a chair beside it when her bedroom doors open.

"Oh Jerry, it's *brilliant*," she says, gliding in. "Quell, Jerry is our senior cartographer."

"Class of '79, simple Shifter." He tips his hat. "Pleasure is all mine."

"Pleased to meet you, sir."

"I've just had the French Quarter redone," she says, indicating the frame. "What do you think?"

I take a closer look and realize it is a map of central New Orleans, but there are streets where structures should be and entrances on the wrong sides of buildings. The lines are drawn with the utmost precision and each place is scaled precisely like the building beside it. My fingers trail the outline of a round structure at the back of what should be the French Market and I tense, realizing I know that place. That's where I saw those Draguns kill that man when the walls changed. Grandmom watches me as if I should say something.

"It's, uh, very impressive."

"Isn't it? Jerry, see my secretary, she'll make sure you're all squared away. And let's do the others in the hall, why don't we? I really like the gold fillet."

"Very good, ma'am." Jerry departs, and Grandmom turns to me. "Now, to you!"

I warm all over.

"*You* will be the talk of the entire Season!" Her words are spun sugar. She hands me a silver wrapped gift box. "Just a little something. You can open it later."

"Thank you. I was proud to do a good job for the House." I'd be lying if I said doing a good job, seeing my Housemates shouting in revelry, Jordan's smile, Grandmom's pride creased around her eyes meant nothing. This place has become a part of me in more ways than I may have fully acknowledged. I'm not sure about staying here, being her heir, but I'd like to reflect my House well.

"Your riband is all a mess. Here, let me." Grandmom resituates my sash around me, which I hadn't even taken a moment to notice.

"Over the right shoulder, to the left hip. And you wear the House sigil here, on the heart. You're going to be circulating in society now; more people than ever will be watching. Think about what conclusions you want them to draw about you, your House."

I nod, dusting off my clothes and checking myself in the mirror. I can't risk a single tilted stare, not just from Grandmom, from *anyone*, getting in the way of Third Rite. If they see through my veneer, they'll begin to question my past. Cotillion is in *four weeks*. I tidy my posture and check myself again, this time in the full-length mirror.

"You look perfect, dear."

"Good."

"Let's take a walk in the rose garden. Sunset is simply exquisite from there."

It takes until we're all the way downstairs and outside before I get the courage to ask, "Is that really my name?" I keep my head straight ahead at the aisles of roses, red, yellow, peach, and . . . black? *How curious.*

"Your mother really didn't tell you much, did she?"

I'm not sure what to say to that. I'm not going to speak poorly of Mom, so I just keep my mouth shut. I run my fingers across the sigil embroidered on my riband, a gold fleur-de-lis wreathed in shimmery stones.

"I apologize for springing it on you right then. I just wanted to ensure things are done properly."

She stops at a coil of thorny roses and plucks a black one, lifting it to her nose. "I need to apologize for something else. I behaved poorly with you after you didn't pass the exam the first time. Quell, you matter a great deal to me. I'd never want you to feel any different."

That doesn't excuse how threatening and downright terrifying she was. It reminded me of Mom some of those times we were on the run. Desperation does scary things to a person. She's opened the conversation to honesty. It's time I share my own.

"I wanted to tell you." I pull at the hem of my dress. "You've mentioned my being your heir, and I'm not sure I'm cut out for it."

"I thought you might feel that way." She hands me the rose. "Smell."

I take it, careful of its thorns, and press it to my nose but don't smell anything. My brows crease as I sniff again.

"It smells like . . . nothing."

"A rose is still, and always will be, a rose." She smiles. "That's probably too old of a song for you."

It's then I notice that most of Grandmom's garden has been taken over by the black roses. "You have so many of them, and they don't even smell pleasant."

"It didn't start that way." She rolls the stem of another between her fingers. "Their stems are twice as thick as those of other roses." She strokes its petals. "They bloom twice as long. And they're fiercely strong, fighters, taking over their weaker counterparts." She gestures at the garden. "It lacks a sweet scent but makes up for it in every other way. It's still a rose. So when you tell me you're not cut out for this, I understand it's all very new to you. But you're more than cut out for it. You were born for it. You're still a Marionne. You have more than proved it."

I shift on my feet and hand her back the rose.

"What exactly is it you intend to do otherwise?"

I have no idea. I think back on my lessons in Dexler's and which type of magic I felt better at. "I'm pretty good at Shifting."

"A Shifter." She titters. "You don't get it, do you?" She pulls another several roses, gathering them together in a bunch, and we keep walking. "Nothing is the same for you."

"I'd like it to be." *She would have me be an outcast here, too.*

"You think that. But do you know what being my heir offers you?"

A home. Security. A place where I'd never have to run again. A history. A lineage. But Mom would never come here. And I'm not even sure Grandmom would want her to.

"Just as I thought," Grandmom says. "You don't really know. You will select Cultivator as your specialty just like I did and every Headmistress of House Marionne before me. Understand? Augmenting magic in others *will* be your specialty."

"You're not listening to me. I'm trying to say—"

"I hear you perfectly well, but you are not hearing me." She gestures for us to make our way back to the garden gate. "I can show you better than I can tell you. Come along." Grandmom takes me back inside, upstairs, and, for the first time, inside her bedroom. I've never seen anything more exquisite.

A bed buried in silky linens is framed by a tall, molded headboard with the House sigil carved into the wood. On either side of her bed are sweeping views of the estate, an ornate writing desk, and a velvet sitting area. Rows upon rows of books frame the sitting area. She runs her finger along the train of spines and plucks a honey-colored one.

"Here." She holds it in front of me, and I flip through pages upon pages of Grandmom in pictures with a flock of debs at her side in tuxedos, regal gowns, and riband sashes. "And here."

I turn the page, and in each Grandmom looks younger and younger. Could Mom be pictured in some of these? I flip until I reach the end, but Grandmom has another few waiting. I don't know how much time passes, but eventually I'm in a chair with a stack of books I've looked through at my feet when Cuthers taps the door.

"Ma'am, Miss Shelby Duncan is waiting to see you."

Grandmom exhales sharply. "What does she need? I'm with my grand-daughter."

"Something about an invitation she was expecting to come in. The Tidwell, perhaps?"

Grandmom waves Mrs. Cuthers away. I flip faster for some glimpse of Mom at Chateau Soleil.

"For what it's worth, it's time I start figuring out a replacement," she says, tugging at the lace of her blouse.

I meet her eyes. "Are you okay?"

She strokes my hands. "Things catch up with you after a while, that's all. Tell me, what do *you* want, Quell?"

To be free of this curse. To make sure Mom is okay. A beach, salty air, sand. "I'd like to travel."

She pulls a trio of leather-bound books. Inside, Grandmom's on a sleek boat of some sort surrounded by blue water that sparkles brighter than a dream. "Where is this?"

"That one must have been on our summer trip one year. We've traveled so much over the years, I don't remember." She flips the picture on the back. "Yes, I was traveling to see one of my débutantes off for her excavating internship. Now she mines enhancers in the caves of Aronya, among other places. And this one." She points to a picture of herself and the other Headmistresses, dressed to the nines with ribands around them in their House colors at some sort of ceremony. "That's the Council and I being officiated as the leaders of the Order."

"You were all made Headmistresses at the same time?" Somehow, I hadn't imagined it that way.

"When the Upper Cabinet were killed in that terrible natural disaster, there was really no other choice." She strokes her pearls. "There were only us four in charge of the Houses and the Dragunhead left. Ruling by Council seemed the easiest solution."

"The Dragunhead. I've heard about them but never met them."

"And you wouldn't. You're not a Dragun."

I stare at the picture again. She and Beaulah are on opposite ends. But Grandmom looks rather chummy with the others. I flip and lose myself once again in pictures from places, a life my mother lived, at least adjacently, that looks like a fairy tale.

"Did your mother tell you we celebrated her sixteenth birthday in the South of France? She's obsessed with the beach. She liked to stay up late and listen to the sound of—"

"The tide coming in."

"So she's told you."

No, she didn't. Only that one day she'd take me to the beach. That's when our jar of savings was born. That's when we penned our plan for the future. Mom only gave me a peep through a crack. Her reasons for that feel less sufficient each time I think of it. There's no harm in me knowing *something* about where I come from.

"We have thirteen homes, Quell. All of which you would inherit. Two in France, one in London, a penthouse in New York, should I go on?"

I can't even fathom—

"Turning out Season after Season of débutants," she goes on, apparently convinced she's winning me over. "While dealing with the politics of the Council is nothing short of an all-star juggling act, I'd endeavor to teach it to you to the best of my ability."

The places she's traveled, the glitz, the glamour. Passing that exam in there today was nerve-wracking. But it also felt like being a part of something big. *A family.* The Order has given me more than just a place to lay my head. But I've been solely focused on surviving.

"Your schedule's already been set up with core classes for Cultivators."

"So *that's* why my schedule changed."

She pats my hands. "So Cultivator it is? You have to formally sign off on it. It goes in the Book of Names."

I wish I had time to think about a decision this big. She wouldn't understand that, so for now I say what she wants to hear instead.

"Cultivator, it is."

"That's my girl. Make sure Jordan gets the paperwork turned in. Everything you need to prepare for Third Rite will be in your room by evening. Stay on top of your mail as well; all rejected invitations should be refused with a prompt, tasteful note and *convincing* excuse." She hands me a fresh pack of newly minted stationery. My name glitters in gold at the top, between two fleurs. "We wouldn't want to snub anyone. Maintaining relationships is paramount."

"Thank you."

"And remember, Quell, it's not your fault."

"I'm sorry?"

"You weren't raised in this House or around the heirs of the other Houses, so of course you have no idea what's expected of someone in your station. I'm hard on you sometimes because I forget that. But I don't blame you. That's on your mother's shoulders."

I flinch at the second dig at Mom. I hadn't thought about the other House's heirs, what they must be like. What it would have been like being raised around them. How helpful knowing that could be as I try to hide myself in this world. I wouldn't be such an obvious disaster if I knew what being a Headmistress's heir *looked* like. Grandmom is more right than she knows.

"How about we invite the heirs here for an evening of fun? I can host it and consult with Dexler and Plume on all the details so it's done just perfectly."

Grandmom sits taller. "*Now* you sound like my granddaughter."

PART FOUR

TWENTY-NINE

YAGRIN

Red hopped off the porch of her parents' farmhouse and started toward Yagrin. Her wide brim hat shielded most of her face, but he couldn't mistake those worn overalls and that bright smile even so far away. Her fingertips skimmed the tops of billowing tall grass as she twirled through the field, making her way to him. The low sun glinted in her auburn hair, and he dug a nail into his palm to be sure he wasn't dreaming.

Her toes were dusty and unpainted. She was barefoot. He shook his head, a grin tugging at his lips. He started toward her, but the phone in his pocket vibrated, tugging at him like a leash.

He halted.

His pulse picked up at the name on the screen.

"Hello?"

"Did you see the announcement in Page Six?"

Sweat broke out on his neck. *He had.* "Mother, how are—"

"What updates do you have on Quell?"

"You said find her, bring her to—"

"I know what I said! What have you accomplished?"

He tensed at her raised tone. "I found her at the Tavern. But it was too crowded to make a move."

"You wouldn't hide anything from me, would you, Yagrin?"

The phone slipped in his slick hands. "No, ma'am." The lie was bitter, an acquired taste.

"And dare I ask, what's the status of your first target? It's been *weeks*."
Pink beanie. "Done."

"Not from where I'm standing. I haven't seen proof."

"I have it with me."

"It's incomplete, Yagrin."

He swallowed. "Yes, ma'am." Would she make him come to her right
now? He bit down. He hated this, so much.

"And where are you now, pray tell?"

Red finally made it to him and curled under his arm, her fingers playing on his face, stroking the little hair he'd managed to grow there.

"I am . . ." He cupped her fingers, kissed them and pressed a finger to
his mouth. She frowned. He put some distance between them.

"It doesn't matter," Mother said. "I expect both assignments done and
soon. Quell's done before she reaches Third Rite. I don't care how hard
she is to get to at that House. Am I understood?"

Red picked flowers and made funny faces at him. He bit back a smile.
"Yes."

"Do I amuse you, Yagrin?"

"No, ma'am. I'm a bit distracted."

"Then *un*distract yourself!"

He turned his back and waved Red away firmly.

"There's one other matter. The Tidwell Ball is coming up. I have some
goods being moved, and I want my people there to oversee it. I'll send
the details securely."

"Got it."

"And Yagrin?"

"Yes, Mother?"

"You're getting sloppy, people are starting to notice."

The line went dead.

His chest squeezed.

"I thought I told you we don't do phones out here." Red pulled his
Order-issued phone from his fingers and tossed it in the dirt. He stroked
her face, then sighed.

"I have to go."

"You just got here yesterday. You said you'd stay the whole week, while my parents are gone. *Yags?*"

"Work."

"Your *work*," she grumbled. "I hate your work. Have I ever told you that?"

He'd never told her a thing about his work, only that he was employed by a small family-owned business and because of that, when they needed him, he had to go. He kept Red far away from the truth, for her own safety. Unmarked weren't welcomed in his world.

"I'm sorry. I have to go take care of a thing and then get all ready for a ball coming up."

"A ball? That sounds fancy." Her teeth tugged at her bottom lip and he kissed her again. Fancy on the surface, maybe. His work would happen in the shadows while the others danced and dined.

"Take me with you."

"I can't."

"You can't or you don't want to?"

"*I can't.*"

"Sometimes I feel like I don't really know you." She looked away, and a flicker of something he'd never seen before gleamed in her eyes. As if her frustration could boil over and turn her into someone else.

"Don't say that." He squeezed her hand. "You know more of me than anyone."

"Then I know you want me on your arm, wherever you're going."

She wasn't wrong. His father had promised Headmistress would help set him up with someone from a "good family" after Yagrin finished his early Dragun years. To further the family lineage. But Yagrin hadn't figured out how to break it to them that *that* was where he drew the line. He could do their Order errands, be the monster that they wanted. But in every other way, he was Red's. For as long as she would have him.

"Take me to the ball, Yagrin."

He hated the way her forehead wrinkled when she was disappointed.

The way her lips pursed out. But he couldn't. It wasn't safe. For now these visits to her farm, moments of escape, were all he'd been able to settle for in the last several months. He wanted more for them. But when had what he wanted ever truly mattered?

"You're ashamed of me," she said, sticking out her lip coyly. "Agree, and I'll put you on your ass." She roped her arm behind his back and pulled him into a headlock.

He wriggled from her hold and threw her over his shoulder. She beat on his back, unwinding the knot he was with her laughter. She was the dusky glow of sunset, a cozy blanket by a fire. Out here in the middle of nowhere he was more at home than he'd ever felt at Hartsboro.

She pulled at his pockets and out came a knitted beanie. He groaned. He shouldn't have brought the hat with him. She wouldn't be insecure about where he'd gotten it. She wasn't like that. Red knew who she was. And never settled. Still, it was weird, carrying around a dead girl's hat in his pocket. He needed to turn it in already.

"Should I even ask?"

He stuffed it back in his pocket.

"Take me! So we can make fun of all the rich, stuffy people. Otherwise, you'll go but not have any fun."

He set her down on her tiptoes and she laced her arm around his. They walked in silence until the sun was an ember on the horizon. He loved that about her. How she gave him time to think. He knew what he wanted to do: make her happy. But it was a risk.

"Are you scared of these people?" She grabbed his jaw and made him look her square in the eyes. Insistence glinted in her sandy brown eyes, where he imagined he saw his true reflection.

"We'll need to get you a dress."

THIRTY

A whole day rushed by since passing Second Rite, and I spent it in session after session. Things are only getting busier. Moonlight glints on the polished floors by the time I'm two turns from my door, where I spot Jordan with an armful of long, rolled papers and envelopes.

"Here to congratulate me again one-on-one?" I haven't seen him since the reception yesterday.

He glances over his shoulder as we step inside my room and find Abby's bed is tidy. She's still out, apparently.

"I don't get why you're allowed in the Belles Wing after curfew."

"I'm technically not an inductee." An uproar of chatter in the hall spins him on his heels, and he closes my door quickly.

I side-eye him. "What was so important you'd break a *rule?*" I tease.

He unloads all but one of the bushel of posters in his arms, setting them on my bed. Then hands me a stack of envelopes, letter after letter with my name on it.

"What is all this?" I flip, tearing a few open. "Invitations? To social events." One is from the Tidwell Committee. "*Oh*, I wonder if I can give this one to Abby. She was hoping to go to that one."

He takes the envelope, opening it. "That's not how this works." He reads the invite aloud. I and a guest are invited. I groan and plop down on the bed.

"If one more person thinks of something *else* I have to do to induct in this Order I'm going to scream."

"That is not how most respond to an invite to the Tidwell, you know?"

I take the invite and set it aside with the others, turning my attention to the long, rolled scroll. "And what is this?"

He stretches it out across my desk, and it's filled with petite renderings of streets and buildings.

Tiny letters at the bottom indicate that it's a map of New York City. Similar to the one Grandmom had the cartographer redo; landmarks, buildings, and streets are all twisted and intersecting. "Does Manhattan really have streets *underneath* buildings?" I peer closer.

"These . . ." He taps four spots on the map labeled *tablinum*, including a block of buildings that appear to have an ice-skating rink between them. " . . . are places members can meet securely in the city." He stretches another map, this one of Los Angeles. "It's the city, but with our world grafted underneath."

"Do I have to memorize all this?"

"Yes." He unrolls more maps. "You have to know where's safe when you travel. You won't be hidden behind the walls of this estate forever."

I search his eyes for knowing.

"And here I thought you came to my room to celebrate with me," I mutter. I let the map curl in on itself. "It's been a *long* few days. Could we, just for tonight, *not* talk about exams or daggers or any of that stuff? Be really good friends hanging out instead of mentor and mentee?"

"We can." His lips thin.

"Oh, come on, today was a victory for you as a mentor, too."

"I suppose," he says, agreeing, but with hollow enthusiasm. "Well, let's get going, then." He reaches for the doorknob.

"I can't go like this!"

I grab a pair of jeans out of my closet and a shirt with satin buttons down the back. "I have to change."

"Right, I'll wait outsi—"

Laughter flits outside the door, whoever's in the hall very much still there.

"Just turn around."

He turns, and I wrestle with my unruly dress straps, trying to slip out of my clothes. Jordan shifts on his feet. "I've been thinking about what you said." He pulls at his pocket. "About my being an orphan."

I still.

"There's some truth to that. It got me pondering maybe home is not a place you can touch and feel but a . . . perspective that defines you. A way of seeing the world. Robert Jordan warred with it when he arrived in Spain."

I've lived in more places than I can recall. But for some reason here at Grandmom's—where I have to keep so many secrets from everyone— *feels* more like home than I've felt anywhere. And I'm not sure that it's the walls and sparkly chandeliers. The having a place to sleep and being safe from Beaulah. It's something else.

"Do you know what I mean?" he asks.

"I do. More than you know." My stubborn strap finally gives, and my dress slips from my fingers, puddling at my feet on the floor. The space between us shifts, and for the first time it's like we are the same song.

He exhales, his shoulders slanting down.

"Hemingway. You consider that reading?" I ask, shoving a leg into my jeans.

"And you say I'm the snob," he says, mirth between his words.

"All book people are snobs in our own way."

He chortles. "Actually, I'm not a huge fan. My parents never liked my take on some of the classics."

"My mother was so consumed with"—*surviving*—"other things, she never even talked to me about school. It was always just, 'don't get in trouble.'" I stand there, staring, hugging around my bare skin, realizing I've never been this open with anyone.

His chin tugs over his shoulder as he waits for me to say more.

"I'm still—"

"Sorry."

"Almost done. No peeking."

"I would never." He rolls his shoulders. "Unless . . . you want me to?"

My skin flushes as I shimmy into my pants and zip them up. I unbutton as few buttons as I can and toss my shirt over my head. "Ready."

"You look really nice," he says, when he finally turns around.

I twist my shirt around my finger as his gaze traces me. Heat flares up my neck when I pull myself to my senses and reach for the door. But he holds it shut and closes the distance between us.

"Until the coast is clear." He leans against the door, listening, his body brushing against mine. He indicates my bare shoulder, where my shirt is slipping from the top few buttons being undone.

"Oh."

"May I?"

I pull my hair over my shoulder and put my back to him. His touch grazes my skin, every spot kindling a warmth inside me that lures like a cozy fire.

"You really should reconsider some of those invitations," he says, feeling for the next button on my shirt.

"I have no desire to go to any ball besides my Cotillion."

His fingers trail down my back and it makes me want to lean in closer to his touch. I close my eyes, but all I can think about is how gentle and careful his touch is. How I could skip this celebration altogether and instead lie here with him, talking about books all night. I clear my throat. "Are you almost done?"

"Two more. And that's a shame," he says. "It's good to get a taste of society before you're thrust into it. See what it's like rubbing elbows with Unmarkeds as if you're not hiding anything at all."

"I'm sure I can hide things just fine, thanks."

"Suit yourself." His breath warms my neck as he does the last couple of buttons. Bumps race across my skin. "I'll be at several of them. It's expected of me, and I do what's expected of me." He finishes with my shirt, and I turn to face him, my foot stumbling over his. I fall against him and he catches me, holding me for a moment against his hard chest. His expression is stoic, but his breath rises and falls quickly.

"Sometimes I think about doing what I want instead of what's expected of me."

There is no space, not a single breath, between us.

"And what do you want, Miss Marionne?"

I listen for footsteps, but the hall is dead silent. Fearing I've been too honest, I push off him gently and grab the doorknob. "Let's get going."

THE NIGHT GUSTS with a chill, and Jordan and I walk close as we round on the Tavern.

"You really couldn't think of anything else you'd like to do?" he asks.

"Hey, you had your chance to weigh in."

Our arms graze as we walk. I hold mine as still as I can, expecting him to put some distance between us before it swings past me again. But he doesn't. So neither do I.

"I have to officially declare my specialty."

"I assume you've chosen Cultivator."

He and Grandmom, I swear. "Am I that predictable?"

"It makes sense for you." His fingers twitch, reaching in my direction as they dangle between us.

"What if I don't want to make sense?"

His brows kiss, my humor completely lost on him.

"I'm still thinking about it, if you must know. And I wanted to know more about your magic. I'm still intrigued." *Why your magic looks so much like toushana . . .*

He moves away ever so slightly but stays silent.

"When you pushed magic into your dagger, was it blindingly bright like that?"

"You're asking if my magic is as strong as yours?"

"No, not exactly."

He straightens. "Then what is it you want to know?"

We walk a few more paces in silence before Jordan stops steps from the Tavern. He faces me and his whole posture oozes his discomfort.

"I'm sorry if I've asked too much."

"No." He takes my hand, his fingers playing on my palm, and a hummingbird takes flight in my chest. "My blade did shine bright like that." He traces circles on my wrist. "But my magic is far stronger than anything you've ever felt."

"How do you know?" I ask, stoking a flame I might be dancing too close to.

"Because." He expression softens. He sighs. "The Dragun work I do requires I summon dark magic."

I snatch my hand away. *His magic didn't just look like mine. It's the same as mine?*

"I shouldn't have said anything. I don't want you to look at me like that." He rakes a hand through his hair.

"I'm surprised. That's all."

His teeth pull at his lip as if there's more he could say. I take his hand this time, determined to find out more. *How do Draguns control it?*

"Isn't that dangerous? Toushana?" I whisper.

"Toushana is mature dark magic that lives inside a person. It flows through them like other magic. What we do is a bit different, the essence of toushana, but not the whole. The aroma of it, a whiff. Like using the steam from a pot instead of the water itself. We summon it from outside of ourselves, use it, and then chase it off. It doesn't stay with us. Which requires a fair bit of . . . managing. So yes. It's quite dangerous." He shrugs uncomfortably as I consider pushing harder and him shutting down.

"It's getting cold out here," I say. "We should go inside."

He tosses his coat over my shoulders before kicking his heel on the cobblestones. The ground opens, and we descend the stairs into the Tavern.

"Ma-Ri-Onne! Ma-Ri-Onne!" The bar is full of familiar faces and several new ones greeting me in a rush of revelry. Casey and crew shout over the crowd, drinks in hand. I spot a few other faces among the bustling energy shoving me to and fro.

"I heard that your exam was *wild*." It's Mynick, Abby's beau. "This one's on me."

I toss back the kiziloxer and offer Jordan half of it, but he turns up his nose.

"Come on, we're here to have fun." We move through the crowd, and I'm jostled by the revelry. Conversations pull at me from every direction, some in admiration, others in curiosity. I smile and the urge to look at my shoes is distant and unfamiliar. The attention doesn't grate like I expect it to, and greeting people doesn't curl like bile in my throat as it used to.

"Could I have a picture?" A rosy-cheeked Electus with a wooden circlet on her head poses in front of me before I can respond.

"Thanks!" She rushes off, tittering to her friends about me being "*so nice.*"

"I'll be over there," Jordan says, and just like that, he's drifting through a parting crowd before I can stop him. I sip my drink and wade through the swell of people bubbled around me, taking in their whispers behind hands, their overeager smiles. I loosen the coat around myself and inhale a sharp breath. *Maybe this wasn't the place to let loose.*

"The *heir* has arrived," a bleary-eyed Shelby says. "What's up, girl? Haven't seen you in a while."

Someone with Shelby tugs at her, but she shrugs them off. Shelby pulls at a blond tendril and pops out a hip, her hand placed firmly on it.

"What do you mean?"

The crowd tightens around us.

"I've just been busy. It was . . . harder than I thought, getting past Second Rite."

"Oh, is that right?" She turns to the crowd. "The heir isn't immortal, ladies and gentlemen. If you poke her, she bleeds!"

Her words lasso my insecurity and pull it down, down like an anchor, my gaze falling with it.

"Oh gosh, girl. I'm kidding!" She shakes my shoulders. "I'm just giving you a hard time. Rikken, another round to celebrate! Seriously, I'm kidding. I stopped by to congratulate you at your reception the other morning, but you looked busy."

I take a sip of my kizi, and a hand touches my hip.

"If you'll excuse us," Jordan says to Shelby. "Dance with me?" He offers me his hand, and I take it. He pulls me away from the prying crowd, from a drunk Shelby, to the dance floor.

"Thank you."

"Rethinking your choice of celebration yet?"

"Shut up," I tease, and that gets me a smile.

Ballroom dancing isn't the only kind of moving Jordan can do, apparently. We move in that way our bodies instinctively know how to. Pressed close. People stare, but I ignore them, playing the part, grafting myself into the Marionne-sized shoes I'm supposed to fill as perfectly as I can. Music pumps through the bar, and I feel it pulsing through my body. I move with it, ignoring the stares, trying to forget what Jordan just admitted to me about Dragun work. The shouts drown out after a while. The last weeks of my life play like a reel in my head, but I let myself go, imagining myself free of all of it.

"I can practically hear your thoughts spinning."

"Just thinking about what we talked about outside. You didn't do the best job of making it sound uninteresting."

The music slows.

"Thirsty," I say, leading him to the bar, and signal the bartender.

"Rikken, a kiziloxer and . . ."

"A water," Jordan shouts overhead before slapping hands in greeting with someone he knows.

Rikken fills a glass. "Fresh meat, glad to see you in here at a normal time of night."

I go cold all over.

"What'd he say?" Jordan nudges me.

"He said . . . uh . . . would you like a soda?"

"Water, I said." Jordan nods, and Rikken gazes between us, stare narrowed at my blatant lie. He slides me a glass and I pull Jordan away from the bar.

"Are you all right?"

"I'm fine." I walk toward the back of the lounge area and fall into a couch around the karaoke stage where it's less crowded, more quiet, my mind still whirring at Draguns using dark magic. Jordan joins me.

We're sitting, comfortable in the silence, as a masked singer onstage belts into a microphone, when I spot Mynick heading our way.

Jordan groans.

"What?"

"Ambrosers. They're all the same. Arrogant know-it-alls."

The irony. Mynick joins us on the couches, glancing at his watch.

"That friend of yours is going to make herself sick over Cotillion. She said she'd be here an hour ago."

"Good luck with that, Abby is *swimming* in preparations. She's down to a couple weeks, I think."

"Twelve days." He sighs. "And I can't escort her. Did she tell you?"

"She's pretty disappointed."

"I mean, you're the heir and all," he goes on. "Maybe you could put in a good word."

I feel Jordan tense beside me at the suggestion of rule-breaking.

"*So!*" I say, before he can open his mouth. "Looks like your training is going well." I gesture at two fresh inked marks on his arm.

"Right, thanks." He pulls his sleeves down. "I'm surprised to see you in here," Mynick says, apparently determined to resurrect Jordan's scorn. "With what's going on with those Perl girls."

I sit up. "Perl girls?"

Mynick's eyes widen. "You don't know?"

Jordan faces him.

"Neither of you know, wow."

"Out with it, Ambrose."

"Two debs were supposed to show up for Second Rite yesterday but never did. Their parents haven't seen them either. It's all everyone's talking about. That and the heir to House Marionne birthing the sun itself out of her blade at exam."

The green in Jordan's eyes darkens. *Two girls from the Order are missing.* The fear I felt the first time I met a Dragun twists in my stomach.

"Is there anywhere they could have gone?" I ask. "Maybe there's a perfectly reasonable explanation."

Mynick shrugs. "Didn't mean to be the bearer of bad news. Congrats again, Quell. I'll see you around."

Jordan stands, and just like that the soft parts of him are jagged. "I have to go." He grabs his coat.

"Jordan, are you okay?"

"This happened in my House. I should have known about it." His green gaze is as gray as steel. "I should be out there—"

"I'm sure Headmistress Perl has people looking into it."

"You wouldn't understand."

"I'm just saying it's not your fault."

His stone expression leaves no room for argument, so I let it go.

"I need to prepare to help, whatever might come. I should ready my magic," he mutters.

"Manage . . . that *thing* we talked about, you mean?"

"All these questions about my magic . . ."

"Jordan, I—"

"You're obviously trying to make a case for"—he lowers his tone—"life as a Dragun, and I won't let you. I'd never do that to you."

"I thought you were proud of your duty."

"I am." He buttons his coat.

"I was just—"

"I have to go, Quell. I'm sorry. Can I walk you back?"

"I'm fine. I hope the girls from your House are okay."

He squeezes my hand. "Cultivator, right?"

"Right."

"Good night." He turns to go, and I try to settle back on the couch, but the mood has passed. The news of Beaulah's girls going missing stinks. I don't like it. The Tavern vibes around me, oblivious.

Jordan's last words dig at me, souring the dregs of the night. I shiver, remembering the way Beaulah's Dragun who stopped me at the convenience store glared with murder in his eyes. Draguns use a form of toushana to kill. They're in charge of protecting the Order's secrecy. It makes sense. And I've never seen anything more destructive than this poison in my veins. But how does Jordan "manage" it, as he called it?

An idea strikes me, and it's so, so foolish. I'm out the door before I can talk myself out of it. I'm going to follow him.

JORDAN STOPS IN the forest farther than I've ever ventured. Thin tall trees, some towering, others in piles on the forest floor surround us like a burned building caving in on itself. There isn't a glimmer of the Chateau or the way to the Tavern in the distance. Like we've wandered to a part of the forest swallowed in darkness that has been altogether forgotten. Dying bushes of flowers in every color curl into themselves and their withered petals litter the ground.

I hook my hands, careful to stay out of sight, watching Jordan navigate through these woods with knowing. He moves like the wind, in a blur of black fog. I follow, sticking from tree to tree, leaves shuffling under my feet as quietly as I can. A deep cold presses in on us. The air tastes of cedar and smoke. Until suddenly he stops and gazes in every direction.

In front of him is a thorny bush with red blooms. He glances around once more before stroking the bush's petals. Then he inhales and stretches his arms wide.

He exhales and tendrils of wispy dark magic appear in his hands, thrashing violently.

I press so hard into the bark in front of me, it scrapes my knees. He shudders, fog suddenly at his lips, and my legs threaten to go out from under me. I blink, but he is still there, holding his wrists together, pointed at the branches beneath him. As the plant crumples in on itself, rotting, leaf by leaf, the writhing wisps of magic in Jordan's hands slow, more deliberate and controlled. When he finishes, the bush and every other one near it are decayed piles of ash. He exhales. Jordan shakes out his hands, then flexes his fingers, rolling his shoulders. His expression has darkened, his mask bleeding through his skin. He hunches forward, turns in on himself, and cloaks, disappearing in dark fog.

I stumble backward, forcing down a dry breath.

I gape into the nothingness of the night, trying to put words to what I just saw. I claw at the roots of my hair, scrubbing a palm down my face, blinking a thousand times.

This . . . this is how he manages it.

Using it, *feeding it*, to keep control.

And he does it here in the dark distant forest where no one would ever notice. I glare at my hands. I have so many questions. If we could just talk about it, if I could ever trust him like that, he could *save* my life. I let a tree hold me up as I realize what I have to do. If I'm going to maintain control, I can't keep fighting it off, denying it air.

I have to use my toushana.

I swallow. The only time my toushana has ever really listened to me was when I destroyed the lab table. As if it suffered of a thirst that had just been quenched. Afterward it did as I asked, listened when I commanded it, which was to lie quiet.

Could this actually work? The woody scent of damp moss fills my nose as I step out of my hiding spot. The silent woods are wreathed in fog, and I follow the pine-needle-covered paths around and through the litter of broken trees. I manage to find a few stumps splintered or covered in fungus. *Here goes nothing . . .*

I call to my toushana, and a chill like death answers in a breath. I lay my icy fingers on the stump and its hard exterior crumbles into blackened sand. I work my hands up and down its long trunk, glancing over my shoulder every few moments, listening hard. As my cold, dead magic rushes out of me, insatiable, the tension in my shoulders eases, like a much needed release.

The sky is somehow darker by the time I finish. I fall to my knees, but my chest is lighter.

"A secret part of the woods," I mutter, a soft smile pulling at my lips as I catch my breath. That's what this place could be for me.

I scatter the evidence until the ashes mix with the deadened leaves imperceptibly. *No one will even know I was here.* I reach for magic again, this time the proper one. And the ache that lives in my side is hardly there, my toushana so sedate I can't even sense it. Instead, warmth unfurls in me, and I play with the leaf of a plant, shifting it into a paper flower.

This is what I have to do.

I try to exhale but can't. Using my toushana on purpose risks strengthening it, because unlike Jordan's, mine is *inside* of me. My chest tightens, and I clutch it, determined to stay calm. *I have no choice.*

I will let my toushana satisfy itself in secret if that's what it takes. Until Cotillion.

Then this cursed life will finally be behind me.

THIRTY-ONE

The next evening when I return to my room, a mountain of boxes, bins, and books awaits. Everything from the geography of speleology, the study of caves, to the Victorian era's influence over Western style and fashion, several history books, and a new list of Latin vocabulary. Abby is at her desk asleep in the chair under a pile of invitations. She startles when the door closes.

"Sorry, didn't mean to wake you." I pull a thin book by Emily Post with a familiar name from the top of the stack on my bed. Then another. *Putting the Charm in Charming, A Member's Guide for Proper Living, The Language of Style*. The list goes on.

"It's fine. I didn't mean to fall asleep." Abby smooths a drip of drool from her mouth but misses the rhinestone stickers stuck to her face. "I need to get these invitations out." She joins me at my bedside. "What happened to you after the Tavern?"

"Do you have to do those tonight?" I ask, removing the first bin from my bed and starting a stack by my closet. A little black journal with a fleur-de-lis on the front slips from the stack.

"My mentor said the calligrapher is running behind. And these *have* to get out, like, *now. The Art of Manners* chapter seventeen: Send an invitation too late and the guest may already be booked. Twelve days is not early. Ugh!"

I peel the rhinestone tape off her face. "I can help you."

"Are you sure? Have you *seen* your stack of things?"

She's not wrong. I pick through the bins and pull out a bound manual thicker than a dictionary. A quick thumb through is telling. "A checklist?"

"Yep."

"It's like four hundred pages!"

"This is Third Rite, Quell." Abby smiles awkwardly. "The kid gloves are off." She plops onto her bed, falling back on her pillow.

"Abby, you need a break."

She hugs her pillow, faux sobbing. "There's no time!"

"All right, that's it." I roll up my sleeves. "I need to learn to do this stuff, too. We're doing it together."

I grab an invite from her stack and toss her sparkly, studded tape. "First off, we're ditching this. Less is more." I wrap a thin ribbon around it. "There, that's enough." I stuff it in an envelope and grab another.

"What happened to you last night after the Tavern?" Abby asks again, joining me to fold. "Mynick told me Jordan ditched early, but then you weren't home for a while." She hands me my invite, trying to situate the ribbon on it.

"Speaking of Mynick," I say, ignoring her question, "I'm so bummed you can't take him."

"Yeah, *that* sucks. I even asked Cuthers if Headmistress would make an exception, and it was a flat no. But Jordan? Last night?"

I hand her a roll of ribbon. "This one is kind of cute."

"Quell! You're not getting out of answering my question." She takes the ribbon and tosses it back at me.

"I just needed some time to myself."

She sits on the bed. "Because you like him, and he likes you, and y'all are pretending like you don't."

That's part of it. "I, ugh . . . I don't know."

"And I suppose you went with Jordan to the Tavern *together* just because."

"He's my mentor. We were celebrating passing my exam."

She makes a face, and I remember the way his eyes light up every time we talk about books. The way he looked at me without surprise when I completed Second Rite.

"Don't look at me like that." I wish I could tell Abby everything. "Sometimes he just frustrates me."

"Is that what you call it? How you get all fidgety and smiley when he's around. The way you can't stop looking at him when he's in the room."

"Abby, shut up! I do not." I gnaw my lip. *Wait, do I?* hangs on my lips, unsure how much to share. "He is the last person in the world I should be thinking about that way." If only it were that simple.

"Why?"

"Because he's rigid. He has zero ability to loosen up. He does everything perfectly. He even has perfect lips. His cheeks slope flawlessly to them. Have you looked at him?"

"No, I don't look at Jordan's lips. But the admission that you do says a lot."

I roll my eyes. "He is wrong for me in every way." In more ways than I can say. "And yet . . . he is all I find myself thinking about. I—"

"Hate him, clearly."

I collapse on her bed beside her. "I'm hopeless."

"Quell, he's a Dragun. Every girl wants to—"

"Abilene Grace Feldsher, I swear if you finish that sentence." I hold up her invitation and a pair of scissors.

"You wouldn't!"

"I wouldn't risk it if I were you."

She snatches the scissors. "Fine, I'll drop it, but that's how I know you *really* like him. My advice? It's your life, and you should live it like you want. If you want Jordan, go get him."

"My feelings for Jordan don't matter. *Not that I have feelings for him!* I like him a little bit, yes, but that doesn't mean— Let's just get these done."

She winks at me, and I pretend to dry gag to show her I mean it. We work, tying ribbons onto her invites, and I tie the first few too tight, distracted entirely by how I wish I knew what Abby really thought. But that would require me to tell her the full truth. That Jordan would kill me if he knew what I was hiding. The thought tugs at my insecurity and I feel the toushana in my body shift.

By the time I finish, Abby is collapsed on her bed in a pile of plum velvet, snoring again. My hands are stiff from all the tying, and I barely have any energy to clear off my bed so I can sleep. I tug Abby's covers over her and switch off her lamp. The quivering chill beneath my skin reminds me it's still there. Reminding me I will need to return to the forest. And soon. Just the thought of using my toushana on purpose makes my insides swim. Memories of Jordan in the forest feeding his toushana loom over me as I drag myself to my covers and pull open my checklist, flipping to the first page.

My plan to use my toushana in order to control it better work.

DEXLER'S SESSION BEGINS with a bang, and I press my hands, still throbbing in frigid warning, between my knees. With as much as they hurt, I was tempted to stay in my room all day until it's dark enough to visit the forest. But I desperately needed to talk to Dexler and Plume about the heir event at the end of the week.

Invitations went out as soon as Grandmom and I figured out a catchy name and description: Summer Blooms Tea, an afternoon of roses and refreshment. And the heirs have each *already* RSVP'd. Hiding the truth from Grandmom is one thing. She sees what she wants to see. But these heirs are the crème de la crème of the Order, the future Darragh Marionnes and Beaulah Perls. I ball my hands into fists.

I have *days* to prepare to put on the best performance of my life.

Dexler's is sparsely filled, with people working at their tables independently.

"All magic, as we know from our studies of Sola Sfenti, comes from . . ." she prods.

"Sun Dust."

"Anciently it was ingested, injected, grafted, and even sewn into the skin. But now—" She gestures for me to finish.

"Magic is in the blood."

Shelby glances my way. I smile, but she goes back to her book.

"Precisely. And discovered when—"

"During the Forty Days of Darkness."

"As a Cultivator, you can sense Sun Dust in people or things and draw it out. But first you'll need to reach your inner kor."

I shake my head, and Dexler presses her glasses firmer to her nose before sitting beside me. "Picture the Dust moving through you."

I close my eyes and imagine my magic burning in me properly. The achiness lurking under my skin shudders. *Please, not now.*

"Draw it to your center. *Really* feel it. Yours should be strong enough now." She taps my diaphragm where my warm magic hums, and I try to forget about my toushana poking me in warning. Dexler quiets a few noisy students when the dull ache in my bones twinges. I eye the clock. I ignore it, tightening from my center, and warmth pools through me, grain by grain, before it zips through my chest in a sharp, searing gust.

My fingertips glow, magic throbbing beneath my skin.

"There you go. You don't need the sun or a candle or any of those things once you can reach your inner kor. You only need to know how to find it. Now *pull it* out of you."

My brows dent in confusion but instincts tell me to pinch my finger. My skin feels as if it's being peeled away from the muscle piece by excruciating piece, and a red flame ignites on my fingertip. I jump but realize it doesn't hurt. "I don't understand."

"That's not fire. It's your kor. You've pulled your own magical energy from inside and deposited it onto your finger." She turns my wrist, admiring the flicker when the flame on my hand grows. I grip the desk, but the world blurs. I tip sideways, and the chilly panic in my veins throbs harder, the dusted warmth I felt earlier diminishing. *What's happening?* I try to say, but my tongue is thick. The flame on my finger has doubled in size.

"*Quell!* The elixir, now," she barks, and someone holds a cold vial to my lips. It goes down, and the world sharpens.

"What happened?"

Dexler clutches her chest. "Are you all right, dear?"

"I think so."

"It's my fault. You can't let your kor burn outside of your body too long or it will drain you."

"Of magic?"

"Of *life*."

I blow out a breath and clench my near freezing hands. Thankfully, Dexler lets me spend the rest of class with my head down, and I use it to slow my breathing and the thump hammering my chest, hoping to settle the chilliness trying to take root in my bones.

As the room empties, Plume appears at the door.

"Are we still meeting?" he asks, and Dexler looks to me. "Are you sure you're feeling up to it?"

"Yes."

Once the class has all filtered out, I explain the Summer Bloom Tea idea. How perfect everything must be. They nod affectionately without interrupting, and by the time I'm done I realize I'm gripping the arms of my chair.

"Relax," Plume says.

"We work for Headmistress." Dexler smiles. "We understand."

"Great," I manage, mildly relieved they think impressing Grandmom is why I need to do well.

"I can come up with some fun games," Dexler says. "And Plume can probably help make it all look just right."

I inhale, exhale, and recline in my seat.

"Oh, most definitely," he says. "I'm thinking crustless sandwiches and light confections on the lawn, perhaps."

They go on about lace tablecloths, place setting styles, and centerpieces, and all I can picture is me sitting there trying to explain myself, where I've been all these years. Why I'm just now meeting them. Whatever I come up with will need to be airtight. I also have to look and speak the part. But most of all, my toushana *must* stay quiet.

As if it's been summoned, my heart stutters in panic, blood pools in my ears, and a cold unfurls in my bones. I stand, my heart racing, and stumble into a chair, the cold bite growing stronger.

"This poor child," Plume says, glancing at Dexler.

"She's stressed herself so sick, she's gone pale. I think we're going to have to . . ." She looks at Plume.

"Yes, I think so, too," he responds. "We'll put the Tea together and make sure your grandmom thinks all the handiwork is your idea." He grins and she winks. "Just give us a copy of the invitation and it'll be done to the nines."

"Oh my goodness, thank you so much!" I say my goodbyes and hurry out the door. Outside, bile burns its way up my throat. That was close. I hate having to do this again and so soon. But I don't see another way. My toushana needs to be fed.

I have to get to the forest.

ON MY FIRST trip back to the Secret Wood of the forest to satisfy my toushana, the bark feels brittle and unfamiliar as it deadens against my skin. I find a patch of thin branches, let my toushana rip through me, and hurry back inside. But I toss and turn all night wondering, if I could destroy more at a time, would the effect last longer?

On my third trip to the Secret Wood, I search for bigger trunks with deep roots and burn them all until I am breathless. Until they lie black and withered like a pile of singed leaves. It takes so long, my fingers are numb, chafed, and stinging. But I leave feeling . . . untethered in a way I've never been. And after it, my toushana lies quiet for three whole days.

But today, on my seventh trip into the forest, I could hardly get through the door because of my toushana burning with an itch, begging to be scratched. I run, tearing through the trees, trying to put as much distance between me and the estate as I can. Trying to bury my secrets far, far away. But the urge to press my skin to something, anything, and feel the soft, dead granules sift between my fingers sticks in my throat like a thirst. I *have* to drink. So I touch the first thing I see, and the next, and the next, leaving a trail of destruction like dead footprints.

Wind whistles, rustling the clawed branches, as I finally make it to the Secret Wood. As far as I can see are blackened branches, dead trees, some in heaps of ash, others withering as if they've been razed. It's desolate and charred as if it barely survived being set on fire.

I glare at my hands, my knees pressed hard in the dirt. My toushana hums in me with a cadence of delight, a bloated contentment. *It is satisfied.*

I pull myself up as my labored breath bleeds through the fog of silence. I force my lips shut despite my raging heart. I'm always most nervous when I finish. What if my senses dull and I miss a crunch of leaves, or hushed breathing?

Ash sticks to my hands. I dust them off and start shifting the blackened trail, transfiguring it into piles of trodden leaves. Covering my tracks. Burying my secrets. Secrets that won't matter in three weeks.

Grandmom's domineering glare hovers in my memory as I work faster to cover the area. She's been on my back so much about this event with the heirs tomorrow that between trips to the forest, the majority of my time has been spent being lectured by her. I'm running out of excuses for where to tell her I've been.

Magic streams from my fingers, controlled and immediate, my proper magic answering on command. My toushana hasn't crept up in surprise all week. As sickening as it is, this is working.

The forest begins to resemble its former state and I make my way back to the door buried in the bushes. My knees are damp with earth. I try to clean them and smooth my hair, sure it's a mess. It feels as if I've been out here for *hours*. My nose is chilled by the time I pull open the hidden door. Inside the passageway I pause to listen for footsteps before hurrying to my room.

I round the corner of my Wing and look for a familiar face lurking in the corridor, but the hall is sparsely dotted with a few Primus. Jordan hasn't returned from his trip to help with the search for the Perl girls. Nor has there been so much as a whisper about them. I twist my doorknob and find Abby fast asleep inside. In what world do people go missing and life just goes on . . .

A chill skitters up my arm. *That could have been me.* I scrub down in a quick shower and tuck into bed with a social etiquette book from my stack. Tomorrow needs to go right. I roll in my covers, reading and re-reading Emily's chapter on conversation.

I have to be perfect.

THIRTY-TWO

———✳———·

The morning comes, and my feet are on the floor before my alarm sounds. The Tea is this afternoon, and after hours tossing and turning I gave up on sleep. First stop is House secretary, Mrs. Cuthers. Her desk is somehow already swallowed by students, and the sun is hardly awake. When her office clears, she gestures for me to come inside and close the door. Behind her is a corkboard with memories pinned to it, smiling faces of elegantly dressed debs, with *You're the best* scribbled underneath. She grabs a stack of envelopes.

"We need a *full* name, Mister Blackshear," she says to herself, tossing an envelope into the trash. "Miss Marionne." She clicks her pen. "How can I help?"

"I wanted to give you these refusals if you wouldn't mind mailing them." I hand her the stack of envelopes in my hand. Coming up with that many "polite" reasons I couldn't attend was no easy feat.

"Heavens." She takes the stack. "Did you say yes to any of them?"

I smile tightly.

"Are you absolutely sure, dear? Not even just one? Society is dying to see you."

"They can meet me after Cotillion." When it's safe.

"As you wish. What else?"

"I also wanted to ensure my mom is on the invitation list."

Cuthers pulls off her glasses. "Little Rhea?" She presses her palms to her chest. "What a delight that would be to see her face around here again." She pulls out the list. "She is not, actually. But I can see to it that she's—"

"Actually, I want to prepare that invite myself."

"I assure you—"

"Respectfully, Mrs. Cuthers, I am going to address it in my own hand with a personal note from me, to ensure my mother opens it." I am going to do this one small thing *my* way.

The door shoves open without a knock, and I don't have to turn around to know who it is.

"Headmistress, so good to see you."

"I was just popping my head in to see where we are with things with Quell's Cotillion. Your dress is the most important part, dear, are you set up with Vestiser fittings?"

"I was actually going to suggest the upcoming merchant festival might be the most efficient route to go," Mrs. Cuthers cuts in.

"*Efficient* isn't the priority." Grandmom turns to me. "This is what you want? To pick your designer at a merchant festival when everyone else does? *From* the selection everyone else does?"

I don't care what my dress looks like. I just want to bind with my magic as soon as possible. "I would hate to delay things for any reason."

"*Fine.* I'll talk to Jordan later today about security for the event just to be sure it's extra tight."

Wait. "He's back?"

"He returned a few days ago."

A hook tugs in my stomach. *He didn't reach out to me.*

"Was his trip successful?"

"So he told you." She tsks. "The girls were found, but that isn't your concern. Are you ready for the Tea today? It's nearly noon."

"Everything's in order."

"It better be." When the door clicks shut behind her, I try to exhale but can't.

⚜

It's TEN UNTIL noon when I rush to the front lawn in my flowery patterned dress, my House riband across my chest. To the backdrop of Grandmom's luscious gardens, the tea party is being set up.

"There you are!" Plume beckons and leads me over to the reception area. A decadent table arrangement is set for six, landscaped in House colors, with flowers and finger foods on fine plates.

"What do we think?"

"It's breathtaking!" I recheck the measurements of everything on the table. The plates, cutlery, and napkins should be one point five inches away from the table edge, no more. In the distance, Grandmom exits the estate with a girl about my age on her arm. I have to lock my knees to still my nervous energy as they cross the lawn to meet me. *Be. Perfect.*

Her heart-shaped face is framed by slicked-back auburn hair with a simple silver diadem arced over her head. Her dull charcoal dress is a sharp contrast to the rest of her. She strides confidently, shoulders back, making small talk with Grandmom. The bright blue riband slung across her is embroidered with three intersecting leaves, and matching gloves cover most of her arms. With gloves that long, no question what they're hiding. She must be the heir to House of Ambrose.

"Nore, this is my granddaughter, Quell."

She sticks out a hand. "Nore Emilie Ambrose. Good to meet you." Her handshake is firm.

"You as well. Please, feel free to explore the gardens while we wait for the rest of the party. Drinks are being passed."

Nore helps herself to the table.

"Heir Drew of Ho—"

"Really, there's no need for all that," the entering guest in a slick pantsuit says, slapping the waitstaff on the belly.

"Hi, Drew, I'm Quell." I offer my hand, trying to make out the sigil on their teal sash, but it's blocked by a long braid hanging over their sharp shoulders.

"You're cute." Drew taps my nose and leaves my hand. "What time do we eat? I'm starving."

Grandmom smooths her hair, groaning under her breath. "Oralia's people have arrived, I see," she mutters. "Don't expect any manners out of that one. Oralia doesn't intend to have any children. So the estate will pass to her sibling, Drew."

I make a mental note not to refer to Headmistress Oralia as Drew's mother. The last guest for the afternoon, also the one I'm most curious about, isn't far behind. Beaulah Perl's heir. Her shiny hair is swept up behind her, curled and cascading, ornamented with jewels. Her warm brown skin is barely dusted with makeup, illuminating her natural beauty. Her ruby dress shimmers in the high sun. Gems on top of her diadem shine radiantly, outdone only by her dark eyes hung like jewels beneath long eyelashes. She is perfection. A black riband is slung across her, and my gaze snags at its cracked column embroidery.

"You must be Quell." She folds into a curtsy that would put mine to shame. "I'm Adola Yve Perl. I was delighted by the invitation. I've heard so many wonderful things about you from my aunt."

"Your aunt?"

"My mother was quite surprised, too." She laughs behind a gloved hand. "But the first girl in the entire family! Aunt Beaulah was delighted. She took me under her wing right away and raised me as her own. You and I appear to have some things in common, I see." She eyes Grandmom with a polite smile.

"Sounds like it." This isn't what I was expecting of the niece of the woman who tried to have me killed. Grandmom glances between us, urging me to say *some*thing. To not be outdone. "I've only heard the loveliest things about your aunt from my mentor."

"Cousin Jordan." Her smile doesn't meet her eyes.

A bell chimes, signaling the start of tea service. Nore and Adola sit on either side of me. Drew, across.

"I'll be just a minute. Please, don't wait," Grandmom says, heading back toward the estate.

"Thank you all so much for coming," I start, gesturing for the servers to begin, trying to remember the proper order of things. Drew slides the sugar over to me.

"Thank you." I scoop the acceptable amount of sweetener into my cup and offer it to Adola.

"No, thank you." She sips from her cup as is. Nore is quiet, eased back in her chair. Her tea sits untouched. And every few moments her gaze falls to Grandmom's seat.

"Is everything all right? I can move your place if you'd like."

"I'm fine," she says, cavalier, finally sipping from her cup. But I don't miss the way it tremors just so before it touches her lips.

I sip from my own cup, and salty hot liquid rushes into my mouth. I spit, spewing the disgusting drink everywhere.

Drew and Adola burst out laughing.

"*Salt.*" I shove the sugar bowl away. "You all *tricked* me!"

"Oh, come on, be a sport. You're the newbie." Drew cocks an arm back on their chair. "We have to make sure you feel welcomed."

Adola grins mischievously. "She's mad."

"She'll be all right," Drew says. "You have a sense of humor, don't you, Marionne?"

"I'm fine. It's fine." But in truth, I burn with embarrassment all over as the servers reset the table linens and all the things. It takes every bit of talking myself down to not let the stress of this reset frazzle me.

"It was all Drew's idea anyway," Adola says, as she, Drew, and I stroll through the roses while the beautiful table Plume arranged is redone.

"Lies!" Drew protests, but a smirk hides behind their denial.

"A sense of humor is better than the best fashion sense, I heard once," I say. "Don't worry about it. It was all in good fun."

Nore strolls on her own as we wait, and I swear I see her eyes roll. But when I look over at her, she's admiring a bush of black roses.

"When did you arrive to Chateau Soleil?" Drew asks.

My heart thumps. Nore tugs at her gloves, pulling at the same threads of her shawl, over and over.

"Is she always to herself like that?" I ask, pretending I didn't hear their question.

"No idea," Adola says. "This is my first time meeting her. Will you be at the Tidwell?"

"I had a conflict. Unfortunately," I add, hoping it's convincing.

"I did too, sadly," Adola says. "I hate to miss it. It's the best one." Her eyes narrow. "Have you ever been to a ball before?"

"No, actually."

"Why not?" Drew asks. Adola watches for my answer as the final utensil is put in place and we're ushered back to a freshly set table.

"These look delicious." I sit back down and tear off a piece of sandwich and stuff it in my mouth so I don't have to answer.

Grandmom finally returns to the courtyard, taking her place at the table.

"What on earth happened?" she asks, eyeing the new setup.

"It's all fine now."

"What did you do before coming to the Chateau, Quell?" Drew asks, annoyingly persistent, before shoving an entire crustless sandwich in their mouth.

Grandmom's stare lassos around my throat.

"There's not much to share that would interest anyone here, I'm sure."

"Try me."

My grip on my glass tightens, and a touch of cold strokes my bones.

"I mean, unless you don't want to talk about it."

"I didn't say that I don't want to talk about it." I twist my riband around my finger. Nore notices, and we share a glance.

"The next round of tea, should we?" Grandmom interjects, and servers swarm the tables. Drew's question is lost in the confusion, and I try to sit back in my seat. Before anyone can fire off any more interrogating questions, I turn to Adola.

"You're finishing this Season, I heard. What color dress are you going to wear?"

"Me?" Adola's dainty fingers stroke her pearls with a lilt of arrogance that reminds me of her aunt Beaulah Perl. Grandmom sighs under her breath.

"Yes," I say.

"In our House, it's tradition to debut in black."

"Right. I must have forgotten."

Grandmom clears her throat. This is going sideways. Drew opens their mouth, but I'm faster.

"*Nore*, how is your tea?"

"It's delicious." She smiles but looks away, bored or irritated or something.

"Was your mother heir, too?" Adola asks, directing the conversation aggressively back to me.

"She wasn't," I say, fighting off a cold sweat.

"Wh—"

"How are things in your House, Adola?" I cut in, an octave too high. "I've been so worried since hearing the news."

She straightens, her composure flinching, but her voice streams out as melodic and sweet as ever. "It's been difficult. You and your mentor must talk often."

"I didn't hear from Jordan. It's been all the talk . . ." *In the Tavern,* I don't add because Grandmom doesn't need to know I've been there.

"I just hope everyone can heal and move on." Adola places another bite of scone with clotted cream into her mouth before crossing her utensils facedown on her plate. Her entire mood has shifted. I prodded a wound. It's shut her up. A small victory, but I'll take it.

Grandmom's watchful eye patrols the table, and for the rest of the tea I'm careful to stick to what I know and avoid being the topic of discussion. The conversation leaves me behind, and perhaps it's better that way. I try to pop in and out of it to at least appear engaged. By the time the final course of pastries comes around, my lower back aches, and all I've gleaned from this group is that the only reason Drew and Adola showed up was to pry.

"You're awfully quiet, Nore," Grandmom prods, as if trying to carefully stir a pot of soup.

"Yes, well, I'd hoped to have more to talk about, but alas, I'm not finding this tea party very inspiring," she says. Adola's gaze swells. Grandmom fiddles with her earring. Drew throws another macaroon in their mouth, apparently entertained.

"How long do you have left before Cotillion, Nore?" I ask, trying to salvage this sham of a party.

"I have just emerged, actually, working on Second Rite."

"And how's that going?" Adola asks.

"Not well." She quickly sips her tea again as if she regrets being so honest.

"Second Rite is a doozy," I say. "Get yourself really organized and chip away at it every day. Good luck."

She thanks me with a half smile, then suddenly her face drains of color.

"Nore?"

"If you'll excuse me," she says. "Which way is the ladies' room?"

"Just to the right as you enter from the courtyard," Grandmom says. Nore pushes up from the table without using her hands and almost knocks into a server. She rushes off in a panic.

Grandmom's brow deepens. She must be wondering the same thing I am.

"If you'll excuse me." I follow Nore inside, but as fast as I'm walking, she is faster. I wait on a scroll-armed chair outside the powder room. Water runs, a toilet flushes, but between them I hear swearing.

"Nore?" I knock.

"Just a minute." Several moments later the door opens, and she's all smiles. Her gloves are gone, and where I expect to see tallies on her arms is bare.

"Sorry, I couldn't figure out how to turn the sink on." She brushes past me, and her arm is bone-chilling cold.

Far colder than is normal.

I swallow my gasp. She stops, and the fear of death burns in her eyes. She puts some distance between us.

"Nore . . . are you all right?"

"I'm fine."

"Your gloves, have you forgotten them?" I watch for some inclination that I'm wrong. Her chest is out, shoulders back, perfectly poised. But ever so slightly she flinches.

"I tore them, by accident. There was a snag, and I should have mended it a long time ago. So I tossed them."

She's lying! The height of her tone says she's desperate to end my questions.

"I was going to thank you for the advice with honing," she says. "Would you like some advice on surviving this place?"

"Sure."

"Choose the people you let into your circle wisely."

I'm not sure what to say to that, so I say nothing.

"I should be getting back." Nore walks off, and her words are choked by the shock of what I *think* I know. I hurry into the bathroom and make a beeline for the wastebasket. *Empty.* I search for some remnant of ash, some whispered footprint of telltale destruction. Tears well in my eyes for reasons I don't have words for. But the bathroom is clean. There's nothing here other than proof she lied about throwing away her gloves. I know what I felt. I know that look in her eyes. It's haunted me my entire life.

She said she's struggling with Second Rite, and I bet I know why.

THIRTY-THREE

———✳———

The next afternoon, after a sleepless night stewing over what I *think* I know about the heir to House of Ambrose, I start my day with a trip to the Secret Wood under the dark dregs of early morning. I am too worked up to focus on anything else. After lunch the day falls into its regular rhythm, and I manage to get away to help Abby.

She slides a saucer toward me with a square of raspberry-filled cake on it as my thoughts drift back to Nore. If another Headmistress's heir also has toushana . . . Tears well in my eyes. The idea that I may not be alone in this chasm, stuck between Grandmom's expectations and a poison that would kill me, nudges a sore spot deep in my chest. I *must* know.

"Come on, one more," Abby prods.

"You're overthinking this," I say, as my thoughts shift to Jordan with an unfamiliar ache. *I wish I could talk to him about this.*

"Fine, I'll go with this one." She indicates a lemon one.

We scoot out of the meeting with the caterer, and I find myself scanning the halls for a familiar brooding face.

"It'll be your turn soon," Abby says, looping her arm through mine. "Which did you like for your cake?"

"I don't know. Does every table need a mini cake? Isn't that a bit much?"

"I think it's kind of glamourous." Abby flips her hair. "Mynick said Ambrose doesn't do that."

Mynick!

"I need to drop off my dagger for polishing and rehearse the dance with my debut-mates." She stops. "Are you all right? You seem a bit off today."

"The heir event was a lot, and Nore was being . . . weird. I don't know." That's as close to the truth as I can get with her for now. "Also, I have an idea. Mynick can be my plus-one for your Cotillion. I know you want him there, and I don't have plans to bring anyone." He is in Nore's House, so maybe he knows more.

"That's brilliant!" She hugs me. "He'll totally go with you."

"Should I notify Cuthers of the additional RSVP?"

"Could you? I'm meeting with Cultivator Tucker. Then the rest of my finishing class is rehearsing the group dance."

"Shelby is one of them, right?"

"Don't remind me."

"She was really nice on my first day."

"To *you*. But everyone's nice to you."

"Uh, sure, whatever. I'll take care of it and catch you later." Back in my room, I grab my stationery.

Nore, I sincerely apologize if I offended you with my insistence. I did not mean to. If there's any chance I am right and . . . you're not okay, please know that I won't tell anyone. Thank you again for coming to my Summer Bloom Tea. I hope to see you again soon.

I add *You're not alone*, then trash that one and rewrite it without it. I write thank-you notes to the other heirs, adding a fleur beneath my signature as Grandmom does, and stuff those into envelopes as well. I quickly drop everything at Cuthers's office and RSVP for Mynick and me. When I return to my room, I find a note slipped under the door in a familiar handwriting.

Meet me at nine.

I try but fail to push away my smile. I should stand him up. *He's been back for days!* A mound of dress swatches covers my bed from pillow to footboard. I'd have good reason to. I read the card again and get that weird fluttery feeling inside.

I . . . missed him.

I wonder if he might know something about Nore Ambrose . . . I scoop up a few armfuls of swatches to take with me, determined to not overthink this dress thing, and rush out the door.

JORDAN'S WAITING FOR me inside the conservatory and seeing him puts a spring in my step.

Whatever frustration I'd brought abandons me entirely when our eyes meet. *I've more than missed him.* He starts toward me, then stops, shifting his weight as if he isn't sure what to do now that I'm here.

I sit on the stone bench, but he remains standing.

"How have your first few days as Secundus gone?"

"Good."

"Did you get the early plans started for Cotillion? You'll want to make sure to get a head start on invitations. Your House is slow with those."

"Yes, we're working on a few new leads now. But—"

"So what did you do with your time yesterday?"

His entire tone is snappy, short, very business. I search his gaze for some explanation. Why it feels like I'm talking to my mentor instead of my *really* good friend, but he evades my stare, pulling at the petals on a nearby flower.

"Quell? I asked a question."

I stiffen at his sharpness. "I've been putting together ideas for where I'd like to intern the year after I debut."

"You'll want to base that on the prestige of the position, not your interest in the work. It's all about networking at this point. Getting to know as many powerful graduates of your House as you can. Running a House requires good relationships."

"Where did you go this past week?"

"I can't tell you that."

I don't know what I expected after not seeing him for so long, but this wasn't it. Have I lied to myself somehow? I can still feel the sand between my toes from when he transfigured this glass house into a living dream just so I could believe in myself. The way he patiently and gently showed me how to hone my blade before my toushana ruined it. How he comes alive when we talk about books. How he listens and sits with the things I say, stewing over them as if they are a treasure. The way his eyes sparkled like a crisp spring day when he saw me pass Second Rite. I look for him, *that* Jordan, my friend.

But lines are carved into his expression that were not there before. He's no more than two feet away, but it may as well be an ocean.

"Quell? Are you listening? Cotillion is in twenty days. What else have you gotten done?"

"I hosted a Tea with the other heirs, actually."

"And? How did it go?"

"It went really well, I thought."

"Elaborate."

I stuff my annoyance down and answer his question because while I don't like his shortness, I *am* eager to tell him. "Everyone came and had a wonderful time. Nor—" A Dragun knowing her predicament would be a death sentence. "Grandmom was very impressed as well."

Jordan listens intently.

"I'm doing well. Even with you not here."

"So Headmistress Marionne is pleased?"

"She is."

"Very good. That bodes well for both of us."

I shift in my seat, irritated. "You're—"

"And you'll want to snag a Vestiser *early*," he says. "Fortunately my mother dabbled in fabric Shifting between Audior studies, so my tails will be tailored in time." He fidgets with nervous energy, and it's equally unsettling and confusing.

I stand.

He steps back.

"What's up with you?"

"I don't know what you mean." He paces, and I can't help but think it's just an excuse to get farther away from me. "Have you started honing the rest of your enhancers? Usually you'll pick up a few extra as gifts here and there."

"I haven't started, but it's on my list." I pick at my skin, but I'd much prefer to pull out my hair.

"And the memory work. I realize it's a lot, but you must know the *full* Order history."

"Jordan . . ."

"I recommend oral recitations, three times a day if you can."

"Jordan."

"I'll expect you to drill with me at least once—"

"Jordan!"

He stills, and a Jordan I don't know gazes back at me, worry tugging at his brow. I close the distance between us, my feet ten steps ahead of my head. And this time he doesn't move away.

I hold his gaze, determined to lasso that piece of him trying to run. *Be here,* he'd told me once when we danced. That's what I want from him right now. That longing to be connected to me. To let me be connected to him.

He stills in my presence, his chest rising and falling faster than it should. But he still doesn't move away.

"What is it? What's changed?"

His expression hardens. His shoulders hang as if they've never known true rest. I wish he would just tell me. Instead of shutting me out. But Jordan strikes me as the helper, not the helped.

Let me in, I want to say. But instead I reach for his fingers, and to my surprise he lets me take them. His fingers play on mine and before I realize it our hands are laced between one another, locked together, braver than our words. I chew the words on the edge of my lips, trying to choke them down. Trying to convince myself these flutters aren't real. But all I manage is to squeeze his hand again and hold on tighter. He squeezes back.

"Is it true you've been back three whole days?" I ask.

He sighs and breaks our touch. "Going to Hartsboro gave me a lot to think about."

We sit together on the bench.

He draws his words as if from a deep well he's never drunk from. His gaze is fixed on the ground instead of at me. "Being here has changed me."

"How?"

"Quell, I'm a Dragun. Do you understand what that means?"

"I do. But—"

"There is no but."

"But." I scoot closer to him. "You're also Jordan Wexton, my *really good friend*. It was a long eight days, and I missed him." I want to hear him proclaim his feelings so I know I'm not alone on this island. But I hesitate to push.

After an ocean of silence: "And he missed you."

He pulls me into a side hug, and my head finds his shoulder. We stay like that for a long while. I hesitate to break it, but now that things feel a little more right between us, there's so much I want to say.

"I was so relieved when I heard the girls were found."

"What do you mean?"

"The girls from your House, they're okay, right?"

"Quell, I didn't find them alive."

My heart squeezes. *The Perl girls are dead.*

He moves the hair out of my face, and I lean into his hand, to offer him some comfort, but immediately worry I've been too bold. His expression warms, and his fingers trace the curve of my nose, my cheeks.

"Talk about something else," he says.

"Did you see your parents?"

"Something else."

"Tell me a story, a fun one from when you were little. And I'll tell you one. How about that?" I should be able to scrounge up a few harmless memories to share.

"All right." He settles against me and pulls a bag of candies out of his bag. He pops a few into his mouth and hands me a green one. I do a double take.

"Doth mine eyes deceive me?"

"You should take it before I change my mind." He smirks, and I pop it into my mouth before resting my head, which fits like a puzzle piece, in the nook of his neck. His shoulders sink a bit as he tries to relax against me.

"I guess I'll start. Once, when I was five . . ." He might not be ready to admit he has feelings for me out loud. But for now, this is everything I need. For now, this is enough.

THIRTY-FOUR

—✳—

It started raining around curfew, so Jordan and I stayed in the conservatory swapping stories. He told me of a time when he'd gotten lost in the forest near his parents' property. And after a long while of searching for the way back, he just decided he'd brave it and live with the wolves. By the time the search party found him, he was so determined to prove he could actually do it, he only spoke in wolf howls for a week. I laughed until my ribs ached and shared morsel-sized snippets of life with Mom with him. Crumbled pieces of who I am. *Who I was.*

By the time we made our way back to our rooms, we were shoeless, breathless, with feet caked in mud. I fell into bed right before dawn fully aware I would miss morning sessions. But my alarm has coaxed me out of bed with just enough time to get ready for a check-in with Grandmom.

I dash up the stairs, picturing little Jordan growling at his parents as I slip into the dining room.

"You're certainly radiant this evening."

I curtsy. "Headmistress."

Her maid sets a tray with tea on the coffee table between us and adds a log to the fire.

"I was worried you weren't coming. Busy day?"

"Quite busy. I'm on top of things though, I promise."

"Mrs. Cuthers seems to think so, too. Do you have your internship list?"

I pull out the list on the Marionne stationery Grandmom had made for me, still not sold completely on this heir business. I can't pretend it's not enticing. I can't pretend making that list wasn't thrilling. But all I could think about was *Where does that leave Mom?* My thoughts drift back to Nore, wondering what she will think of my letter. If I'm right, I wonder how she makes it all work. Her family isn't in pieces. Hopefully, today I can broach the topic with Jordan.

Grandmom eyes over my paper, then snaps at the air, and her maid puts a pen in her hand.

She writes on my wish list, crossing something out several times, and I groan under my breath. I'd picked each place carefully, all near the beach.

"There, now that's a good start. I'll go over it with the Council. It should be no trouble, but we all vote on heir assignments. So I like to be methodical." She hands the paper back to me, and she's written in "In-House internship" in the number one spot and shuffled the places at the bottom to put those in closest proximity to Chateau Soleil higher up.

"I don't understand. I thought . . ." *It was up to me.*

"Yes?"

"Nothing." I take a sip from my cup. It won't matter. Once I finish, Mom and I are leaving.

"Invitations, where are we with those? I sent over a recommended guest list, did you get it?"

Yes, three hundred fifty people I've never heard of in my life. "I did, thank you. I noticed that my mom wasn't on there. I added her. I hope that's all right?"

Her teacup stops just before her lips. "Yes, yes, of course. That must have been an oversight. She should absolutely have been on the list. Forgive me."

Good. I set my cup on the saucer so that it doesn't make a sound, nodding with a smile. I don't entirely know that she's being honest about her excitement. But at least she knows what I expect. That I'm paying attention. I can't wait to see Mom again once it's safe to.

The check-in wraps without much more interrogation.

"Same time tomorrow?"

"Wouldn't miss it," I say, trying to infuse some excitement in my voice. I did enjoy these meetups at first. But as they've morphed into her brow-beating me into planning *her* vision of my future, I look forward to them less and less.

"Before you go." She hands me an envelope. "This came for you today." Silver letters shine against a bright blue paper, closed by three leaves intertwined pressed into its wax seal. "It's from Nore Ambrose, I presume."

My stomach twists.

"It's good to see you making friends with others of your stature, Quell. Keep it up."

I tell Grandmom goodbye and hurry out into the hall, where a familiar blond-haired, blue-eyed Secundus is sitting.

"Shelby, hey."

She crosses and uncrosses her legs.

"Is everything okay?"

"What's it to you?"

She goes back to her notebook, ignoring me completely. I leave her there. I've got ten thousand other things to worry about. Once I'm alone, I pull at the seal.

Meet me where the trees are dead.
At midnight.

I read the words again and again. The sun's glow is dipping below the trees outside the nearest window. My thoughts spin, winding me up. I descend the stairs, rereading the note, when I crash into Jordan.

He catches me around the waist, pulling me into his orbit. "You're in a rush."

"Oh, hey, I've been meaning to talk to you more about the Tea I had with the heirs."

"Then come to my room tonight."

"I didn't realize girls are allowed in the Gents Wing."

"I'm on duty tonight."

"Jordan Wexton, are you *bending* the rules?"

He holds up two fingers barely apart.

"Okay. But I, uh, have to get out of there before midnight to study." I hold tight to the note from Nore at my back until he's out of sight.

JORDAN'S ROOM IS a corner suite on its own hall between the Gents and Cultivator Wings. He ushers me inside, and I'm greeted by the scent of garlic. There's a separate bedroom and a bathroom. All prim and tidy. He doesn't appear to have a roommate, which isn't a shock.

I sit at the table, which he has set properly with all the settings and a tiny flower on the plate next to a card with my name. He fills my glass with sparkling cider and pulls something out of the oven.

"I really didn't take you for a chef."

"I'm not." He dangles a recipe. "This is the one dish I can make pretty well. I learned it from my grandmother's mother. My parents would leave me with her—"

"For summers, I remember." He told me the other night all about his stern great-grandmother with her penchant for extreme punishments. He slides a pan of flaky golden bread rounds onto a trivet on the table, and it smells heavenly.

"What is it?"

"Popovers. Or Yorkshire puddings, as Gran called it."

"I didn't realize you were close with her."

"I wasn't, but I watched her closely enough." He doesn't say any more, and I don't push.

"So the Tea was interesting." I dive right in, Nore's note needling me. "What do you know about the heirs of the other Houses?"

He slips a bite into his mouth. "I know Adola fairly well, obviously. Never met Drew. But I've heard they're sharp. And I don't deal with Ambrosers if I can help it."

"But do you know anything about the Ambrose heir?" I hold in a breath.

"Nore Emilie Ambrose. Born of Paul and Isla Ambrose. She lives in Idaho at Dlaminaugh Estate, the training grounds of House Ambrose. She's set to debut in one of the upcoming two Seasons. She's a fair Shifter and a decent Retentor, I heard. She's of course going to be a Cultivator, so none of that matters."

Wow. "I figured you didn't know them well. She must be someone you and your Dragun friends have discussed . . ."

"It's my job to know things and not mention them."

His tone sends a chill up my arm. A chill I haven't felt around him in a long time. "So why would they discuss her? Any reason in particular?"

"They haven't." His brows dent as he holds out a cheese tray. "Did something happen at the Tea?"

"*No*," I say a bit too quickly. I clear my throat and take a bite of food. "Any leads on who harmed the girls from your House?" His next bite of food halts at his mouth as I grab a few olives and some cheese.

He sighs, dabbing the corners of his mouth with a napkin. "I didn't invite you here to talk about my work." He stands. "How about some music?"

"I'm just asking because—"

"No more, all right?"

"Fine." I join his side at a vintage record player and pick up a black-and-white record cover. He puts the vinyl on when I notice a polished box beside it engraved with a cracked column. I flip open the top. Inside are six golden lapel pins, each with a different word inscribed on them.

He takes the box out of my hands before I can read them. "Please."

"What are they?"

"A tradition we have in my House. I had to earn each one." He cups an angry scar on his elbow before closing the box and setting it on a high shelf.

"So a gramophone?" I pivot, realizing I've poked a wound.

"I got it from our home in Ascot the last time we visited. It was my great-grandfather's." He grabs the arm of the player and sets it carefully on the black disc. "The Ink Spots, heard of them?"

"No." Tunes bellow from the horn speaker.

"What about William Congreve?"

"That sounds familiar, but I couldn't say from where."

"'Music has charms to sooth a savage breast.' *The Mourning Bride.* He was a seventeenth-century English playwright." Jordan works his magic toward the ceiling. "You know how I feel about the classics, but they were of course required reading." The white above us bleeds black, the ceiling shifting into a night sky full of stars. "Will you dance with me?"

I *want* to ask him more about Nore. "My food is going to get cold."

He reaches for me, and I give in, fitting my hand into his. "You need to practice."

"It's okay to like me, you know?"

"No, it's not."

I pull away.

"I'm sorry. That came out wrong."

"Or did it come out right?" I scoff, irritation triggered by his insistence on locking away the things he doesn't want to talk about. First his magic, then his work, the girls from his House, and, of course, his *feelings*.

"What do you want me to say, Quell?"

"I want you to tell me what you really want."

"I *want* to have a nice meal. I *want* to dance."

"You *know* that's not what I'm asking." I put more distance between us. "What do you want, Jordan?" I look at him, deep in his eyes, and dare him to look away.

"Quell, you don't know what you're asking."

"*Yes*, I do."

"No, you *don't.* Because if you did, you wouldn't ask it!"

"This isn't only hard for *you*, Jordan." I eye the time and snatch my sweater from the chair.

He keeps pulling me in, but he won't acknowledge that he feels something. Letting me in but keeping me at arm's length. As if he wants to *have* me without *having* me. And I'm sick of it.

"It *almost* felt different with you. *Almost.*"

"Quell, please."

I grab the knob. "I don't understand how you're content living with so much of yourself in shadows."

He rushes at me in a blur of black. "I *am* the shadow, Quell."

"Well, I've lived a life in the shadows." I pull open his door. "And I don't recommend it."

I SHOVE AWAY the frustration of Jordan and hurry to the foyer, then broom closet, and race down the corridor with minutes to midnight. Humid air welcomes me as I dash through the forest until the trees close in around me and the Chateau is a memory in the distance. My toushana curls in my bones, stretching itself awake, eager to be fed. *Not now*, I tell it.

I still, listening. But hear only wind.

"Nore?"

The Secret Wood is bleak, as still as a graveyard.

"Nore?" I say once more.

But she doesn't answer.

No one does.

THIRTY-FIVE

I t's been two days since I stormed out of Jordan's room, and my annoy-ance with him still simmers. Fortunately, Abby's last-minute Cotillion preparations and my own have kept me busy. And now that her day is finally here, I can count on hopefully getting some answers about Nore from Mynick.

"How are you so relaxed? I've been a ball of nerves for *weeks*." Abby turns both ways in the mirror, checking and rechecking every vantage point of her gown.

"You think I'm relaxed?" I've spent the last two nights thinking about Nore and that letter. I'd hoped she'd write again, letting me know that we missed each other. But nothing has come. The last few days have been mind spiraling, heart racing, toushana thirsting. Not to mention I've gone back to the forest to use my forbidden magic. Octos's warning to keep my dark magic in check has haunted me, worrying me that I may be using it more than is okay. "Abby, I am far from relaxed."

"Well, you play it off well." She grabs her riband. "Help me with this, I can't lift my arms."

I lay the satin over her and adjust the fleur so it's on her chest. "You look perfect."

"Really? Don't lie to me because I'm your friend."

"Stop it. You couldn't be more beautiful."

"My dagger, where's my—"

"It's here." I grab it, careful to hold it in the cloth it's wrapped in, and hand it to her.

"Okay, I *think* I'm ready."

"You have the oath in your purse in case you get stuck?"

"Yep."

"Duct tape and pins?"

She pulls out a flat fold of tape and pins from her bag. "Wardrobe-malfunction-ready, yep."

"Lips?"

"Painted."

"Diadem?"

"Polished." She tilts her head down, and I double-check.

"Boobs?"

"Pushed together."

"Okay, you're definitely ready."

"Oh, Quell." She throws her arms around me. "Promise you'll come visit. A year is a long time. But the Healer facility where I'm interning allows visitors, so you *have* to come."

The reality that this room won't ring with Abby's voice tomorrow night twists me in a knot. I'm going to miss her. "I will do my best." But the truth is it's probably easier this way. That she leaves first. Because I don't know where I'm headed after my own Cotillion.

Someone knocks at the door.

I open it, and three cameras flash at once.

"Oh, sorry. You want her," I say, ducking out of the way and blinking away the white spots.

Mrs. Feldsher rushes in with a bunch of other people who all resemble Abby. Their arms are full of flowers, and her father's face shines with a sleek mask. I back up as they swarm her with cheers and look for Mynick.

"Whoa, watch it." It's Mynick I've backed into as he comes through the door.

"Abs, we should probably get going," Mr. Feldsher says, before checking his mask in the mirror.

"See you two out there," Abby says as she and her family hurry out the door.

"Hey, thanks for the invite." Mynick offers his arm. "Shall we?"

"Why, thank you," I say, taking it, mocking the formality of it all.

He snickers. "Thanks again for doing this. I owe you one."

"I'll be sure to think of a way you can repay me."

By telling me all you know about Nore Ambrose.

THE GRAND BALLROOM is decked out in hues of blush and gold. Arched windows have been sheathed in shiny fabric that cascades to the floor. Everything shimmers.

There are six chairs on the small center stage but only five daggers. I skim the program.

"Shelby's missing."

"Who?" Mynick asks, snaking his way between the tables toward the one marked with Abby's surname.

"Nothing."

We find our seats when music booms and the lights dim. The audience quiets as the doors part. I lean into Mynick, whispering, "So tell me about Nore Ambrose."

He teeters off the edge of his seat, craning for a glimpse of the debs as they enter and stream right into their group dance. "What about her?"

Abby catches us looking, and we wave.

"Oh, you know . . . what is she like? Is she in any of your sessions?" *Does she have toushana?*

"You ask that like it's someone I actually know."

"So you don't know her?"

"I know you more than I know her." He laughs. "No one gets close to Nore. Headmistress would lose it."

"So she's sheltered?"

"To the extreme."

Before I can get another question in, we stand with the whole room, applauding as the group dances finish and Abby takes the floor with her date. Mynick reclines in his seat and decides to butter his bread instead of watch.

"You were saying?" I lean forward.

"Why are you so interested in Nore anyway?"

Because she may be a mirror of survival in this world I haven't conceived of. Because I've never even met someone who's afflicted like I am. Because knowing there's another heir out there, broken like me, makes my footsteps feel lighter. Makes the air a bit crisper. Makes me feel *less* broken.

"I have my reasons. Besides, you owe me."

He grins. "No, but I never see her."

"She's inducting, she said. You don't have sessions with her?"

"She doesn't live inside the estate."

"Wait. *What?*"

Pinched stares glare in my direction as Abby's dance comes to a close.

"She hasn't set a foot inside Dlaminaugh in years, I heard."

The ballroom erupts in raucous applause, and a bell chimes. The crowd goes silent as Abby finishes her dance and approaches the stage to bind with her magic. A spotlight follows her to a small dais shrouded with floral arrangements.

"Abilene Grace Feldsher," Grandmom bellows into the microphone, and Abby steps forward.

Nore hasn't set a foot inside Dlaminaugh in years.

And yet she came to the Tea and acted like nothing was wrong.

I keep my eyes ahead, digging my nail into the fabric of the chair, trying to sort out what that means for me.

"It is my distinct honor," Grandmom says, raising her volume, and I watch as Abby climbs the stage. But the rest of what she says blurs into a haze in my head, which is fully consumed with Nore. The dagger disappears into Abby's chest with a crack; the lights flicker. I almost miss it.

"On behalf of House of Marionne, the Prestigious Order of Highest Mysteries formally welcomes you, Abilene Grace Feldsher, into our fold. *Supra alios.*" Grandmom curtsies to Abby.

"*Supra alios*," the crowd says.

"*Supra alios*, Headmistress," Abby mimics, and Grandmom embraces her.

I wave at her from the crowd, hoping she sees me as she faces everyone, smiling but a bit dazed. Her mother sobs into her arms, and Mynick punches the air, radiating excitement. Abby blinks a few more times, rubbing the tiniest scar where her dagger disappeared. For a moment, the skin beneath it seems to glow or something before Grandmom ushers her offstage and calls for the next debut.

Mynick rises from his seat to get to her. I grab his arm. "Is there anything else you can share?"

"Look, I really don't know a lot. She has her own cottage on the grounds because she takes her lessons privately. But she never comes out. Like she's scared to socialize or something. At the start of Season, Headmistress told everyone she was supposed to be going on a diplomatic tour. *Debs Daily* was supposed to be following the whole story, but nothing ever came out in the paper. Everything about Nore is just weird."

Dread nudges me. "Mynick, has the Council ever, like, leisurely visited Dlaminaugh?"

"Once, and not the whole Council. Just one of the Headmistresses."

"Who?"

"Headmistress Perl. Sorry, I wish I knew more." He shrugs before walking off to find Abby.

The ceremony drones on but Mynick's words pin me in my seat. I could sniff Nore's secret at a short luncheon, Beaulah would be much more savvy at recognizing the signs. My grip tightens on my chair as the ballroom empties. The walls close in.

Did Beaulah get to Nore? If so, she could get to me.

THIRTY-SIX

T he next morning, Thursday, a note slides under my door, and my heart skips a beat. But it's only a note from Jordan telling me I looked nice last night. I rip it up and toss it into the trash can. Friday no mail comes, and I can't take it anymore, so I send another letter to Nore Ambrose. This one much simpler.

Are you okay?

On Saturday morning a firm rap at the door nearly knocks me out of bed. I grab a robe and turn on a light, realizing it's so early it's still dark outside. I snatch open the door, hopeful it's a response from Nore Ambrose.

"Morning, dear."

"Grandmom?"

She pushes her way inside, and it takes me a moment to realize she's not alone.

"It's . . . six a.m."

"Yes, and today's the first day you'll be consumed by the public. It must be done right."

Consumed?

"Our annual Magnolia Merchant Festival is today. And the parent reception tonight."

Oh, right. Vendors will line the courtyard offering their wares to débutants. Debs who won't debut for years still travel here from all over to stock up on goods, collect business cards, and rub elbows on the Marionne estate. In addition to picking a dress, I made a whole checklist of all the things I still need to do. A beauty Shifter with Grandmom sets up a chair and lays out a stack of magazines.

"Is this really necessary?" I ask Grandmom, but she's too busy flipping through my closet.

The Shifter pulls at my bonnet and gestures for me to sit in her chair.

Grandmom holds up two dresses I'd intentionally stuffed into the back of my closet. "What do you think?"

Her brow rises with a challenge. I don't have fight in me this early in the morning. Not with Nore on my mind and Abby being gone. And other annoying people sending me notes I don't want. I accept defeat and sit in the chair.

"Up or down?" the Shifter asks.

"Whatever's fastest." I slump down in the seat as much as I can. It takes an hour to finish my hair and makeup to Grandmom's liking. Thankfully she at least listened to my color choices, and I don't look like a clown. Grandmom's been working at the desk in my room the entire time despite my telling her she's welcome to go. If this is what she's like at the top of the day, this is going to be a *long* day.

"Now, I'll miss the first hour of the festival or so because I have a tea with the Daughters of Duncan. They think I'm their key to reinstatement, but they're gravely mistaken. I'll catch up with you mid-morning, and we can finish up whatever you have left."

"You're not coming with me?"

She smiles, interpreting that the opposite way I meant it.

"I'll see you soon, though."

The door shuts. *An hour, she said?* I grab my checklist. I'll just have to make sure I'm done by then.

THE COURTYARD IS packed with people even at the top of the morning. Nore is the only thing on my mind. *She has a private cottage on her estate.*

So does that mean Isla Ambrose knows about her toushana and is trying to
help protect her? Or is Nore hiding her truth from her Headmistress like I am?
Vendors line the front lawn, tent tops as far as I can see. Slow, soft music
plays from a live band and delicious smells warm up my appetite. I'd
thought getting here before breakfast would help me sift faster through
things. But lines snake from each merchant table. Parents and family
members have come from far and wide to peruse the festival's finds. This
isn't going to be efficient or easy. I check my list again.

First a Vestiser. I also need shoes, cake stands, and some sort of party
favor for all three hundred whatever of them. This is to be a circus, and
I'm the star of the show.

I find the blue tent marked VESTISER VICTOR where a portly fellow in a
tailored suit is handing out cards to everyone who passes.

"Monsieur Victor Laurent." He kisses the back of my hand. "Vestiser
at your service." His stare lingers on my diadem. "You must be Quell
Marionne."

He rolls a rack of dresses in bags over to me and hands me a glass
of champagne. I almost fumble it, Nore tumbling through my memory
again. Last time she responded so quickly.

"Ma'am?"

"Sorry." I gulp down my entire champagne. There is nothing I can do
about Nore until she responds. "You were saying?"

"What sort of color or style are you looking for?" He rocks back and
forth on his heels.

"I'm not sure."

"We have a fine selection." He rolls two more racks out and lingers
eagerly.

"What would you suggest color-wise? Convince me and I might not
need to keep my other appointments."

"A green or blue would do wonders with your eyes." He holds out an
intricately beaded dress on his arm.

"Meh."

"Or how about . . ." He unzips another dress bag and pulls out an ombré blush gown trimmed in sparkles. "I modeled the magic of the sparkles after actual constellations. I can pull it exclusively for you."

I hold it up to myself, twisting in the floor mirror, and hardly recognize the girl staring back at me. "I don't think I realized a dress could leave me speechless. I'll take it. Wait. How much does this cost?"

He laughs. "It goes on the House account, Miss."

Dress done. I finish up with Victor, and if they're all that easy, I'll definitely finish before Grandmom can harass me.

With centerpieces, party favors, and shoes done, nearly an hour has passed when I hustle to my final stop—flowers. The floral vendors are set up on the courtyard nearest the rose garden, and I smell them before I reach them. Tables lined with bouquets, corsages, boutonnieres, and sample centerpieces are covered in a swarm of debs and their families. I pull a familiar white flower from a barrel of loose blooms sold by the stem. *Oleander.*

"Oh, these are very special, madam," says a gentleman in overalls and a wide-brimmed straw hat. "You must be Quell Marionne."

"Yes, I need . . ." I check my notes. "One boutonniere, a *lot* of centerpieces, and two arrangements for the stage."

"Oh, then you must use the finest blooms." He hands me a deep purple flower, and I cough at the price tag. "The black dahlia. *Extremely* difficult to craft. A lady of your stature should have something both as rare and as beautiful as she is."

"Good morning, sir." His attention shifts to someone behind me, and he tidies his clothes. I don't have to turn around to know it's Jordan.

"I'll take these and the oleanders," I tell the flower guy. "You'll have to get with Mrs. Cuthers, Headmistress's secretary, on the exact number of centerpieces. But everything should be billed to the House."

"A fine choice, madam." He bows and I walk away, in the opposite direction of Jordan.

He follows.

"What do you have left?"

"A dagger polisher."

"Use Rollins Shine. They've been in business a long time."

I sigh and stop to face him. "Okay, thank you. Is that all?"

"Quell."

"Jordan." *Walk away.* But my feet don't listen. I pull at a few dresses nearby just to avoid looking at him.

"Did you get my note?"

"I did. And I decorated my trash can with it."

His jaw clenches, and I savor it. *See how it feels to have your feelings toyed with.*

"Jordan!" someone calls. "Jordan, is that you?"

"Oh god," he mutters, and I turn to leave.

"Quell?" the same high-pitched voice says.

"Who is—" But one look at the woman answers my question. Jordan's mother isn't much taller than me. She struts toward us in a fancy checkered blazer and pointy heels. Her coiled hair is luscious and twisted out perfectly. Massive jewels hang from her ears.

"It's a pleasure to meet you. I'm Lena, Jordan's mother. He's told us much about this mentee of his. Though he didn't say you were so beautiful."

"You're so kind, thank you."

Behind Mrs. Wexton, with a phone pressed to his ear, is a ghostly pale version of Jordan. Mrs. Wexton tries to get his attention but is met with a finger from his hand.

"Work never stops." She smiles.

"Why are you here, Mother?"

"You say that like you're not happy to see me."

"That's not an answer."

"I saw the piece in Page Six! *Well* done," she says, ignoring him completely.

"And who is this?" Mr. Wexton joins the conversation and Jordan's expression hardens.

"This is Darragh Marionne's granddaughter and *heir*, Richard."

He glances at me dismissively, then back at Jordan. "Is everything above board here, son?"

The condescension in his tone curdles my stomach.

"Richard! I apologize." Mrs. Wexton squeezes my shoulder.

"If this mentor thing is getting out of hand, I'll talk to Headmistress," he goes on.

"I'm sorry, what are you presuming exactly?" I ask, crossing my arms.

Jordan touches my wrist. "You will talk to no one." Jordan spits the words, meeting his father's eyes for the first time. "Headmistress Perl is pleased with my work here."

"As long as you're sure." He turns his snarl in my direction. "And as long as she understands her place."

The shock of his crassness loosens my tongue. "Excuse me, sir, but I do believe we are standing on *my* family's estate."

Jordan groans.

His father glares so sharply I brace for his next words to cut. But his virulence isn't fired at me.

"Jordan. The Dragunhead is eager to meet you next week to discuss placement. I hope I don't have reason to hesitate when your name is brought forward."

"You don't. And you won't."

"Perhaps." He meets his son's glare with a challenge. Jordan's jaw tenses, but he stays quiet.

"Lena, we're leaving, and you"—Mr. Wexton points at me—"watch yourself, young lady." He departs, and Mrs. Wexton follows with no more than an awkward glance between us.

"My son's honor won't be stained by the bastard child of some prodigal— " he says to his wife as they storm off.

"Quell, I'm sorry. Ignore him. Ignore them both. I try my best to."

I stuff down my rage the best I can as Jordan steps in front of my line of sight.

"Please."

"What is he talking about anyway?" I fold my arms.

"Once I leave here, I'm being looked at to run the Dragun brother-hood under the Dragunhead himself, which is unheard of for someone of my age. But because of my skill and my taking on a mentee to demon-strate leadership, my chances look good. My father's promised to endorse me as well."

"So what's he suggesting? He's not going to support you anymore?"

"Getting involved with people is highly frowned upon for Draguns." His words are measured with the calmness of a brewing storm.

"He would seriously take all that you've worked for away?"

"He's warning me to not let us . . ." He looks off. "Get out of hand."

His parents have disappeared in the crowd and he glances in their di-rection. "I have to go deal with this."

"Do you?"

"I should."

"You shouldn't. He is entirely out of line." I want to be angry, but the only emotion I can tap is pity. Mom and I might not have had much. She is far from perfect, but she'd never manipulate me like that. Hold things over me to control me. She gave up her entire life to protect me. I wish that for him. That kind of love.

"You wouldn't understand, you don't have—"

"Parents?! Is that what you were going to say?" I reach to shove him right in the chest. But he catches my wrist, and I realize I've missed his touch on my skin.

"I was going to say you don't have to deal with Dragun politics."

"Don't go after him, Jordan. Don't play his game."

"It's not that simple."

"Isn't it?" My pity morphs into frustration rekindling my annoyance with the way he's been. "Jordan, for once in your life do something for yourself." I snatch my arm away and leave.

⚜

EVENING HAS WOUND down. Its golden pink glow dips below my bedroom window, and a yawn scratches my throat. With no response from Nore, and the irritation from earlier still stinging, I retreated to my room to bury myself in what matters: Cotillion studies.

An expected soft tap at my door stirs me from my covers. Grandmom never caught up with me; I was done with my entire list before she'd finished her tea brunch. There's no way she was thrilled about that. I pull open the door and fold in a curtsy when I spot polished men's shoes.

Jordan.

I shove the door to shut it, but he stops it with his hand.

"Why are you here?"

"To talk."

"Jordan—"

"To apologize."

"Shouldn't you be running after your father? I assume he's still here for the parent reception or whatever."

"I didn't talk to them. Instead, I thought long and hard about what you said."

"And—"

"May I come in?" His brows pull up in pleading and it tugs at my heart.

"Please," he says.

I should shut the door and never look back. But I part it wider instead. "Briefly."

He steps in, and I retreat to my bed.

"I was wrong for not being more forthright with my father about how I feel about you." His eyes trace me, and I can feel him searching for some hint that I accept his admission of fault. That I forgive him. But I'm not sure apologizing afterward is good enough. His gaze falls to my legs, curled over one another. The knot at his throat bobs, and I pull my covers over them.

"My father is a difficult man to please. But he wields a lot of control in the Order. I don't give a damn what he thinks, not truly. But I need him to think I do."

"But you do."

"I don't. It's bigger than him."

"So it's the Order you care about? Not his opinion?"

"Quell, this is my life. For now, he's the gatekeeper. You have to be able to see that."

"So what are you saying? You wouldn't have done anything differently?"

"No, I—"

"It sounds like that's exactly what you're saying. Coming in here like I'm your pet you can keep and appease with the right words." I hop up and head toward my door. "Because if that's what you're here for—"

"Stop." His fingers tug at my wrist, more in demand than request. He pulls me into him and there's no air between us. "I don't see you that way. I could never." He sighs. "It's *because* I respect you and know I can't give you everything you may want that I keep a distance." His heartbeat picks up, and I can feel it against my chest. "It's that reason only that I stop myself from saying, doing *stupid* things." His gaze falls to my lips.

"Jordan, I need to know that it's not just me imagining whatever this is."

The strap on my thin nightshirt slips off my shoulder, and he pulls it back into place, his touch soft as summer rain. His thumb finds my jaw, kindling a flame deep inside me, throbbing with a heat, a wanting, I've never felt.

"It's not."

His fingers trace down my neck as if they move to music, brushing my skin feather soft. Across my collarbone and over my bare shoulder as if he's admiring a fine sculpture. His arm tightens around my waist, and his gaze glows like a drunken sunrise. Because I know him, I can see there are more words hanging on his lips.

"Say it. Whatever you're thinking."

"I can't."

I force his eyes to mine. "You can."

He bites his lip. "I want you," he breathes, and somehow we are closer. His breath is warm on my lips, and I hang on them, teetering on the edge of a cliff, daring him to jump with me.

"Let yourself go," I tell him, as he once told me.

He hesitates, then gives in to the fire kindling in his eyes. His fingers curve around my hip with the knowing of how it must make me feel. I lean into his touch as his other hand runs through my hair, then down the back of my neck. "May I kiss you?"

I lean in, and his mouth meets mine, tender and warm. I shudder at the sweet taste of him, and the world melts away. He pulls at my lips, hungrily urging me to deepen their bond. I tremble all over with an ache deep inside, like a magic I've never felt. We meld as one and it's like dancing with him all over again.

He breaks the kiss, hunger unfurled in his eyes.

But his appetite has bled into me and I lean back in for another moment where there is no world, no poison in my veins, no Cotillion, no Headmistresses. Only me and him. Our lips crash together again, a bit clumsy from eagerness, and I let it consume me.

Heat, passion, *life* rushes into the darkest, most desolate parts of me, suturing what was broken. I open my mouth wider, giving all of myself to this feeling, to this moment, and it touches me deeper than my magic has ever thrummed.

THIRTY-SEVEN

⸺ ✳ ⸺

I wake the next morning sure yesterday was a dream. I kissed Jordan. I *kissed* Jordan! I roll in my covers and frown at Abby's empty bed before burying my head back in my pillow, trying to remember something besides yesterday. But it's impossible. So I force myself up and out of bed and out to sessions.

Dexler's voice drones on, but I'm somewhere far away, back in my room with Jordan's lips soft against mine. Depositing my magic onto my finger is easier this time. My index is dancing with red flame when a familiar face pops his head into class.

"Cultivator Dexler," Jordan says. "Just checking in on Miss Marionne if that's all right?"

She parts the door wider, and he rounds on my table. I let my kor sink back into myself and the flames shrink, then fade.

"How did you sleep?" His mouth moves, but I'm distracted by his hand at the small of my waist. How it makes me wish I could kiss him again.

"Are you all right?"

"Yes," I manage bashfully, trying to remember where I was in the cultivating lesson.

"Did I do something wrong?"

"No." *I've never kissed anyone before.*

He smiles knowingly. "You were perfect."

I chew my lip, embarrassed that I'm that transparent, and skim the notes on cultivating again. "You never visit me in Dexler's. What's so special about today?"

Jordan slips a note into my hand. It's signed by Grandmom, allowing me off the grounds tonight until curfew.

"I was listening. Yesterday." He takes both my hands. "Let me take you out?"

"Out? Like on a date?"

He nods.

"Jordan, I'm in class. Couldn't this wait?"

"No, I don't think it can or should."

"Jordan Wexton interrupting a lesson for something frivolous," I say. "Have we met?" I offer him a handshake. His thumb draws circles on my skin.

"Where are we going?"

"It's a surprise. Is that a yes?" He leans toward me, his expression brimming with anticipation. He wants to take me somewhere away from here, away from the pressure of Grandmom, away from worrying about Nore? To leave it all behind for even a second, to breathe?

"When do we leave?"

"Meet me in the foyer at seven. Wear a gown."

I HADN'T WANTED to go back to the Secret Wood again so soon, to continue using my toushana, but I can't risk having issues tonight. The air outside is thick and hot, hotter than it's been, reminding me Season will be coming to an end in weeks. Jordan's already outside the doors to the Chateau when I arrive. He's in a tux with his House jacket, stitched with red threads and tiny suns along the lapel. His tux has never been more dapper. His gold House pins line his lapel. I threw on a gold sequined gown and pulled my hair up with a few tendrils hanging here and there.

"You're breathtaking." He hands me a rose and I thank him, looking for some hint of where we might be going but seeing none.

"We're not cloaking to get there?" I ask when a car coated in a fine layer of familiar dust rolls up.

"Where we are going, there will be Unmarked. Tonight, we play the game of blending in."

I glance at his pocket watch. *July 10.* "The Tidwell Ball is tonight!"

His lips curl in a clever grin as his driver opens the car door.

"The minute I'm over it, we're leaving."

"You have my word." Jordan slides into the car behind me, and the door closes. Chateau Soleil is in the rear window when the world shifts and Grandmom's neighborhood bleeds into glittering lights of towering buildings. The city throbs with life, people darting in and out of traffic, car horns blaring in the distance. I press my nose to the window. We're not anywhere near Louisiana anymore. Jordan's hand folds in mine. Tonight, I let it all go.

Tonight, I will be free.

THE DOORS TO the Q hotel part as we approach, and Jordan's arm threads around mine. His House ring's rubies glint in the lights from the line of photographers at the door. Several held back by velvet ropes shout our names to beckon us over.

"Ignore them," he whispers to me, his lips brushing my ear.

"Mister Wexton," the doorman says. "Should I have the penthouse prepared? Is your father with you tonight?"

"Just myself and Miss Marionne. No need."

Inside, the hotel drips with elegance. Columns and oiled furniture, polished floors and sparkly dim lighting. Inscriptions along the crown of the ornamented ceiling remind me of Chateau Soleil.

Jordan sees me gawking and points at carved suns along the perimeter of a gilded mirror near a lounge area. Every other sun is darkened in the middle. "Dysiian influences, alongside Sfentian."

"Wasn't Dysiis that Order member who was barred from studying magic?"

"Dysiis believed to understand the full breadth of magic's capacity to do good, we have to understand its darker parts. He studied toushana until he died. That's where everything we know about it comes from."

"Oh, he sounded like some sort of rebel."

"He is. To some." Sleek black elevator doors open, and we step inside.

Jordan squeezes my hand as the doors close. When they reopen, we follow a sign for the Yaäuper Rea Ballroom. It's expansive and a burst of color. Sweeping fabrics, sparkling candelabras, silver trays, and a lavishly dressed crowd. I hold tighter to Jordan's arm.

"Mister Wexton." A curly-mustached fellow with a big barrel belly who looks oddly familiar grips Jordan by the shoulders. "I was just talking to Charlie and Sand about you."

"Marcius Walsby, good to see you."

"And this must be Miss Marionne." He reaches for my hand, and I oblige, resisting the urge to grimace as his lips touch my skin.

"Pleasure to meet you." *I know his face.*

"The pleasure is all mine. The picture in the paper did not do justice to your full regality, young lady."

I snatch my hand away.

"Good to see you, as always," Jordan says, pulling me away. "We should make rounds."

"Is he in the Or—?"

"A *member* is the term we use away from home. And no, he's not a member. Walsby is the governor."

"I *knew* I'd seen him somewhere before. He's—"

"A witless jerk, corrupt, and disgusting. So naturally he's quite popular and powerful."

"Does he know about . . . us?"

"He knows we are an exclusive group with extensive means. And to a politician that's all he needs to know to care."

When a server with bubbling flutes on a tray passes, I grab a glass, still rocked with disbelief. This whole world, the wealth, the access, the power—it all exists because the Order *wants* it to.

"And what about him?" I point at a neatly shaven fellow in a dark suit with silver streaks in his hair, my curiosity piqued at stepping into the other side of the world I used to live in.

"Emerson Tidwell, himself. Member. House Oralia." Jordan's words brush my ear, his body pressed hard against my back. The music shifts to a slightly slower tune, and he hugs around me, swaying.

"You know him?"

He turns my chin in the direction of Emerson, who is using his teal handkerchief to clean his glasses.

"Look closely."

We dance in Emerson's direction, and I spot the embroidered sigil of House Oralia on his handkerchief.

"What about her?" I point at another, a girl about my age with a swan-like gait as she glides from one conversation to the next.

"House Marionne."

"Her fleur earrings?"

Jordan smiles.

"And him?"

"You tell me."

I stare as inauspiciously as I can for several minutes but come up empty. "I can't tell."

"Okay, that was unfair. He's Unmarked." Jordan snickers and I elbow him playfully.

"She's House Perl, am I right?" I indicate a girl with radiant copper skin and dark eyes that sparkle like gems. Her dress is black sequin with a gather of red fabric on one shoulder. He glances at her, then promptly turns me in his grip, and we dance, facing one another.

"You know her *well*, I assume."

"I didn't say that."

"You didn't have to."

He shifts uncomfortably in my arms.

"There are no swans; Abby will be so relieved she didn't miss them," I say to lighten the mood. But his gaze is darting in every direction.

"Jordan, I don't care about some girl you—"

We stop dancing and he leads me to a shadowed corner near a table with an ice sculpture. "Are you comfortable? Do you want to leave?" he says, looking everywhere but at me.

"Do *you*? What's going on?"

He skims the crowd with a harried expression.

"You have to tell me things. That's how this works."

"I think there's a raid happening tonight," he whispers. "There've been more lately because of all the concerns about the Sphere. We never should have come."

"A raid?"

But before Jordan can respond, I spot a familiar dark-haired man with a low shave. He's dressed nicer than the last time I saw him that afternoon at the Market, but I couldn't mistake that face. Beside him is another I faintly recognize. I steady myself on the hard wall as the hazy memory of a man bound to a chair screaming rattles in my mind. The smoke that choked him, the way his head lolled. That man there, across the ballroom, is who stood over him, puffing on his cigar.

If those other men from the Market are here, the Dragun after me must be, too.

THIRTY-EIGHT

YAGRIN

Candlelit chandeliers swayed ever so gently from the ceiling of the Yaäuper Rea Ballroom. Yagrin tugged at his tux jacket, then eyed the seam of the doors for any indication of tampering. There was none. He reared back ever so slightly on his heels, pushing his magic up through his body to his head to sharpen his Dragun senses. If there was even a whiff that tonight's exchange of Headmistresses' goods downstairs could bleed into this ballroom, he would run out of there right now. Mother be damned. But it appeared all at the Tidwell was in order, glittering and decadent. He glanced at his watch. *Ten minutes.*

"Your heart's racing." Red worked her hand into his clammy fist.

"Yours is, too."

"You really don't have to be so nervous. I'll be fine."

He escorted her through the crowd, smiling at the familiar faces. "Don't make eye contact with anyone unless it's completely unavoidable."

"Yagrin, just because I like living on a farm doesn't mean—"

"This is *not* a game, Red." He ushered them to a dark corner.

"No, it's a party." Her finger traced the slope of his nose and it melted him. How he wished none of this mattered. That having two left feet could be the worst of his anxieties tonight. But the veil he wore when he was with her had been ripped off when they stepped through the Q's doors.

"The rules, tell them to me again."

She sighed. "Don't talk to anyone; if they try to talk to me, make a quick excuse and hurry away. If someone asks how I know you, I should say that I don't. Not even your name. And not give any explanation beyond that. Let's see, oh, and under no circumstances am I to leave this ballroom."

"Promise me."

"Yag—"

"Promise me, please."

"I promise."

He tried to exhale but couldn't. He wanted to believe he could have this moment with Red, give her what she wanted and appease his Head-mistress, too. His two worlds could coexist without colliding, even if tonight would be a near miss. He checked his watch again and looked for his peers or the freckle-faced girl who Mother had reminded him twice may be here tonight. But when a portly fellow walked toward him with wide eyes, Yagrin swept Red in another direction.

"Go over to the ice sculpture. Stay there until I come back and grab you." He left her there, and shame twisted his insides. This wasn't what Red wanted when she insisted on coming. But it was the best he could offer. Word could not get back to his family or anyone from his House that he was there with someone. They'd begin to ask questions, find out she was Unmarked, and assume he'd shared the secrets of their world. His stomach soured at the thought of what they would do then.

The big-bellied fellow plucked a slender purple-leaved cigar from a shiny case embossed with a cracked column as he caught up with him. "I thought that was you. They keep it so dim in these places. How have you been, my boy? I didn't realize you all would be here tonight."

"Fine, sir." He craned for a glimpse of his Dragun brethren.

"All in order?"

Yagrin smiled politely. He wasn't foolish enough to affirm or deny their private business.

"Well, I won't keep you, I can see you have things to attend to." He watched Yagrin for a response, but Yagrin remained stoic as he told the nosy House alum goodbye.

He was headed toward the sculpture to rejoin Red, who was poking holes in the ice, when he spotted a black and red gown from the corner of his eye. He glanced that way for his Housemate, but she was gone. *Where were the rest of them?* He peered through the crowd. The ballroom was massive, twice the size of the ones at Hartsboro. He navigated through the bodies of chattering people, head down, grateful at least the size of the crowd was working in his favor. He spotted another Housemate with mussed-up dark hair and a tailored suit. The fellow tapped his watch and held up three fingers at Yagrin.

Downstairs in three minutes.

Yagrin flipped his coin and blew out a breath before quickly checking on Red. She'd broken off a chip of ice and was stirring it in her drink.

"Okay, problem," she said.

Yagrin's heart hiccupped. "What?"

"My feet hurt. These heels, I—"

"Just blend in, *please*. I have to go handle a thing. The rules, remember." He left her there swearing to himself he'd never do this again and somehow, after they left, he'd make it up to her.

Yagrin stepped into the elevator, and three of his peers joined him without a word, all Draguns who'd finished with him last Season. The one beside him crossed her arms.

"What's wrong?" He pressed the hidden button to the lowest garage floor of the Q, the one only accessible by members.

"Nothing's wrong," she said, clearly lying.

"Whatever's clouding your head, forget it," he said. "We're doing this clean tonight; smooth, no screwups, no escalations. *Officium est honor quis.*"

"Keep talking like that and people might believe you actually want to be here," she said. The two beside her smirked. When the doors opened, Yagrin hustled out of there as fast as he could and followed a long hall to a glass-encased meeting room.

"Yagrin," their leader for the night greeted him, his mask already on his face. "Surprised to see you."

"Charlie." He shrugged, confused.

Charlie's glare hardened but he turned his attention to the others, and Yagrin was finally able to swallow.

"Bring it in," Charlie said, and everyone huddled around him. "We're here to exchange those packing crates"—he pointed at a plastic-wrapped tower of wooden shipping pallets in an adjoining room separated by a glass window—"for payment. Once the deal is done, if you sniff out any toushana among their men, have at it. But only maim as needed. That's from Mother herself. Dragunhead gets no word of this one. Questions?"

His Housemate in the long dress flexed her fingers. "He never lets us have any fun."

"Who's the customer?" Yagrin asked.

Charlie sucked his teeth before answering. "Old man Manzure."

Yagrin shifted on his feet. Manzure was a snake. "We *have* to maintain the upper hand."

"No shit, Yagrin." Charlie shrugged him off. "Let's go." He pounded his fists together and then to his chest.

"Aye," Yagrin barked with the others, and where it usually rang hollow, tonight he meant it. He would be the monster, not for Mother, for Red. As he walked off, Charlie pulled him back by the hem of his coat.

"Just stay out of the way, all right? Before you mess something up."

The lashing stung, but Yagrin rolled his shoulders and followed them into the room.

Inside, a petite fellow with a crown of white hair and a matching mask on his face sat, alone with a small briefcase on his lap. Yagrin's stomach twisted. *Manzure hadn't brought a single bit of muscle to meet with a group of Draguns?* Something was wrong. His peers all watched, impassive.

"It's good to see you again, Charlie," Manzure said. "How have you been?"

"We're here to do pre-agreed business. Not to talk." Charlie squared his shoulders. "Payment?" He held out his hand and Manzure's tightened on the briefcase in his lap.

"You have grown so much, *inches*, I dare say," Manzure said, now running his fingers across the length of his briefcase.

Charlie checked his watch. "You have three minutes to deliver on this deal or the offer to purchase is permanently rescinded."

Yagrin clenched his fist.

"You know, obsession with youth is what drives most to madness in their old age." Manzure crossed his arms. "But I don't think that makes sense. You see, when you are young, your strength is in the way, your magic answers more quickly, you can zip around faster, flex your brawn. But when you are old"—he touched his temple, rimmed in receding hair—"your strength is in your wit. If you survive long enough, you'll see what I mean."

"Two minutes," Charlie says.

"I have reconsidered the terms of the offer and have decided the price for the liquid kor is exorbitant. I will take the same quantity for half price." He played with the locks on his briefcase, and Yagrin's heart leapt.

"You—"

The *thrung* of Maznure's briefcase clicking open shut Charlie's mouth and sent shivers up Yagrin's spine. Out of the suitcase he pulled a nail clipper and file, then proceeded to manicure his nails.

"And as you consider siccing your dogs on me, if I am not back upstairs by the stroke of the hour, my Shifters—strategically placed around this hotel—have instructions to seal the exits and shift the air to methyl chloride. The entire ballroom, all your lovely guests, would be dead within minutes. And not to mention the legal implications for dear Mister Wexton and his precious hotel. It would be the top news in all the papers. The *scandal*." He cupped his cheek, as if smitten with himself.

Yagrin and the others gape at each other first, then Charlie.

"It's as I said, Charlie." Manzure tapped his temple. "When you are older, you will plan with your head, not just muscle."

Yagrin's gut lurched as he looked to the others for some sort of direction. Each of them wore blank stares. His heart thrummed. They had to do something. Fast. Red was up there.

"Charlie, this guy is a bluffer," Yagrin whispered in his ear, but his Dragun brother was frozen with indecision. He could sit there and wait for someone else to decide Red's fate or he could do it himself.

Yagrin pulled at the cold dead trickle of darkness and twisted his torso until he disappeared. Charlie glared in shock as Yagrin encircled the room in a dark fog. The world darkened at its edges as he lassoed his shadowed self around Manzure. Yagrin jerked his body and his cloak cinched tight, squeezing Manzure's neck, choking him with darkness. He swatted at him, but Yagrin was no more than air.

Manzure may have been older and wiser, but he was human, and like anyone else, when it came down to it, he would save himself. Everyone was a coward in the end. Just as he was.

"Let . . ." He coughed. "Me . . . Go!"

Yagrin squeezed. He hadn't brought a single person of protection into the meeting room. He was all bluff. The Shifter threat was a bluff, too, he would bet.

The world's color faded, and for a moment Yagrin's grip on Manzure slacked as his cloaking magic drained him, as if he'd been hanging upside down too long. Manzure grew woozy. But Yagrin wasn't much better. He needed to let go, *soon*. Once Manzure's will buckled and he sagged in his chair, Yagrin reappeared, breathless. He staggered, then steadied himself and grabbed Manzure in a Dragunhold, hand cupped on the back of the neck, thumb pressed up into his chin. Manzure wriggled like a fish caught on a line, then stiffened as the paralyzing magic set in.

"His phone," Yagrin said to Charlie, who tossed it to him. "Call them now. These Shifters of yours. Go on."

Eyes around the room darted in every direction. Charlie's lips thinned. But Yagrin tightened his grip. He knew what he was doing. There were no Shifters. This would prove it. He released his hold on him, and Manzure sank in his chair. Then tapped Call on his phone.

"Sir?" the voice on the phone said.

Yagrin's heart leapt. *He wasn't bluffing.*

He had to salvage this.

"I—" Manzure started, but Yagrin was faster. He summoned all the magic he could muster. Heat pooled in his gut, and he shoved up into his chest, into his head until magic burned behind his ears, down his throat, and onto his lips. He blew, air rippled through his fingers, and he pictured himself plucking the notes of Manzure's voice one by one, mimicking their pitch and tone.

Manzure opened his mouth, but it was Yagrin who spoke.

"The deal is done, abandon your positions," he said, in Manzure's voice. The man's eyes widened as if he'd seen a ghost, and his briefcase slipped from his lap. Yagrin's Housemate with the long dress plucked the envelope from the fallen briefcase.

"Thanks for the charity," she said.

Yagrin collapsed in relief.

BY THE TIME he could stand without swaying, almost all of Yagrin's peers and Manzure had been cleared out. He checked his watch. *Past midnight.*

"Come on, then," Long Dress said, roping his arm around her shoulders to lug him up. "I misjudged you, I guess."

"Did you?" A scowl stained Charlie's expression as he appeared behind them. "Or did you peg him just right?"

Yagrin steadied himself on his own feet and dusted off his jacket. He needed to get back upstairs to Red. "Manzure was going to take out the whole ballroom. I did something good."

"Since when do some Unmarked in silk suits matter more than getting Mother her payment?"

Red's face was on the back of Yagrin's eyelids. "Some of our people are up there. They're not all Unmarked." An excuse, but still true.

"Look around, Yagrin. *Our* people are all down here."

He went cold all over. Mother's people. Their House. The unspoken rule: House first.

"I should go," Yagrin said, brushing past Charlie.

"Where you off to tonight?" Charlie asked at his back.

He ignored him. When the door closed, he took off in a full sprint toward the elevator. Back on the ballroom floor, Yagrin sifted through the thinned crowd for sight of Red. They needed to get out of there. He was naive to think tonight could work. He spotted her tittering behind her gloved hand with a sinewy blonde in a teal flowered dress. His throat thickened.

"Excuse me, sorry to interrupt." He tugged her along.

"Slow down." She had to walk-run to keep up with him.

"I told you, talk to no one."

"You left me up here for *forever*. I almost went home."

He rubbed his temples. "Look, I'm sorry. Let's just get out of here." He turned and bumped into one of his Housemates from downstairs.

"Sorry to interrupt, Yagrin," his blond-haired brother said. "And you are?"

Red gaped at the Dragun's outstretched hand. She looked at Yagrin.

"You didn't tell your own brothers that you had a friend, Yags?" Blondie said. "We're supposed to be family." He jostled Yagrin's shoulders.

"We just met," Red said.

"I have it on good authority you've known each other for some time." He glanced over his shoulder at the girl in the teal dress Red had been talking to.

Red's eyes darted.

"Yags, Mother called. Something urgent popped up. She needs to see you."

"I'll go to her as soon as I get Red home."

"We'll see her home." Blondie stepped forward. Charlie and the others were suddenly at his back. "You should get to Mother. There's a chopper on the roof, waiting." Charlie tried to pull him along but Yagrin shoved off their hands. People started to watch.

"Don't make a scene," Charlie warned.

Yagrin huffed. He shouldn't overreact or they'd know there was more to him and Red.

Red wore a smile. But Yagrin could only see worry in her brown eyes.

"It's fine, I can get home on my own. I hope your mother's okay." Red started toward the door, but Blondie stepped in her path.

"I'll escort you out," he said, offering his arm. She swallowed before looping hers around his.

"Let me know when you make it home." Yagrin hugged her goodbye. "Get away from them as soon as you can," he whispered in her ear. She broke the hug and smiled tightly before they were off. Yagrin resituated his coat around himself as he, too, was ushered out the door.

THIRTY-NINE

※

Heads turn at commotion near the ballroom doors, but the crowd is so thick, and the entrance is so far across the room, I can't make out what the trouble is about.

"Stay here," Jordan says, eyeing the crowd in that direction.

"No." I lasso his wrist, scanning, fearing the worst.

"If there is a raid happening, these things can get ugly."

I tug at him, then halt when I spot a familiar head of brown hair on a set of broad shoulders. His deep-set brow is unmistakable.

The Dragun who cornered me at the gas station.

The Dragun after me.

I stagger backward and bump into a table. A few gasp. My pulse races as I watch the Dragun getting what appears to be a stern talking-to by two House of Perl men and a girl with red hair. The discussion escalates to an argument, and I am careful to keep my head down. I yank Jordan, pulling him in the opposite direction.

"Is there somewhere else we can go?"

"I know just the spot." He takes me by the hand and leads me through the room to a back door where waitstaff go and come. The service entrance of the ballroom empties into a long hall. We traipse through the bowels of the hotel and finally arrive at a service elevator. "I hope you don't mind taking the elevator. Cloaking here is a risk."

"Jordan, when I'm not with you, I take the elevator and stairs everywhere."

That gets a laugh. We exit the elevator onto a rooftop veranda where there is lounge furniture, a glittering overlook of the city, and a grand piano. A helicopter takes off in the distance. The commotion in the hotel appears to have moved to the sidewalk below. But my hold on the lip of the balcony slacks as the men disappear into a car. Jordan watches intently beside me, until it speeds off.

He tugs at his coat. "Well, whatever was going on, it's done now."

I exhale, feeling a bit more relaxed. I join Jordan on the piano bench. Tonight could have gone completely differently. And yet I am here, in a dress, dancing, having drinks.

"I'm glad I came tonight."

"The Tidwell is . . ."

"It's not the ball or any of that. It's being out here in the . . . open." Able to move in a world where I used to have to be a shadow. "You don't know how much that means."

"I'd like to."

I pull at my earring and press a few piano keys. We laugh at how terrible it sounds. It unspools the tightness in my posture. I slide closer to him on the bench.

"There's so much I want to tell you," he says. "So much I've wanted to say to you for so long." He sighs. "I can't figure out what tomorrow looks like and that doesn't work for someone like me. You understand? Everything I do has to be careful, calculated. And with you it's like . . ." He leans toward me, insistent, and I warm all over at the adoration in his eyes.

"Like what?" I play with the ends of my hair to do something with the angst buzzing through me.

"When I'm with you . . ."

I squeeze his hand. "Go on."

"It's like . . . there is no tomorrow or yesterday. Everything about you pins me in the present." He smiles hesitantly. "You're powerful but it doesn't possess you. You fit in this world as if it was made for you. But somehow on your own terms." His gaze moves to the city beyond us.

"I . . . envy it." He stares as if I'm a puzzle he needs a few more pieces to suss out.

Heat rushes to my face.

"You will run a quarter of the Order someday. It makes me hopeful that it could be . . ." A gust of wind steals whatever he was going to say. He shakes his head.

"Continue. Please."

"Our world is made of glass, Quell." Something hides in the cracks of his words, as if it could shatter the very glass he speaks of.

Our fingers find each other, crossing themselves.

"I have kept you at a distance, on purpose. I'm sorry for that. Ask me anything, I'm an open book."

He fidgets, his hand slick in mine, with a nervousness that suggests he's never trusted someone like this before. I could exploit this moment, dig into him to find out all the things I've been dying to know about toushana. *No.* He will know that his worth to me isn't in any information he gives me or what he's able to do for me. But in who he is. And no more.

"Just talk."

"About anything?"

"Anything."

His brow slashes in thought. "You were right the other day about my father." He stares down at the piano. "I guess I just thought by now it wouldn't matter so much."

I trace the edges of his hair, and I can feel him relax against my fingers. If home could be a moment, a feeling, I'm pretty sure this is it.

"I moved a lot when I was little." I let out a huge breath. "My mom was always afraid . . . someone would find out about my magic." My heart ticks faster as I skirt so close to the truth.

"Well, I'm glad you've found your way back to us."

I set my head on his shoulder. "Play me something."

His fingers dance along the piano, and the strain permanently etched in his expression melts away. The melody races my pulse, low and fast at first, then high and soothing. I sway to the rhythm. The song rises to a pinnacle of notes clustered together like a starry sky before it ends with a crisp, sharp finish.

"Where did you learn to play like that?"

"I was eight, in piano lessons when Audior magic came to me for the first time. I'd—" His expression darkens for the second time tonight as he thinks of home. "Seen something earlier that day and was trying to get it out of my head. Playing so fierce and fast, my fingers stopped, but the music went on, my magic transfiguring the sounds in the air. My parents had me tested right away."

"Tested?"

"Yes." His shoulder tense beneath my touch. "I was able to reach two forms of magic so young that I was moved in with Headmistress Perl that same day." *He's never truly known a home either.* He meets my eyes, his narrowed in concern. "I didn't learn about my third strand of magic until I'd left home."

"Toushana."

"No, Quell. That's something we touch when we have to, not something we nurture to grow."

"Oh, you didn't exactly explain it to me." I laugh to keep the mood light, but as he turns to me, I grip the wood of my seat.

"I don't talk about these things because I don't want you to fear me."

A flutter of chill raises hairs on my skin. "It doesn't scare me."

His thumb grazes my jaw. "It should."

I swallow. I cross and uncross my legs, commanding the cold angst coiling in me back down. Nothing is ruining this moment.

"There's a reason Draguns only really socialize among themselves. It's easy to lose yourself in all of it. The power. The proximity to forbidden magic. Toushana is different because it feeds off of a person to grow stronger. Poisoning their ability to reach their real magic. Part of the reason the Order is so adamant about hunting people with toushana is that the bounds of its power are unknown. It's not clear when it stops growing. But once it takes a person over completely, the person is no longer in control, the toushana is. Many of Dysiis's findings were actually burned."

I twist the end of my skirt, teetering on the edge of my seat. "Why?"

"Darkbearers."

The diadems in the glass cases on display all over Chateau Soleil. "Toushana worshippers. Early Draguns—Sunbringers, I believe they were called back then—hunted them." I hug around myself.

He nods. "Centuries ago, some magic students found Dysiis's teachings and distorted them completely, saying toushana wasn't to be feared, it was to be *used*. A weapon the Marked were blessed with by Sola Sfenti to use as they pleased."

Is that what they worry I'll do? Is that why they'd kill me?

"That's of course not at all the point of Dysiis's teachings. But that's when Sunbringers were born. That's *why*."

I've stopped breathing.

"So yes, I can summon toushana outside of myself and use it. But it takes much intentional focus and *lots* of training to keep it from seeping into my bones and binding with me. To not bend to its will but keep it bent to mine. But judging by the Sphere's crack, there are many more using toushana out there."

Nore's face flits through my memory.

"Killing those with toushana is also what keeps the Sphere in balance. We think."

My breath snags on the word *kill*. I want to plug my ears or tell him to keep playing.

"My peers have been busy lately trying to find more with toushana." He twists his mouth.

"Yes?"

"Brooke and Alison, the girls from my House, were killed by someone on suspicion of having it. And they didn't, Quell. There have been so many like them over the years."

"So many . . . ?"

"*Hundreds* of members, maybe more, who've been killed over *decades* with no explanation. The assumption is that it's members who fashion themselves Sunbringers come again taking matters into their own hands against those they suspect of having toushana. Instead of letting us do our work, which has a due process of how to handle it."

Is that what Beaulah thinks she's doing, helping . . .

"But I'm not sure if I buy that. Brooke and Alison were innocent. There was no whiff of forbidden magic." He screws his lips, ruminating on his words like two pieces of a puzzle that don't quite fit together. He laughs, and my heart stumbles over the suddenness.

"What?"

"Do you know what my brothers would do to me if they knew I was telling you all this?" He rakes a hand through his hair. "I swear I don't know what you're doing to me."

"You don't have to if you don't want to."

"I'd share all I am with you if I could, Quell." He exhales, and it's like the weight of the world rides the wave of his breath. "You know, I finish at the end of summer. And the position I'm taking means I'll have more freedom than most. From what I've heard, the Sphere will be my main focus. It has to be located so we can figure out how it's been cracked." He bites into his knuckle and something in his eyes takes him far away.

"Maybe we shouldn't talk about any of that anymore." I fold my hand into his.

"Part of me wishes I was already out there, you know?"

"But then, how could you be here?"

"Exactly." His eyes drift off, and he's gone again.

"I want cake." I stand, willing him to come back to me, desperate to hold us in this moment.

"I'm fairly sure the kitchens are closed, but—"

"Come on." I pull him up and take the stairs.

"Quell, we shouldn't make a scene, really . . ." He has to hustle to keep up with me as I fly down the stairs. He reaches for me, but I twist through the stairwell door and spill into the lobby.

"Mister Wexton," says someone behind the reception desk. "Is there something you need?"

"No—"

"Could you tell me where the kitchens are?" I blurt out.

"What are you doing?" Jordan whispers, but the concierge points and I pull Jordan in that direction, down an aisle of rooms, through another small lobby, and into a dining room with a few late patrons. The kitchen is through an open doorway behind the bar, and I hurry that way, cutting a corner too close, bumping into something.

"Oh!" A waiter dashes out of my way, tray wobbling on his hand.

"Sorry," I yell as I stumble into an empty kitchen. "Now, cake." I pull open fridge door after fridge door until I spot a brown round layer cake coated in creamy chocolate.

"Are you going to—"

I fold my fingers around the messy chocolate, sticky between my fingers, and bite into it. "Mmmm, oh my goodness. It's heaven."

Jordan's eyes double in size.

I hold a piece at his lips.

"Qu—"

I tip the cake into his talking mouth and frosting smears on his lips. I snort, laughing as he chews.

"That's really . . . good actually." He tries to clean his mouth but only smears the frosting more. "I feel like I have something on my face."

My ribs ache with laughter as he paws at his face.

"Do I have—? Is there something?"

I shove another piece into his mouth. Laughter bursts from his lips and the wall holds me up from giggling so hard. I take another bite before licking some of the icing off his finger and pressing my lips to his. His mouth melts into mine and our bodies press close. He softens in my arms.

"My father's going to be furious when he hears about this."

"Good."

By the time Jordan and I return to Chateau Soleil, it's an entire hour past curfew. Thankfully we were able to make it inside without running into Grandmom. He drops me off at my door with a long, slow kiss good night. Inside, I reach to pull back my covers, where I spot a familiar envelope on my bed. The envelope I sent Nore.

Return to Sender. Undeliverable to Recipient.

FORTY

❋

YAGRIN

Gravity bore down on Yagrin as the city grew small beneath the chopper. He could swear it was his own heart he heard swooping faster and faster overhead. He turned his phone in his hands as the pilot, Charlie, eyed him in the mirror. *He'd just met Red. He had bound at Third Rite like everyone else.* He rehearsed his lies. He would act like nothing was wrong until they had proof there was.

The world tipped like a yacht caught in a storm as they turned and he spotted the sprawling Hartsboro, but the aircraft didn't descend. It kept going. When they touched down, a copper glow kissed the Cape's waters beyond them. He'd only ever visited Mother's Massachusetts home once before.

"Headmistress will meet you in the library shortly."

Yagrin checked his phone. Still no sign Red had shaken the others and made it home. Nerves swam in his gut as he hurried inside.

"*Fratris, fortunam,*" someone said.

"*A fortuna.*" He spun. Felix.

They shook, then pressed fists together and to their chests.

"Thought you'd be here. I saw your father here a bit ago."

"My *father?*" His heart stuttered. Facing off against Headmistress was one thing, but his father could always tell when he was lying. "And what are you doing here?" Did Felix know anything about this interrogation Yagrin was about to endure? "I thought the Dragunhead had you out West on a big assignment over the Duncans."

"Mother called in a favor." Felix glanced over his shoulder, then lifted the tail of his coat where ruffled papers were shoved into his pants pocket. "Tracking coordinates," he whispered before unfolding them. His eyebrows bounced.

Tracking . . . "She's looking for the Sphere?"

"Aye. Got a list of the previous places it's been. I'm starting with those."

Mother was looking for the Sphere . . . why? "Anything else you can share?" Yagrin pressed.

"Nothing to report yet. She's intent on getting some eyes on it to see what's causing the shift. No one wants that thing to break." Felix was a bit wild, which made him a very effective Dragun. But he was naive when it came to Mother. If she had him privately looking for the Sphere, it wasn't just because she was curious. Rikken's warning about a Headmistress trying to find the Sphere sludged through his memory just as Charlie poked his head into the hall, and Yagrin went cold all over. "I should get going."

He and Felix shook again. "Tell your father I said hello."

Yagrin stepped into the sitting room outside of the library, and his heart stopped. There in a leather wingback was his father, flipping through a hunting magazine. He cleared his throat, and his father's gaze floated up and down him, unmoved, before he returned to his reading.

Just like that, Yagrin was turning seventeen all over again at his birthday dinner. That year his father managed to attend. He'd even brought him a gift. But when he found Yagrin had earned three nights in the cold as punishment for low marks at Hartsboro, he hemmed him up right there in public in front of everyone and no one. He told him if he botched things up again, the family was done with him completely. He decided his father was dead to him that moment.

Yagrin checked his phone. Still nothing from Red. His blood boiled. *If they hurt her . . .* The doors to Headmistress Perl's library opened. Yagrin stood. His father did as well. But only her assistant emerged. She leaned into his father's ear, whispering, and his scowl deepened.

"Tell him," his father said gruffly, tossing the magazine aside before leaving.

The assistant cleared her throat. "Headmistress Perl had something urgent come up. She still needs to discuss an important matter with you. But she'll summon you again very soon. In the meantime, she asked me to give you this message." She handed him an envelope before retreating inside the double doors.

Yagrin's breath should come easier knowing he didn't have to face Beaulah Perl and his father today, but his heart stammered as he ripped open the letter.

Duty is the honor of the willing.

She knew. She must. He shoved the note in his jacket pocket, his pulse thundering. *Air, he needed air.* He flagged one of the maids. "Get me a pilot to the front lawn to ready the chopper."

"Sir, you are welcome to stay for—"

"Do what I said, *now.*"

She hurried off and guilt twisted in him like a corkscrew. He shouldn't have yelled at her like that. He rushed out to the grass and looked for an aircraft light. Frustration tangled in him like a nest of barbed wire. He was glad he didn't have to see Mother today. Whatever she knew he wasn't prepared to face. He needed to make a decision, for once in his life. To stand for something or to not. Because the next time she summoned him, he'd have to answer to her and his father.

The tip of the sun disappeared below the horizon and it reminded him of golden red hair. He could finish his job, apprehend the freckle-faced girl before she debuted, obey, like a good Dragun. *Or . . .* an idea struck him.

The bird's lights clicked on and he rushed toward it, checking his phone again, tapping Red's name and ramming the End button when he heard her voicemail.

If he could find the Sphere's location before Felix, he could barter it with Headmistress when they next met. He could come clean to her about what he really wanted—*out* of the Order. And she would have to grant it to him. He slid into the bird and clicked his safety belt in place. Tracking the Sphere was the only thing Yagrin had outscored everyone on in Dragun training. Even his own family.

He weighed his choices, checking his phone again. He fired off a text to no response. He bit down. He couldn't keep this up much longer. They knew about Red now. It would only be a matter of time before they knew what she meant to him. And found a reason she should die.

The pilot's voice buzzed in his ear, "So where to?"

"To the Tavern." He needed to meet with a Trader. He'd made his decision.

FORTY-ONE

—*—

I wake to Grandmom's hand on my back.

"What are you doing here?" I sit up. "I—I mean, good morning, Grandmom."

"You came in quite late last night. Past curfew."

I swallow.

"The consequence for that is usually three lashes."

I wince.

"Not to worry, that practice has been done away with, in our House at least. But I want you to know curfews exist for a reason and I won't take my heir setting a poor example. People are looking to you as the standard. You are to be . . ." She gestures for me to finish her sentence.

"A cut above the rest."

She sits beside me on my bed, her posture heavy. "There is one more thing, and I wanted you to hear it from me first."

Her shoulders sag with a weight that unsettles me. I scrub the crust from my eyes.

"Nore Ambrose has gone missing."

My blood curdles. My mouth falls open, a gasp stuck in my throat.

"I have to know, Quell, when she left in a rush at the Tea, did you notice anything out of the ordinary?" Grandmom's pointed stare pierces my insecurity.

"She'd torn her gloves and had to throw them away. But that's all I really noticed."

"And what about the letters you've exchanged? Did she mention anything that gave you pause?" Grandmom's sulk has stiffened and I look for some hint of why she's asking me this, but all I find in her eyes is unyielding insistence.

"She wanted to meet up again. It didn't strike me as odd." I look somewhere else other than Grandmom's stone expression.

"It would be unfortunate if Nore was in trouble and she told someone and that someone didn't say anything. It might look like that someone wanted her to be hurt."

"I swear I don't know anything."

Her jaw ticks. "So she didn't confide in you? Or tell you anyone she was scared of?"

"No, none of that."

"Very well." She stands, and I push the trash can with Nore's letter under my bed when her back is turned to avoid things I don't want to have to explain. "The Council has postponed all events, including your Cotillion, until Nore is found. I'm sure you understand."

"Yes, of course."

"I'll be in and out traveling for a bit to be hands-on with the investigation. If you need anything, you'll have to see Mrs. Cuthers."

"All right. Thank you. I hope she's okay."

Grandmom glances off, then at me. "Right, yes. I hope so, too. Oh, and this came for you just now." She hands me an envelope, and I rip it open.

"It's from my mom," I say before realizing there might be things in the letter Mom doesn't want Grandmom to know.

"Thank you again." I hold the note to my chest, and her nostrils flare as she lets herself out.

Remember, stay put. See you soon.

I clutch the letter to myself in relief before sticking it in a drawer as the knowledge that Nore is missing tugs at my conscience. Once I'm sure

Grandmom's farther away, I bolt out the door. I have to find Jordan. The halls are full, but I'm numb to their rotation. There's no sign of Jordan in the dining hall or the security booth. I even go to the Gents Wing and bang on his door. Nothing.

Panic seizes in me, and my toushana wakes to greet me. I tense, willing it back down, but I can still see Nore's face draining of color. I rush to the foyer, through the broom closet door, and down the corridor toward the forest, trying to choke down the bile rising in my throat. I push through the doors, and outside morning fog hugs the trees.

My chest is tight, my bones colder as the Dust in me fights back but fails against my snowballing panic. *Jordan, I need to find him. I need answers. But first—* In the privacy of the Secret Wood, I fall to my knees and sink my hands into the earth and let the cold burn through me. Decay spreads around me like a swelling pool of blood, and my pulse slows. I blow out a breath and sit there until my knees ache, until my toushana finally settles like a feather done being blown about by the wind. My black diadem pricks my memory. I hope I don't regret this.

I inhale the woodsy morning scent of cypress and earth, reminding myself I'm still alive. I'm still here. I rise and start my cleanup, dusting my shame from my pant legs.

"Quell?"

I turn and there's Jordan. My heart stops.

"What are you doing out here?"

"I . . . was looking for you."

"Here?" His mouth twists in suspicion.

A bit of truth is the only way I'll get out of this. "I followed you here, that night after the Tavern. I—I saw what you did with your . . . you know." My gaze hits the ground for fear he might see how much I'm holding back.

He sighs. "I hate you saw that. I hate you know that's what this place is."

"What do you mean?"

"Look around."

His words seep into me like a sieve, and for the first time I really take in the forest in morning light. It's littered with broken trees as far as I can see. But most are more than broken, they're bent in half, bits of them decayed. The ground is blotchy, not just where I'm standing, but more or less all over.

I'm not the first to come here to use toushana. Nor is he.

I hug around myself.

He steps closer to me, misreading my discomfort entirely. But it's a balm I cling to, a shield I will use.

"I heard about Nore from Grandmom, but she wouldn't say much." My chest squeezes, awaiting his answer. "Does she have . . ."

"You will repeat this to no one."

I nod.

"We've heard whispers about her. But we didn't have orders to officially pursue her, so we haven't. But Quell, this feels like an inside job. I'm going to volunteer to help with the investigation. It's not my House, so I have no grounds to, but—"

"You want to."

"Yes."

"So you're leaving again."

"It's the right thing to do. This reeks of treason."

The more he's with them, the greater chance he could rub elbows with the Dragun after me. *I don't like this.* I want to keep him in my presence, plug my fingers in his ears. I want to shield his eyes from a world that would tear us apart. I want to hold what we have, selfishly, with both my hands. And I refuse to feel wrong for that. "Stay, *please.*"

"I won't be gone long. She is probably . . . you know."

Dead. I swallow and nod.

"And if so, I intend to get to the bottom of who killed her and why. This has got to stop."

I tense in his arms, and he wraps me tighter in them.

"Please, remain on the grounds while I'm gone and . . ." He pulls away from me. "I need to show you this. But you can't tell anyone." He presses his hand firmly to himself. Then his fist disappears into his chest. I gasp as he pulls his hand back out. His kor flickers on the tip of his finger. With his free hand he gathers a fistful of air. Fog forms at his lips and in seconds shadows appear inside his palm. He joins the toushana to the red flame and it flickers silver. "I can shift my kor from just an energy source to a magnetic one. It's called Tracing."

"I've never heard of—"

"And you wouldn't. It's a mystery, written into the folds of Dragun lore."

"What does it do?"

He holds the silver fire to my chest. "Magic is strongest in the heart, that's why when you bind, you press your dagger into it. If you let me put a piece of my kor inside you, our hearts will be like poles of a magnet, tethering us together, so that anytime you're experiencing extreme distress, I can sense it and come to you immediately."

"You think I'm in danger?"

"No, but all it takes is an overly ambitious fool," he snaps. "Please."

"Does it hurt?"

"It shouldn't. It just can't be removed. Ever."

I can think of a thousand reasons to say no, but I can think of several others to say yes.

"Okay."

He holds the silver flame to my chest, and pressure gathers at the meeting of my ribs. He flicks at the base of the silver fire, and a single lick of flame leaps from his hand to my chest. He places his palm over the spot, and his kor seeps into me, its flicker glowing beneath my skin. He replaces the rest of the flame back into himself. For several moments, I'm a bit woozy. Then I wriggle as it settles deep inside with a shudder, the metallic glow dimming. I touch the spot where his magic disappeared. There's no going back now. I have to keep myself under control, calm. And get through Cotillion.

"Promise me you won't leave the grounds until I return."

"I promise."

He turns to go, and my heart pounds faster.

He stops. "It's going to be okay."

"You can feel that?"

He smiles and walks away.

FORTY-TWO

—————✳—————

The walk back to my room is cloaked in dread. I can't stop think-ing about Nore. Did Beaulah get to her? Is that why she didn't show the other night? Should I have told Jordan? But how would I have explained being so obsessed with Nore in the first place? My pulse picks up. But I blow out a breath. Calm, I *have* to stay calm so Jordan doesn't pop up on me at the wrong time. That has to be my entire focus. I fall into my bed and bury myself in the covers, wishing I could wake up again and find out this has all been a terrible dream.

The first full day with no news, I manage to make it to Latin and work on my Cultivator specialty. But sensing magic in others is so much harder than it sounds. It doesn't help that I'm majorly distracted by Shelby shoot-ing daggers at me all through class. I still don't know why she was slated to debut but didn't or why she is being so mean.

The session ends, and despite an invite from some Secundus to hang, I spend the rest of the day in my room, hoping for some word from Jordan. Some news of what is going on outside the gates of Chateau Soleil. Abby's empty bed taunts me. *I should write to her.*

The next day with no news from Grandmom or Jordan, I do one ses-sion of etiquette practice before retreating back to solitude. It's the people who make this place feel like home. And right now, those closest to me here are all gone. My thoughts spiral at the whirlwind of silence, my panic trying fiercely to take hold.

Once the fifth day has passed with no word from Jordan and only a glimpse of Grandmom before she is off again, the thought of even getting out of bed makes it feel like the walls are closing in. So I don't leave that day. Or the next. The sun rises and sets for days. The only thing that keeps me sane is sitting in my room working on my magic with no questions or stares, or people I have to pretend in front of.

I've locked myself in like a cage.

Because I can't imagine a world outside of it where I am safe.

A WEEK OR more passes before Dexler comes knocking on my door.

"Quell, dear, there's a call for you from Abby, your old roommate."

I untangle myself from bed.

"It came to me because I guess she knows you're in my sessions. It's in my office if you'd like to take it?"

"Yes! I would." I stick to her heels until the phone is in my hand.

"You are *difficult* to get ahold of," Abby's voice comes through, and it warms me like a sun peeking through the clouds.

"It's so good to hear from you. I'm just dying to hear some news. Everything is so bleak."

"I know what you mean. When I heard about Nore Ambrose, I was with a patient and accidentally snapped her bone in half."

"Oh, geez."

"It's getting so strange out here. The things I'm hearing. The Sphere has everyone wound up. Everyone is desperate to do something, anything, to fix it."

"I've heard similar." I glance at a watchful Dexler and bite my tongue. "But you're okay?"

"Homesick, but yes. I can't believe I have to be here an entire year."

"You said you'd love it."

"I do . . . I just, I miss Mynick and you, Deda's lectures, and even my mother, if you can believe it. No one's had time to visit."

A disturbance breaks out in the hall, and Dexler peeks her head out of the door.

"Jordan's gone off to find Nore," I whisper. "He thinks it was an inside job."

"That's so scary. It's like everyone's accusing everyone these days—" She doesn't finish. The noise in the hall grows, thundering like a stampede.

"What's going on?" I ask a pinched-face Dexler when she slips back inside.

"The search has ended," she says. "Headmistress is back. She's called a meeting."

"Abby, I have to go." I hang up and follow the crowd streaming into the foyer. Grandmom stands behind a podium, and the room is packed with my peers and a smattering of concerned parents.

I'm too nervous to sit, so I hover in the back. *Please be good news.*

"Nore Ambrose has been found, *alive*," Grandmom says.

The audience expels a collective sigh of relief.

"As you can imagine, she's been through a lot. So she will be on sabbatical for the foreseeable future."

"Headmistress, might I ask a question about the Sphere?" an Electus asks.

"No questions about the Sphere at this time. I do have one more update. It has been a long week, but I'm happy to say our upcoming presentation for the Season is back on. Cotillion will proceed as planned. We're not altering the date or time. So those debuting, please ensure everything is in order. I'm truly relieved on the heels of such a tragedy to bring you such refreshing news." Grandmom exits the stage, ignoring a barrage of questions. I watch as she whispers something to Mrs. Cuthers. The dutiful secretary nods and departs.

"Grandmom." I hurry to catch her.

"Quell."

"Good to see you're back."

"Yes, did you hear?"

"That Nore is okay, yes! That's wonderful."

"That your Cotillion is back on. You have six days."

"Oh, yes." I search her expression for more than she lets on, some hint of what the last several days were like for her. But she doesn't appear very relieved.

"Well, don't dawdle," she snaps.

I curtsy and she walks off. She doesn't say a word to anyone else in the crowd. I head straight for Mrs. Cuthers. Since the ticking timeline leading up to debut is back, I need to be sure everything's in place. Mrs. Cuthers's door is cracked when I arrive, and she waves me in.

"I just wanted to check to see if anything has arrived for me."

She checks her record of deliveries. "I'm showing three dozen cake stands." She runs her finger down the page. "Shoes . . . gloves . . . no dress. I'll check in with the Vestiser."

"What about RSVPs?"

"You're at . . ." She flips a few more pages, and I peek over her shoulder at name after name of every person who received an invitation and their response. "Two hundred seventy-four."

"May I see that?"

"Sure." She hands me the tablet, and I flip and flip for one name . . . the only one that I'd recognize—my mother's. But it's not there.

"Mrs. Cuthers, I don't see Rhea Marionne on this list. I gave you an invite to send her."

"Oh, that's right you did." She takes a closer look. "That's so odd. Headmistress wanted to mail them herself. And that's the final list she gave me."

I see red. "I need to borrow this list." I leave and head up the stairs to find Grandmom. She might be hiding things, but this she's going to explain.

FORTY-THREE

——✳——

There's no one waiting to greet me at Grandmom's door. I turn the knob, but it doesn't give. It's locked. I try turning it again, but its resistance only churns my irritation. She didn't mail Mom's invite. On purpose. I shake the handle in frustration, my fingers prickling with chill, and twist harder. The door clicks open.

"Grandmom, hello?" I step inside. A fire burns, a newspaper is parted on the chair. "It's Quell." But no one answers. She must be in here or will be back shortly, so I sit and wait. I fold and unfold the newspaper and flip through the books on her coffee table, my curiosity getting the best of me. An arrangement of black flowers ornaments her writing desk. I press my nose to them, reminding myself they have no scent, and a card slips out.

I'm sorry, I can't.

It's unsigned. I put the card down and back away from Grandmom's personal things. The clock ticks on, still with no sign of her. I peek my head into the hallway, but it's vacant. I try her bedroom with a gentle tap.

"Grandmom? It's Quell. I came to have a word with you." But my voice is answered with silence. I push open the door and peek into Grandmom's bedroom. It's just as it was before, her velvet sitting area framed by a view of the grounds through an arched window. Her bed is tidied perfection as if it belongs in a palace museum. I step inside, and my heart thuds in my ears. I shouldn't be snooping in her room when she's not here.

I pass her vanity, and my fingers trace her golden brush and hand mirror. I glance over my shoulder and pick them up, imagining myself in this room as a girl growing into Season here. What should have been my home, if I weren't broken. I slip open a drawer of her dresser. It is velvet lined and filled with sparkling jewels and a tiny golden key. I hold a necklace to my chest, a stud to my ear, twisting in the mirror. The reflection stills me. Not because I'm surprised by what I see, but because I am not. The rise of my chin, the set of my shoulders—slightly back—the lush fabric decadent on my skin. I look like I belong here.

Did Mom ever feel like this? My attention moves to the shelf of albums Grandmom showed me. She has so many. Her entire sitting room is lined with them, her bedroom, too. I replace Grandmom's jewels and cosmetics and trace a row of spines on one of her towering shelves before taking one with a leather cover. In it are pictures, like before. I flip quickly through, trying to glean some indication of the dates. But the only photos are of Grandmom when she was much younger. I need something more recent. I put the book back and grab another, breezing through the pages. *Still too long ago.*

I set it on the table and grab a few more, anticipation rushing through me. After I've cleared half a row of one shelf, I finally spot a picture of Mom with a regal gold diadem flecked with green gems. My eyes fill with tears. She wears a long satin dress with a riband around her in House colors, ornamented with a fleur sigil. Her arms are looped with a masked guy. I stare, drinking all of her in. I smooth the tears from my cheeks, staring back at a whole life kept secret. I squint to see which sigil the guy wears, but the picture is too old and fuzzy to tell. I study his face, but it doesn't look anything like mine. Mom's never mentioned who my father is. It was just her and me from what I remember, after we left here. I turn the page and the next, but that's the only one of her.

I rush back to the shelf for more but find nothing more than historical texts. I wander over to another wall of floor-to-ceiling glass shelves full of leather spines with tiny gold writing. These are behind lock and key. I pull at the latch, but the locked glass doesn't give, and I recall the golden key among her jewels.

I bet this is where she's chronicled all of Mom's childhood. She loves her despite how she keeps her at arm's reach.

The key from Grandmom's vanity slips right into the locked wall of shelves and my bones chill in warning. I pull out a stack of three or four from what must be a dozen identical leather-bound albums.

I part the pages, teeth pressed to my lip in anticipation. But there is no photo. Only a name, scribbles of notes I don't understand, and what looks to be a red ink stain. The Book of Names I signed to enter induction was full of blank pages and a short group roster. These are full. I check the spine again for a name. There is no title page. I flip and flip, but it's more of the same, pages with red dots. I bring one to my nose, and the ache in my bones grows at its rusty scent.

Blood.

I turn a few more pages, but it's more and more records. So many names. I rip through another book, hoping to make more sense of why she'd have records and blood samples. But it's just more of the same. And another. And another. Blood rushes to my head, dizzying me, until I spot a book just like the one in my hands on Grandmom's bedside table.

My heart thrums faster. The urge to get out of this room bites at my heels. But my feet move toward the book. I open it and flip past names and more names until I reach a page with the most recent entries.

Brooke Hamilton, House of Perl—0624
Alison Blakewell, House of Perl—0624

The girls from Jordan's House. The numbers next to their names look like they could be dates.

Grandmom has records of dead people . . .

I try but fail to still my trembling hands. I take another glance at the page, hoping I don't see what I expect. But there it is in black ink.

Nore Ambrose, House of Perl—0710*
*afflicted

July 10. Next to Nore's name is a dark red spot, and there is no question in my mind. *That is Nore's blood.* Grandmom said Nore was on sabbatical for the foreseeable future. But she's not. If her name is in here with the other dead girls', she's dead.

Nore is dead.

That's why her letter returned. I glare at the rows and rows of books just like this one and the truth cuts me sharp. *So many records. Names upon names of dead débutants. There must be years, generations of records here.* I pore over three, four, ten more registries to be sure I'm not losing my mind. But it's all right here. Hundreds with dates and red spots. I blink and see a forest of dead trees. I blink again and remember Jordan telling me about the *hundreds* gone missing. I bar my mouth shut as if that could keep me from the weight of what this means.

I drop the book and back away. The supposition forming on my tongue chokes as the pieces of Grandmom's facade click into place. The way she didn't actually seem relieved when she made the announcement of Nore's return. The way she insisted on knowing if Nore had mentioned anyone she was afraid of. She was trying to see if I was on to her. The way she wanted to be "hands-on" in the investigation. A perfect cover for making sure no one caught on to her. Grandmom killed Nore.

Tears form in my eyes at the warning glimpse Grandmom gave me of her cruelty when she'd thought I wasn't ready for Second Rite. The way she threatened me without a flinch.

I skim the page again as if there's an answer that could actually make this okay. Only a handful have an asterisk, indicating they have toushana. Jordan had said Draguns have attributed the hundreds who have gone missing to members taking the rules into their own hands.

But this isn't *any* member—it's a Headmistress.

The walls seem to close in around me as I search for some other way this makes sense. Some reason Grandmom would have walls and walls, years upon years of dead debs' names cataloged under lock and key in her private bedroom. *There isn't one.*

I run.

Out of her bedroom and out of her door, down the hall, my feet racing my pulse. Down the stairs, I have to reach Mom. The world darkens around me, and Jordan appears.

"Quell."

I struggle for words.

"Are you okay?" He reaches for me. People are staring. Listening. I grab him by the wrist and lead him through the doors, through the courtyard. When the air hits my face, I break into a full-out run toward the conservatory.

"Quell." He rushes after me, but I can't stop. I can't. If I stop, I might break. I reach the glass door, and to my relief it's unlocked.

I throw myself inside, fall to my knees, and scream.

FORTY-FOUR

——✳——

"Quell, what's happened?"

I rock back and forth, trying to erase the last few hours. I hug myself all over, tears rushing harder. I can't stay here anymore. I've pushed past any reasonable reason to make it work. Even if she doesn't discover my secret, even if I finish, I can't be the heir to a monster.

"Quell, please, you're in so much distress."

I don't look at him. I can't move. He joins me on the ground in the dirt and puts his jacket around my shoulders.

"What happened?"

The words forming on my tongue don't make sense.

"So many deaths."

He shakes me and I startle. I meet his eyes and throw my arms around his broad shoulders, wondering if they're strong enough to hold the weight he's asking me to put on him. The world sways. He pulls me tighter to him.

"Whatever it is, I will fix it."

"You can't."

He pulls us apart, smoothing my face with his hands.

"Try me."

"Jordan, my grandmother . . ." I choke on words that want to come out. That want to be told so I don't have to carry this horrid burden on my own. "I think she's responsible for all the missing members."

He narrows his eyes in disbelief.

"I found death registries in a locked cabinet in her room." My voice cracks. I can't believe my ears. The next words come out mixed with sobs, but I've opened this well now and I can't turn it off. "Nore. The two girls from your House. And hundreds of others. I don't think it has anything to do with toushana."

I look for shock or anger or something in Jordan's expression but find neither.

"She just announced that Nore—" Jordan stands, his lips thin with doubt.

I pace. "We have to get out of here. Leave with me. Let's just go anywhere, we can find my mom and sleep in the woods for all I care."

I stop and he hugs me tighter. "There has to be an explanation. I know Headmistress Marionne to be a woman of great moral fortitude."

I wrap myself in his words even though they reek of foolish optimism. I know what I saw. He strokes my hair and I try to slow my pulse, but the ache in my bones rises, threatening. I pull away from him, just in case.

"If this is true," he goes on, "she can be held accountable."

"No, Jordan, no one is going to hold *Darragh Marionne* accountable."

"We can't leave." He scrubs a palm down his face. "Dear Sfenti, I pray you are wrong about this."

"I'm not!"

His mouth bows with skepticism. "If you're right, the Order needs us now more than ever. You see that, don't you?"

"I didn't come here to get into a war with my grandmother."

"There's a way things are done. We honor the Order, Quell, at all costs. Listen to me. Do you trust me?"

"Listen to me!" I reach for him, but the ache in my bones spasms and my arm goes cold just as he grabs it. Fear shudders through me at Jordan holding on to my arm as my toushana burns through me with frigid chill. I try to pull back but his grip on my arm tightens, his stare widening.

"Let me go." I snatch away and put distance between us, hoping I was fast enough. Hoping he was distracted enough to miss the abnormal shift in my body temperature. But his expression is frozen with something I've never seen in him.

Devastation.

My heart stops.

He knows.

"Quell?" he whispers.

I glance at the door. *Running would never work.* "Please," I utter, vulnerability shattering every urge of reason. I chill entirely, my toushana taking over fully, drowning my will to fight. A lump rises in my throat and my heart rages as I stumble back to put more space between us. But there's nowhere to go.

His eyes flicker with knowing. *He can feel me panicking.* There's no way I could deny it even if I wanted to. A tear steals down my cheek. "Please, anything. Just say something, Jordan." My voice is as broken and weak as I am.

He shakes his head and rakes a hand through his hair, pacing.

"You . . . lied?" He grasps for words, his throat bobs, his eyes glassy. "I . . ." He shakes his head. Then his nostrils flare. "I thought you were different. I thought . . ." But he chokes on the next words and turns his back to me.

"Jordan." I chance reaching for him, grabbing him with my cold hand. But when he turns, his pained expression has hardened to a glare. His chest heaves, but his brows draw together, unable to hide his grief, his eyes a watery sea. He stares at my hand on his arm. I snatch it away, stepping backward.

He steps toward me.

And I can feel the distance between us closing like a crush on my throat. His edges harden, anger mangling the hurt in his expression. And the chill in my bones seizes me, not from my toushana but from bloodcurdling fear.

He steps toward me again, and fear prickles my spine. Jordan's mask bleeds through his skin and his jaw clenches. I look for some glimpse of the boy who held my hand. Who gave me green candies and saw more in me than, at the time, I saw in myself.

But that boy is gone.

Only a Dragun stands before me now.

"Jordan, please."

He meets my eyes for the first time since our touch, but in his gaze is a ghost of the person I knew, hiding beneath a veil. Dying an excruciating death.

He's going to kill me.

The space between his breaths shortens.

"I only did it to protect myself. All of this was to—"

His lip quivers as he summons his magic. Black dances on his fingertips.

"Jordan, I love you. And you love me!" My voice tears and his gaze falls. "I know those are big heavy words, and it's confusing and feels wrong in a way. But it doesn't change that you do. You love me, Jordan Wexton, I *dare* you to deny it." I fight out the words between tears. "Please don't do this," I breathe.

Jordan looks away once more.

Before his hand closes around my throat.

And the world disappears.

PART FIVE

FORTY-FIVE

⸺ ✳ ⸺

I blink, wondering if this is the afterlife, black fog around me. But then I breathe, realizing my lungs fill. I am not dead. Jordan surrounds me in a cloud of black, the world hardly perceivable through its mist. His hand is tight around my neck, not squeezing but holding me there, and however it works, I can't move.

There is no love in his touch. Not anymore. But because I'm stubborn and hurt and lost, so lost, his name lingers on my lips. I want him to look at me one more time with the sunrise in his eyes. To promise me after this dark night there is a morning. My entire body is stiff when the air clears and Grandmom's double doors appear.

His grip on me makes it impossible to do more than think. I try to glimpse his features to glean what he's doing. He didn't take me to Beaulah.

"What is this?" Grandmom looks past us, down the hall in both directions. But there's no one else up here. No witnesses to my impending death.

"In here, now," she says.

We move, though I don't feel it.

"Release your magic, Jordan, now!"

He does and life rushes into my limbs.

"What is the meaning of this?" Grandmom's entire sitting room is different than it was a moment ago. The fire that burned is out. The newspaper I left strewn about is gone. The bouquet that sat on her writing desk is gone, too. *Her bedroom.*

"Jordan, the records. They're all in here." I rush at her bedroom doors and halt. The floor, which was just a mountain of books, is cleaned up.

The shelves are neatly arranged with ornaments, plants, and doodads. There isn't a single leather-bound book in sight.

"Quell Janae Marionne, is there something I can help you with?" Grandmom hovers in the doorway, and her composure shifts with knowing, a single brow raised. *Now she knows it was me.* Jordan's gaze darts between us with a flicker of doubt.

"It was all here. It was all just—" *The books. The shelves.* I pull at the bookcase doors, but they're locked.

"I apologize for bursting in, Headmistress," he says. "But I've come into grave news about Quell and needed to tell you immediately." He holds my gaze for one more beat, but when he breaks it, it shatters my heart. "A private word, please."

"Your granddaughter is afflicted," he says beyond the door, and my heart hammers, imagining Grandmom's face. "She has toushana. I felt it myself, just a moment ago."

They step out of earshot, their voices too low to hear, and I tear through Grandmom's things for some glimpse of the truth. Grandmom, with Jordan as her shadow, reappears and my fingers dig in my pockets, squeezing my key chain. Wishing I could tell Mom I'm thinking of her one more time. There's no escaping. Death is my fate and has always been, I suppose. One I foolishly hoped I could outsmart. Grandmom grabs my wrist so tightly I yelp. She runs her nail along my finger, and it feels like fire is attached to my fingertip.

"Ow!" I try to tug away, but her grip on me is iron as a dot of blood pools under my fingertip, answering to her magic. She smooths her finger over it, and it feels like rubbing sandpaper into a fresh wound.

"This is not possible," she mutters to herself. "I took a sample when you arrived."

I writhe in her grip, the pain rippling down my spine, into my head. She steadies me with an aggressive shake, and I squeeze my eyes shut to manage the pain. The blood under my finger shines bright red a moment before gleaming black. She sucks in a silent breath. "How did I miss this?"

she mutters, then her lips part in understanding. "The test shows what was last used," she mutters to herself.

My heart thuds in my ears, and I can't find a single word to say. I glance at the door, but there is no way out of here that doesn't end in my death. For several moments the only sound is the beat of my hammering heart. I glare at the floor, trying to think of something to say or do. My toushana unwinds, but I don't even try to calm it. I can't muster the strength.

"Jordan, I'll take care of this. Please see yourself out."

"Headmistress, I said I could do . . . what's required of me." He clears his throat. I look for some glimpse of scheme in him but only find resolute duty. I shake my head, my heart grasping for straws that aren't there. *He wouldn't!*

He would.

He did.

"I would never doubt your sense of duty, Mister Wexton. You have served me well. Please, see yourself out."

I wait for him to look at me, to shatter the fragments of me left into nothingness, but he doesn't. And somehow that hurts more.

"I'll be outside the door should you need me." He hesitates a moment, his gaze lowering before he turns on his heels and takes the last bit of wind in my lungs with him. The world swims as Grandmom motions me to her velvet armchair beside the fire in her bedroom. She fills the hearth with flames and motions for me to sit. I back away.

"Closer to the fire, Quell. Relax."

I hesitate. My heart pounds, but I can't ignore the lure of the fire that could chase away this poison. I step closer, tentatively, and a sigh shoves its way up and out of my mouth. The heat is an undeniable relief. My toushana soothes, beginning its retreat. Grandmom hovers near it too, warming her hands.

"Better?" She offers me tea. I ignore it.

"I'm surprised I didn't see the signs. Sometimes we're so good at seeing only what we want to see. Your coming back here, Quell. I can't put into words just what that means for our House. For me, too, yes, but for our House. And now to learn this." She sips from her tea again before retrieving a hair clip from her drawer. It's a tiny butterfly clip with pearls for eyes, one missing. "I am grieved. But fortunately for you, grief is something my shoulders have learned to carry well."

"What?" I manage.

"I was ten when my mother burst into my little sister's room in the middle of the night and caught me trying to help her warm her hands by the fire. I didn't know what it was called then. I just knew my sister was in pain and cold." Grandmom stands just feet away but she's somewhere else entirely. "I didn't have the ache then, but Moriette did." She strokes the clip. "I'll spare you the details, but I saw then what happens to those with toushana. So imagine my surprise when on the night of my own Cotillion, *after* I'd bound with my magic, my limbs turned to ice."

I sit up. I can't have heard her correctly.

"I knew it was toushana, even though it shouldn't have been possible since I was already bound. But toushana is an ever-elusive mystery. There's only so much we understand about it, still. From what I understand about it now, my situation is extremely rare."

I sit straighter, hanging on her every word.

"That night, I lied to my mother, said it was a migraine, and buried myself on the bathroom floor. It took some time, but I figured out how to manage it."

"You have . . . toushana . . ." The words break something in me.

"Closer to the fire, dear. It really will help."

I scoot closer to the heat, trying to untangle what this truth means.

"It's been my life's work to keep it secret and create a fortress around myself and my House. You're lucky yours has shown itself before Third Rite. We should have some options."

I swallow, gaping at the woman I thought I knew.

"My duty is to House of Marionne. *Not* the Order. That was my mother's mistake." She lets out a huge breath and meets my eyes, hers full of prideful defiance. "So I added a bit of magic to Third Rite for all who debut from my House. Whenever someone plunges their dagger into their heart here, it will bind them not only to their magic, but to this House, in servitude."

My pulse quickens.

"Plume coming over from House Ambrose had its benefits. Nabbed one of their best-kept discoveries—a way to cloak the ceremony stage with reverse tracer magic."

"Tracing magic . . ." I hold my chest, remembering the silver flame. "How?"

"A tracer on one person tethers them to another, allowing them to go to them wherever they are when they sense extreme emotion. House Ambrose stretched the bounds of that magic somehow to trace many at once and reverse the direction. Thanks to Third Rite, I can summon any of my graduates and they will come to me in an instant. They are tethered to this House. That way I can use them, their magic, how I see fit and against whom I see fit." She tidies the collar of her dress.

I scoot away from her.

"The Sphere is under great duress, Quell. And with the tensions between the Houses, finger pointing is only growing worse. The Headmistresses have banded together before to commit atrocities. I wouldn't put it past them to do it again. Should the House relationships come to blows, Marionne will stand with an army at her back."

Chills skitter up my arms. "None of that explains all those names of people who have died. In your books." I point a shaky finger. "You tried to hide your dirt, but I saw it *all*."

"See, that all started with an accident. I am a Cultivator, dear. When I first took this post, inductees would enroll here and I would work with them. But my toushana would on occasion be deposited by mistake. I couldn't very well let it grow in them." She shifts in her seat. "I've had to clean up things a bit."

She's so close to me I can smell her. She is honey and lavender, jasmine, and yet her heart is made of rot.

"But I hired Dexler and now she does the hands-on cultivating. Not me. I did that to fix this, can't you see? To stop being the one working directly with inductees."

I shake my head, not believing my ears.

"I had hoped your mother would fill that role, but alas . . . she left."

"Because she didn't want the Order to kill me!"

"Your mother has never understood that I am on her side."

"And I wonder why? The Perl girls and Nore weren't even in your House!"

Grandmom crosses her legs, and I can feel her burgeoning irritation.

"Nore had toushana, Quell, and I think you know it."

I look away.

"So there's more than one liar sitting here."

"We are not the same." I don't know what she's playing at, but nothing she can say makes this okay. I refuse. "You didn't have to hurt her."

"*I didn't* hurt Nore."

"She's in your death log. I saw her name."

"You are right, she's dead. I lied about sabbatical because I was asked to. That's the end of that topic." She sighs, exasperated. "I wish you no ill, child, and I understand you have questions, but my patience is wearing thin. I am not your enemy. What else do you want to know?"

"So that's what the Order does, then? Just kills whomever gets in their way?" I feel sick. "Why keep records?"

"Because . . ." Now it's Grandmom who breaks our gaze. "I began to notice changes in the Sphere as I cleaned up things."

I cringe at her word choice—"cleaning" as if she did a favor, picked up someone's mess. She *murdered* them.

"The bookshelf being visible was an oversight. I received a delivery to-day that I had to follow up on immediately and neglected to disguise it." Grandmom's lip flinches. "And for the Perl girls. They have been snooping around safe houses for some reason, on Beaulah's orders, I suspect, and they got a little too close to the truth of the Third Rite tracer I have in place. If that got out, it would dissolve our House on the spot. All the other Houses would turn against me. Even our own. I *had* to do something. And they were already rumored to have toushana, so."

"You build a fortress around yourself to protect your toushana but condemn others for theirs. You're a hypocrite *and* a liar. A monster. No wonder Mom left."

"I've heard enough of this. Bind with your proper magic at Cotillion. You will go through with everything as planned. It'll bury your toushana and we can put this nonsense behind us!"

That's been my plan the entire time. But how can I stay here now, knowing all this?

"No, I won't."

"You will."

"I won't!"

She snatches me up by my collar, but I manage to pull myself away. I grab a letter opener from the table. It's the sharpest thing I see. The air ripples black from her fingertip. The letter opener rots in my grip. I look for something else. A book. A vase. I kick an ottoman into her path as she pursues, but with the stroke of her hand, that turns to black dust, too.

"I have done *nothing* but give you more than you've *ever* had!" She reaches me and grabs me by my neck like Jordan did. Everything in me stills, her magic paralyzing me head to toe. "Jordan would have killed you if I'd ordered him to. Don't you doubt otherwise. I *saved* your life tonight and *you would judge me?* As if I'm anything but in *your* corner! *Our* corner." She pulls open a door and shoves me inside a small room. I hit the ground hard, pain rippling up my spine.

"You will do as I've said or I'll turn you over to the Dragunhead and let his flock have its way with you. Your choice." The door slams.

I curl up in a ball and crumple on the floor of my cage.

This has to be worse than death.

FORTY-SIX

———*———

Time is an illusion in a world without windows. Darkness has become my blanket. I've cried so long the ache of sorrow wrings dry as bone. At a certain point, the desire to cry was lost, buried by the desire to feel nothing at all. To be nothing at all.

Meals have come, but I've refused them all. I won't take anything else from her hands.

Anger simmers through me the more I stew, exhausting and consuming. Sleep is how I quiet it. But my mind is awake now in the dark with no respite in sight. I rise from the covers I've tossed and turned in and switch on a lamp. The room Grandmom locked me in used to be a bedroom of some sort. It's sparse, with tiny indentations of furniture that used to live here imprinted on the carpet like ghost footprints. Why she has a bedroom off her bedroom, I don't understand.

I run my fingers over the carved edges of a stately dresser, lamenting the choices she has set before me. I call to my toushana, just to feel something powerful. Jordan's face flits through my memory and my toushana groans to be quenched. It's been a long time since I've gone to the forest. What I wouldn't give to go there now, even if it wasn't in secret.

I hate Grandmom for doing this to me. For personally knowing what it's like and still forcing me into this. And Jordan. I see his face, and I ache deeper somehow. I don't have words for what I feel for him. The wound is too raw. The hurt is too fresh.

I pull open one of the drawers on Grandmom's fine furniture and slam it shut. The clatter of the wood against itself satisfies. My toushana nudges me, pleading to be free, and I let it. I trace my fingers along Grandmom's antique cabinet, leaving a trail of blackened wood in their wake. Once the wood top is seared like it's been caught in a swarm of flames, I let my toushana loose on its legs. It buckles under the weight of itself and crashes to the floor. I have no idea what this means to her. How long it's been here. How special it is. But I savor the broken wood at my feet.

I look for something else. Locked behind these bars of rage, my toushana's appetite grows. The mantel on the fireplace is ornately carved. I pull it down, decaying it until it's mangled and unrecognizable. The chair and desk are short work. The carpet, a bookshelf, a rocking chair, a porcelain statue. I even try the walls. I would burn this whole place into a heap of ash in this moment if I was outside this room. A scream rips from my throat, and I claw at the wall that should be a door.

"Let me out!" I bang and bang, but there's no use. My chest heaves. Ash from my destructive handiwork swarms in the air, and my heart delights in it like freshly fallen snow. My toushana flutters in me with satisfaction, and an odd sensation tugs at me as I realize something.

"You've never let me down," I say to my toushana, and she answers in a wave of chill.

My first memory of meeting her is when I was eight. I was about to cross the street as a car was speeding past. My toushana unfurled in my bones so sharply I had to stop from the pain. The car rushed past, just missing me. I was in such a panic I hid behind another parked vehicle, trying to catch my breath. I was so wound up, just sitting there trying to calm down, I destroyed half of that sedan. Though we said goodbye to that city, that school, in that moment my toushana kept me safe.

She's never lashed out at me. She was calm when I emerged. Helpful when I stole the bauble for Octos to make my diadem look acceptable. She was wary of my dagger as I worked toward honing because she could sense I was intending to use it destructively. But my toushana has never hurt or lied to me. She is the only thing that's been true to me.

She is fury and determination, insatiable at times, and intensely powerful. She is also destruction.

But some things deserve to be destroyed.

I hide her because I have to. But now that I understand her, she isn't out of control. In some ways she's the only thing I do have control of in my entire life. I flicker with her chill, and it's endearing.

She burns colder and I give in to her call, and it fills me in a way only she can. I stare at my hands in delight that I feel something. Can do something. And it hits me. I think I know what I have to do.

I will not be relegated to the whims of my grandmother. I will not be chained to her—or anyone's—version of my fate. Going through with Cotillion to bind with my proper magic would tether me to Grandmom, to this House in servitude forever, stepping from one cage into another. Destroying my toushana means destroying a part of myself. A part of myself that's *powerful*. Perhaps I've been coming at it all wrong. Perhaps I should have been chasing courage instead.

Perhaps the only way to truly be free . . .

Is to stop fighting against who I really am.

The truth makes me steady myself on the wall. I brace myself against it and try to piece together what I think I'm saying. What I think I've decided. I knock on the wall.

"I've reached my decision, Grandmom, please."

I will go through with Third Rite.

And play along with Grandmom's wishes.

But on that stage, I will bind with my toushana.

With her, I am free.

FORTY-SEVEN

The door to my room parts open tentatively, and I glimpse Grandmom's face.

"I'm ready to talk, please."

Grandmom is in a blazer and skirt, with a fleur brooch beside her neck, gloves on her hands. She comes inside, light streaming in behind her. And I suddenly realize I'm not sure how long I've been trapped in here. She takes in the room and her expression twists.

"You're on your way out?"

"To a meeting, yes." She tightens her mouth at the mess I've made of her precious things. "I didn't want to keep you waiting in the event you've come to your senses with Cotillion tomorrow."

Tomorrow! My chance isn't lost. "I have."

"I'm listening." She faces me, rigid and unreadable, her classic expression. I stare at her a moment and realize I could be looking in a mirror. But because I didn't grow up here, shellacked by this world, I am not beholden to it. Not yet.

I can tell by the way her hands hook together, the draw up of her shoulders, she's nervous. Cautious. Whatever I say has to convince her completely. She can't suspect I'm lying or who knows what she might do. I know her dirty tethering secret now, and she's proven she doesn't balk at getting rid of those who can cause trouble for her. I clasp my hands behind my back, digging my nails into my skin as if in them are buried roots of courage.

"You were right." I paint on a sad veneer and fidget with my hands. I even pace a little bit for good measure. "The shock of everything threw me. I can't imagine a safer place to be. Home. With you, here in Chateau Soleil."

The word sticks in my throat.

Home is Mom. Home is my toushana. Home is wherever I choose it to be.

My forbidden magic flickers in me, and its chill soothes.

"I will complete Third Rite and bind with my magic, erasing my toushana forever."

Grandmom circles me, and my heart thrums faster.

"Forgive me, please, I still want to induct if you would have me."

Her fingers play on the pile of wood that used to be a dresser. "King Louis XVI gave this to my great-great-great-grandmother. A gift at her Cotillion from his own collection."

I knew it was special; it was too fancy not to be. But I refuse to feel guilty.

"He was big into the arts back then and was enthralled by magic. Something he never could get to conform to his will. So he befriended our family. People like to be close to our world. But it takes much to be *in* it."

Grandmom faces me, scorn and question burned into her expression.

"I don't know that he would have had the stomach to induct. Too weak. Their monarchy fell at his hand, you know?" She runs her fingers across the pile of rubble and its ashes stir, as if unsettled by a gust of wind. She pulls back on the pile with her fingers, and the broken pieces of the dresser cinch back together, shedding their blackened finish for its former gilded veneer.

I gasp.

"I keep it here as a reminder." A knob that had rolled across the room snaps to the dresser and it sits perfect as if it had never been destroyed. "Kings can be brave; they can do wonderful things. Beautiful things. And yet their monarchy can still fall. Their legacy moving on without them." She glimpses herself in the mirror, which has re-formed as well. "A hundred years from now, House of Marionne will be *more* than fancy dressers and gilded ballrooms."

She steps toward me.

I don't step back.

"Running the Order isn't unlike running a kingdom. You do what you must for the greater good. And in this case, that is our family. Our bloodline. The future of this House. Do you understand that?"

"I do."

She's unmoved and turns away from me.

"Which is why binding to the House with the tether is so important," I say, hoping to dent her doubt.

That swivels her head around.

"It ensures my loyalty is unwavering, that I'm committed to serve this House, whatever comes."

She folds her arms.

"If I am in this, I am in it all the way."

"Then prove it. Give me your key chain. Rhea would never accept you grafting yourself into this world. You have to let this dream of her and you go. If you're in this, as you say . . ." She holds out her hand. This I didn't expect.

If I do this, I have no way to communicate with Mom. But it would seal Grandmom's trust that I mean what I say.

"Well?"

"Yes, of course, Grandmom." I dig the key chain out of my pocket. There has to be some other way to find Mom when I leave this horrid place. I set it in her hand, and she turns it to dust in an instant.

A piece of me fractures. I hope that wasn't the wrong decision.

"Very well." Her chin rises. "That dresser was fortified with protection magic. Your toushana is untrained, but it runs strong in you. It might give you a fight on that stage. Your heart must be sure or it'll turn to metal. You *must be* resilient and resist *hard*. While maintaining poise. No one must know what you're battling."

"I understand," I tell her. "I can do this."

"I hope you can see how much I love you, Quell."

"And I am so grateful." I slide my foot behind the other, one knee inside the other, and fold in a perfect curtsy.

Grandmom opens the door. "You should get yourself some proper rest.

Cotillion is tomorrow. I expect you in my room by six a.m. Do not make me have to come to find you."

"Yes, ma'am."

She slips on a ring from a desk drawer. Then smooths her hands over my face, beneath my eyes, and over my hair, and nausea rises in my throat at her touch. "Now run along."

I pass a mirror and glimpse her Shifting handiwork, her gift for hiding the truth. Looking at me you'd never know I'd spent days locked away crying my eyes out.

It's late evening and most are in bed as I hurry down the hall to my room. I offer a plastic "Good evening" to a handful of onlookers. Some ask where I've been, to which I just smile. Inside my room I bar the door closed. The minute I leave here, I don't know how long I'll have before Grandmom outs my toushana to the Dragunhead. I have to find Mom fast.

And I'm going to need help.

There's only one person I'd trust to help me with something so dangerous. But I'm not sure how to send him a message without knowing his full name. I crack my door open but find one of Grandmom's Draguns standing sentry outside it. Sneaking off to the Tavern won't work.

Who else can I trust? Abby? I grab a note to write to her, but I hesitate when the pen hits the paper. I've never asked anything of her more than advice here or there. I chew off my nail, hoping I'm making the right decision.

Abs,

I have so much to tell you. It's not safe here anymore. For now, do exactly what I say. Go to the Tavern and find a trader by the name of Octos. Tell him I need his help. He will come with you. Don't come to Cotillion. Meet me afterward in the forest on the usual trail we would take to the Tavern. I'll explain everything.
—Quell

I grab another paper and write to Mom, telling her there's been a change of plans and asking her to meet me in the same place as Abby.

Butterflies swarm in my stomach as I seal the envelopes and write their names on the front. I stuff the letters into my shirt and reopen my door. The Dragun doesn't say anything, so I don't say anything to him. I recognize him as the one who's occasionally outside of Grandmom's door. I slip past him and he stalks me, like a shadow.

"Just going to Mrs. Cuthers to be sure we're set for tomorrow."

He gestures for me to continue on, but when I take another step, he sticks to my heels. Mrs. Cuthers's door is unlocked when we arrive. The Dragun hovers in the doorway watching as I rummage around inside, pretending to look through stacks of boxes she has. Her desk is mostly tidy, and I pretend to shuffle through the few things she has there, careful to angle my body just so, to block his view of the wooden tray on her desk. My heart hammers as I slip the envelopes out of my shirt and into the outbox. They disappear immediately.

FORTY-EIGHT

———✳———

Grandmom sent staff to gather my dress, shoes, accessories, and things late last night. The next morning, I wake before my alarm, painfully aware that tonight I leave this place. The comfort of this bed, the security of these walls, the laughter held within this room. *It's over.* A part of me aches, wishing I could live a moment longer in this nightmare and still pretend it's a daydream. It's a naive thought, but undeniable.

I grab my dagger, some enhancers I have left, a few books, and my postcard of the beach. Once my bag is full I exit and pull the door to my room closed. My fist tightens on the knob. *I've left countless places. But this feels different.* Because I believed this place would be different.

The clarity unsticks my fingers from the brass, and I force myself to back away. To see this for what it is. I was seduced by Chateau Soleil's glitter, the allure that I could fit in a place so magnificent. That being here would tell me who the girl in the mirror is, when it's *how* I saw her that needed to change. I'm still figuring out who she is.

But whoever that girl is—she is free.

The House is as quiet as it was when I went to bed. I glimpse the hall that leads to the Gents Wing as I pass, and my anger mangles with sorrow. I don't want to see him until I absolutely have to. I'm not sure how I'll bear to even look at him or how it will feel. *Forget him. Forget it all.*

I climb the stairs and knock on Grandmom's door.

"Right on time," she says, her hair still up in curlers. "Well, you don't look excited. Today's your big day."

I reach for a smile but my gut swims with irritation at having to pretend all over again. She and her puppets will fawn over me and I'll have to bear it. I'll have to play the part of the obedient heir. One more time. I swallow it down and it burns like bile. But this *is* the beginning of the end. My lips tug up a bit easier.

"Much better." She opens the door wider and I step inside.

My dress hangs from the window in Grandmom's sitting room, caught in the morning's glow. I run my fingers across its fabric, every speckle intentionally placed, and imagine what it would feel like to put this on and not know. To go out there wrapped in the beauty and perfume of Grandmom's world oblivious of the rot hidden between its layers. How glorious that must feel. Did Mom get that far? I'm going to ask her. I'm going to ask her a lot of things when we get back together.

I survey the rest of everything set out for me. Sparkly shoes and a handbag in satin blush with a fleur clasp that was specifically made for tonight's ceremony. It's all so gorgeous. Maybe I'll pretend, tonight, that all this get-up, the pomp and circumstance, is a toast to freeing myself. Grandmom watches me closely, from her breakfast table, and for a moment, I worry she's heard my treasonous thoughts.

A wooden box engraved with the name COLLINS is set next to a boutonniere made with black dahlia and pink peony. I crack it open and my blade gleams at me, shinier than I've ever seen it.

"All in order?" Grandmom asks.

"I think so."

"Plume is managing the setup downstairs. I peeked at the centerpieces; they're beautiful."

"Thank you."

I'm summoned for a bath by beauty Shifters who fawn over me with elixirs to decorate my nails, soften my skin, and give it a glow. When the bath is finished, the Shifter does something else that makes me smell like a garden of roses. Once I'm dressed, I cover myself in a robe and join Grandmom in the sitting room, where a meal awaits.

"Have you eaten?" She slides me a plate and I take a few bites, too distracted by what's ahead to eat. A bell chimes and the door opens. It's Mrs. Cuthers with an envelope, with Abby's name in slanted letters on the back.

"This came for you, Quell."

I wait for my toushana to strangle me with panic, but it only flutters below my skin in a hushed calm. She knows I'm not trying to get rid of her and she is completely at peace.

"Isn't Miss Feldsher going to see you tonight?" Grandmom inspects the letter, tugging at its seam, and my heart pounds. But the magic works as it should and it doesn't open. She hands it to me, flustered. "Well, go on. What does she want?"

If I open the letter, Grandmom will read it. My toushana hums in agreement. If I lie, she may see through me. My dark magic burns colder. *No, I don't think that's a good idea either.* The best thing I can do is try for an earnest distraction. The chill in my veins hums, content, as if in agreement.

"I'm not sure," I say to Grandmom, tossing Abby's letter aside. "Mrs. Cuthers, before you go, you *have* to see my dress!" I hop up from the table with more zeal than I feel and pull her over to the window to behold the magnificence Vestiser Laurent created for me.

"Oh, Quell, it's exquisite." She pulls the hanger down and holds it to me, and I spin.

"And the shoes!" I drag her from item to item, doting until Grandmom's pulled into a conversation with her own beauty Shifter for the day. The excitement drones on and when Grandmom's not paying the least bit of attention, I slip the note into my bag and stuff the whole thing in a corner.

Grandmom checks her watch. "It's about time to start your makeup and hair. Pictures will begin two hours before the ceremony."

I climb into the chair and recognize the beauty Shifter as the same one who helped me on festival day. "Sam, is it?"

"Yes, Miss." She blushes and works her magic over my face, reminding me ten thousand times to look at her instead of at the corner where I hid my bag. When she's done, she moves on to my hair. I opt for a simple updo since I'll be donning giant earrings from the House's parure. While Sam works my hair with her magic into different styles until she finds one she likes, I spot Grandmom slipping out into the hall for a private word with the caterer. I hop out of the chair.

"Miss, I'm not—"

"Just a second!" I hurry to my bag, dig out the note, and rip it open.

Oh my gosh! I hope you're okay. I'll do as you say. And there's something I need to tell you. I heard Nore Ambrose might be dead! See you tonight. —Abby

The door to Grandmom's room clicks open, and I call on my toushana to turn the note to ash. I hide the mess in my bag and return to my chair.

"We're about done, I hope?" Grandmom says, checking her watch again.

"Yes, ma'am." Sam hands me a mirror.

Grandmom takes it out of my hand. "No time. Everyone out, please!" She pulls down my dress as the room empties. "It's only fair that I get to see you first in your gown." She winks.

I swallow the lump in my throat as I slip the gown over my head.

Grandmom's lips twist. She taps them.

"Is something wrong?"

I turn for a glimpse in a mirror, but she snatches me forward.

"No, no, I don't think so."

I gaze at the sea of sparkling chiffon swishing around me. "I think it's stunning, Gran—"

"Get Vestiser Laurent here, *now*," she says to someone outside the door.

"I really don't want to make any trouble, this is fine."

"Nonsense, Laurent was told to stand by for last minute changes."

Last minute changes? The snag in what I *thought* was happening unsettles me, but I bite my tongue as Vestiser Laurent enters.

"My apologies, Headmistress, is something not to your liking?" he asks, his expression pinched with concern.

"This is not going to work."

"I don't understand. I handstitched this gown with my four-thread twine, the absolute best for magical conduction. The fabric is lined with Cultivator agents, so any magic she uses while wearing it lasts longer. There's Retentor resistance worked into the inner sleeves, masked by those sparkles, to ensure her magic cannot be easily removed. I've put all the bells and whistles on this thing."

"What use are bells and whistles if it's ugly? It's too humdrum. Too *expected*." Grandmom turns me and I catch a sweeping glimpse of myself. I look fine. More than fine. Really pretty. But I keep my mouth shut. This is her show, and she has to believe I'm fully compliant.

Vestiser Laurent smiles at me bashfully, and I try my best to smile back in a way that says, *It's really okay, don't be embarrassed.*

"I need you to fix it to my liking. Or I'm afraid you will not be compensated."

"I can do it just like you wish." He pulls off his coat and fluffs the end of my gown. "Now, tell me what you're thinking."

Grandmom reaches for words as if she could find them in the air. "Quell is the *heir* of a great House. No one will remember this dress. Quell should be a sight others *miss* when she's gone, like a fine piece of art. I am not *missing* this!"

Vestiser Laurent's hands work furiously over the fabric, sweat beading on his brow. I watch stunned as his magic transforms the thin breathy fabric into a thicker one with fleurs that shimmer when the dress shifts a certain way.

"Perhaps . . ." He taps his lip. "More moon illuminance could give us better shine than the rhinestone beading." He pulls his magic as if poking with tiny pins at each speckle, and one by one they shine brighter.

The corner of Grandmom's mouth tugs up.

"Do you know," she says to me, her tone decidedly lighter, "a Vardena Toussaint?"

"The first débutante of our House, I believe? Daughter of Bradley Toussaint, Upper, Two of Twelve, founding member of the Order."

"She *set* the standard thereafter of what debs would aspire to in her day." She pulls at my chin. "*You* will set the standard. You hear that, *Vestiser* Laurent? You're not making a dress. You're *defining* an era."

Laurent finishes and Grandmom tugs the zipper.

"Well, what do you think?" he asks.

Grandmom's silent, motioning for me to turn around and take a look. I glimpse myself in a full-length mirror and gasp, searching for words, but they don't come.

"Quell?"

"It was beautiful before, truly gorgeous. But this . . . this . . . I—I—"

She is breathtaking.

Me.

I am breathtaking.

"Speechless. *Exactly* the response we're going for." She turns to thank Laurent, and I chance another glance in the mirror. The pale blush fabric glimmers with a sheen, and every twist I make, the fabric sparkles brighter than a starry night sky. The scoop neckline dances on the edge of my shoulder, and crystal beading cascades down my arms as if on an invisible piece of tulle. If I was dressed for a nice dance before, I'm fancy enough to be crowned queen of something now.

Laurent departs, and I gape in the mirror until Grandmom pulls me away to help me with my shoes. I can't let whatever this is seduce me. I have a plan, and no matter how dreamy the veneer looks on me, I won't be fooled by it.

"What about the tether?" I ask, focusing on the matter at hand. "How does it work exactly?"

"Just make sure when you bind with your magic, you're standing in the center of the stage so that it takes," Grandmom says, pulling at the ties on my dress to cinch them tight. "The magic is veiled over the stage."

I nod. *So bind offstage. Got it.*

She grabs my shoulders, forcing me to look up at her. "Today is the first day of the rest of your life, Quell. A very different life than you've had. I'm so proud of you. Are you ready, dear?"

"More than you know."

"Well then, shall we?" Grandmom opens the door and there is Jordan in a tux, holding my corsage.

FORTY-NINE

••——✳——••

"Headmistress, Quell." He bows and I can't move. He wears a tux with a coat more ornately trimmed with red embroidery along the rim of the sleeves, nicer than the one he wore to the Tidwell. Gold pins line his lapel, a white bow tie cinches at his neck, and his House riband is slung across his chest. Heat licks the back of my neck and my insides twist, burning through my anger. *I hate him.*

I'm surprised he went along with all this. I'm surprised he'll have anything to do with me at all. His tall frame eclipses the doorway, and I feel small again. Weak. Reminded of how I took refuge in that shadow of his. How I craved it.

"You're breathtaking."

I want to tell him to shut up, but that crack in my composure can't show. I have to be resolute and focused. I refuse to feel anything for him after what he's done. He takes my wrist and affixes the flowers he brought to it. I want to cringe at his touch.

"Now, I believe it's your turn." He grabs my boutonniere from the table and hands it to me. Forever two steps ahead of me. He looks at me, and I'd forgotten what this felt like. To stare into the sun on the horizon and not blink. I bite my lip and pin the flower on his chest, making short work of it. I'm pretty sure it's crooked, but I don't care.

"Are we ready for pictures?" I ask. *Let's get on with this mess.*

Grandmom smiles, doting on my hair, my dress. She reaches to adjust Jordan's boutonniere, but he jerks away ever so slightly. *He isn't as on board with Grandmom's plan as I thought.* Even if I could talk some sense into him, opening the floodgates with Jordan is too risky. I can't dig through the quicksand of emotions I've buried, or I risk drowning with him. The best thing I can do is keep him in the dark like Grandmom and get this Rite over with.

"Shall we?" Jordan offers his arm, and I loop mine through his to keep her from asking questions. We move through the estate in silence and descend the stairs. The photographer is set up in the foyer and low music plays somewhere. We pose and smile, and every time Jordan looks at me, I make it a point to avoid looking his way. It takes an hour or more, but once we finish, my chest is tight. My toushana burns colder, urging me with encouragement. I blow out a breath. *I can do this.*

Grandmom waves goodbye at us and disappears into the ballroom, which is swarming with guests hurrying to their seats. A line of ball gowns and masks in tuxedos snakes up to the door.

"Congrats," one of them says. His date curtsies to me, and because Jordan is on my arm and I don't want him to suspect my true plan, I go through the motions.

"You both look lovely," I say to them. "Good luck with First Dance."

She blushes, and the couple in front of her turn, realizing the Headmistress's heir is in line with them. They offer Jordan and me congratulations.

"And to you," Jordan answers, before I get a chance to.

"I can respond for myself, thanks."

"You're wound in a knot. I can feel it," he says. *The tracer.* Oh, how that complicates things. Confidence is my shield. This only works if I keep him in the dark.

"I couldn't reach you the last few days."

I fiddle with the beading on my gown.

"I hoped I was wrong. Or there was an explanation. Or . . ." He moves closer, not with his body, but with the warmth of concern in his words. *Too close.* He shakes his head and the lines of frustration deepen. I shift on my feet as the first couple's names are announced and our short line moves forward. They go right into First Dance and my stomach twists with dread. I'm not looking forward to this. Silence hangs between us, and it pulls at me with an urge to fill it. I meet his eyes and glimpse the boy I knew. The boy I love. *Loved.* I can't entertain his sympathy, be seduced by his hopes. A fissure has opened between us, wider than a lifetime. But it's better this way.

After the next two couples' names are called, there is one more before us. I consciously tell my shoulders to relax. This is almost over.

Jordan tires of waiting for a response. "But it appears I was right," he says. "I should have known something was off when Headmistress Perl asked me about you."

I try to bite my tongue but can't.

"What would Headmistress Perl say if she knew your loyalties have shifted to Darragh Marionne?"

"Introducing!" The announcer motions for us to step forward. "Quell Janae Marionne, sixth of her blood, Cultivator candidate, and heiress to House of Marionne." The ballroom stands, welcoming us with applause. "Escorted by Jordan Richard Wexton, thirteenth of his blood, Dragun candidate, Ward of House Marionne, House of Perl, and as of yesterday, understudy to the Dragunhead himself." I look at him, speechless.

The Grand Ballroom is layered in fine fabrics, beautifully folded napkins, satin-wrapped chairs, and luscious flower arrangements in every direction with glittering tiered lights overhead. There's more of everything than at Abby's ceremony: chairs, cakes, tables, people. Servers work their way through the crowd, passing out champagne. Wine bottles with the House name monogrammed on them sit at every place setting. A live band plays adjacent a stage, which is wreathed in dahlia blooms and fresh roses from Grandmom's garden.

I spot my dagger onstage beside four others. I blow out a big breath as the music beckons us, and our feet answer its call effortlessly. Jordan pulls me to him, our hands fit together. He dances and my body echoes his movements, gives in to the requests of his hands as he spins me out, back to him, hugs around me, then replaces his hand at my hip. The melody shifts to the slower part and I press hard against him, our chests, our hearts, beating to the same rhythm. His cheek caresses mine.

"I don't want to fight with you, Quell," he whispers. I long for the slow cadence of the music to pick up so I can put some distance between us. "I understand what finishing Third Rite must mean to you." His words twist in my stomach. "And yes, this plan of Headmistress's is wrong. But I get why you're doing it."

I meet his eyes.

"This is a home, safety. Tell me I'm wrong."

The melody shifts into a faster rhythm and our bodies break apart, to my great relief. I take the lead, pushing my hips, moving with the next motion before he gets a chance to. Confusion staccatos his steps, and it takes him a minute to adjust to my flow. He falls in line with me and we're in sync again, but we move to *my* dance. *My* song. His brows dent in confusion as I spin him out. The crowd's faces crease in curiosity as well. I pull him back.

"Quell, what are you up to?"

"Shut up and just dance with me."

His lips part in realization and he misses the next step, our hand-holding breaks, and he spins out far away from me. The ballroom stills. His eyes narrow, and my breath quickens. *He knows.* I smile, curtsying as the music comes to an awkward finish. Jordan bows where he is. And we exit the dance floor.

Backstage, he sticks to my heels.

"Quell."

I walk faster toward the powder room before I have to go out there again for binding.

"Quell!" He re-forms in front of me. "You think you're the only one who can see through people? *What* are you planning?" A raging war brews in his eyes. He doesn't want to believe that I would do something so terrible—bind with my toushana. And if I am, he doesn't know what to do.

"Say I am wrong. Say . . . you're going to do what Headmistress expects and put this behind you."

I say nothing, but my heart rams in my chest, telling on me.

He sucks in a breath and stumbles back, and the boy behind the mask finally stares at me. I turn to get back to the ceremony before my name is called to do my binding.

"Quell, *please*." Desperation crackles his words, and for some foolish reason, I stop and turn to look at him. "If you do this, it would fall to me. I'd have to—find you and . . ." A single tear streams down his cheek. I close the distance between us and smooth away the answer to any questions I had about what I mean to him.

"Quell, I—I love you." The words break from his lips like a cracked bit of concrete. Brittle, hard, heavy. *And true.*

I relish hearing him admit it. I reach for him.

"I need you." His thumb grazes my jaw, and his chest heaves with a patter as if the admission alone may shatter him into pieces.

"To your seats, everyone. If our débutants will make their way to their seats, we'll start the ceremony and finish with our group dance, followed by a reception and guest performance by Audior extraordinaire from the class of '15, the lovely Lomena." The crowd applauds, calling to me, but I am frozen face-to-face with a boy who loves me. And just found the courage to say it.

His finger traces my face, and I turn into his palm, savoring its gentleness.

"I could find a way to amend the rules, I bet. We could be together, Quell. We can have everything we couldn't before."

I could have it all. In one swipe of a blade, I could do away with my past, erase my history. Forget who I am and become who they want me to be.

But that is not freedom.

Another tear forms on Jordan's face, and for a moment I consider trying to get him to come with me. But his heart doesn't want to be free of this prison, he wants me stuck in it with him.

I gaze back down the corridor at the audience decked out in jewels, expressions glazed with awe. They all deserve to know the truth. Binding with my toushana isn't enough. I must tell them about the tracing tether.

If this world is made of glass, I will dance with a hammer in my hand.

Jordan's fingers try to lace between mine, but I pull them away and press my lips to his, savoring his love, imagining I could fit it in my hand, take it with me in my pocket. His arms tighten around me, and I wish that I could hold on to this feeling forever. I break the kiss.

"I can't live in a cage, Jordan." I leave him there.

His composure breaks. And it's the wall that holds him upright on his feet. "Where will you go? What will you do?" His voice cracks.

"I will dare to claim the sky." I hurry toward the stage as my name is called.

Grandmom is there when I spill out of the corridor, and another débutant is onstage with their hands gripped on the hilt of their blade up against their chest. Grandmom waits as they exhale and the handle disappears. Their chest glows a moment. *A symptom of the tracing tether.* Applause follows and Grandmom's gesturing for me to join her onstage.

"And now for a very special débutante, our last but certainly not least, my very own granddaughter, the heir and future leader of this great House, Raquell Janae Marionne." Applause drowns my steps as I join her onstage.

I stand at Grandmom's side as she hands me my dagger, and I look for some indication of the invisible tether around the stage, some tear of magic or ripple that shouldn't be there. "If you'll refer to your program, you'll see all of Raquell's distinguishing accomplishments, including the enhancers she's infused into her magic. She also received the highest marks on Second Rite this House has ever seen." Her cheeks push up under her eyes. "Raquell will be interning here as my understudy in Cultivating." She turns to me. "Please raise your right hand and place the other on your dagger, then recite your oath."

"By blood and trial, I swear to keep and protect the Order's truth. To honor and serve and never divide. Should I desert the way of Rule, my brother's blade should make me true. For service is for life, and a broken oath is only righted by death."

"When you're ready, you may bind with your magic to complete Third Rite." She hands me my dagger. I glance out at the crowd, the generations of members, parents, grandparents. Histories and lineages. I am shattering it all because of one woman's treachery. I force down the lump in my throat.

Some things deserve to be destroyed.

Let's do this, I whisper to my toushana. I call to my magic, the one I trust. *There is magic enveloping the stage. Show it to me.* I hold my side, urging my toushana awake, and she unfurls from the place where she slumbers. Black curls from my fingers. Whispers swarm as darkness coils in the air like a plume of smoke, swelling until it encircles the stage, filling an invisible barrier Grandmom has bubbled around it.

"Your Headmistress has a tracer affixed to this ceremony," I start, and the truth rushes out of me like unclogging a drain. "So that your binding is to not only your magic, but a tether to this House!"

Grandmom reaches for me, but I dart out of the way, holding tight to my dagger.

"Now." I tighten my core, tuck my elbows, and urge my toushana through me entirely. Cold seeps into my bones, flowing to my every extremity, into my arms and then to my hands. The darkness around me thickens. The barrier groans against the strain of my magic. *Destroy it.* I bite down and exhale, sinking into the lull of cold, keeping every muscle in my body relaxed to avoid fighting the expelling of my toushana in any way.

The barrier bubbled around the stage shatters into a cloud of smoke.

I'm breathless when I jump off the stage and shove my way between the barrage of people clamoring over each other. Vases shatter. Tables topple. Shouts and cries blare like a siren. But I tune it all out. *I'm not finished.* With my dagger tip to my chest, I call on my toushana again. She rushes through me into my hands, icy, ready, and waiting. I urge her into the blade, and it throbs with light.

Now push it in.

My hands shake.

Through the haze, I spot Jordan, stilled with shock. He holds my gaze. I can't bear to look away from him, to let go of this last glimpse of what we were, what I hoped we could be. I hold him in my sights and push the hilt of my dagger into me, sealing our fate. It pierces my skin without even a pinch. Its hilt slams into my chest bone with a shudder.

Exhale. I try to, timidly, expecting it to hurt as my toushana rolls through me. But when the breath leaves my lungs, there is no pain. There is no feeling at all. Fog forms at my lips at my next breath as a numbing chill as cold as death settles over me like the comfiest blanket. The dagger hilt dissolves into nothingness in my hands.

The world darkens at its edges, and I stumble sideways, catching myself on a table. I swallow, blinking, patting myself down, inspecting the place the dagger disappeared. I run my finger over the jagged scar there, which has already healed. As the cold settles in my blood, suddenly the colors of the ceremony ripen. The voices in the room swell and somehow untangle. I can hear each conversation and all of them at once. And the smells, so many. I've never felt more alive.

I gape at my empty hands but am distracted by my dress. Its pale pink fabric has turned black, its sparkled embellishments shining like stars. The tulle on my arms has shifted into leather, and I reach for the diadem on my head, feeling a few new gems as I dash for a glimpse of myself in a polished plate.

My black diadem sits on my head.

I look at the spot where Jordan just was. But he's gone.

Get out of there.

I grab a shawl from a chair, throw it over my head, elbow my way through the chaos, and shove the ballroom doors open. I'm two steps from the broom closet when a hand hugged in rings reaches for my throat.

FIFTY

◦◦──✳──◦◦

I jerk backward and grip the wrist at my throat. It starts to blacken. I blink at the face attached to the arm trying to apprehend me. *Headmistress Perl.* She winces, releasing her grip.

"I know what you've just done," she says, eyeing the shawl over my head, clutching her hurt hand. I put distance between us, keeping my hand raised in warning, and realize my fingertips are bruised. Whatever I did to her, I also did to me. *But I'll do it again if I must.*

"You mistake me," she whispers, glancing in both directions before handing me a note. *"Alea iacta est."*

The die has been cast.

"If you ever need refuge," she says. "My address."

I glance at the paper before rushing off through the broom closet door, hoping to find Abby, Mom, and Octos waiting for me.

The forest is chilly under the moonlight. The shock of everything that's happened hits me and I have to steady myself on a nearby tree. The trail to the Tavern cuts its way through the forest up ahead. Abby isn't anywhere in sight. I realize my debacle cut the ceremony a bit short. My fingers prickle, yearning with a thirst stronger than I've ever felt before. I have time.

I dash toward the Secret Wood. I arrive, panting. How many have come here terrified and desperate to hide a secret they never wanted? How many died because they couldn't?

A rustle in the leaves pins me in place.

"You said if I got you in to meet with Marionne," a guy says, "you'd be on that stage tonight debuting as her *heir*."

I creep along lower, careful to stick to the shadows, to see who's there.

"And I tried. *You* told me you'd get rid of the girl that Headmistress Perl was after."

I peer around the tree I'm hiding behind and see Shelby. And Felix.

"You could have tried harder to befriend her instead of letting your feelings get in the way."

She shoves him, and I dig my nails into the tree that covers me.

"My feelings?!" Her voice cracks, and Felix pulls her into him.

"It's all right," he says. "Just calm down." He peers around, and I press harder into my hiding spot.

"I feel like you're clouding my judgment."

He strokes her face, which is pressed against his chest. "Don't talk that way. You love me."

"I do, but this is about my House. How Duncan was to replace Marionne. And I was close, so close, like a daughter to her, until *she* came back." She pokes his chest. "Darragh Marionne was grooming me!"

My eyes widen.

"*Shh.*" Felix pets Shelby but she pulls away from him. His jaw clenches.

"I mean it, Felix. What am I supposed to do now? I can't go anywhere else. I want what was promised."

"Darling." He fingers her hair. "Calm, calm, it's going to be okay." He pulls her into a hug and she exhales, resting against him. "You'll have everything I promised you, that and more. I just need time to think."

She folds her arms. He lifts her chin, running a thumb across her lips. She turns her face away, but he tugs it back to center and she gives in to him, their faces joined in a quick kiss.

"You should've trusted me," he says, smoothing away her tears.

"I'm trying to."

He holds her face in his hands dotingly, then his expression hardens. Shelby crumbles in his hands in a cloud of dust.

Felix kicks leaves over her pile of ash before vanishing on the spot. I stumble up and run, trying to scrub what I just saw from my memory. Once the trail to the Tavern and the Chateau are visible again I slow, panting, when I spot Abby.

"Quell?" She gazes past me with curiosity.

"You came!" I throw my arms around her, and a dam inside me breaks. Maybe I won't be alone in this. Maybe I've not abandoned everything that mattered to me. But once she knows the truth, the full truth, she will probably hate me, too.

"Of course I came. You're as pale as a ghost. Are you okay?" Her nose scrunches, eyeing my dress. "You debuted in black?"

"I'll explain everything," I say, and then I realize someone's hovering behind her. *Mynick.*

"I hope it's okay I brought him."

I stuff my shaky hands in the pockets of my gown.

"Were you able to find Octos?" I ask, rubbing my arms, imagining I can rub away the horror I just witnessed.

"She was," a voice behind me says.

I turn and sigh at the sight of him. I could hug him. "Thank you so much for coming."

He nods, keeping a distance. Almost everyone's here. I look for Mom through the trees, but don't see her. Abby sets a hand on her hip, watching expectantly for an explanation for all this. I pull her aside.

"Abby, I don't know about Mynick." I tighten my hand on the shawl. "He's not—"

"He came here with me. He broke the curfew rules. He's in this with us. Whatever we're doing. You can trust him."

"You don't know what I'm about to tell you."

"If it's a problem I'm here, I can go." Mynick folds his tattooed arms, and I notice he has several more marks than before. Octos eyes him out of the corner of his eye, but whether it's in contempt or admiration, I can't tell.

"No, it's fine," Abby says to him. "It's fine, right?" She presses me.

I can mention the tracing tether—that gossip will spread soon enough—but I have no idea how he'll react to knowing about my toushana. If Abby insists on his being here, then I can't tell her everything.

"Sure, fine." I explain what I found on Grandmom's bookshelves, the Perl girls, Nore Ambrose, how Grandmom has fixed Third Rite, what happened at Cotillion. But not about my toushana. Once I'm done, Abby clings to Mynick in shock.

"So I'm . . . tethered?" Fear wells in her eyes.

"You are."

Octos's expression glints.

Mynick paces.

Abby nudges him. "I told her she could trust you."

"She can. I was just thinking. It would be good to tell Headmistress Ambrose."

"My grandmother told me that she lied about Nore being on sabbatical because she was asked to. Any idea who would ask her to do that?" My pulse ticks faster at still no sign of Mom.

I glance at Octos, who still hasn't said anything, and I realize that gleam in his eye is ambition. Opportunity.

"So what are we going to do?" Abby asks, pulling at her sweater.

I crane for a view of some indication someone's coming but see only darkness. "First I need to find my mom. Octos, I was hoping you could help with that." My gaze falls to his sleeves, which are rolled all the way down today.

"She will expect that," he says.

"Who?"

"Darragh Marionne. She can influence any of those she's tethered to her House, whether they want to be or not. Including those who have gone on to become Draguns. I would wager she will circumvent the Dragunhead and have her Dragun graduates hunting you after what you've done." His posture shifts with knowing, and he glances at my still-veiled diadem.

"Outing the tethering secret, I mean," he clarifies to a perplexed Abby. "I imagine they'll expect you to try to find your mom."

"He's right. It's what I would do." Mynick pulls back his jacket, revealing a talon stitched at his throat, like the one Jordan wears.

"You were invited to be a Dragun of your House!" Abby slaps his arm. "When were you going to tell me?"

"I wasn't. Until I was sure. I haven't finished yet."

Abby's eyes well with tears. "How could you?"

They argue, and Octos steps closer to me, whispering under his breath.

"What you need to spend your time doing is focusing on getting control." He holds up my bruised fingers. "Before you lose yourself completely. I can teach you."

I trust my toushana, but I don't know how to wield it with control. I need to in order to protect myself and Mom. *He's right.*

"Abby, can you and Mynick look for my mom?"

She side-eyes him. "I will, but he can't."

"Abby, please," he says. "I'm sorry. I'll turn it down, okay? I—I'll fail the exam or, I don't know."

"So you'll do it, then?" I ask.

"Yes," Mynick says emphatically. "If that gets my Abs talking to me again."

"What about you?" she asks. "What are you going to do?"

"Octos is going to help me strengthen my magic."

Abby's brow dents.

"Since she won't be able to hone her skills here anymore," he says, veiling my secret.

"But what could he possibly know about magic? He didn't even finish."

"Take off your shirt, Octos," I say. "Let them see you."

He groans but pulls at his sleeves and slips out of his shirt. Mynick's eyes widen. There isn't an inch of skin not covered in tally marks. Mynick's lips purse with something he wants to say, but only silence grows between us.

"So it's a plan, then?" I ask.

Everyone nods in agreement, and I hug Abby tight once more, thanking her before they head out. At some point I need to come clean with her fully. That's what a friend would do. But I don't know Mynick well enough, and I can't bear to lose her help if I scare her.

"Thank you," I say to Octos once Abby and Mynick are long out of sight. "I'm truly in your debt."

"I was glad to hear you thought of me again. I meant what I said, though. We need to get you more familiar with your toushana. You don't know what you're up against."

"And you do, I suppose?"

"I know enough to be dangerous."

He digs out a piece of paper from his pocket. "This is one of the last standing safe houses. I'll meet you there."

"You're not coming with me?"

"I have to take care of something first. Cloak yourself. Traveling any other way at this point isn't safe."

I hadn't quite expected to be going it alone, right away. To somewhere where I know no one. "How do I cloak?"

"Lean into your toushana, urge it to make you disappear. Set your mind on where you want to go. Your magic is stronger now that you're bound. It should do the rest."

I nod, replaying the instructions in my head.

"Any questions?"

"No, I think I've got it."

"*Festina lente.*"

"Careful, I'll be careful."

"Good. See you soon." Octos disappears in a cloak of black. I reach for my magic and she stirs, cold and sure. I hold the address firm in my hand and take a last sullen glance at Chateau Soleil in the distance.

I suck in a breath at how it's changed.

What was once a sprawling palatial architectural masterpiece is decrepit and old. Lights don't sparkle from its ramparts. Instead, they are battered and caving in on themselves. I blink, and it's like a veil has been lifted from my eyes. But the realization bleeds through like a gushing wound.

This is what Chateau Soleil always was.

I can just see it now.

Thanks to my toushana.

I close my eyes and call to her, my only trusted friend, and she answers with an iciness that's comforting. *Take me.* I mutter the destination, and the world disappears in a cloud of welcomed darkness.

FIFTY-ONE

——✳——

YAGRIN

One Month Later

The Sphere gleamed in Yagrin's eye, and he dropped his bag before taking a drink. The hike up Mount Eurajny had been long and arduous. The mountain peak was fortified in a magical force field that wouldn't allow him to cloak himself and appear near it. And now, on top was a mile or more of desecrated wasteland littered with bones and remains as far as he could see. Broken barrels of kor elixir where others had tried—but failed—to use a concentrated amount of the liquid energy to break through the Sphere's defenses, he guessed.

The sun beat down on him as he latched his water back at his side and shouldered his bag. He'd found it, finally. But now he had to do the job. A job that curled his insides with delight instead of dread for once in his life. A delight he'd steeped in anger mangled with sorrow the last few weeks. A delight saturated with Red's blood.

They'd killed her.

He fiddled the edge of the picture in his pocket of her grave and headstone. Taped on the back was a tuft of her bloodied hair. They'd sent it to scare him. Still he couldn't manage to toss it. Who killed her, exactly, he wasn't sure. Any of his Dragun brethren could have run back and told on him. Or maybe it was that stone-hearted man who'd sired him. Or Headmistress. He wouldn't put it past any of them. But they were all dead to him now. As dead as Red was.

A deep ache sank in him like a stone that was too heavy, too settled to ever be moved. His sorrow was a new sort of anchor. There was no freedom in this life without her. There was only vengeance. Yagrin reached for anger, but he was a dry well of emotion. The only thing he could seem to find was iron-willed resolve. He would shatter the Sphere today. In one stroke he would end the use of magic for half a century at least *and* put a knife at Beaulah's throat. Of all of them, he hated her the most.

He lassoed his magic out to the glowing Sphere, which hovered ahead of him like a low-hanging moon. Black matter weltered violently inside it. Since he'd started his search, he'd found it twice but lost it.

He'd almost given up until he got the call on the emergency burner phone he'd given Red. Someone had found it. She was missing. It had been four days. Yagrin knew. Right then, he knew. Yagrin sent a truckload of flowers to her family farm. He couldn't bear to go there again in person. But it didn't bring Red back. Nothing could. She was just another casualty of the Order's sociopathic narcissism.

The Sphere shook as his magic attached to it, and the ground trembled, unsteadying him.

He needed to be a bit closer to unleash his fury on its surface. He pulled himself toward the Sphere, careful to keep his hold on his magic, which held it in place. If he let up at all, it'd vanish, relocating to protect itself.

He grinned at the tiny crack already on its glass, though he couldn't take credit for it. That was someone else's handiwork. It arced upside down, and he imagined it was a frown on the Sphere's facade. As if it was upset to be destroyed.

"You don't want this," he muttered. "Look how unhappy you are trapped in there."

He was setting it free. And making those he hated most rue the day they took his life from him.

He skirted a landfill of skeletal remains before getting close enough to the Sphere to do anything. How many had died on a similar mission? He wasn't sure, but it wouldn't be him.

When he got up close to the Sphere, its glow reflected on his sooty skin. It was also quite bigger than he'd imagined, the sun eclipsed behind it. It was a sight to behold. The epitome of power. The representation of the balance of magic. Or imbalance, as its dark sloshing insides suggested. But the taint of its appearance didn't rob it of majesty.

What would she look like when she cracked all over? When she started bleeding and the time clock on their magic ran dry? Would she gleam with power then? One day, someone would appreciate his brilliance and thank him.

"Don't do this." Yagrin didn't have to turn to know his brother's voice. Had he brought their father, too? His knees felt like they might falter under him for a second, and anger burned in him for letting himself feel it. But when he turned, his father wasn't there.

"Brother," Jordan begged. "Please, don't do this."

He should have known he'd come. *The trace.* He'd let his brother put it on him as a prank when they were kids. But because of it, his brother could always tell when he was feeling distressed.

He rested his hands a moment, giving Jordan a chance to catch up to him. Jordan, more than anyone, needed to see the Sphere crack and bleed. His younger brother's usual swagger was full of dignity and prowess, but today, a deep fatigue hung his shoulders. As if he was in every possible way exhausted. Yagrin almost didn't recognize him.

"How'd you find it so fast?" Jordan asked, shoring himself up beside Yagrin, keeping his hands loose as if this might come to blows. He wouldn't put it past his brother to try to hurt him to protect the Sphere. He was determined to follow in Father's destructive footsteps. To whom, duty to the Order was his altar of worship. Yagrin was done with that. Revenge would be as good as freedom.

"A fortuitous trade brought me a dagger and a Location Enhancer," Yagrin said. "Traded the dagger for the last of the ingredients I needed for a reverse summoning elixir."

"Please, turn away from here and go. I don't want to stop you, but I will if I have to."

"You didn't bring Father. Why?"

Jordan's gaze hit the ground. "You know why."

"You're just like him. You spare me nothing by not having him here."

Jordan wrung him by the shirt. He could fight back. He knew his brother's tendencies. His left flank was always open. He reacted emotionally without thinking when he got upset, which made his moves hasty, leaving him vulnerable. Yagrin was the older brother, but he'd spent his life watching Jordan, forever in his prodigious shadow, and he knew him better than anyone. Better than he knew himself.

He could pound his face bloody, give him a good brotherly ass-kicking, which he probably needed. But that would still pale in comparison to the hurt Jordan stood there with right now over the girl. It bled through the droop of his posture. It hung in his sullen glance, which he tried to shadow with anger. And it had been *weeks*. Jordan still sitting with that pain was more satisfying than anything Yagrin could ever do to him.

And not because he didn't love his brother.

Because he *did*.

"I hoped that girl would change your cold heart," Yagrin said.

"Don't speak of her."

"But you seem determined to make Father proud."

Jordan let him go with a shove. "I came here to stop you from making a mistake."

"You won't stop me with your words."

Jordan's composure hardened, but Yagrin could see right through him. The fury that burned in Jordan was no more than an ember. He was more wounded than angry. More confused than determined. He was still too broken over that girl to do anything to Yagrin. He didn't have the grit to stop him. That was a good thing, Yagrin supposed. Meant his brother had some semblance of a heart. It hadn't yet all rotted.

He rolled up his sleeves to get on with his plan, picturing Beaulah's face. The devastation that would stain it when she heard what happened to the Sphere. How she would fear for her life every day until it ended. A dark smile curled his lips. Yagrin wished he could be there to witness it. But he had other places to be. Other duties that called.

"Yags," Jordan pleaded, with his boyhood nickname. But that tender wound had long since scabbed over. *It wouldn't work.* He would empty the Sphere.

Yagrin's magic stirred in him like a brewing storm. He raised his hands and unleashed it at the bobbing orb above them. His brother's knees hit the hard ground and weeping sobs scratched at Yagrin's ears, but he couldn't tear his gaze away from the dark magic assaulting the Sphere's glassy surface.

It cracked like an egg, and breath stuck in Yagrin's lungs. Tight in his chest. He held it in, waiting for the first piece of it to fall to the ground and its innards to bleed out. But she glowed brighter. He flinched with frustration, and he drew the destructive magic to himself again, this time with more force. He unleashed. The Sphere cracked more, into a tapestry of spiderwebs, but still its form held. Irritation burned through him, and fatigue weighed down his shoulders. He pulled at the remnants of toushana, all he could muster, the last of his strength, and unleashed once more. But it held, still. Broken, fractured beyond repair, but not a single trickle of matter fell from it.

"Bleed, dammit!" He pounded his fist to the ground and found a glisten of hope in his brother's green eyes. "Well, it's a start."

Jordan's lips parted as if he were reaching for something to say, but it came out as sobs. Yagrin considered embracing him, but his brother was like their father—it would take more than momentarily wallowing to change his heart.

"I'd stay and chat, but I have someone to train." Yagrin pulled at his Anatomer magic, and a ripple ran down his body as he slipped into his other skin, the one he'd grown comfortable in as of late. Ever since he'd found an impressionable heiress in a Tavern. The face the girl wasn't scared of—Octos.

After meeting her close up, her getting away, he wasn't convinced she deserved to die. So when they crossed paths on the stairs of the Tavern, he'd shifted into one of his personas to get to know her. Form his own opinion. When he offered her the potion to tempt her ambition and she turned it down, that's when he knew she was different. When he saw his brother come to her aid, he wondered what drove him.

Yagrin had decided then he would think hard before bringing the girl to Beaulah as she'd requested. But it was when the girl emerged and chose to trust him, when she'd said she was sorry he wasn't allowed to finish his training—*him, a nobody*—that he'd made his choice. She would live, and he would help her get away with it. When she wrote looking for her mother, who was being held captive by his Dragun brothers, he wrote back forging her hand, to urge her to stay under her grandmother's protection. And when he'd finally mastered her mother's face, he paid Quell another visit to drive the point home.

She wasn't only different, but she would be powerful.

When he later realized his brother was falling in love with her, he knew she needed to survive and be protected more than ever for the sake of not only her life, but Jordan's. He'd been pondering a way to do just that, stewing over a letter, when her friend Abilene found him. Her binding with her toushana was an unexpected delight.

Yagrin could be credited for many egregious, harrowing things in his life but not loving his brother wasn't one of them. The girl was good for Jordan. She was good for them all. He glanced at the Sphere, his work unfinished. She would be able to do far more than he ever could. He rolled down his sleeves over Octos's marked arms.

"Until we meet again, brother." Yagrin departed to the melody of his brother's sobs.

APPENDIX

THE HOUSES AND THEIR HISTORIES

MEMENTO SUMPTUS

HOUSE OF PERL

Est. 1822

At Hartsboro Estate

Territory: East and Northeast

Hartsboro Estate, located in Connecticut, was originally the operating Headquarters of the Order's governing body: the Upper Cabinet. In 1822, on the heel of the Sorting Years, to support the development of the Order's growing member numbers, Upper established a formalized magic-studying system using a boarding school model. Members would continue in the débutante tradition, which had been in practice since the onset of the Industrial Revolution, but be organized into Houses and territories. Houses would be overseen by a Headmistress.

The Upper Cabinet relocated their Headquarters and commissioned its first House: House of Perl, naming Beatrice Perl inaugural Headmistress. At the time, Beatrice had been serving in the Cabinet. Before agreeing to sign on, she insisted that the seat of the House pass down in family lineage by the matriarch. Upper agreed, and so it remains. The House of Perl sigil is a cracked column.

HOUSE OF MARIONNE

Est. 1874
At Chateau Soleil
Territory: Southern

House of Marionne was the second established House of the Order, as their numbers swelled with more and more showing a propensity for magic. The origins of the philosophies that shaped House of Marionne are rooted in the Era of Indulgence.

After the fall of Yaäuper Rea Universitas, the Silent Years followed. Formal magical education had come to a screeching halt as it was forced to shift to underground. It is said generations of magical people lost their magic because of sparse access to training, study, and development until a lowly but studious Order member, Loken Delosu, was sought out by King George I of England. He was courting Loken's affections, as he'd heard rumors his family dabbled in sun magic. George was at a long-standing war with the French and wanted any edge he could get. Around that same time, King Louis XIV, the "Sun King," heard of George's interest in Loken and sent his own parties to sway Loken. Louis, being a man of abundance, showered gifts and hospitality at the feet of Loken and his family, his friends, anyone he knew in exchange for one thing—his company.

King Louis XIV was incredibly ambitious and eventually pressed Loken directly to know more about magic, but Loken refused. He held to the age-old tenet that magic should be kept far away from government. Louis beheaded him. The Order was divided on how to feel about the French and English years of courtship. But the years dabbling in French culture had left its mark evident in House of Marionne's architecture, culture, traditions, and art. The Upper Cabinet commissioned Claudette Marionne as inaugural Headmistress. The House of Marionne sigil is a fleur-de-lis.

COGITARE DE PRETIO

HOUSE OF DUNCAN

Est. 1875
At Wigonshire Estate
Territory: West & Midwest*

House of Duncan was established on the heels of House of Marionne at the urging of Upper Cabinet members who were rumored to favor House of Perl's Dysiian influences. The House was intended to be a replica in culture and architecture of House of Perl but located in Colorado. The estate's inaugural Headmistress was Maisie Duncan. In 1938, an explosion in the Midwest killed thousands of Unmarked. The news reported that the accident was the result of an industrial explosion. However, House of Duncan, whose new Headmistress was experimenting with using toushana to mine gold, was behind the tragedy. The dark magic she'd been illegally using spiraled out of control, and twenty-three hundred barrels of kor elixir leaked into an oil shipment being transported west. The result was catastrophic. The Upper Cabinet shut down the House immediately and required each within its territories to reapply. Most were denied on grounds of distrust. Maisie Duncan was publicly beheaded, a rare but symbolically vicious act at the time. The House of Duncan sigil was a scale and darkened sun.

* The Midwest territory, formerly under House of Duncan, was initially moved to House of Ambrose. In later years the Midwest was split, its northern side under Ambrose territory and its southern side under Oralia.

INTELLECTUS SECAT ACUTISSIMUM

HOUSE OF AMBROSE

Est. 1877

At Dlaminaugh Estate

Territory: Northwest & parts of the Midwest

House of Ambrose, nestled in the tallest peaks of central Idaho, was the fourth established House of the Order. Its inaugural Headmistress was Caera Ambrose, a well-known member of the Order who had built her reputation on leading efforts to push the bounds of understood magic. Her views were seen as outlandish, but she received the votes needed from the Upper Cabinet. Caera's ancestors were immigrants to America with a strained and hostile history with Europeans. Thus, Dlaminaugh Estate was erected as a neo-Gothic replica of Yaäuper Rea Universitas and commissioned to be the first House in the Order that defined itself as distinctly separate from European influence. Caera desired to usher forward a generation of débutants who would be known for their supreme intellect, not ostentatious shows of wealth. The House of Ambrose sigil is three yew leaves intertwined.

UTI VEL AMITTERE

HOUSE OF ORALIA

Est. 1942

At Begonia Terrace

Territory: West & parts of the Midwest

House of Oralia was the fifth and final established House, located in northern California. Donya Oralia was its inaugural Headmistress. Her grandmother had been a candidate for Uppership but was ultimately passed over because of her progressive views on women's rights at the time. In 1942, House of Oralia was commissioned by a slim majority vote as the world was engrossed in World War II. They are known for using magic as a means of artistic expression and enjoyment, believing magic serves the wielder and not the other way around. The House of Oralia sigil is two smudged dollops of paint.

ACKNOWLEDGMENTS

———✳———

House of Marionne is a story I dreamed up long before I was able to pen a single word of it. And it would have never come to fruition without the love and support of many people.

I am so grateful to God for giving me this gift with words. Thank you to my husband, who is constantly cheerleading and supporting me as I wander awestruck in this author life dream. Extra-special thanks to my three little people, who are free, wild spirits, each in their own way. Mariah, you inspire me to pour myself into my art the way you do. Daniel, you inspire me to be my goofy, loud, sensitive self, unapologetically. And Sarah Grace, you inspire me to do everything with joy.

To my grandfather, who is as blown away each time I churn out another one of these as the first time. Your unconditional love, Grandma, and your determination to fill in the gap, showed me the power of giving a child the opportunity to freely explore who they want to be. I miss Grandma, but I know she is proud.

To Emily, who dragged me through the creation of this book with her bare hands. There aren't enough words or tears to convey how much *Marionne*'s existence is largely because of you. You are the second half of my writing brain. I could not have crossed that finish line without our senseless polos, my sobbing sessions, fuzzy socks, binging shows, PEAKKYYYY, your help navigating the general chaos that just always is my life, ha ha. Your reminders to be kind to myself and take care of myself first kept me afloat when I was drowning. Thank you for always being in my corner as #TeamJess first. I cannot wait until it's your turn to do this and the world gets to experience your writing brilliance!

To Jodi Reamer, my extraordinary agent, who not only changed my life, but fights for me to have the freedom I write about. You are a treasure. And yes, we will get you on a horse in Texas one day. To Rūta, who is fiercely brilliant, and the most incredible advocate and editor. In true Cancer-Sag fashion, I am going to go super emo and hopefully make you feel very awkward, ha ha. Thank you for all you do, tirelessly with such enthusiasm and joy. I cannot imagine going on this journey with these characters in this epic world with anyone else. I am literally teary-eyed typing this! You've breathed new life into my hope of being able to tell a plethora of stories.

To Jen Loja, Jen Klonsky, and Casey McIntyre, who each passionately believed in *Marionne* from the very beginning, thank you for seeing what this book could be! I hope she's made you proud. To Simone, my fellow Cancer-loving, romance-reading, fuzzy-sock wearing, curly-haired book lover—thank you for swooning over the dance scene, ha ha! You are a gift to work with. Publishing is very lucky to have you.

To the rest of the editorial, publicity, art, digital, sales, and marketing teams—Kaitlin, Jaleesa, Shanta, Felicity, Shannon, James, Theresa, Alex, Emily R., Carmela, Christina, Bri, Olivia, Laurel, Michelle C., and those who I haven't had the chance to meet one-on-one—I am so grateful for each moment you spent bringing this book into the world. Special thanks to Virginia for this beautifully gorgeous map! We have truly made magic together, and that wouldn't be possible at all without you adding your unique dash of sparkle! <3 <3 <3

To Sabaa, who continues to hold me together, thank you for looping your arm in mine and being there in the ways that matter and mean the most. To Ayana, my sister, who I love fiercely, thank you for the endless phone calls, love, and support. To Stephanie Garber, whose sweet heart is so rare, thank you for being so encouraging through the ups and the downs, always having such clever thoughts and so much industry wisdom. I am so fortunate to call you friend. To Nic, my twin, who always wants to see me win—you set the example of endurance I aspire to. Love you, girl. To Nicola and Karen, who always find the time to remind me that my stories matter, thank you! To my Jessicas—Olson, Froberg, and Lewis—where would I be without y'all?! Certainly not still in publishing, that's for sure.

To my family! Diarra, who holds me down always; Jennifer, whose idea for princess crowns sparked the diadem concept; Andonnia, for being there always and without notice; Stephanie Jones, for being my ride or die; Sandra B., for your marketing genius and constant love. To cousin Roslyn, Rocqell, Aunty Regina, Aunt Jackie, Kotomi, Trent, Mom, Paige, and Naomi, you hold me together. Laura W., Amy D., Alyssa, Uncle Chuck, Micah, Sydney, and sweet Sara Kate, who has been so excited about this book since its inception, thank you for being such a positive influence on the uphill journey to get this story out.

To my other author friends who have been kind enough to express their excitement, offer a word of encouragement, be willing to read, comment, like, or share a social media post. Rachel, Alexandra, Schwab, Dhonielle, Marie, Tiffany, Leigh, Victoria, Shelby, Adalyn, Brigid, Kerri, I am so very grateful for all of it, no matter how seemingly small. It is not! And to Marissa, who has been there with me from the beginning, I adore you! To everyone and anyone whose name I may have missed, I am endlessly grateful. You are an integral part of this story's success.

And last but certainly not least—the biggest of thank-yous goes to you, my incredible readers, who faithfully come back to my stories over and over again. You are the greatest gift. Thank you for your support! I look forward to breaking your heart (and maybe putting it back together) many more times.

Hugs!

~Jess